Eye of Truth

P.G. Badzey

Stone Owl Press

4th Edition

Copyright © 2025 by P.G. Badzey

A STONE OWL PRESS BOOK

ISBN-13: 978-1-7328627-9-1

For Michael and Joshua
Two True Heroes for God.

Novels by P.G. Badzey

The Grey Rider Series

Whitehorse Peak
Eye of Truth
Helm of Shadows
Assassin Prince
The Skull Gates
Gate of Stars
Tower of Light

Contents

Acknowledgements   VII

Song of the Grey Riders   VIII

Maps   X

1. Fate of the Prophesied   1

2. To Face Cold Fire   10

3. Pit of the Dragon   22

4. Enigma in Grey   35

5. Thicker than Water   46

6. Eyes of Earth   56

7. Undying Light   64

8. Eye of Truth   76

9. Witch Storm   88

10. Captives   102

11. From an Unexpected Source   113

12. Hunted   123

13. Seek and Ye Shall Find   132

14. The Arm of the Law   141

15. Justice is Blind   158

16. Out of the Shadows   168

17. Rumors of Shadow   181

18. A Dish Served Cold   194

19. New Destinations   212

20. Tempest Gathering   218

Sneak Peek – Book 3: Helm of Shadows   220

Glossary   224

About the Author   240

Acknowledgements

The author wishes to acknowledge the following people, without whom this novel (and in some cases, its predecessor) would have been impossible to produce: Dora Badzey, publicist and proofreader extraordinaire; the good people at Wavecloud who have generated two terrific book covers; Gene Badzey, who proofread and caught the mistakes other readers did not;Veronica Badzey, whose typesetting skills saved this author's sanity, and C. Dale Brittain, for her encouraging advice and friendship over the years, thus showing this author how all other authors should take good care of fledgling writers.

Song of the Grey Riders

Seven they are, the Riders Grey,
who come to serve the Holy Way.
Seven they are of varied flight,
on winged steeds of dark midnight.
The Riders Grey, the warriors brave,
who seek to stem the Evil Wave:
One with sword from dwarves of old
and one fair maiden with hair of gold.
To aid the ones who follow the Three
comes another of the Silver Tree.
One with hawk of sharpened claw,
one forest guide of Christian law.
One small and swift, silent and light;
another the same with magic bright.
North they go to face Cold Fire
to battle the dragon and quench her ire.
When ogre's rage meets its end,
then does their true quest begin.

In tower cold and cavern deep,
the Diamond Eye they now must seek.
For good or evil all must choose
or choosing none, their lives to lose.
When gold to red at passage end,
then Halfling toy upward must send.
Golden sorrow, heart's true Love,
pray to God in Heaven above.
That she may see, and all may learn,
what Truthful Eye cannot discern.

Holy relic, giver of life,

meant for tresses of carpenter's wife.
Ancient Evil, Good to slay,
seeks to thwart the Holy Way.
Relic's might of love is wrought,
so evil's will avails it naught.
One Dark Rider fights seven of Grey,
yet Queenly Crown shall win the day.
Seven they were, from varied flight,
on winged steeds of dark midnight.
Seven they were, the Riders Grey,
who came to serve the Holy Way.

Maps

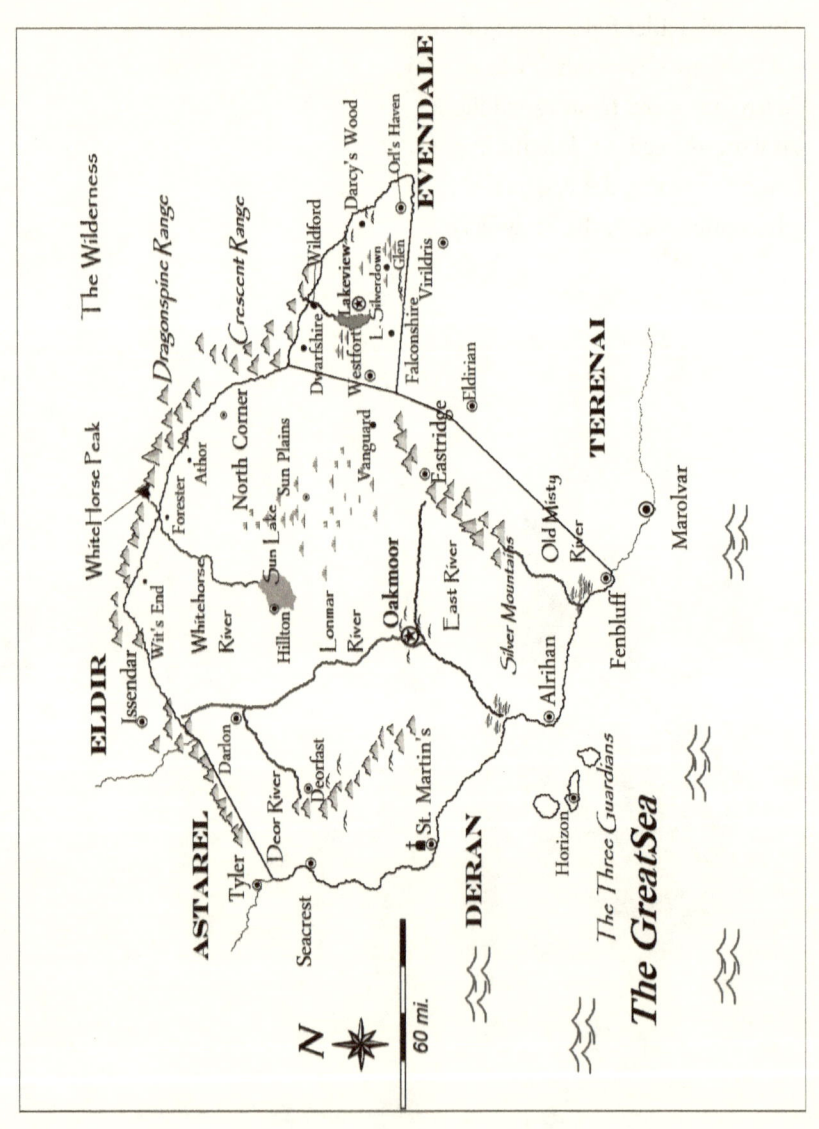

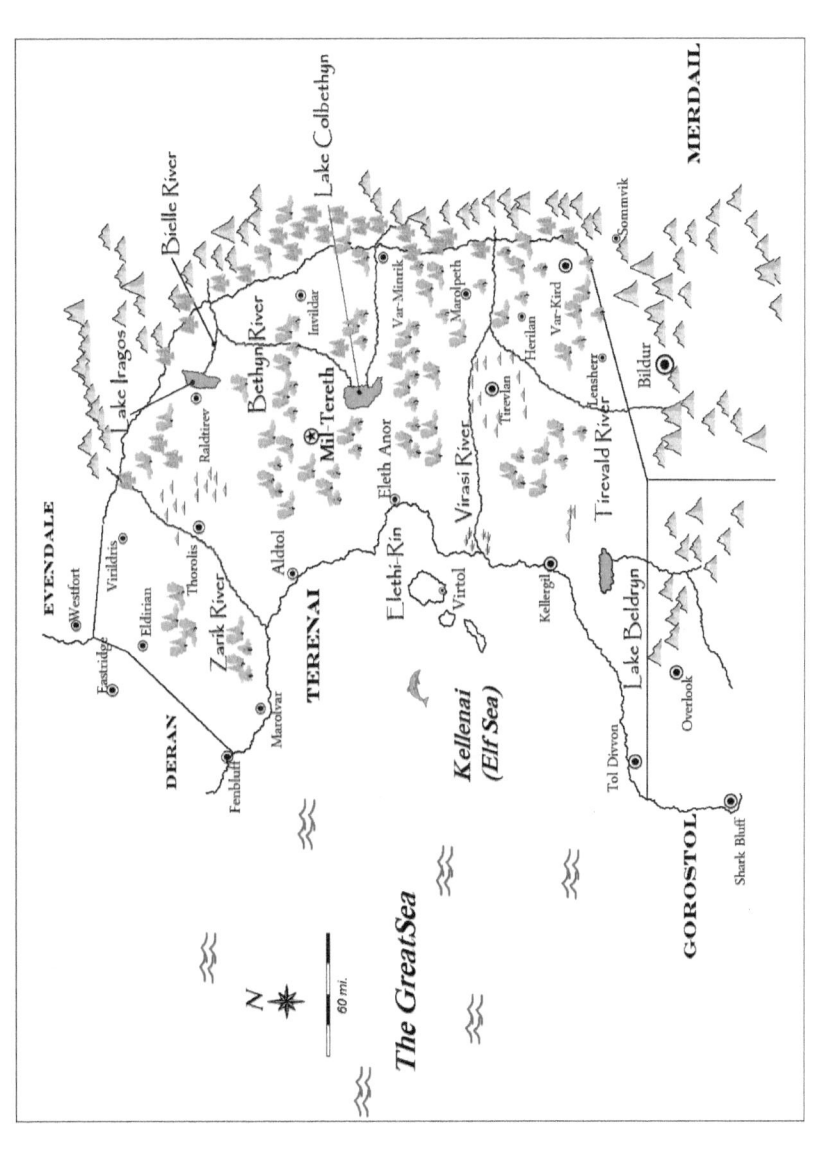

Chapter One

Fate of the Prophesied

With a sigh, Andyn Eleandir tossed her helmet and weapon-belt on the quilted bed-covers. She leaned a hand against the window sill and looked down at the street below. A burly man pushed a hand-cart full of tools down the avenue. She watched as he trudged next to a stone sewer-cover that wound down the middle of the cobbled street.

In front of one of the stores, a circle of four children swirled around their parents. Their shrill voices echoed in the street as they pleaded to go look at the horses at the stables. Andyn watched them with a little smile.

She eased the shutters and curtains closed. With a wave of her hand, a candelabrum on the bureau next to a tall mirror flared into life.

Andyn removed her hauberk and tossed it on the bed. She took extra care unbuckling her chainmail armor, wincing a bit as she did so. She wriggled out of it and the underlying padding. Then she pulled off her mail leggings, her boots and the rest of her clothing. She looked at her nude reflection in the mirror.

Ogres sure hit hard.

A blonde - woman gazed back at her with tired amber eyes. Those eyes — and the little point at the top of her ears — marked her as a *Kired-Nai*, or half-Elf in the Elven tongue. Her physique, toned and fit from years of training, could have marked her as a laborer or soldier, yet her background included years in study and meditation, learning the ways of the Elven god Verian.

The scar under her left breast and the bruise on her right thigh appeared to be fading, finally. She frowned, turning sideways. *Well, I may be a battered wreck, but with all this crashing around in the wilderness, I'm staying in shape.*

She turned away from the mirror and dropped a couple of soap beads into a full bathtub at the foot of the bed. A handful of fragrant herbs followed the beads. She dipped a finger into the water and frowned. *I'll have to talk to the maids about this.*

She spoke a gentle word and waved her hand over the water. A faint wash of red light rippled over the surface. Steam rose from the tub and she tested it again. *Perfect.*

Andyn let out a sigh of complete satisfaction as she eased herself into the steaming water. She lay there unmoving for a while. Her eyes followed carvings in the ceiling beams: centaurs and Halflings in a wooded glade.

The men complained about spending the extra gold to stay here, but even they have to admit it's worth it. Just because we're free-lance sell-swords doesn't mean we have to live like brush tramps all the time.

She closed her eyes. Thank Verian for a chance to take a breath. Hunting down a gang of Ogre bandits in the borderlands isn't easy work and it's even tougher in the summer heat. At least we got the job done. Buck and Connor should be happy. Lord Nolan rewarded us well.

Cloth brushed on wood behind her and she tensed, then relaxed, shaking her head. "Connor Lomin, if that's you trying to steal my clothes again, I'm going to bounce your little Halfling rump all the way back to Forester."

Andyn opened her eyes. A leering, bearded face hovered over her. A dagger plunged downward.

She gasped and twisted sideways, grabbing a hairy wrist and twisting it. She heard a grunted curse.

She sensed something behind her and she ducked into the water. A blade whistled over her head. Giving the first attacker a final twist of the arm, she jumped out of the tub and half-slid, half-fell on the bed. Grabbing her two maces from her weapon-belt, she spun to one side as a knife thumped into the headboard. She stood on guard, naked and dripping.

Two short men stalked her intently, each about four feet tall, bearded, and dark-eyed. Dressed in servant's garb, they bore short curved swords and dirks. *Gnomes?*

One of them charged and jumped on the bed, bouncing behind her. She took a swipe at him. He sprang backward out of the way, hitting the headboard. The second assailant charged, swinging and stabbing. She parried each blow. Her first assailant lunged and she leaped to the side. He hurtled past, slamming into the wall next to the window with a curse of frustration.

The second charged again. She dropped a mace on the bed and pointed at him with a short arcane word.

A pair of glowing darts shot out and hit him in the chest, detonating with sharp cracks. He staggered, grimacing in pain.

The other Gnome stepped in, swinging. She vaulted the bathtub. He jumped after her and she gave him a hearty whack in the legs, throwing him to the floor. Andyn skipped around the tub and grabbed her second mace from the bed.

The one she had shot with the firedarts lunged forward. She slammed aside the sword and crushed his skull with a right-hand blow of her mace.

A searing pain lashed across her ribs on the right side and she gasped, lurching forwards and hitting the wall. She spun aside and a dagger bit into the wood where she had just been.

The limping Gnome pressed his advantage but Andyn brought her knee up in a vicious kick and he flew backwards. A wave of weakness and colored lights danced in front of her eyes. She tried to steady herself against the wall. *Oh Verian's mercy! Poison blade!*

The Gnome hurled himself at her with a shriek and she felled him with an overhand stroke.

Her vision blurred. She collapsed on the mattress, hearing her door crash open. *Assassins. Others will finish me off, I guess. Larad, my love, I'll be with you soon.*

Strong hands lifted her up. Though she struggled, someone snatched her weapons away.

"Andyn! It's us! What happened?" asked a concerned male voice.

A young human man with dark eyes and short-cropped dark hair peering at her with alarm.

"Dar. Poison," she whispered.

"Poison? Oh great! Eric!"

Another male voice came to her, sounding strangely distant. "Okay, okay," it said. "I got it."

A cool smoothness caressed her wound. Instantly, the pain receded and she the fire diminished.

"Oh, Lord. Eric!" said Dar, "Get it all over the place, why don't you?"

3

"Relax," replied the other. "I'm not a medic. Just be glad I know what to do with this stuff. Besides, I think I got it."

The pain faded to a mere memory. Andyn opened her eyes. Dar Cabot, in travel clothes of dun and brown but without his chainmail, knelt on the bed next to her.

He helped her sit up, his face still worried. He slipped off the bed, then picked up a long-handled bastard sword and sheathed it. "Are you okay?" he asked, looping the sword belt over his shoulder.

She nodded, then shook her head, clearing the last of the colored lights.

A blond half Elven male gave her a measuring look with intense violet eyes as he replaced the top of a tiny white jar. He wore a dark green tunic and matching trousers, a longsword at his hip.

"Sure, *she's* okay, but *we're* not going to be when she lets us have it for breaking in on her bath," Eric Indidarc said. He closed the door.

Andyn put her head in her hands. *I can't get a moment's peace! We killed Halkith months ago and still the Ja'al hunt us.*

Dar's gentle hands settled on her shoulders. "Hey, are you sure you're okay?"

"Yes, I'm sure," she said, her frustration and irritation boiling over. She shook him off. "Stop pawing me."

Dar's mouth dropped open. "Hey, Andyn, I'm not—"

Tolan's Tears! Why did I do that? I'm such an idiot. She felt instantly ashamed. "Dar, I'm sorry. Please... It's just that I'm *so* tired. We thought we were free of the Ja'al after we found the pegasi, and now this. I can't even have a bath in peace."

Dar sat down next to her and handed her a towel. She began drying herself off, then looked at him sheepishly. "Friends again? I'm really sorry. I didn't mean it."

Dar gave her a wry look, then grinned and stroked her hair. "Yeah, friends again, though I'm sure I'll regret it soon. You had me worried, Andyn."

Eric sat next to her on the other side and patted her hand. "I'm tired myself, Andyn, but I don't blame Nolan or the King's other lords for trying to get as much use out of us as they can. We're kind of rare, you know: pegasus riders and free-lance blank-shields. But it won't last forever. As soon as we've paid off the debt we owe for the pegasi, we'll be on our own again."

4

She sighed. "You're right. I know you're right, but it's not only that. That prophecy haunts us wherever we go, this Dark Rider is lurking out there somewhere, and the Ja'al would just love to make us into wall trophies."

Dar gave her a gentle shove in the shoulder. "You wouldn't be our Andyn if you didn't get worked up over this."

Eric grinned. "Naw. Actually, she's just upset because we saw her naked."

Dar looked shocked and Andyn giggled, realizing again that she wore not a stitch. *Fine Christian lads. Remarkably calm about this, but then again, they've known me for a while.*

She whipped her towel at their heads. "All right, now get out of here so I can get dressed. The city guards are going to be all over this place and I have no intention of meeting *them* without clothes."

"You're right." Eric winked as he and Dar headed out. "The last thing we want is trouble with the locals."

Trouble? thought Andyn, looking at the mess of her room. *How could I possibly get into more trouble?*

"I need information," said the young sandy-haired man.

The bearded young Gnome smirked at him from across the table. "Doesn't everyone?" His black eyes glimmered in the dim light.

Buckminster Bydecy, free-lance warrior and pegasus rider, shrugged. "I guess. Can you get information from Tyler, in Astarel?"

"Information about what?"

Buck leaned forward, his voice dropping to a whisper. "I need to know about someone named Derek Feller, a jeweler's apprentice. And also about a warrant for someone named Buck Bydecy."

The Gnome shifted the hood of his cloak forward, over his brown hair. "That wouldn't happen to be you, would it? Never mind. Don't answer that. It'll be fifty in advance, with a hundred extra when I finish the job."

Buck slid a purse of coins to the Gnome. "Just be sure you wait for me to return here and don't tell anyone else what you find."

The purse slithered out of sight into the Gnome's dark clothing. "You can count on it," Buck's new hireling stood to go.

5

"Wait," said Buck. "I need to be able to find you. What's your name?"

The Gnome hesitated for a moment. "Hlerv," he said, then slipped into the crowd of people swirling around the worn wooden tables and chairs.

Hlerv? thought Buck. *Sounds like a disease.*

The room smelled of ale, roast meat, sweat and an occasional whiff of perfume. He leaned back in his chair, lifting a tankard of ale to his lips. His eyes roamed over the young serving girls with appreciation. *The blonde one with the white blouse is nice: a good shape, pretty smile, and very quick reflexes.*

He enjoyed the opportunity to relax by himself for once. *It's easy to blend in here. Not that the others are insufferable, but if I'm going to go to the more adventurous parts of Darlon, I can't have Andyn, Dar and Eric around. No offense to them or their religions, but their ideals are stifling.*

Four men and women wearing tunics of forest green and white over scale mail heralded the entry of the Darlon city guard. The roiling, dense river of customers curled around them as if they were rocks in a stream.

Buck stared down at his mug, watching the guards through hooded eyes. After they passed, he stood, buckled on his sword belt, and lifted a backpack hanging on his chair.

A young red-headed barmaid swung by and he stopped her, pressing a couple of silver coins into her hand. Stepping through the tavern's double doors, he blinked in the afternoon sun, then moved to the side. Traffic flowed past him: wagons, carts, many pedestrians and the occasional horse-man, usually an armored warrior or a military officer. Then, convinced no one paid him any heed, he slipped off to a side street.

Only a grubby drunk eyed him for a second as he passed down the alleyway. Buck stopped at the next corner. Looking up, he put his fingers to his mouth and gave three short, sharp whistles.

A grey-and-white pigeon fluttered down to land on his shoulder. He patted the bird on the head, feeding it a bit of crusty bread.

"Come on, Puup," Buck said, scanning the area. "Let's see what everyone else is up to."

With that, he joined the traffic on the next major street. He wound through wide boulevards, junk-crammed alleyways, and meticulous avenues decorated with trees and flower-boxes.

He followed a torturous path, changing direction often and counting his steps. Finally, he emerged on a nearly empty street in a respectable part of town. There, he stopped in front of a leatherworker's shop and pretended to look at the new saddlebags in the window.

Instead, he watched the reflection of the Saber's Edge Inn behind him. Three city guards lounged next to a horse and cart in front of the porch of the establishment. A few moments later, a sergeant stepped out of the lobby, waving to someone inside and nodding. The guards clambered aboard the cart and headed off down the street away from the inn.

Buck waited until the cart turned a corner, then strolled across the street to the porch.

A notice on the bulletin board caught his eye and it took a lot of effort not to jump in alarm. His heart racing, he read the other notices, then reached into his backpack and withdrew a blank sheet of paper. Pretending to post it next to one of the notices, he fumbled with the other notice, dropping both onto the boards of the porch. He replaced the printed paper with his blank sheet and stuffed the notice into his pack.

Can't be having that around for casual bounty hunters to find.

Dar Cabot looked up as he entered the lobby. "Buck!" He said with relief. "Thank God. Come on, the others are waiting."

Buck followed him into the empty tavern, where Andyn and Eric waited at one of the tables. Andyn looked lovely as usual in dark green livery and chainmail, her golden hair bright against dark cloth.

"What's going on?" Buck asked as he slid into a seat.

Andyn smiled at him. *She looks a bit sad*, he thought.

"We have to leave," she said.

What? Buck raised his eyebrows. "But we just got here."

Dar plopped into a seat next to Buck. "Andyn was attacked by two assassins in her bath. She killed both of them but got poisoned. It's a good thing Eric carries that healing ointment around with him or we'd be minus a group member."

"Assassins?" Buck asked. He felt a chill, remembering Hlerv, then dismissed the feeling. *That would be too much of a coincidence. Besides, the Saber's Edge and the Golden Lady are on opposite sides of the city.*

A voice at his elbow startled him. "Bloodswords, or at least that's what I've been able to find out."

A dark-haired male Halfling vaulted into the seat next to Buck. Unlike Hlerv the Gnome, he sported no beard or mustache. Black leather armor protected his vitals and a cloak, colored black on the outside and patchy with camouflage colors on the reverse side, covered his shoulders. A broadsword hung from his left hip.

"Bloodswords, Connor?" asked Andyn.

Connor nodded. "An established assassins guild, favorites of our friends the evil religions." He reached for Andyn's ale tankard. "Bloodswords don't come cheap."

Andyn slapped his hand away. "Do we know who hired them?"

Connor turned a brilliant grin to her. "*That* would have been pricey *and* dangerous. I've had enough of dangerous for a while. Just be glad I found out what I did."

Dar leaned back in his chair. "The bottom line is that we have to find another inn, and quickly. We need some rest before we go see this Count Telmin tomorrow. The owner of this place doesn't want us here. Pitched battles are not great for business."

Buck spoke up. "I know of a great inn down in the south of town, the Golden Lady."

Andyn shot him a withering look.

Buck sighed. He already knew her opinion of the south end of town.

"Let's get going then," said Dar, rising from his seat. "I'll see if maybe the barkeep has any recommendations while the rest of you get your gear together."

Buck and Connor stayed at the table, the Halfling sipping Andyn's ale. Buck absently fed Puup a bit of bread. The bird gulped it down and began cleaning his feathers.

"You know," Connor noted, paying a lot of attention to the designs on the tankard, "I've seen your name in print lately."

Buck felt a chill. "Have you?"

Connor fixed him with sharp black eyes. "Look, Buck, I don't know what kind of trouble you had in the past, but you'd better come clean, and soon. It'll be worse for you the longer you hide it."

Buck gauged him, then looked down at the table. "Can I trust you not to tell anyone?"

Connor grinned. "Always."

Buck had his doubts, but he shrugged. "Derek Feller was a friend of mine and a jeweler's apprentice. One night, he showed up at my father's house, telling me he had just gotten a great break. I asked to see it and he showed me a bag of gems. I knew he had stolen them from his boss. Unfortunately, the city guard were right on his heels. I told Derek to get lost and he did, but not before planting the gems in the house. They caught him later, but he fingered me and claimed I was the guy they were looking for. I didn't have time to break his nose, seeing as how I was already heading south on a fast horse. I found out later that Derek slugged his master from behind and lifted the gems. When the guards started searching, he decided to stash them at my place, but blamed me when he got caught."

Connor said nothing.

"I was framed, honest," Buck continued. "The gems weren't worth that much anyway. Derek was just being stupid."

"I believe you," Connor said, "You haven't given me any reason to doubt you, but the others follow Verian and Christianity. I don't have to remind you those faiths have pointed ideas about stealing and lying. The sooner you tell them, the better it will be."

Buck looked out the tavern window that looked out onto the street. An old man shuffled past, gnarled fingers gripping his cane. "But will they believe me? And why should they risk everything just to help me, especially after I've kept this from them all this time?"

Connor gave him a wry grin and hopped off his chair. "If you don't know the answers to that, it was somebody else named Buck Bydecy who fought alongside them, saved their lives and helped beat Halkith and the Ja'al. You're one of the reasons we even have pegasi to ride. Don't sell yourself short." He clapped Buck on the shoulder and left.

Buck Bydecy sat there long after he departed. "You know, Puup," he said to the pigeon, "I should have turned west instead of east back at Wit's End those months ago."

CHAPTER TWO

To Face Cold Fire

D ar Cabot tapped his foot against the ornate, carved baseboard and paced back to the others for about the hundredth time. He cast his eyes around the anteroom, lined with cherry wood paneling. Paintings of country scenes hung on the walls and an inlaid ceramic vase sat on a side table.

The paneling alone is probably worth the price of my parents' old house in Forester.

Andyn and Eric reclined on an immaculate white divan in front of one of the two windows in the room. She had opted for her finest dark green tunic over chain armor but disdained long breeches in the warmth of late spring, instead leaving her legs bare from mid-thigh to shin. Twin steely maces hung from her weapon-belt and her holy symbol, a silver tree, rested between her breasts, winking in the sunlight. She and Eric occasionally cast glances down onto the castle courtyard and made quiet comments to each other. Buck stood next to them, the ever-present Puup on his shoulder.

Dar shook his head. *Of course, we had to bring the bird. He's just the size to fit in Buck's shoulder sack, luckily enough. The guards wouldn't have appreciated it — and even less, the housekeeper.*

Buck leaned his rangy six-foot-two frame up against the window-frame. A sandy-haired fellow, observers often mistook his lazy grey eyes as a sign of boredom. He, too, wore his finest: dark grey hauberk over chainmail, his boots shined, and the Dwarven sword Khelios polished to radiance at his hip.

Eric nodded at something Andyn said, smiled, and stretched.

Dar noted Eric's blue hauberk with a white cross. *In honor of his absent lady, Brandawyn.*

He wandered back to the vase on the table, examined it, and wandered back to the window. *Brandi and Megan. When will I see Megan again?*

Connor perched on a nearby windowsill and gave him a wry look. "Pacing won't make this move along any faster," he remarked, turning back to a map in his hands.

Dar sighed. "I know. He's a count. He's got important people in there. We're next in line. Etcetera, etcetera. I just hate waiting."

Connor grinned. "Boy, are you going to have an aggravated life. Wait until you have children."

Dar's eyebrows rose, his interest piqued. "And how would you know about that?"

A click echoed in the room. A pair of tall double doors chased in silver opened on the other side of the narrow room.

A purple-liveried servant held the doors open. "His Excellency will see you now."

The companions smoothed their clothing and followed the servant into an office. Bookshelves lined the walls. A massive, polished table and matching chair dominated the center, on top of a huge rug woven with capering centaurs.

A slim young human with a thin mustache eyed them as they entered, a parchment in his hands. His splendid forest green doublet and black trousers caught Dar's eye, as did a heavy gold chain of office and four rings on his fingers. His ornate jeweled dagger could probably cut bread but little else. The man looked at the companions and sniffed.

Dar disliked him instantly.

The servant indicated Dar and his friends. "Your Excellency, these are Dar Cabot, Eric Indidarc, Buckminster Bydecy, Connor Lomin and Andyn Eleandir, the Grey Riders, in the service of Lord Nolan of Forester. Riders, this is His Excellency, Count James Telmin, Lord of Riverbend, Vassal of the Duke of Darlon."

Telmin waved a hand and the servant departed, closing the door.

"Well, well," he said in a droll, affected voice. "Grey Riders is it? I wonder, were you named in 'ancient legend' or is it some backwoods folk tale? Or maybe a minstrel's tale?"

Andyn's eyes flashed for a second, but she bowed. "None of the above, Excellency. A dragon wizard, Iron Thunder, named us."

Telmin's eyes widened and he coughed. "Yes, quite. Well, I see from Baron Hanford's letter that you are his air squadron, trained pegasus riders. Good. I have need of your services."

He stepped around the desk. "There has been some unrest in the mountains on the northern Astarel-Deran border," he continued, walking over to a map of Deran on one wall of the office. He swept a languid hand at a region north and west of Darlon. "Brigands, Kaftu, Trolls and similar rabble. There is a bandit prince in the region who seems to have designs on carving out a territory for himself. The Duke has sent two air squadrons along with a couple of his regiments to root them out."

Dar looked at the map with interest, noting where Darlon sat between the confluence of the Deor and Lonmar rivers. *That area is at least a day's flight away. If the squadrons have to keep pace with ground units, it's more like a week.*

Telmin stepped away from the map. "Simply put, with regard to air cavalry, we are undermanned. There seems to be a virus or other pestilence in some of our feed grain. Most of the pegasi and griffons are under veterinary attention. You are the closest squadron in the vicinity, which is why His Grace the Duke decided to send a message to Lord Hanford by Tele-Post."

He watched them for a reaction. "However, your mission has nothing to do with the bandits. There is a region immediately north of Darlon, along a minor trade route to Kareth, in Astarel. A patrol and a small caravan have disappeared in the area. Whatever is attacking them is leaving nothing behind but pools of water, dried blood and a few bits of armor."

Dar blinked at the strange combination of evidence, especially the pools of water. He looked at Andyn.

Telmin cleared his throat, toying with the medallion against his chest. He looked down at them. "You are to find out the source of this trouble and eliminate it. Do you think you can handle it?"

Andyn nodded. "Of course, Excellency."

Telmin raised an eyebrow, smirking. "My, confident, aren't we? No matter. The reward is two thousand gold crowns for the lot of you to divide up as you see fit, along with anything you might manage to procure on the way."

Eric looked at the others, who nodded. "That is acceptable."

"I dare say," the Count replied. Now he looked as if he had tasted something bitter. "Were you one of my elite units, you would be doing this for your nation, not gold."

Yes, thought Dar, *so elite that they didn't have their feed grain inspected by clerics before giving it to their mounts.*

Andyn smiled. "We are doing it for our nations, milord. Since we are free-lances, we just get paid less regularly."

The noble sniffed again. "Quite. Well, that is all." He waved a hand to dismiss them.

What an idiot. Dar considered telling him where to put his attitude, but kept his mouth shut. A servant escorted the companions out to another room, down some stairs, through a grand hall and out into the sun-splashed courtyard.

"Sword of Saint Michael!" Dar exploded as they stopped next to the castle well. He cast a baleful eye up at the tower. "Are we sure he doesn't work for the Ja'al?"

Eric smiled. "You may have something there."

Dar shook his head. "Those kinds of people really bother me. I guess growing up with Lord Nolan and his father kind of protected me from smug blockheads like that."

Andyn blinked in the afternoon sun. "Well, most nobles I've met have been somewhere between the two, more towards Nolan's side. They try to treat most people with some kind of respect, even if they feel otherwise. After all, they can't do everything themselves and people are more educated nowadays than they were back in the time of the Paragon Kings."

"Let's get going," Connor said, heading for the main gate. "Whatever it is that's attacking people doesn't care how arrogant Telmin is."

The others followed him.

—◆◇◆—

Kalar Cintos, courier of the Ja'al, wound through the dark, web-filled corridor, cursing both his luck and his superiors. *Why can't Margoth find a better place to hide out? And she insisted I come alone. Why?*

He imagined all manner of reasons why the undead sorceress would want him to come by himself. He conjured more vicious epithets as he ducked under a fallen beam.

Being the liaison between the Ja'al command and Margoth probably won't count for much if it's bad news, he thought sourly. *The old bitch probably wants to fry me anyway.*

The hallway yawned above him: tall, wide, and decrepit. At the far end, massive arched stained-glass windows had once stood above a throne dais. Now, empty window frames gaped, replaced by creepers and vines where designs and figures once caught the sunlight. Boulders from the ceiling stones lay among the shattered, dusty floor tiles, and more plants coiled up around massive marble pillars.

Kalar surveyed the scene, faintly impressed. *Well now. This must have been quite the showplace in its day. It isn't Thul Mardil - that old palace has long since crumbled to dust and it's much farther south.*

He picked his way down the hall, avoiding the more noisome-looking growth. The hall remained deathly quiet. Dim moonlight mingled with the flame of his flickering torch and the place spelled of musty, rotting things.

His skin crawled in that unnerving quiet. Despite the wild and verdant forest outside the confines of these ruins, he heard no animals or insects. The silence felt heavy, as if the stones resented any sound.

A hiss sounded from his left and he jumped into a defensive stance. He whipped out a short sword. The weapon flared with red light. He stared.

A skeleton in ornate plated armor stood before him, bearing a massive two-handed sword. Tiny balls of flame burned where its eyes should have been and a filthy crown sat on top of a yellowed cranium.

14

The thing bowed. "Captain Cintos, from the Ja'al High Command, I presume," it rasped.

Kalar swallowed. "Y-yes. I have a report for Her Highness."

The skeletal creature straightened. "Wait here." It stepped away from him with fluid grace and headed off to a side door.

Kalar felt the sweat run down his back. *I can summon skeletons to do my bidding, but that creature moves much faster and more gracefully than the mindless automatons I can command. What the hell is it?*

Before he could give it a second thought, the side door opened. Four hulking Ogres entered, glowing orange eyes locked on him and halberds at the ready. At least eight feet tall and horned, their tusks protruded from black lips. A skeletal figure in rich purple and gold floated in after the guards, a glowing crown lighting her features.

Kalar fought against an overwhelming feeling of panic. Even though he knew it was a spell effect, he still had trouble preventing his hands from shaking. Instead, he bowed low. "To Zhinia Margoth, Princess of Thul Mardil, Priestess of Garon-Zith, I bring respectful greeting from the Ja'al High Council."

He brought his eyes up and shuddered.

Margoth's eye sockets, unlike those of her knight, burned from within with tiny points of purple light. Her skull still retained some few strands of hair, as if to make a last, desperate attempt to deny her un-living state. She wore a high-necked gown in richest purple with thread-of-gold symbols and piping along its hem and seams. The diamonds and rubies in her twelve-pointed tiara glittered with some kind of weird inner fire.

"I accept your greeting," she said in a musical, feminine voice, raising a skeletal hand. "I extend the hospitality of this glorious estate bequeathed to me by your liege lords of the Ja'al."

"I am honored," he replied. He couldn't miss the ironic tone of voice as she noted that her current hideout came courtesy of Kalar's masters.

Margoth extended her hand to the side and spoke a word. A glittering vertical strip of light appeared and in the blink of an eye she held a staff of intertwining black wood with a large clear crystal at the top.

"So, how do the Ja'al's recruiting efforts go?"

"We can provide two thousand mercenaries," he answered. "We have signed on a few new free-lances from the academies and universities. There are also three more Goblin tribes who have sworn fealty to Your Majesty, bringing their total to sixteen hundred."

She nodded, taking a seat in the throne. "Does Philip of Deran suspect anything?"

"We do not think so. The escapade with the pegasi of Whitehorse Peak seems to have distracted him. They think they have thwarted our latest plans. Our sources indicate the Deranese leadership feels the pegasi were the ultimate goal and, since Halkith is dead, that particular battle has been won."

Margoth chuckled but said nothing.

"As for our other efforts," Kalar continued, "Many minstrels and troubadours are favorably disposed to our agents. Some artists, as well, appear to be ripe for subjugation with the correct inducements. Certain elements in the artistic professions apparently have felt suppressed under Philip, who has insisted on certain, shall we say, standards. None of them know the true source of our suggestions. Some songwriters have begun to insert lyrics into their latest works intimating that Philip is an oppressive tyrant."

"As for the brothel owners and drug smugglers, they have been very cooperative. They are a prime source of income for our effort. Two assassins' guilds, the Crossed Swords and the Shrikes, have tentatively agreed to support us when the time is right."

Margoth stood, nodding. "Excellent. Your cult may yet redeem itself after the bungled pegasus project. Now, tell me the bad news."

Kalar shuddered. *How does she sense what I'm going to say?*

He kept his eyes averted. "Even though our allies in the communities of Deran are well on their way to lulling the populace into complacency, our enemies have not been idle. The Order of Saint Thomas, from the Christian church, and the Followers of Mindra, of Verian, have sponsored various artists who oppose our efforts. We have tried various subtle means to discredit them, but they are attaining a strong following."

She rapped the heel of her staff against the shattered tiles and spun away from him. "Cursed lap-dogs of Mindra! How are this 'Order' and the Followers being dealt with?"

He tried to respond with deference. "There are various avenues. Some of our sympathizers in the government are endeavoring to bribe the local town-criers and printers to refuse to advertise them, a route which has had some success.

Many of the people in those professions already sympathize with our cause. We have also organized free-gift offerings to the more famous of the artists communities to entice them to support our agenda."

Her eyes flared. "Why do we not just slay their leadership?"

Kalar nodded. "Ah yes. We could do so if Your Majesty were already in power. However, in the current climate, we cannot move openly. Philip would suspect something and, whatever you may think of *him*, his lady queen is no fool. No, Majesty, persecuting our enemies subtly from popular and admired segments of society is the best course of action at this time. Rest assured, any amount of confusion and internal bickering can only help us. When you finally strike, they will feel your power."

She nodded and turned back, a nimbus of fairy-flame coursing over her tiara. "Quite so. I will make additional funds available for your use if the need arises. But there is more, I can tell."

"Darlon's duke has responded to our forays in the northwest of Deran, as we expected, but our assassins were unsuccessful in slaying Andyn Eleandir. We have word that the Grey Riders were seen at the court of one of the Darlon counts, which could bode ill for us if we are to conduct any searches in the mountains north of there."

She hissed. There were a few moments of silence, then she shook her head. "Veriani bitch. First she and her band of simpering mercy-workers take *my* pegasi for themselves and now they blunder right where we don't want them."

Kalar shrugged. "There is always the alliance with the Fallen Elves, Your Majesty. The Grey Riders *are* heading into their territory. Your agent there, Liander Tolin, could set up something for us."

She considered this, stroking the crystal on the staff. "Yes. The Dark Elves need something to do while Darlon's army is off chasing our bandit friends."

Kalar shrugged. "I would recommend that Your Majesty not delay. The opportunity is ripe, with the Riders in the north of the country. The prophecy of Irial states, 'North they go, to face cold fire...'"

A vise-like band constricted around his throat and he wheezed. He stumbled backwards, then an unseen force lifted him up and slammed him into the nearest pillar. When the spots cleared from his vision, Margoth stood not five feet from him, eyes lit fiery purple.

"Do not mention that blasphemous drivel in my presence!" she shrieked.

He fought for air, then the force on his throat vanished. He collapsed to kneel on the floor, gasping.

"I am well aware of the prophecy and all it contains, idiot!" Margoth swept away from him and spat on the ground. Her spittle smoked and sizzled where it contacted anything living, eating away at the vines and creepers.

Kalar held his tongue. He too, knew many of the verses, only because the High Command made it part of his training. The Song of the Grey Riders foretold of a Dark Rider of great power — he was sure it was Margoth — but they also prophesied her eventual destruction at the hands of seven grey riders.

And that's what she fears more than anything. She knows they could take her down if they ever figured out whatever the hell that damned Song means.

She spun back to him. "Is that all?"

Kalar stood and nodded. "Yes, Majesty."

She raised herself to her full, skeletal height. "Very well, then. Report back to your masters that I have received their information and concur with the approach. I will have Liander contact Queen Ildrisana of the Dark Elves and strike an alliance: magic, gems and gold in exchange for the capture of the Grey Riders."

She turned away. "You are dismissed."

Kalar bowed and slipped away down the hallway, towards the passage and freedom. As he left, he shot a look back at the ruined and now-empty throne room.

I have to get into a new line of work, he thought, feeling his throat.

———◄O►———

Dear Verian, I hope not, thought Andyn, looking down at the village from her vantage point high in the air.

She pulled Medianox into a hover and waved a hand at her companions. Her pegasus slowed some five hundred feet above the ground with even strokes of black wings.

The other Riders gathered around her.

"Look!" she pointed. "The village!"

Dar nodded and wheeled Virasi, heading down. The others followed.

About four feet above the ground, Medianox beat her wings hard and stopped for a split second, then dropped into a canter, folding her wings next to her ribcage, over Andyn's legs.

Andyn reined in and petted the pegasus on the neck, her mouth set in a grim line.

A shattered blacksmith shop greeted her eyes first, then a collection of leaning timbers and burnt wood that might have been another shop. Dark figures lay on the ground nearby in either pools of water or mud. Jumbles of cloth, paper, weapons, bodies, and wood littered the main street.

The other Riders landed ahead of her in the village, looking for survivors. Andyn dismounted and picked her way forward, checking the bodies. She slipped into a spell trance and tried to gauge the time of death. *Dead more than twelve hours. Why hasn't the water evaporated by now?*

She looked up at the bright sky. The sunshine made this little roadside place warm, at least a hundred yards from the nearest shade.

"No luck, Andyn," said Dar, walking his pegasus towards her. Sunlight glinted on his helmet. "There are sixteen people, all dead, and parts of about six others."

She sighed. "Well, at least we know we're on the right track."

Buck, Connor and Eric joined them.

Eric took off his helmet and ran a hand through his hair. "The street is so churned, I can't pick out any prints."

Dar nodded. "The ground is really wet."

"Rain?" asked Buck.

Andyn shook her head. "Haven't had rain clouds over this part of the range in a month. Why would there still be water? Unless it was ice —"

A memory clicked in her brain. Her eyes widened. "By the Tree..."

Connor looked around quickly. "What, what?"

She took Eric and Dar by the arms. "Look for tracks, really big tracks. Back, away from the ruins, closer to the trees." They strode off.

Buck petted Puup, who flapped his wings in agitation. "What's going on?"

Andyn waved him to silence and he looked at Connor with a shrug. She moved off to check other bodies.

Dar shouted to them and Andyn raced to his side, joined by Buck and Connor. Eric and Dar waited for them away from the main street, behind ruined shops and homes.

Dar shook his head. "You called it, Andyn."

Eric knelt down to touch a deep, three-clawed footprint in the earth, fully two feet long.

"What is it?" asked Connor, patting the nose of Phantom, his pegasus.

Dar and Eric exchanged a look.

"A dragon," Dar said, toeing the track with his boot. "Too small for a True Dragon or a Drake, but by the size of it, probably a Balar at the least."

Andy's heart clenched. "Ice Balar."

"How do you know that?" asked Buck.

"These people have been dead for a long time, and with no rain, the only way we'd have water here is if there were a great amount of ice."

"But why an Ice Balar here?" asked Eric. "They don't even like warm climates. It should be far away in the north this time of year."

No one spoke for a long moment. Eric stood, eyeing the silent forest behind the town, then the towering peaks a few miles away. They heard only soft scurrying sounds among the wreckage and the occasional call of a raven.

"North they go, to face cold fire, to battle the dragon and still her ire," whispered Andyn.

Connor smiled. "You've memorized the Song of the Grey Riders, haven't you?"

Andyn shook her head. "How can you be so sanguine about a prophecy that was supposed to predict our lives? And possible demise?"

He shrugged. "I think it's fascinating."

Buck kicked a rock. "Damn prophecy!"

"Wait a minute," said Eric, "Let's have a look at the thing."

Andyn sighed, removing her backpack. "Connor's right — I've memorized it. And no, there isn't anything else about a dragon. Just that we're supposed to encounter and defeat one. And it's a female."

She handed him a bone scroll case and he pulled out a roll of aged vellum. Eric's eyes scanned the page, then he rolled the paper up.

He looked worried.

I don't blame him, Andyn thought with a twinge of apprehension. To be summoned by some kind of prophecy to fight evil and then find events in your life headed the way the prophecy predicted— it would worried anyone.

"All right," said Connor, "How do we find this dragon then?"

"Follow her tracks," said Dar from behind them.

Eric sighed. "Balar fly, Dar."

"This one didn't."

The companions joined him. He knelt next to a partial claw-print in the soft, wet earth. He looked off into the mountains. He pointed. More claw prints marched off into the forest.

"Now why didn't she just fly off?" Andyn mused.

Dar stood and looked at Eric, who shrugged. "Maybe someone got a couple of arrows into a wing. Maybe she just felt like it. All I know is that I have tracks."

Buck squinted, looking up at the mountains and foothills. "Where would she live?"

"There," said Dar, pointing at the foothills. "Close to the road, and deep underground."

CHAPTER THREE

Pit of the Dragon

I'll sure be glad when this is all over.

Megan Alenar tried not to fidget. Peering out between the graceful branches of the low-hanging willow, she watched the silent glade for signs of her aunt Daphne. Low fingers of grey mist hovered above the tall grass. A black bird darted across the meadow. Perversely, the day turned out cloudy and damp, another indignity for Megan, who hated both. She patted the neck of her pegasus.

"How long until we go after her?" Brandi asked from behind her.

"Another turn of the sand," said Uncle Stephen. Slim and dark-haired, he placed a gauntleted hand on her shoulder. Shiny chainmail glinted underneath his brown-and-green mottled cloak. A longsword and mace hung at his side. He smiled, his thin mustache curving.

"It's not as long as you think," he said, holding up a tiny hourglass on a chain around his neck. He let the device drop back onto his forest-green tunic. "And don't worry, my sister can take care of herself."

Brandi led her pegasus next to Megan to watch the glade. She, too, wore armor under a camouflage cloak. She settled her helmet and rested her hands on the two short swords at her hips.

"I don't doubt Aunt Daphne's abilities, Uncle Stephen," she replied, "I'm just worried. The last time we tried to get 'secret information' we almost lost all of our gear to a con man."

"Ah," said Stephen, putting his arm around her shoulders. "But we didn't. And that's the most important part. We soundly defeated that rascal. Glorious, wasn't it?"

I wish I could be so confident, Megan mused, thinking over spell lists in her head. *I have to be ready no matter what.*

She rested her hand on a silver dagger at her belt, hidden behind her own camouflage cloak. Her finger traced the patterns of the gold-chased pommel for a few seconds. *Dar Cabot's grandmother's dagger, and she a free-lance like him.*

Stephen's eyes flitted to the dagger. "I'm sure Dar is doing fine."

Megan gave a little smile. "Me too, but he lets his quest drive him too much."

Stephen nodded. "That's a determined young man, to be sure. He'll find out what happened to his grandparents. Seventeen years is a long time, but I've known ranger scouts who have managed to pick up even older trails by careful research, patience and their ability to read people. I have confidence. You should too."

Megan sighed. *Family quests brought us together and now they break us apart. I'm here to find some ancient secrets about the southern nations and he's up in Deran, still looking for clues to his grandparents.*

She tried to ignore the pain on her heart. Despite the urgency and importance of their current mission, she missed him more, not less, as time went on. *Does Dar still love me? I know I love him.*

She wondered if she would ever see him again. *God,* she prayed, fighting tears, *please take care of him until I return.*

Stephen's hand squeezed her shoulder. She looked up in surprise, realizing he had been watching her.

Drat. She smiled sadly. "It's that obvious?"

Stephen gave her a hug. "Don't worry, Megan. I have a feeling you'll see him again, and he won't forget you. If everything you and Brandi told me about him and Eric is true, you have nothing to worry about. As long as they hold out hope for you, they will be waiting when you return. They are not the type of men who take love lightly. Besides, after we're finished, I will help you find them again."

"Here she comes," said Brandi.

A woman in chain armor trotted back towards them through the glade, casting an occasional glance over her shoulder, naked longsword in her hand. Daphne Alenar's countenance and the reddened blade in her hand gave them grim testimony of what had transpired.

"Are you hurt?" asked Stephen, slipping a long bow off his back.

"I'm fine," said Daphne. She ducked under the willow branches. "It's the three lying in the grove over there that are going to need some help. Or actually, the last rites, if their religions do such things."

"What happened?" Brandi asked.

Daphne made a face as she thrust her blade into the soft earth to clean it off. "Birimon showed up just like he promised. Except instead of bringing information about the Ancients of Torosc, he had two assassins. I guess he thought I was the only one interested."

Megan shuddered. "That's the second time. It's a good thing they don't know there are four of us or they'd send a lot more."

Stephen nodded. "It won't take long for them to figure it out." He tapped Daphne on the helmet with the tip of his bow. "What now?"

Daphne finished cleaning her blade and sheathed it. "Mil-Tereth. There are a lot of colleges and academies in the capitol. We're sure to find a sage somewhere. What we really need is enough information to tell deceptions from the truth. We can't keep stumbling around like this."

Megan wondered again about their mission. *Finding legendary texts about the ancient Paragon-Era kingdoms in Torosc is a tall order*, she thought. *I know Aunt Daphne and Uncle Stephen are dedicated to this quest, but I don't have a lot of hope that people were able to bring out a lot of important documents before Torosc fell. The Ja'al and the Vardish had a lot of incentive to destroy all mention of the old ways.*

Stephen nodded. "Let's move as fast as we can."

Daphne slipped a necklace out from under her armor. The silver medallion of an owl glinted in the misty light She stepped out from under the willow and placed it on the damp ground.

"Paractus!"

The medallion glowed, filled out and grew to an amazing eight-foot height in a few seconds. A tremendous owl blinked and stared at them, massive claws gripping the sodden earth. Daphne and Stephen climbed into the large, two-seated saddle on the creature's back.

Brandi sighed and mounted up. "We won't get anywhere standing in this swamp. We can probably make it to Eleth-Anor tonight if we move fast."

Megan vaulted into Larinor's saddle. *Dar, I hope you're having an easier time than we are.*

"Dar," whispered Buck. "We've got to strike a light or something. It's as dark as a Daemon's arse in here."

Dar grinned in the darkness. "Connor will be back in a little while. Just hang on."

"Besides," Eric added, "Lighting a torch won't do us any good if the last thing we see is an ice Balar freezing us solid."

"I'll freeze solid anyway," muttered Buck, but the others either didn't hear or ignored him.

Dar sat back on his haunches, bastard sword across his knees. After a hard day tracking the dragon's prints, they discovered this enormous shaft in the ground. Formed by steam, volcanic activity — or creatures Dar cared not to think about — it descended vertically from the surface. He barely made out rough ledges on the other side of the shaft, ramping downwards like the one they rested on. Now, almost a hundred feet in, a small grey circle of fading afternoon light at the top of the shaft seemed to mock their downward trek. Here, they crouched on the winding shelf, waiting for Connor to finish his reconnaissance.

These damn ramps must have been made by Goblins, he mused. Some of the paths faded into the side wall without warning, making them backtrack several times to find more stable footing.

"Are we sure the pegasi are all right?" Andyn asked. "After all, they aren't familiar with the area."

"They'll be fine," Eric said. "They know enough to find a high place that's safe. They'll wait until I signal them to return with another magical flare. Don't worry."

He shot a grin at Buck. "Puup is with them, after all."

Buck rolled his eyes at the mention of his pet pigeon. "You should thank me. The pegasi like having him around and you have to admit he's been a good luck charm."

"I'm just not sure how he's survived all this time," Dar added. A whisper of sound alerted him and he started.

Andyn held up a hand, her eyes glimmering light green in the dark. "He's coming," she said.

A few heartbeats later, Dar saw another pair of glimmering eyes. He felt a momentary jealousy of Halflings, Elves and Dwarves with their ability to see short distances in total darkness.

Connor's voice floated back to him. "There's a blue-white Balar down there all right, a female, in a big cavern at the bottom of this shaft. She's got a pretty good wound in one wing. I'll bet my shorts she's the one we're looking for."

"There's a bet I want to lose," Buck muttered.

"Can we use lights?" asked Eric.

Connor hesitated. "It looks like she's asleep so it should be okay. Just keep it dim and don't make a lot of noise."

Dar reached for a tinderbox but Buck stopped him. He drew his sword and raised Khelios. Buck's eyes glowed a mild gold color and a dim blue fire raced around the edge of his blade. A soft glow lit the area. Dar's companions looked back at him with shadowed, tense faces.

"I'm not sure we're used to your eyes glowing like that every time you use one of Khelios' features," he said to Buck and got a grunt in response, "It makes you look, well, never mind."

Connor drew his broadsword and turned down the rough rampway. Buck and Dar crept behind him, followed by Andyn and Eric.

Dar took special care to watch his step. To the left he saw a long way down, probably terminating in very hard rocks.

After inching downwards for what seemed like years, Connor's gloved hand shot up. Everyone stopped. The Halfling stepped to his right and disappeared.

Dar blinked. So concentrated on not falling, he didn't notice they had reached the rough, boulder-strewn area at the bottom of the shaft. He followed Connor.

They slipped between massive rocks and four-foot tall, black mushrooms with yellow stripes. Connor waved at Buck and Dar, then slipped into the shadows.

Dar peeked around a boulder and took a deep breath.

A slender, reptilian form about the length of three carts laid end to end lay coiled upon a veritable mountain of silver and copper coins. A pair of bat-like wings folded against the creature's sides, rising and falling with the rhythm of her breathing. Three long horns and a ruff of smaller ones crowned the head. Fangs protruded down from the upper jaw, and sharp talons the size of knives glinted in the light of Buck's sword. The dragon's pale-blue, almost white scales shimmered like frost on grass in the winter.

Dar saw a few jewels, a sword and mace wink at him in the dim light cast by Khelios.

Now how do we—wait a minute. Sir Tan said something about this.

Dar motioned to the others and they joined him. "We can jump it," Dar said. "If we knock it unconscious, we can take it back to Darlon."

Buck stared at him. "Are you crazy? How are we going to take it to the city? We'd need iron chains to hold it down!"

"Shh!" said Andyn, wide eyes locked on the dragon. "He's right. I've heard of people subduing dragons before. It's tough, but not impossible. If we just kill it, we won't be able to find out what's been going on. If it's our captive, maybe we can make it talk."

Buck looked dismayed when Eric nodded. "But, but—" he sputtered.

Dar cut in before he could continue. "Sir Tan, my mentor, said he had done it himself once. I think we can do it. Come on. There's not much time."

He ignored Buck's muttered oath as they crept towards the Balar.

The four gathered in a ring around the treasure pile and Dar saw Connor's small figure perched on a rock behind and above the creature. Dar raised his hand to signal the attack.

Both of the Balar's eyes popped open.

Dar blinked and lowered his hand.

The creature grinned. "Stealthy you are, but not stealthy enough."

Andyn bowed low. "As we expected, Your Grace. It would be foolish to think that we could approach a frost Balar so, without her so much as knowing we are about. The tales of your kind are true."

The Balar smiled wider and drew herself up, head towering ten feet above the floor of the cavern. Deep blue eyes flashed. "They are indeed true. What do you seek here, little fools?"

Eric now got into the act, bowing as well. "Only information and service, Great One. We have heard that you are ravaging the countryside and would join you or the one whom you serve. How may we call you?"

"Hideges," the Balar answered after a moment. "Yes, that is a good short form. Hideges." She rose and stood astride the treasure pile with forepaws clasped before her. "But what makes you think you are worthy? The quest for the Tower of Undying Light is not for the faint of heart."

Tower of Undying Light? What the hell is that? Dar refrained from the obvious question at a warning look from Andyn.

Buck looked a little pale. Dar almost jumped in surprise when Buck stepped forward and sketched a quick bow of his own. "My...I mean, Your Greatliness... I too wish to join you in the quest for the tower."

Dar stared. *Well, that's a sudden change of heart for someone who didn't vote for this approach.*

Again, Hideges bent her neck in a regal nod. "If you are worthy."

Andyn took a step to the side. "How may we prove ourselves?"

"You will have to do a task for me," Hideges said. "I would have your names."

"Well..." began Dar, wondering if he should lie, then decided against it. *Who's she going to tell? Anyway, if we can capture her, it will be a moot point.*

"I am Dar Cabot. This is Eric Indidarc, the lady is Andyn Eleandir and the other gentleman is Buck Bydecy."

The Balar whirled, eyes flashing. "Bydecy!" she hissed, then opened her mouth wide. The air crackled with frost.

Dar leapt to the side. A blast of the coldest air he had ever encountered shot by him. He rolled and popped up, drawing his sword.

The other Riders dodged. Some rocks and mushrooms behind them took the brunt of the blast.

A small shape hurled down off a boulder behind the dragon. Connor landed on the Balar's back and stabbed. A shriek of pain rang out. Then, with a flickering, sinuous motion, Hideges slipped and rolled, snapping her tail. The tail strike smacked Connor Lomin into the air and he landed in a heap in a corner. He dragged himself to his feet, grimacing.

Dar charged forward. He slashed at a massive leg. His sword bounced off. Hideges snapped down at him and he used the return stroke to swat her on the side of the head.

She swung a claw and he tried to twist away. The heel of her paw struck him full in the side. Air woofed out of him as he crashed to the stony floor, banging his helmeted head on a rock.

He rolled over and tried to get out of the way. *Saint Michael! That hurt!*

Hoping he didn't have any broken bones, he struggled to his feet. Hideges swiped her tail at Buck and Eric. They leaped over it. Andyn shouted a word and a thin green shaft of light shot out from her hand, striking Hideges full in the chest. A mild greenish radiance covered the Balar.

Hideges' eyes glazed over and she stumbled. She shook her head, muttering an oath in some draconic tongue and blinked, looking disoriented.

Here's our chance. Dar jumped into the fray.

Buck stabbed a foreleg, drawing dark blue blood that made a cloying fog. Hideges shrieked and tried to bite him, but he slipped out of the way, deflecting her teeth with his shield. Eric darted in, thrusting with his spear. It struck home and caused another cloud of white mist.

Hideges jerked the spear away and cast it aside. Buck dashed in, stabbing upward with Khelios. The Balar slapped him aside with a claw and he tumbled into Connor, racing over to help. Both went down in a heap.

"I've got it!" yelled Eric.

What is he shouting about? Dar thought, too busy dodging a lashing tail. He swung at her hindquarters. This time he drew blood and Hideges grunted.

A flare of orange light sprang up behind him. Dar whirled.

Eric held two tongues of flame in his hands. He hurled both at Hideges. The Balar cried out in terror and backed up. Dar stumbled out of the way of a dragon leg, tripped, and landed on a pile of money.

One flame-tongue landed on Hideges and her scream shook the very stones. Flesh began melt off the creature's shoulder and chest.

The other flame bounced off the Balar and landed on the tangled pile of Connor and Buck.

"Holy Tree!" shouted Andyn. She barked a couple of sharp words. Connor and Buck stood, cursing in pain as the flames engulfed their cloaks and Buck's shield.

Then, several things happened at once. Hideges took a deep breath. Andyn finished her spell. A wall of water crashed down on Connor and Buck just as the Balar breathed.

An immense cloud of steam erupted. When it cleared, Dar gaped in amazement and shock. A solid block of ice encased Connor and Buck, both of them frozen in mid-motion.

Hideges stared, eyes wide.

"Damn!" cried Eric. He raised his right hand and spoke sharp words. A thin stroke of lightning seared out and hit the Balar full in the chest.

Hideges cursed. Her jaws clashed on empty air as Eric rolled out of the way. Andyn followed Eric with a lightning spell of her own. The Balar shrieked again, weaker this time.

Dar stepped in and slammed his blade into her. Hideges reeled and crashed into a wall. Dar thrust with all his strength. He heard a loud pop and his sword sank to the hilt into Hideges' side. The Balar gave a gurgling sigh and collapsed in a heap.

Dar followed her, flopping down on the stones, panting. Everything hurt and he felt like he had run ten miles.

Andyn raced over to her frozen compatriots and examined the ice wall.

"Nice move, Eric," Dar gasped. He limped over to join her. "Now what do we do?"

"Actually, it was a good move," Andyn murmured, brow furrowed in concentration. "Ice Balars are afraid of fire, as you saw, and with good reason. It was just poor timing that got them into this."

Eric looked worried. "Are they alive?"

Andyn tapped her chin. "Probably. They were hit with the cold blast so quick their bodies probably didn't have time to even feel the shock."

Dar looked it over. About four feet thick and seven tall, the block looked clear and smooth, just like the walls of ice that mages made for grocers and butchers in Forester and Hillton. *Except now, instead of keeping food from spoiling, it's keeping Connor and Buck alive—I hope.*

"Well?" Dar asked.

Andyn shook her head. "I've never seen this before. I guess we have two options. Either we wait for them to thaw out, or we warm them up and melt the ice."

"I vote for the second one," Dar said, running his hand on the ice wall. "It'll be dark soon and we don't want to be caught in here when night falls."

Eric nodded. "Just tell us what we have to do."

Andyn sighed. "Okay. Eric, do you know a warming spell?"

When he nodded, she continued. "Use it. Dar, get ready to catch them when they get free. I'll try to use healing spells to get them to wake up."

Eric closed his eyes and placed them on the ice. An orange glow suffused his palms. In seconds, the whole block steamed. Then, whole sections fell away with loud cracks. Dar caught Buck as he slumped out of the collapsing ice and lowered him to the ground. Connor's smaller size made him a lot easier to handle.

Andyn placed a hand on each man's heart and concentrated, a yellow glow covering their chests. Then she and Dar and Eric heaved a sigh of relief when the two began to cough, shiver and blink in confusion.

"Wha...wha.. what h-happened?" Connor stammered, hugging Dar's cloak around himself. Andyn explained and his eyes got wide.

Buck shivered. "W-w-ell, at least she's not going to bother us any m-m-ore."

Eric's eyes narrowed. "Yes, but no thanks to you, Mister Bydecy. We had her until she went crazy. Why does she hate your name? And what was that about a Tower of Undead Light or whatever it was?"

Buck squirmed. The others waited. For some reason, Connor fixed Buck with a look and the human wouldn't meet his eyes.

"Maybe she had me confused with someone else," Buck muttered.

Dar looked at Eric, who shrugged.

Andyn raised an eyebrow. "Talk, mister, or you're going to need more than thawing out when I'm through with you."

Buck sighed from his boots and sat down on the dragon's treasure pile with a loud clink. "I was going to tell you guys this when I was sure about what to do, but I guess I might as well do it now."

Dar sat next to him, interest piqued.

"There's a guy in Tyler named Derek Feller," Buck explained, pulling a cloak tighter around him. "He and I used to be pretty close when we were teenagers, always trying to put the moves on the girls, sneak into our fathers' liquor cabinets, play pranks on the city guards. The usual stuff."

Dar hid a smile. *I could tell him a few tales from Forester.*

"Well, he and I grew apart a bit after I went to the Academy. He became an apprentice jeweler with a fellow named Sarago," Buck continued, "Just a little while after I graduated from Joko's Academy, Derek sneaked in the back window of my father's house one night. I thought that was kind of odd until he showed me a fistful of gems. He winked and said we had it made. I didn't understand for a second but then figured out he had stolen them."

Dar exchanged a glance with Andyn. *And I know what's coming next.*

"The next thing I know, someone's pounding on the door. I told Derek he was an idiot and to get the hell out of my house. Of course, there were two city guards at the door. They were looking for Derek but I told them I hadn't seen him. They just barged in and searched the place but Derek was gone by then."

"So, what's the problem?" asked Connor. "It's not like they're after you."

"But they are."

Eric shook his head. "Wait a minute. Derek stole the jewels."

"Yeah," said Buck wryly, running a hand through damp, sandy hair. "They caught him. He didn't have the gems anymore, but Sarago had him arrested anyway. Then Derek told everyone that I had stolen the gems. He said they could find them in my father's house, under a floorboard. That's when I knew I shouldn't have left him alone when I went to answer the door."

Dar shook his head. "So, you're wanted for theft."

"It gets better," said Buck, flicking a copper coin. "I skipped out of Astarel, but on the border, some bounty hunter and an agent of the government ran into me and I had to fight them to get away. Didn't hurt 'em a lot, but they were mad."

Andyn sighed. "But why didn't you go back and try to prove your innocence?"

Buck gave her an exasperated look. "There were no other witnesses. Besides, I went to Sarago's shop that day to drop off one of Joko's jeweled daggers for repair. I had the opportunity. Sarago was hit from behind, and Derek was his apprentice and, er, I have a bit of a reputation."

Connor began drying his hair with the cloak. "But what about the Undead Light Tower or whatever it is?"

Buck sat without speaking. After a long pause, he sighed again. "You may find it hard to believe, but one of my ancestors was a wizard, a very long time ago. He built a place called the Tower of Undying Light, somewhere out here near the Astarel-Deran border. There's supposed to be a diamond there called the Eye of Truth. If you look through it, you can see the true nature of things, including whether someone is lying or not."

Eric and Andyn gasped. "Do you know how powerful an item like that is? Good Lord!" Eric exclaimed.

Buck frowned. "Yeah, I can guess."

Dar nodded. "And you want to use it to clear your name."

Buck nodded back, silent for a few heartbeats. Then he sighed and stood. "Well, I guess I'll be going."

Andyn stood with him, confused. "What do you mean?"

He blinked. "Well, I can't expect you to throw in with me. I don't have the money to pay you all."

Eric and Connor looked at Dar, who shrugged. "Hey," said Dar, "we might not like the situation and we even might be mad at you for not telling us this before, but you're still one of us."

Andyn nodded. "We're friends, Buck, or at least I thought we were."

Buck looked from one person to the other. "Really? You mean it? And you don't want anything from me?"

Eric clapped him on the shoulder. "Really. And no, we don't want anything, except that you tell us about these things beforehand—and that you don't get the lot of us killed. Now dry off and let's grab some of this loot for ourselves."

Buck looked thoughtful as the companions began sorting through the dragon's treasure pile.

Dar shook his head. *He still can't believe we'd help him for nothing.*

"I'm wondering," said Andyn as she counted out gold pieces from a small sack. "How did Hideges know about this Tower of Undying Light?"

Connor shrugged, hefting a small round shield and rubbing dirt off the metal banding. "Who cares? Dragons know a lot of stuff."

"Dragon stuff, sure," she replied, closing the sack, "and legends certainly, but specific things about a human family? I don't think so. And assuming she was after the Eye of Truth as well, it's unlikely she just happened to come across it. I think we should keep looking."

Dar kept searching the pile. All told, they filled several sacks with silver and gold coins, a couple of items of gold jewelry, a purse full of aquamarines, some arrows, the sword, mace and a potion bottle that Andyn thought were enchanted. In all this, Andyn refused to leave, urging the others on to keep looking.

Finally, Dar turned to her. "Look, we've tried everything. We've got to get back to a town before it gets dark."

She shook her head, then stopped, eyes on the dragon's body. "What's this?" She knelt next to a white-scaled claw and fiddled with something.

"Ha!" She stood and walked over to Dar.

She carried a golden necklace in her hands. A small golden plate etched with elegant writing hung from it.

"She was wearing it?" asked Eric, coming over to her. "That's strange."

Andyn shrugged. "Why not? It's the right size to fit her wrist joint. And if it's something important, she'd want to keep it with her always."

"It looks like it's in Elven." Dar peered at the script and furrowed his brow. *Thank God Megan tried to teach me Elven. Too bad I'm not that great at reading it yet.*

Andyn nodded.

"What does it say?" asked Connor, standing on tip-toe to see.

"The eye in the earth to the eye's home leads," she read, "Beneath the Tower of Undying Light. To the brave, a wall of fire and tower cold are not barriers real. Seek the blue of sky and not the red of flame and therein lies the truth."

No one said anything for a long time. Buck finally stepped forward and took the plate and necklace from Andyn. "Dar's right. We'd better go. We can think about this back in town." He met each person's eyes. "You don't have to do this you know."

Dar gave him a warm smile. "Yes, we do. You're one of the Grey Riders."

CHAPTER FOUR

Enigma in Grey

This will make a nice trophy. Eric leaned back in the chair and put his boots up on the windowsill. He polished a four-inch white talon on his sleeve and blew on it. "Do you think this is enough evidence?"

Dar shrugged and undid the straps on his chainmail. "We have five of them from her claws and there aren't any other white Balar around here. Besides, when the attacks stop, they'll know we did our job."

Connor held up his black leather armor and made a face. He poked a finger through a blackened hole and eyed the water stains. "Sure. I'm made of money. I'll just buy another set of enchanted leather armor."

Buck lay back on the bed with a sigh. "You guys worry too much. And we'd have a lot more evidence if we had brought the head."

Eric made a disgusted face at Buck. "That's nauseous."

Dar grinned and pulled out a drawer. "But excellent proof."

Buck saluted him from the bed.

Connor pulled on a dark green shirt with loose sleeves and began buttoning the front. He needed loose-fitting clothes; despite his small size, his torso, chest and shoulders showed corded muscle.

And I can attest to that personally. He beat me more than once in arm-wrestling.

Eric gazed out the window at the last pink glow of sunset. Far in the distance, from one of the towers of the city wall, a trio of winged creatures took flight. He saw their silhouettes: hindquarters of lions, foreparts of eagles, and each bearing soldiers.

Griffons with riders, Eric thought.

35

"Why do we have to all share one room?" asked Connor, finishing with his shirt.

Dar grinned, slipping into a shirt himself. "Isn't it obvious? Andyn's the only woman."

Connor's expression radiated innocence. "So? You and Eric have already seen her naked."

Buck snickered.

Eric ignored him. "What's our next move, by the way?" he asked instead, tossing the dragon talon in his hand. "I know this 'Eye of Earth' place is supposed to lead to the Tower, but if anybody has any ideas where the 'eye' is, they'd better speak up."

Dar pulled up another chair and looked out the window with Eric. "I think we'd better start with Hideges. She wouldn't have been on the search here if she didn't think there was a chance of success. The question that worries me is why."

Why indeed. Eric wondered. *Did someone put her up to it? Or it could just be a case of draconic curiosity — which is a real thing, according to what Grandpa told us.*

"I know one thing," said Buck, stretching. Puup preened himself from the bedpost. "We're going to get the tar kicked out of us if we go subterranean any more. This was a chore with only one medium-sized Balar, plus had a ton of trouble with Halkith's hobgoblins. We need someone who knows his way around underground."

Connor hopped onto the bed, startling the pigeon. "Great idea. If we could find a Gnome or Dwarf, we'd have no trouble."

Eric looked at him sidelong. "Don't Halfling homes have extensive cellars and things like that?"

"My people only dig down deep enough to extend our homes and provide an escape route. The rest is above ground. If you come to Evendale with me someday, I'll show you. Dwarves and Gnomes wouldn't even consider our workings more than scratches in the earth."

Dar spoke up. "Darlon's a big city. We'll need to post some notices, hire a town crier and maybe advertise in one of the city publications. We could get an agent to interview people for us."

Buck bit his lip and cleared his throat. "Oh, er, actually, I might know someone."

Eric raised an eyebrow. "From where?" *Knowing the parts of town Buck liked to frequent, I'm not sure I trust whoever he might know.*

Buck sat up. "Well, when I was down in town, looking for some help with my, er, problem, I met a Gnome who might help. Not sure what he does for a living, but he seemed to know how to find information, so he might be a blank shield like us."

Eric considered this. *A Gnome. Half-breed between Dwarf and Halfling... almost as good as a full-blooded Dwarf underground.*

"Fine," said Dar, rising. "Why don't you go get him and bring him here to the Silver Griffon? We'll interview him tonight or tomorrow. Now, who's for an ale?"

Connor hopped off the bed. "I thought you'd never ask. Mister Bydecy, care to join us?"

Buck lifted himself up with a groan. "My poor bones might be able to make it."

Dar laughed. "Coming, Eric?"

Eric shook his head. "Go on without me. I'll catch up."

Buck nodded. "Just doesn't want me to drink him under the table again."

Eric grinned and slugged him in the side. "More than likely they'll be hauling your carcass up here before too long! Get out of here."

Eric turned back to the view from his second-story window as the door closed behind him. In the street below, workmen used long hooked poles to remove the covers of the streetlights that marched down the avenue. As they did so, magical light flared, illuminating the darkening streets.

A light breeze ruffled Eric's short-cropped hair as he gazed out at the city of Darlon. All along the battlements of the outer city, lights glittered like motionless fireflies.

He tossed Hideges' talon in his hand, then shoved it into his backpack and reached inside for a steel tube with two end caps. He popped a cap off, unrolling a parchment.

The gathering dusk made it hard to see. He waved a hand and a ball of light sprang up next to the open window shutters.

He ran a finger over the postal stamp and address on the outside: Eric Indidarc, care of Lord Nolan Hanford of Forester, mailed on the third of Augustus, about two weeks ago.

He scanned the words again, hearing her smooth voice in his head:

My Dearest Eric,

Megan and I are well. Naturally, as in my first letter, I cannot tell you where we are right now, for fear that this could be intercepted.

Aunt Daphne and Uncle Stephen are fine. They are much like I remembered them, except wiser and more thoughtful perhaps. They still will not tell us the background behind our quest. They say it is for security purposes, in case we are captured, but I think it may be because there are too many uncertainties.

All I can say is that we've been visiting a lot of colleges and academies and talking to a lot of sages. The fees for those people alone would be enough to retire on. Daphne and Stephen don't seem to mind. I don't know where they keep getting it, but there's always money to be used for expenses like that. I want very much to tell you where we've been, but I'll have to wait until I see you next to tell you everything in person.

It hasn't been easy. I won't lie to you. I miss you terribly and pray every night that Our Lord will let me be with you again. Megan tries to concentrate on her tasks, but I can tell she thinks of Dar often. I remember those weeks after we all defeated Halkith and recovered the pegasi. Those were the happiest days of my life. I was able to be at peace and, more importantly, to be myself. I'm glad you were there with me.

I know you are probably still wrestling with your past life and whether to tell the other Riders about it. I can only ask that you pray over it and be honest with them. They are good friends and true. The longer you wait, the worse it will be. Secrets are always like that.

Give my best to Dar, Andyn, Connor and Buck. Please take care of yourself. I will continue sending letters to Lord Nolan as long as I am able, then I will only be able to send prayers to Our Lord and His Mother, asking them to watch over you and guide you. I will look forward to the day when I can see you again.

I love you. Brandawyn."

A tear somehow sneaked its way out of his eye and rolled down his cheek. He wiped it away before anyone could see, then remembered he was alone. *Melinor rescued me from my family. He and Ann and Saren — and Terenil —were the only ones who ever really cared for me. Until Brandi.*

He stood and replaced the scroll in the tube and dropped it back in his pack, thinking of Connor, Andyn, Buck and Dar. *Actually, these court jesters care too, in their own strange way, even Buck*

He leaned on the windowsill, eyes following the lights of the city, listening to the faint music from a tavern down the street.

He lifted a silver crucifix from under his tunic. *Her crucifix. God, please let her come back. I don't know what I'm going to do if she doesn't.*

The door opened behind him and he turned.

Dar Cabot looked at him, sheepish. "Uh, can't buy any drinks if I don't have any money." He knelt, inserted a key into a floorboard. There, he tapped an iron box with the key and whispered a word. In seconds, he stood after closing the trap door, a jingling coin purse in his hand.

Eric felt the crucifix and a familiar loneliness came over him. "Come to think of it," he said, "I will join you guys for a drink after all."

Buck had already left to find the Gnome when the other men awoke the next morning, nursing slight headaches. Andyn came down late to join them in the morning for breakfast, complaining about the temperature of her bath water.

Eric grinned. *We received the same bath water that morning and it was warm enough for him. She certainly does like her creature comforts. I wonder if she's part Halfling.*

He sat back in his chair and pushed his plate away just as Buck arrived at the tavern entrance with a small, hooded figure in tow.

Dar raised an eyebrow. "Is there a price on this guy's head as well? Saint Michael, we don't need two fugitives!"

Eric grinned and slugged Dar's shoulder. "Give him a chance, for crying out loud. We haven't even talked to him yet."

The new arrivals pulled up chairs. Buck gestured at his companions.

"This is Andyn Eleandir, of the church of Verian, Dar Cabot, scout of St. Kira's Order, Connor Lomin, agent, and Eric Indidarc, scout and mage. Everyone, this is Hlerv."

Eric almost choked on his ale, instead turning away to give a slight cough. *Hlerv? What the hell kind of name is that?*

"Pleased to meet you," said Andyn.

The figure nodded.

Connor spoke up. "We understand you may be looking for employment as a freelance."

Hlerv shrugged. "Perhaps."

Andyn flashed a brilliant smile. "Well, then, perhaps also you would like to join us. We are in the employ of the King of Deran as officers-at-large under the command of Lord Nolan Hanford of Forester. We hold the rank of brevet-sergeants for his lordship's army. We need someone who has experience in underground expeditions. The rewards promise to be great."

The figure slowly nodded. "I might be interested. What is the mission?"

Eric set down his tankard. "We're looking for a lost tower," he said before any of the others could jump in, "The key to finding it has something to do with the underground. None of us are very good in that environment so we need help."

The figure was silent for a while. "What are the terms?"

Dar chuckled. "We'll get to that when we know a little more about you. Where do you come from?"

"Oakmoor."

Why am I not surprised? thought Eric. *At least three hundred thousand in that city. No way to check on him, even if we wanted to waste our time in the first place.*

"What sort of experience do you have?" asked Dar.

"All kinds," countered their erstwhile partner. "I assume you have plenty of experience yourselves."

Dar shot an irritated look at Buck. "Of course."

"Then so do I." Hlerv sat back in his chair.

Dar opened his mouth but Eric coughed and shook his head.

"We just want to make sure you know what you're getting into," he interjected. "We've run into some pretty tough customers lately."

"I can take care of myself."

Connor toyed with his tankard lid. "Have you ever heard of the Whitepaw?"

Buck opened his mouth to correct him when Eric kicked him under the table.

Hlerv shook his head. "No. What are they?"

"They're an assassin's guild and they're really called the Whiteclaw," Andyn answered. "They've paid us a visit or two."

Buck turned to Hlerv. "Let's make a deal. We'll offer you an equal share of any freelance-bounty we collect, plus add you to our contract with the Crown."

Hlerv sat quietly for a few heartbeats, then nodded. "Sounds good. I accept."

"Wait a second," interjected Dar, raising his hand. "We haven't agreed to anything. We still need to know what skills you bring with you. What kind of professional training do you have?"

After a momentary silence, Hlerv shifted in his seat. "You will see when the need arises."

Eric bit his lip. *Dar is just itching to give this Hlerv a stout smack in the side of the head.*

"Well, no deal then," he said, smiling and rising. "We'd rather spend money to look for someone else than accept a total unknown who's not willing to be forthcoming. Good day, Mister Hlerv."

Buck looked pained at the mention of spending money, but rose with the others. Dar had a disgusted look on his face.

"Wait." Hlerv stood with them. "Let's not be too hasty. I have to be careful in my profession. I'm a spy, like Mister Lomin there."

Dar nodded. "Better. Now, we have to be able to recognize you in the day-light, so lose the hood so we can get a look at you."

Hlerv hesitated so long Eric thought he would refuse. Finally, a pair of browned hands lifted the hood back. A young Gnome regarded them with piercing black eyes. Dark brown hair and beard framed a solid, blunt-looking face, typical for the gnomish race.

In contrast to the few Gnomes Eric met in the past, Hlerv's eyes bore only a flat, suspicious glint. *Most Gnomes are cheerful and optimistic but with a penchant for mischief. Hlerv looks like he expects someone to swindle him any minute.*

Hlerv's eyebrows rose. "Satisfied?"

Eric nodded and stood. "We will be meeting in one hour's time at the stables behind this inn. We start today."

Hlerv appeared a bit taken aback, but he nodded. "Done. I will meet with you then." He slipped over alongside the wall and peered out the front windows before leaving out the front door.

"Saints and angels!" Dar exploded. "What a paranoid little—"

"Dar, Dar," said Andyn, shaking her head. "We don't have to know everything about everyone right away. If he works out well, we'll find out plenty about him soon enough."

Connor cleared his throat. "I think you all ought to know something. Before he left, I saw a white symbol of some kind under his cloak."

Dead silence greeted that comment.

Eric felt a chill. *The symbol of the Whiteclaw is, of course, a white claw...*

"Are you sure?" asked Andyn.

Connor nodded. All eyes turned to Buck.

He held his hands out. "Hey, listen, I don't know that much about him. He's been giving me info about Derek and the warrant for my arrest. That's it."

Dar shook his head. "Well, we've got to find out for sure or just not take him. Especially after what happened to Andyn."

The Verian priestess looked down at her hands. "I don't have any magic that could help us. I'd have to be able to read his surface thoughts and impressions and I just don't know how to do that. As for anything else, we'd need to look through his things while he's asleep."

Connor snapped his fingers. "Wait a minute. That's it. Andyn, you can use magic to put people to sleep, right?"

When she nodded, Connor spread his hands out wide. "So, you put him to sleep, we strip-search him and find out for sure."

Eric laughed. "That's ridiculous."

Dar's face lit up. "Great idea!"

"Wait a minute," Eric said. "That's not right. It would be an unprovoked attack on him. It's unethical at the very least."

Buck shook his head. "You're looking at this wrong. We've got to protect ourselves. This guy could be a spy for the Whiteclaw."

Dar nodded. "We've got to be sure. He's been too secretive for my taste."

Eric looked at Andyn for support. "Surely you can't think this is okay. Maybe he has a good reason for being secretive."

Andyn shuddered. "I know, but if it's a choice between this and being attacked in my bath again, I'll take this."

Eric protested, but to no avail. In the end, the others overruled him. He relented, seeing the look in their eyes: scared and nervous. Everyone knew they needed someone like Hlerv and didn't have the time for an extended search.

He sighed and threw up his hands. "All right. I just know that no good is going to come of this."

———————◄O►———————

Eric glanced over his shoulder. Dar, Buck, and Connor clustered together, awaiting Hlerv.

"I don't like it," he muttered to Andyn.

She looked down at the dust of the corral. "I know. I don't either, but we've got to be sure."

Of anyone, she has a right to be wary of secretive Gnomes.

Eric looked over his shoulder again.

"Did you remember to put the counterspell on yourself?" Andyn asked. "I don't want to put you to sleep too. Though you might need the rest."

"Yes," Eric replied. "And I know the plan. I go to meet him, you cast the spell, we search him. Done."

"There he is," said Connor.

Hlerv materialized from behind the corner of the stables in an excellent display of stealthy maneuvering, using the corral posts as cover.

Eric went to meet him.

Hlerv, still hooded, nodded at him. "Are we ready?"

"Almost," Eric in a cheerful voice.

Andyn spoke a single word. Eric steeled himself. A cloying lethargy passed over him. His counterspell went off. He blinked and managed to stay awake.

"I'm waiting," said Hlerv. Then his eyes rolled back in his head.

Eric caught him before he hit the ground. The others crowded around. Dar stood next to him, a concerned expression on his face. "How is he?"

Andyn checked him and smiled. "He'll be fine," she said, "but you'd better hurry. He'll only be out for a few minutes."

Eric sighed and stood. "Let's get this over with."

Dar and Andyn exchanged guilty looks, then shrugged. Together, the men helped haul the comatose Gnome inside the stable and over to one of the stalls.

Andyn watched for anyone interrupting them, partly because Connor insisted he knew what to look for and partly due to Eric and Dar's insistence on modesty. Eric joined them in the search, if only to hurry up the process. For the next few minutes, the only sounds in the stables were the ruffling of cloth, muttered discussion, and a few clinks of metal.

Soon, Dar sat back on his haunches, looking chastened. Eric tossed one of Hlerv's boots down on the hay and eyed Connor in disgust.

"Well?" asked Andyn, still facing away.

"Nothing," Dar answered, "The symbol on his jerkin was the emblem of the leatherworker who made it, a white hawk in a white circle."

Eric snorted. "Well, I hope you're satisfied, the lot of you."

"Hey," said Buck, brushing hay off Hlerv's tunic, "we had to be sure, so go easy. Let's get him dressed and awake."

As it turned out, Hlerv swore a blue streak under his breath as he checked all his equipment. Despite Dar's assurances that it was all there, the Gnome made a painstaking inspection anyway.

Eric tried to explain their reasoning. Hlerv replied only in clipped sentences and glared at the Riders. Finally, after Andyn sat next to him and told him about the attack of the Gnome assassins in her bath, he relaxed and nodded. She even let him in on Buck's troubles and the quest for his ancient family tower and the Eye of Truth.

Hlerv listened, eyes interested, then with one last glare at the group, stood and brushed hay from his clothes. "I understand the reason," he said with a cold stare, "but that doesn't make it right. I can be secretive if I want to."

Dar threw up his hands. "Hlerv, we didn't know what else to do! The Ja'al almost wiped us out a few months ago, assassins poisoned Andyn and almost killed her, and God only knows what more they might try to do to us. This is only the fifteenth of Augustus—I don't need to remind you that the Ja'al have far longer memories than that."

Hlerv snorted. "Well, just think what your 'God' thinks of this whole thing. And Christians are supposed to be so trustworthy."

"That's hitting below the belt," said Eric. He looked down at Hlerv. "We deserve it, but it's unfair. We're trying to stay alive and we didn't know what else to do. You weren't being honest and we need the help."

Andyn looked at her hands. "We don't blame you if you don't want the job."

Hlerv stared out the stable doors at the horses drinking from the trough. Finally, he shrugged. "I can't lie about it: I need steady work. Part-time spying isn't cutting it. And you guys were honest with me after all this crap, I'll give you that."

"You'll stay with us?" asked Buck.

Hlerv paused for a long moment, then nodded. He turned back to them and flung his cloak over one shoulder. "Well? Are we going to sit here in the hay or are we going after the Ja'al? Unless you'd like to try some other spell on me?"

Andyn put a hand on his arm. "I'm sorry Hlerv. Really, I am. We'll make it up to you."

The Gnome's expression softened and he looked out at the horses again. "Right," he said. "Well, what do we do now?"

Dar spoke up. "I was thinking of looking for old maps in the city Hall of Records to see if there's anything that resembles an Eye of Earth. It's a long-shot but we can try."

The Gnome nodded. "Fine. Let's go."

The others followed him as he marched off into the corral.

"At least he stayed," Dar said to no one in particular.

CHAPTER FIVE

Thicker than Water

Dar's eyes popped open. He reached for his sword in the darkness. *Where? What?* A vague feeling of uneasiness dogged his mind. Then it all came back to him.

Yes. We're in the Silver Sword tavern. We go to the Darlon University tomorrow to look for clues about the mysterious Eye of Earth.

He scanned the room, letting his eyes adjust to the dimness as best they could. *It looks like early morning, maybe two or three of the clock.*

The darker lumps of Buck, Eric, Connor and Hlerv rose and fell in disjointed rhythm, like some silent bagpipe quartet. Eric stirred and sat up. Dar saw the faint greenish glimmer of his eyes and put a finger to his lips.

Clad in only his tunic, Dar stood and writhed into his trousers. *Something woke me up. Could be only late-night revelers, returning from a pub crawl but...*

Eric arose as well, slipping to the door that led to the exterior hallway outside their room. He listened, then pointed and made a "man-walking" motion with his fingers. He held up four fingers.

Dar's heart began pounding. *Another assassination attempt?*

He stepped into his boots and saw Eric doing the same. Eric drew his sword and reached to shake Buck when a piercing scream cut the night.

The others jerked awake. Eric and Dar charged out into the hall.

They ran to Andyn's room, but she already stood in the doorway, mace in hand and clad only in her shift.

"That way!" Eric raced down the hall, Dar on his heels.

Andyn cursed and darted back into her room as the men pounded past. Another scream echoed down the hall, a shriek that choked off.

Eric skidded to a halt at the corner and crouched, then leaped out with a suddenness that startled Dar.

Something hummed past like a massive bee and thudded into a plank next to him and Dar rolled again. Another object zipped past, thumping into the wall. Dar stared in amazement at a crossbow bolt barely as long as his hand. He rolled, then popped up into a ready position, blade up. Eric knelt next to the wall, pointing his hand at a group of dark figures clustered near the railing of the outer corridor that overlooked the inn's central garden. He spoke two quick words.

Four darts of flame leapt out from his fingers at the knot of dark forms, striking one of them with sharp cracks. A man screamed and pitched over into the darkness. Following an unseen cue, the other figures sent a hail of tiny crossbow bolts at Eric and Dar, then vaulted the railing.

Dar twisted out of the way, then cursed. He raced to the banister and climbed over as well.

"Dar!" came Andyn's shocked voice from behind him. He had eyes only for the three men in black cloaks picking themselves up from the garden pathway.

Dar scooted down and dropped. The attackers jerked up from inspecting their fallen comrade and swarmed towards him.

Three flashing blades surrounded him. He backed up, using his blade defensively, unable to mount an assault.

A figure floated down at him. For a fraction of a second, he thought it was another attacker, but Eric alighted on the stones at his side.

Magic helps.

"Can't even get a good night's sleep these days," Buck Bydecy growled as he took up a position next to Dar. He swung Khelios Giantbane in a wide arc, driving the dark figures back. The blade glowed brightly.

Well, if Khelios is afire like that, we know they're evil.

Eric slashed. One of the figures cried out and stumbled back. The remaining enemy swordsmen defended with clever moves to cover each other, but did not press the attack.

The wounded intruder knelt, drew something from under his cloak, and tossed it down. A brilliant flash erupted. Dar staggered backward into a wall, swinging his blade left and right in short, defensive strokes. He blinked desperately, trying to make sense of the blotches of color and dark in his eyes.

When he could see again, the dark figures raced away towards the garden gate. Dar took off after them. A pair of small shadows leaped from under a stairway at one of the intruders and all three tumbled in a heap, blades flashing the night. Dar didn't stop running, hoping Hlerv and Connor could handle one assailant.

"Come on!" he shouted to Eric.

Andyn's voice rang out and four fire darts slammed into the wounded attacker. He stumbled and crashed into a bench, tumbling to the ground to lie still.

One of the dark forms hurled a glittering object at the wall of the inn to Dar's right. It hit the door to a room and exploded into flame. A woman's terrified shriek rang out from inside the room.

Dar snarled in anger and raced ahead, Buck right on his heels. Another one of those little crossbow bolts sang by his head. He dodged, then stumbled on a bush and fell onto another bench.

"Eric Hylar?" cried a voice from the gate.

Dar scrambled to his feet, gaping in astonishment.

Eric stood as still as a rock, a strange expression on his face, somewhere between horror and disbelief. Only one of the intruders faced him in the flickering firelight. The man pulled off his hood, revealing a dark face with glittering black eyes and a pale scar from forehead to chin.

"It *is* you!" he said in amazement.

Eric shook his head. "No…"

"Yes!" the dark man said, smiling. "Yes! This is amazing! We thought you lost all those years ago! Gariil's own luck! Come, join us!"

"I'm not one of you!" Eric said in a choked voice.

"Nonsense!" the dark man retorted. "Reclaim your birthright!"

Eric's handsome face twisted in such rage that Dar felt a palpable fear and shock. "Never!" he screamed and launched himself forward. "I'll never go back!"

The dark man cast something onto the cobblestones. A cloud of smoke and sparks leaped up.

Eric slashed through the cloud, but hit only empty air. He leaped to the gate. The assassin joined two other figures waiting with prancing mounts and the trio rode off.

Eric leaned against the gatepost, head hanging down.

Dar leapt to his side in an instant. "You okay?

Eric nodded.

A shriek from behind them brought them back to the present and they whirled.

The inn burned. The Grey Riders joined a bucket brigade with people from the inn. Andyn used a water spell to good effect and the fire disappeared in a cloud of steam, but not before the door, windows and front of the guest room were blackened and charred.

Pounding hooves, shouts and the jangle of armor sounded from the street outside, receding in the distance.

Andyn tossed her hair over her shoulder. She had had the presence of mind to slip on her trousers and boots before coming down to help.

"What was that all about?" she asked.

"Assassins."

The innkeeper sank in exhaustion on one of the benches. A round, bearded man named Darvin who reminded Dar of a plump bread-roll, he held one of the intruders' dark cloaks in his hand.

"How do you know?" asked Buck, dropping his bucket with a splash of water. Hlerv dodged out of the way, shooting an annoyed look at Buck.

Darvin held up the cloak. He showed them the symbol of two silver crossed swords with bloody tips, embroidered on the inside of the collar. "Crossed Swords, see? Besides, Hirvath the gemcutter lies in his bed upstairs, gutted like a fish, with all his gems still intact. No, this wasn't a simple robbery."

Connor looked unconvinced. "So sure, are you?"

Darvin eyed him. "Sure as you're a Halfling, my friend. I heard down at the Leaping Hart that Hirvath owed some people money for loans. Seems his gemcutting couldn't keep up with his gambling."

A clatter of hooves sounded in the street outside. In a few moments, a group of eight Darlon guards shoved their way past the crowd.

Their leader, a tall, well-muscled soldier in chain armor, nodded in a self-satisfied way as he peeled off his gloves. He wore the deep green and silver of the Ducal Patrol and the double gold daggers of a sergeant on one shoulder. "It was a rough ride, but we got them," he announced.

Dar blinked. "How?"

The sergeant winked. "We have a few tricks up our sleeve too. You folk set up such a hue and cry that some of the boys—and one of our mages—were ready for them. It wasn't easy, but they paid for their crimes."

Eric's face was pale. "Were any caught alive?"

The sergeant looked at him. "Are you joking? These were Crossed Swords. They fought to the death, and good riddance."

Eric's expression looked very odd, somewhere between guilt and relief. Dar's suspicions and dread deepened.

"Who was the first on the scene?" asked the guard.

Dar explained his and Eric's role in the fight, omitting Eric's conversation with the assassin leader. Eric averted his eyes, only nodding in affirmation.

Satisfied, the sergeant turned to Darvin. "Now, innkeeper, I'll have an accounting of what happened here, in your words."

They disappeared into the tavern while the other city guards took positions around the courtyard.

Dar caught up with Eric at the foot of the stairs up to their room.

"What was all that—"

"Shhh!" hissed Eric. He looked hunted. "Not here. In our room."

Saint Mary and all angels. He looks like he's headed for the gallows. Dar beckoned to the others. "Come on."

At their puzzled looks, he realized no one but him heard the exchange between Eric and the dark assassin. Connor pulled at his sleeve but Dar shook his head. "Eric will tell us."

They gathered in the men's room. Andyn sat on one of the beds while Eric stood by the window. Buck slid Khelios back into his scabbard and leaned against the wall while Connor sat on the windowsill. Hlerv coiled up into a dark form in the corner.

They waited. Eric finally moved, closing the shutter and drawing the curtains. The room darkened, but he put up a ball of light just below the ceiling with a whispered word.

"Okay Eric," said Dar. "What's all this about?" *This is really worrying me.*

Eric leaned his hands on a chair back. "The lead assassin said something to me before they escaped into the street. I have something I wanted to tell you all, something that's been burning in me for months, and this is the best time,

I guess. I tried telling you back when we were hunting down Halkith and the Ja'al, but there was always something in the way. I just can't hide it any longer."

The other Riders froze. Dar hardly breathed, fearing the worst but not daring to think of it.

Eric looked at all of them. "I'm not going to mince words. The guildmaster of the Crossed Swords is named Harkin Hylar. I'm his fourth son."

Dar's mind spun. *An assassin? Eric? Worse, son of a guildmaster?*

Buck stepped back a pace, reaching for Khelios. Connor hopped down to the floor, his mouth open in shock. Hlerv scuttled towards the door, sword flickering out.

Andyn went white as a sheet and caught herself on a chair.

Oh my God. Andyn's husband! The Crossed Swords killed him.

"I left my family when I was a young teen," Eric continued, as if he would lose courage if he stopped. "I... I couldn't take it anymore. I wouldn't do as ordered and the beatings were getting worse. They killed one of my cousins and a sister died in a fight with city guards on an assignment. I left."

He looked up at them. "I ran into Melinor Indidarc and tried to steal his purse, but he caught me."

No doubt, thought Dar.

"The family searched for weeks," said Eric, voice sounding very tired. "By that time, Melinor had shielded me from all but the most powerful magic sensing and I was safe. The Hylars forgot about me and I started a new life and I thought I was free of them, until tonight."

"Bastard!"

The shriek of fury made Dar jump. Andyn stood in front of the bed, fists in tight balls, eyes blazing and tears streaming down her face. "You killed him!"

"Andyn," Dar said in a calm voice, "It wasn't Eric who killed your husband six years ago. He wasn't even part of the family at that time."

"You killed him!" she shouted as if she hadn't heard. "I can't believe I trusted you! You're one of those evil, murdering—"

Dar put a hand on her shoulder, but she shook him off. Her expression changed from fury to abject misery, staring at Eric. Tears streamed down her smooth cheeks. "Eric, why?" she sobbed in a broken voice. "You're my friend..."

She pushed her way past Hlerv and stumbled out of the room.

Eric deflated and slumped against the chair. "At least she didn't try to kill me," he murmured.

Connor started for the door, but Dar stopped him. "I'll talk to her," he said.

Connor gave him a long look, then nodded.

Her door was unlocked. Dar entered.

Andyn stood with her back to him, staring out the window of her room at the city lights. She braced her arms against the window frame as if she would hold up the entire building by her strength alone.

"Andyn?" he asked.

"Why?" she said in a forlorn voice. "Damn that bastard, why?" Her voice broke and her head hung down.

Dar went to her, turned her around and held her.

She sobbed into his shoulder for a long time. "How could he do this to me?" she said finally, partly furious and partly despairing. "How could he become my friend, how could he let me care about him when he's one of those foul, hell-spawned..."

"Shhhh, Andyn," Dar said, stroking her golden hair. "He isn't one of them anymore. He never was. Did you hear what he said? Melinor Indidarc helped him. You know a lot more about Melinor than I do. Do you think Melinor would let Eric go down the Dark Path if he could help it?"

She shook her head, then raised it and tried to wipe her face. Tears streaked her cheeks and she looked so miserable Dar's heart ached.

"Dar," she whispered. "Why Eric? Oh, Verian, why! He can't have been party to Larad's murder." She buried her face in his chest again.

Dar sighed. "Maybe there's some other reason, some other purpose we can't see right now."

She sobbed once and shook her head. "How much longer does this have to go on? I can't keep reliving that agony! I want a new life."

"I know you do," Dar replied, "Anyone who hears your story can see that. I do know this: God can bring great good out of great evil. If Larad hadn't died, you wouldn't be here with us. If my grandparents hadn't disappeared, I wouldn't be either. Buck wouldn't be here if it weren't for Derek's betrayal, and on and on. In any case, Halkith would have the pegasi and the kingdom would be in jeopardy. Maybe there's a reason that Larad and the Crossed Swords keep coming back into your life. We can't truly know until later."

She stilled. After a little while, she raised her head and gave him a little smile. "What are you now, a philosopher?"

He chuckled. "Me? Don't say that out loud to anyone. It'll take them an hour to recover from laughing."

She gave him a tremulous smile, then sighed. "I know, you're right. You and I don't worship the same, Dar, but I also know Verian doesn't let people suffer needlessly. I'm just so tired of feeling that pain over and over. Can you understand?"

He gave her a quick hug. "Don't let it get you down. Something right will come of all of this. Just don't try to handle it alone."

She smiled up at him, lovely face sad and relieved all at once. "How can I? You guys are around constantly, even in my bath."

He chuckled again, then turned serious, looking into her eyes through her tears. "Andyn, you and I both know what kind of a man Eric is. I believe him. His actions speak louder than anything his old family could have done. He's just lucky none of those assassins survived to take word to his father. And can you imagine Brandawyn? Do you think she could fall in love with someone evil, someone who kills for a living? I think Brandi's too wise and insightful to be fooled. She loves him and believes in him."

Her hand went to her mouth. "Oh Verian's Tears! Poor Brandi! This will crush her..."

Dar remembered the way Brandi and Eric looked at each other sometimes, in a way that showed they shared a secret knowledge, something more than their romance.

"Andyn," he said, "I think she already knows."

They stood in silence for a while. Then she sighed. "I've heard many stories about Melinor too. And you're right: Melinor couldn't form any kind of alliance with murderers, unless they wanted to repent."

He tipped her chin up to look at him. *She has a beautiful face,* he thought, *and bright eyes... just like Megan.* That thought made him stop and release her, confused.

"Look Andyn," he said instead, "you'll have to make your peace with Eric."

As if in answer, the door opened a bit and Eric slid inside.

Andyn turned to meet him.

They both spoke at once. "Eric... Andyn... I'm so sorry... no... pardon... you first."

A ghost of a smile flickered on Eric's face, forlorn now.

Dar felt sad. *We see the cheerful, smiling Eric so often that this one is so very hard to deal with.*

"Me first," Eric said to her. She smiled back.

To Dar's and Andyn's amazement, Eric went down on one knee before her and held his sword out. "I have dreaded this for months," he said. "I knew you would hate me, but please, Andyn, know that I had nothing to do with it. I didn't even hear about it in my father's halls. I promise you, Andyn Fallbrook Eleandir, widow of Larad, that I will not rest until either my last breath has left me or the family Hylar has paid for the murder of your husband to the last assassin. I promise you with God and Saint Michael as my witness."

Andyn stared at him in amazement, then turned teary eyes to Dar. "What do I do?" she whispered.

"Kiss the sword and return it to him," he said, very surprised himself. "And tell him what you feel."

She took the sword, gently kissed the blade and offered it back to Eric, hilt-first. "I... Eric, I'm so sorry for what I said. I...I was just so angry. All my feelings about Larad came back again. Please forgive me. And you don't have to make such a promise to me. I can't ask you to turn against your family."

Eric took back his weapon and rose, sheathing it, his eyes bright. "Andyn, there is no one there who ever cared for me. Not my father, not my mother. I was just a tool, someone to carry on the family tradition. Anyone who had a spark of compassion died early. It will be an honor to bring them to justice."

"But they're your family..."

"No." His eyes were softer now. He put a hand on her shoulder. "Melinor, Anne, Saren, Terenil: they are my family. *You* are my family. Let me fight for you."

Andyn wrapped her arms around him and gave him a tight hug. "Oh Eric."

It isn't all about Larad, Dar realized. He slipped out of the room and rejoined Buck, Connor and Hlerv.

A couple of hours later, Eric returned. No one asked him any questions or made any racy jokes, not even Connor. It would have cheapened something they all knew was noble.

Dar took a long time to fall asleep.

CHAPTER SIX

Eyes of Earth

"This had better work," growled Buck Bydecy.

Connor raised an eyebrow and looked up at him. "Relax. I know you think books are used to move children higher at the dinner table, but some people find meaning in the little black marks. The old guy knows what he's doing. He better, with all the gold we're paying him."

He hopped up onto the bench next to Buck, stood on the seat and leaned back against the wall. Buck flicked leaves from a branch he had torn from a nearby flowering shrub.

"Besides," Connor said, gesturing at their surroundings, "Isn't this a great place to sit back and enjoy a summer's day? Unless you'd rather be off in a stinking tunnel somewhere?"

Buck grunted and tossed the now-bare branch down on the stones at his feet and sat back, closing his eyes.

Connor shook his head, looking out at the university square. Manicured lawns stretched away from him towards brick buildings. Stately trees towered overhead. Flower beds of intricate design, bursting with color, dotted the landscaping.

Connor hid a smile. *It's a strain for Buck to be involved in anything academic, even if it also helps him. Probably more aggravating now, since he's itching to get out into the mountains ever since breakfast.*

A few students hurried away from him towards a monolithic white tower to his left. He watched an elderly woman in a professor's black gown shuffle down the pattern of cobblestones towards a fountain in the center of the sward.

I wish we had a college like this back in Glen, Connor mused, then dismissed the idea. *Probably wouldn't work. Glen is too small.*

He glanced at the tall, arched doors to the Darlon University Library and considered going in.

"Maybe we should help hurry them up," he suggested.

Buck shook his head. "I've had enough research for a while. Lord Nolan's library is okay and all, but digging around in old scrolls and books for the location of the Eye of Earth is the job of mages and scholars, not spies and warriors."

Mention of the library in Forester brought back thoughts of their first mission and Connor shuddered. "I hear you. I still have chills thinking about what we discovered in Lord Nolan's library."

Buck shot him a look, his lazy grey eyes sardonic. "What, you mean finding out that an undead sorceress from a bygone age might be hunting us unnerves you? Or that the Song of the Grey Riders predicts that we'll have to fight her? Don't be such a worry wort, Connor."

Despite the somber memories, Connor grinned back. "Yeah. I'm worrying for nothing. Hey, we avenged the massacre at Westhaven, beat the Ja'al cult to a secret weapon — a herd of battle-trained pegasi frozen in time, no less— and then killed the Ja'al high priest who ordered the massacre. Zhinia Margoth will be a walk in the park. Even if she is an undead sorceress."

Buck smirked and leaned against the wall again. The bell in the university clock tower rang out with deep, sonorous tones, marking three of the clock.

"Oaks and mistletoe," Buck sighed. "Are they reading old books and maps or are they writing them? They're taking forever."

Connor nodded towards the library clock. "It hasn't been as long as you think. Just relax."

Connor tried to relax as well, but the memories of Margoth agitated him. *Sure, Lord Nolan took us off the case after that and turned it over to the Royal Intelligence Ministry, but Margoth is still out there. And she probably isn't happy.*

Connor laced his fingers behind his head. *Best to leave all that in the hands of the powerful and the knowledgeable. The King's men are alerted. It's not our problem.*

Familiar voices made him open his eyes. Andyn, Eric, Dar and Hlerv walked out of the library doors next to a spindly figure in professor's robes. Andyn spoke with him and the sage bobbed his head, white hair waving. Eric handed him a small pouch while Dar and Hlerv pored over a parchment scroll.

"Well?" asked Buck when they came to the bench.

Andyn shrugged. "We got something. I don't know how good it is, but it's a start."

Hlerv snorted. "It cost enough. It better be worth it."

"What did you find?" Connor asked.

"The professor let us make a copy of an ancient map," Andyn said. "It was originally on a piece of tanned leather."

Dar pointed to a spot on the map. Next to the drawing of a tower, the symbol of an eye glared back at Connor.

"The professor says that mountain is called the Devil's Finger," Dar continued, "I checked a few other maps and it looks like a three-day ride by horse, one by pegasus. It's near the source of the Lonmar River."

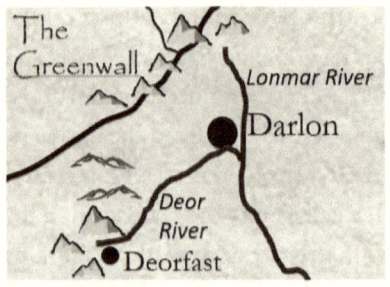

"That's it?" asked Buck. "Nothing else?"

Andyn smacked him in the shoulder. "Just pay attention."

Eric took the parchment from Dar and laid it in his map case. "The professor has been looking ever since yesterday. This is the only reference to an Eye of Earth he could find, and he admitted it was obscure. The question is, do we want him to keep looking or do we want to try this one out?"

Anything's better than sitting around. Connor nodded. "Let's go after it. We'll find something, even if it's the wrong place."

Everyone turned to Buck, who looked martyred but nodded.

"Hey, why so glum?" chuckled Eric. "It's your family heirloom we're looking for."

"I was hoping for something more descriptive."

"Sword-swingers!" said Andyn, heading off down the walkway. "Do you want everything handed to you on a plate? Come on, we've got a bit of traveling to do."

"Report," Margoth ordered, glowering at her chief of espionage. "I expect something positive. The last couple of days have not been encouraging: one of my spies in King Phillip's court was arrested yesterday and two whole platoons of goblins deserted in the middle of a fight with Dwarves near Dorn's Hall."

Zadar bowed low, his half-baboon features controlled. Scuffed boots made a scraping sound on the lowest step of the throne dais. "Our agents report seeing the pegasus-riders leaving the city of Darlon, heading northwest."

Margoth tapped her staff with bony fingers. *This is better. If those fools are traipsing through the mountains, they can't interfere – or try to fulfill that drivel in the so-called Song of the Grey Riders.*

She shifted in her ruined throne, feeling the empty sockets where sapphires and diamonds once decorated the worked marble. Her finger bones caressed the twisted figure of a woman writhing in agony.

"Good," she said, watching Zadar. *He's a Hobgoblin, but their tribes are more important to them than almost anything. I wonder if he really is loyal or not.* "Tell me about the search for the Halfling toy mentioned in the Song of the Grey Riders."

A twitch from Zadar now. He ran a hand over his chainmail and bowed lower. "We have found nothing, Great Majesty."

"Why not?"

Zadar straightened, placing one hand on his sword hilt and one on his mace. "There are many Halflings in Deran, Majesty. Because of that race's well-known nervousness around larger peoples, we have to move very cautiously in any Halfling communities. Also, recruiting Halflings to our cause has been difficult. So far, none of our searches have yielded anything about a magical Halfling toy that can fly."

She stood and he watched her with black eyes. "What about the search in Evendale?" she asked.

He shrugged. "That is even more difficult. The Halflings apparently have a spy network of their own and suspect something."

She gritted the few teeth she had left. *Patience. They will make a mistake.*

Margoth stood in the glow of magical lights, watching the glint of broken stained glass on the tiled floor. Two skeleton knights flanked her throne at attention. Next to them, trying not to look nervous, stood her mage assistant, Ralis, and her military aide, Jerran.

"Ralis," she asked, "What do you think? Is the Halfling toy critical to the Grey Riders?"

Ralis, a rotund human with even beadier eyes than Zadar, stroked his beard. "It certainly is, according to the prophecy, but we have been searching for what, over a year, Your Majesty? I agree with Zadar. A toy made for a Halfling child, even a magical one, is difficult to find indeed. No one even knows what it looks like. Because of their proximity to the Empire of Terenai, the Halflings in the Dales would have ample access to magical playthings of all kinds. If it is indeed that hard to find, the Grey Riders will have equal, if not more, difficulty finding it. It appears we are safe for now. If Your Majesty recalls, we have already searched the Dales after our epidemic, going through all the cast-off items from the dead. Nothing."

She nodded, making a note to have him flayed alive if the stupid gewgaw turned up anywhere. "Jerran."

The warrior, a seven-foot-tall giant of a man, wrapped his cloak around himself and bowed.

"Get me a courier and a squad to escort. We are going to send a message to Ildrisana and our good allies in Essergil."

Jerran straightened, looking annoyed. "The Dark Elves?" he rumbled. "Why do we need them? Our forces are more than enough to handle six free-lances, no matter what they ride."

"Because, dear general," she said, sitting back in her throne. "It is much better to have someone else do our work for us than it is to spend any energy on it, if we can help it. We have many other preparations to make. Besides, Liander Tolin will have a vested interest in our little flying friends."

She smiled and stroked one of the empty gem-sockets on the throne. She imagined it was the eye-socket of Dar Cabot's skull.

———— ◄O► ————

Connor wiped rainwater from his face, trying to keep Dar in sight. Even with his waterproofed hood up, the windblown rain got into his eyes.

He looked to his left wing. Andyn's Medianox struggled to move through the air, slowed by the storm.

He patted Phantom on the neck. "Hang on! Just a bit longer," he shouted to the pegasus, trying to make himself heard above the wind.

Rain and grey clouds swathed the mountains below. Leaden skies glowered down at him. Buffets of wind forced Connor and the other Riders to pay constant attention to formation to avoid collision.

A storm in northern Deran in mid-summer? Something's not right, Connor thought.

He heard a muttered curse from Hlerv, sitting in the saddle behind him. "Are we insane?" Hlerv complained. "Why don't we land?"

Connor shrugged. "Where?" he shouted back, pointing down. "There's no good place down there!"

Only steep, craggy canyons and rocky slopes greeted their eyes.

Connor flew on, trying to feel where Phantom was going with the wind. Slowly and gradually, the rain turned to a downpour the closer they got to the mountains.

Dar's hand shot up and he pointed down, then wheeled Virasi into a dive. Buck, on Shadowbane, and Eric, on Falcon, peeled off and followed, then Andyn and Connor.

In a minute Connor spied their destination. A small ledge beckoned to them, just in front of a wide cave mouth. The mountain itself looked like a tall spire, but Connor didn't care. *I'm soaked, tired. And getting hungry.*

The Riders executed a bit of tricky maneuvering to get onto the ledge one at a time and then into the cavern, but they finally stood there, shaking water off their clothing and trying to keep the pegasi calm.

"They're not comfortable in here," Andyn said, placing her hands on their heads.

"Do you blame them?" Eric said, brushing rain out of his hair. "They're creatures of the air, not caverns. They wouldn't be caught dead in here if we didn't lead them in."

The size of the cavern surprised Connor. From the outside, the entrance spanned about thirty feet wide and ten tall, but the cavern soared to twice that width and equally deep, towering above to a height of thirty feet.

Hlerv looked around, eyes glinting. "This is better."

Connor grinned. "I expected you'd like it."

Dar came over, carrying a lantern. "Let's put the pegasi over there," he said, pointing to the right, "It's close to the exit so they can at least see the sky. We can camp next to them."

Connor nodded, ruffling water out of his hair. "Hlerv, let's set up a few surprises in case anything comes visiting."

He and the Gnome constructed a few simple traps using cord, rocks and a couple of tree branches.

Connor put his hands on his hips, surveying their handiwork.

Hlerv frowned. "With such limited material, they won't do much to anything of substance, but they'll at least surprise intruders and give us a chance to react."

Connor clapped him on the shoulder. "You're wetter than the weather. Come on. They've got a fire started."

Somehow, Dar and Eric coaxed a small campfire out of what scattered tree branches they found in the cave. Andyn laid out her bedroll next to the fire. She sat on it, taking a wrapped paper package out of her backpack. She opened it, taking a bit of jerked meat. "Storms like this aren't common in summer, are they, Dar?"

The ranger shook his head. "Once in a while, there's a light rain, but not like this. This is more like fall or early spring."

Connor suppressed a shudder. *There's something weird going on underneath the surface of this. I just know it.*

The companions ate in silence. Connor tossed lots with the others and drew second watch of three, his least favorite.

Next time, he thought, bundling up in his blankets, *I use my own dice. Hlerv's are loaded.*

Connor's watch passed without incident. He sat at the cave mouth, using his heat-vision and listening to the rain. After the change of watch, he fell asleep with the image of Eric sitting at the cave entrance, his back turned to him. He awoke to a grey morning sky devoid of rain.

They ate a quick breakfast.

Dar stood at the entrance, looking out at the canyons and mountains, biting his lip. "We should be close," he said, looking down at a map in his hands. "It's the right area, but with the storm last night, we could have been blown ten miles off course."

Buck came up next to him. "Then we'd better get started."

Connor looked up at him. Buck wore an intense demeanor these days, focused on the idea of his ancestral castle.

He didn't even grouse about the lack of bawdy houses back in Darlon. Yes. Very intense.

After giving the pegasi a ration of feed from their saddlebags, they led the flying horses out on the ledge one by one and lifted off. Connor and Hlerv went last.

Connor looked back at the cavern as they climbed away, noting its odd shape. Hlerv looked back with him.

Hmm, Connor mused, turning to face forward. *Looks like...*

Sudden realization hit him and he straightened.

"Oaks and mistletoe!" he growled, then urged Phantom forward. The pegasus raced ahead, catching up with Dar at the head of their formation.

Connor made the "landing now" sign and Dar's face grew annoyed, but he followed Connor down.

The Halfling found a semi-level spot on a wide slope, scattered with pine trees. The others joined him there.

"What?" asked Andyn, struggling to keep Medianox on even footing, "What's the idea?"

Connor pointed back at their former camping spot. "Look!"

Andyn gasped and Buck's jaw dropped.

The cave entrance stared back at them, just like a giant eye.

CHAPTER SEVEN

Undying Light

B uck Bydecy eyed the tunnel. *So, this is it.*

"Nice place you have here," commented Dar.

Buck grunted in response.

The group gazed at the tunnel with growing interest. It stretched away from them, smooth and clean, with none of the usual flotsam and cobwebs they found in underground warrens. Along the walls, on the right-hand side, a strip of mild white luminescence lit the entire hallway.

"But are we sure this is the right place?" asked Eric, touching the bright strip with a gloved hand.

"A tower of rock, an eye of earth, and light that doesn't die," Andyn said, "Can you doubt it?"

"Based on how hard it was to find the door, it seems almost like we were meant to come

"I don't," replied Connor, moving to the head of the formation to join Buck, "Step lively at any rate. We know some creatures managed to get in here somehow."

Buck remembered their path up to this point: a difficult time finding the secret door in the cavern, followed by a lot of fiddling with the mechanism by Connor and Hlerv and then a silent trek through clean hallways with ornate carvings. He also remembered the sundered tiles and blackened bones in several chambers.

Connor's right. We have no idea what's in here. He bit his lip, caught between excitement and fear. *But it's Moridan's ancient tower! Where would he have hidden the Eye? Probably down lower somewhere.*

Buck touched the light strip and pulled back his hand, surprised to feel a tingle.

Connor looked at him. "Something wrong?"

"Uh, no," Buck replied. "Let's go."

They marched three abreast in the wide tunnel, with Eric joined Buck and Connor at the front. Andyn, Dar and Hlerv brought up the rear in the second rank.

They followed the passage until it turned, then entered a chamber. On the left and right sides, dusty stone benches rested against the walls. Along the rim of the walls, near the ceiling, a strip of gold letters followed the path of the light strip.

"It's in Elven, I think," whispered Dar, "But the lettering is unfamiliar."

Buck shook his head. *Languages. Not my specialty.*

"It's an older script style," said Eric. "Enter ye now the domain of Moridan Bydeky, Lord High Archmage in the service of the Imperial family of Esten. Good welcome to all of peaceful intent. May Irial provide thee bountiful blessings."

"Well, if that doesn't remove all doubt," said Connor.

They exited through an archway on the other side of the room and passed into another hall. Every thirty feet or so, they came upon a small alcove with a bench and a potted plant, green and vibrant.

Buck shook his head in wonder. *Live plants? It's been hundreds of years! What kind of magic could old Moridan do in order to make that happen?*

They reached a four-way intersection.

"Now what?" asked Andyn, hands on her hips.

Connor bit his lip. "Any ideas?"

Buck looked left, right and straight ahead. Only a smooth passageway greeted his eyes each time. The way ahead looked like it turned right after about eighty feet.

He put his hand on the glowing strip of light. His fingers tingled and he felt a slight pull ahead. "Straight," he said.

Connor regarded him for a minute, then nodded. "Come on, guys. I think we have a key for finding our way around in here."

Buck barely heard him and strode forward, hand brushing the strip of light. The others followed him. The passage turned and led to an arched opening.

"Okay," said Connor, "Now we're getting somewhere."

They approached. Beyond the entrance, a stone fountain sparkled with clean water.

Buck put out his hand to the strip along the wall and he felt a very strong tingle.

"Wait," he said.

Connor looked up at him.

Buck shook his head. "Don't ask." He stepped forward, hand on the strip. He peeked around the corner, then jerked back, heart quickening. *Now it gets dicey...*

"Get ready, gang," he whispered, drawing Khelios from his scabbard.

"What is it?" whispered Andyn.

"Some kind of twelve-legged lizard," he replied, lifting his shield off his back.

He stepped inside. A two-foot thick, multi-legged lizard, light blue and white, coiled around a statue of a maiden in one corner. Long horns curved back over an armored head with three closed eyes. Its tail looked like a bony club.

Buck lifted his shield and looked to the three exits. *If we can just sneak past it to one of those doorways...*

The reptile's central eye snapped open. It flared blue light and the other two eyes opened. The creature uncoiled itself—and continued uncoiling to a full length over twenty feet.

"Nice," said Dar. "One of your grand-dad's pets?"

The creature's eyes narrowed and it bared its fangs. Tiny electric arcs danced between rows of sharp teeth.

"Look out!" Dar shouted. The creature opened its mouth wide and a bolt of forked lightning lanced out.

Buck lifted his shield just in time. A powerful blow staggered him. He saw the other fork hit Eric's shield. Both men staggered backwards, slamming into the wall.

Buck recovered and leaped forward, Khelios extended, blue fire glittering on its razor edge. Dar joined him, slashing with his blade. The lizard snapped at Khelios.

Buck heard Andyn chanting and a ball of light popped in front of the thing's eyes. It hissed and turned aside.

Buck hacked at its head. The sword bounced off. Dar's blade sliced into its side, drawing dark blood that sizzled on the floorstones.

Connor and Hlerv appeared behind the thing. Buck took another whack at its head and it ducked this time, sweeping at him with its horns. A powerful blow slammed him to the side and he barely retained his grip on his shield.

The creature opened its mouth again. Eric stepped up, thrusting with his spear. The point jabbed the roof of the creature's mouth and it screeched, biting down and wresting the spear away. Hlerv and Connor jumped on it from behind, stabbing with their swords.

The creature went wild, thrashing about madly, eight of its twelve clawed legs and club-like tail lashing at anything that moved. Buck and his companions waded in but its whirling claws and lashing tail hurled them back. Buck took a slash on one arm, narrowly missed a horn in the eye, and managed to stab it deeply in the side. It screeched again.

A flick of the tail cast Hlerv into a corner, then a mace-head whirled in and smacked the lizard's head. It reeled and Andyn struck again with both her weapons.

Five blades plunged downward. The creature writhed once, then convulsed and lay still. Buck let out a deep breath, then jerked backwards as a strong electric shock burst out from the corpse.

"Hey!" yelled Dar. "It's falling apart!"

Buck stepped back, leaving Khelios in the body, eyes wide in amazement. Arcs of electricity raced around the outlines of the lizard thing. As he watched, the tail began to disappear. The body followed, fading into the air. Bolts of electricity melted into the floor stones and disappeared. The entire corpse vanished.

"What *was* that thing?" asked Dar, holding a hand to a claw wound on his arm.

Andyn shook her head, getting out her medical kit. "Whatever it was, it's gone. It's a good thing Buck was so cautious or we would have blundered right into it."

Buck turned away but Connor stepped in front of him. "Exactly why were you so cautious?"

"Well," Buck said. "I can feel something in here. I get these, er, warnings and directions." He shuddered.

Eric shook his head, leaning on his spear. "Why didn't you tell us earlier?"

"I didn't understand it," Buck said, sheathing Khelios. "It's weird and magical and I don't know much about magic and stuff like that. You and Andyn are the ones who deal with that department."

Andyn smiled and put a hand on his shoulder. "Buck, it's probably something that Moridan set up to recognize anyone with his lineage. That kind of magic is so advanced I wouldn't be able to do it in a hundred years. It would make *me* feel weird. But no more secrets, okay?"

He nodded.

Hlerv snorted. "Well, where is your Bydecy lineage sending you now?"

Buck lined up a particularly acid retort but forgot it when something pulled at him from the right-hand exit.

"Oh," he said instead, rather surprised, "I guess we go that way."

"This seems familiar, which makes me nervous," Dar whispered.

"I agree," Buck replied. "It looks weird, and we've seen plenty of weird things."

Hlerv snorted. "Weird is commonplace in this Tower of Undying Light. Miles of passages, a rotating chamber with multiple doors, a glass room with crystals floating in mid-air. Only this really tops the list."

Buck eyed a wall of blue fire bisecting the room exactly in the center, its flames roaring with arcane life. *There's no way around* that.

"Did we take a wrong turn?" asked Eric.

Buck shook his head. "I can feel the pull right now. It leads across the room."

"Well, it's certainly a fire wall, and magical." Andyn conferred in whispered tones with Eric. Buck heard many unfamiliar arcane terms, most of which he ignored.

"We can't go through it and we can't go around it," Eric concluded. "We're going to try to douse the flames with water spells long enough for us to get across."

Buck licked his lips. Even from twenty feet away he felt the heat.

Andyn and Eric began chanting, their voices blending together. The Riders tensed, waiting for the right moment. The air went bone-dry and a wall of water crashed down on the center of the blue flame-wall. Buck charged forwards, hearing the others near him.

An immense cloud of steam erupted and blinded him. He couldn't see anything for a split second, then the blue flames appeared out of the cloud, unaffected.

"Stop!" he shouted, skidding to a halt.

His companions rattled to a stop next to him, Hlerv skipping nimbly around to avoid ramming Dar into the flames.

They all stared at the wall. Eric's eyes narrowed and he gazed at the flames, running a hand over his chin.

"Didn't even reduce it," Connor said in wonder.

No one said anything for a while.

How do I get past this? thought Buck. The inexorable pull still tugged at him, urging him onwards, right through the flames.

"There's a trick to this," Eric said slowly, walking a little closer to the flames. "We just have to figure out what it is."

A thought came to Buck. "What did the verse say?" he asked Andyn. "Wasn't there something about a flame?"

"Yes. A wall of fire and tower cold are not barriers real."

Hlerv scoffed. "It most certainly is real. I could cook a boar on that."

The pull became more insistent. Buck set his jaw. "It's not real."

Dar looked at him. "Are you kidding? What makes you say that?"

He shook his head. "He wouldn't have put something in here to pull me on into failure. Besides, Moridan was a wizard. He could make illusions, right?"

Eric leaned on his spear. "With thermal components? That's really advanced. I don't know if Melinor could even do that."

Without another word, Buck stepped into the flames. The others gasped and called out to him. Andyn screamed.

He emerged on the other side, unharmed. He felt no heat. His friends gaped at him, open-mouthed. He chuckled at their expressions.

"By Blessed Mindra!" Andyn exclaimed, hand on her chest. "Warn us before you do that!"

Buck motioned towards a door in the opposite wall, "Are you coming or not?" He didn't wait to see if they followed.

He led the way down another smooth passage, ending in an archway that glimmered with arcane sigils all along its arc. He stopped at the opening. "Well, this is, um, different."

In a circular room before them, a massive, bluish-white cylinder with a door faced them. The door had no handle and the cylinder reached from the floor to the ceiling. Only a few inches of floor space curved around to the other side.

Bone-chilling cold radiated from the cylinder.

"Andyn?"

She didn't even pause. "... and tower cold are not barriers real..."

"Go ahead, Buck," Dar said. "We trust you."

Buck felt a strange combination of gratitude, pride and affection. *They're waiting for me to lead. And the only reason they're even here is because of friendship, because I'm a Grey Rider. Boy, was I wrong in not confiding in them months ago.* It humbled him.

"Is this the right way?" asked Eric.

Buck felt the pull and nodded. Above the door, he saw a few symbols carved into the stone.

"That's the Irial script for 'he who commands'", said Connor.

They stood in silence for a while.

"All right," Buck said finally. *Tower cold...*

"Open," he commanded into the chill air. The door slid sideways, revealing a wide hallway beyond and an open archway leading to another passage. Buck's mouth felt dry. The others stared at him like they'd never seen him before.

"Holy saints, Buck," said Eric, "Are you really a wizard in disguise?"

"Not by a long shot. Come on." Buck motioned them forward.

The hallway stretched at least thirty feet to either side and forward for about eighty. Neat, arched doorways marched down the left and right walls at regular intervals. Two glowing strips of light ran down the center of the hall, one red and the other blue. At the end of the hall, the blue strip led to the left door and the red to the right.

Buck scanned the area, gripping Khelios. Many small ledges lined the thirty-foot long hall, holding the life-sized forms of creatures.

Mostly gargoyles, he decided, then froze. Bones lay scattered on the floor, along with many shards of stone.

"Now what the hell does that mean?" murmured Connor at his side.

Hlerv stepped to one side, surveyed the area, and grunted. "Who cares? Let's get through this place, fast. It gives me the shivers."

Buck nodded, feeling the pull leading him to the far door. By this time, he knew the words by heart.

"Sapphire blue and not ruby red," he murmured in the silence. He drew Khelios and followed the blue strip.

After about twenty steps Andyn screamed behind him. "Run!"

He whirled. The gargoyle statues stretched and grew. They extended their wings, blinking glowing red eyes. Muscular limbs flexed and claws opened. Some of them had dark grey or blue fleshy skin where others appeared to be made of solid rock.

Buck dashed for the door at the end of the blue strip, hearing the rush of wings behind him. He jerked the door open and motioned the others through.

Appalled, he stared at the hall as his friends ran past. At least twenty gargoyles swooped down at them, shrieking. Dar and Eric whipped their bows out. When they reached the door, they each fired twice, aiming for a single, fleshy gargoyle. The creature screamed and dropped.

Dar spat an oath and popped through the door with Eric. Buck slammed it shut. Hlerv and Connor whipped iron spikes out of their backpacks and jammed the portal.

Howling and shrieking resounded in the passageway. The door shook. The stones rumbled under his feet. The Riders stepped back, weapons at the ready.

"Well," said Eric, "At least they can't get through."

A stony, clawed hand shot up out of the floor, flailing around. Buck's eyes widened in horror. *Some of the gargoyles looked stony!*

The Grey Riders attacked without even thinking, hacking and slamming at the creature as it pulled itself out of the floor. More claws and fanged heads appeared in the walls.

Buck's breath came in gasps as he swung Khelios. By the shrieks, he knew he hurt them but only chipped pieces off the creatures. Andyn, however, crushed a skull with her maces and the creature fell apart. Buck wished for a stout club.

Despite their efforts, two gargoyles stood before them, lashing with sharp talons while others emerged from the stones and began to tear the door apart.

"Fall back!" shouted Dar. Buck gave way, shield up, beating a fighting retreat.

Andyn and Eric shouted arcane words and balls of light sprang up on the noses of the foremost attackers. They howled in frustration and flailed the air.

"There's a room back here!" said Connor.

They slipped back towards Connor. In despair, Buck saw the door splinter under the double assault of the fleshy and stone gargoyles. A veritable sea of limbs and wings surged through at them.

The companions reached a circular room and formed a ring at the entrance.

Buck deflected a claw with his shield. "Exits!" he shouted. There was no time for anything more.

"One back here!" called Connor. Buck heard Andyn and Eric mutter magical sentences under their breath.

A flock of tiny glowing comets arced out at the first stone gargoyles in their path. They hit the creatures and detonated, hurling them back to lie in a pile of shattered stone.

"Walls!" yelled Dar.

"They can't!" answered Connor. "The walls are set with some kind of metal leaf, with carvings and everything. The floors and ceiling too."

Behind the two stone gargoyles, more of the fleshy variety leaped at them, howling.

Damn it! It's like fighting a windmill with claws. Finally, Buck saw an opening, ducked a wild swing and thrust. Khelios glowed bright blue and impaled the beast.

Behind the fallen one, three more stone monsters advanced.

Buck's arms and legs felt like lead.

"Wait!" shouted Hlerv. "Everyone, draw back to the exit door on my command."

The stone gargoyles attacked and Buck slammed two of them back with his shield. At his side, Dar kicked one in the knee and it dropped, howling.

"Now!"

They legged it to the opposite doorway. Hlerv held both hands out at the charging, infuriated swarm, murmuring softly.

The room quickly filled with a thick grey fog.

"Connor!" he yelled, drawing his sword. The Halfling joined him and they leaped into the cloud.

Buck started after them but Eric held him back. "I think..." he panted, "I know... what they're doing."

Clanging noises and enraged howls rang out from inside the fog. Then snarling and screams and ripping noises filled the room.

Connor and Hlerv slipped back to them out of the fog, both sporting many bloody claw marks.

They leaned against the walls. "Go," Connor gasped. "Let's get away from here."

"The gargoyles..." Dar protested.

"...are busy killing each other," Hlerv said, hands on his knees. "We slashed them from behind in the fog and they thought it was each other attacking. They're ripping themselves to shreds in there. Let's hope none of them wanders out of the fog and comes after us."

They moved away as fast as they could, following the blue strip of light down a twisting, downward-ramped passageway to a set of double doors. Beyond this, a chamber with two exits and a set of benches greeted their relieved eyes. A bar fit on the opposite side of the door. Buck and Eric slipped it into place.

Connor and Hlerv downed healing potions and mild golden light covered their injuries.

"All right!" snapped Andyn. She turned on Hlerv, eyes flashing. "Why didn't you tell us you were a mage?"

Hlerv actually squirmed, his usual snide bravado vanishing under her glare. "Er... um... slipped my mind?"

She whacked him on the shoulder. "I'll slip your mind right out of your head if you 'forget' to tell us something that important again! All this time we could have had extra help from you!"

"I didn't see that you needed extra help," he protested. "Besides, I'm a dabbler compared to you guys."

Her eyes narrowed. "Well, dabbler or no dabbler, that fog back there was very useful. Are there any more little surprises we should know about?"

Hlerv's eyes glittered. "No."

She glared at him for a few heartbeats, then turned away. "Buck, which way?"

Buck pointed and she stalked off. He slapped Hlerv on the shoulder as he went past. "Don't worry about it. If she didn't yell at you, she wouldn't care. You're part of the family now."

Dar grinned at Buck as he headed for the right-hand passage.

"I usually get the brunt of it," he whispered to Hlerv. "I know I shouldn't bait her, but it's fun. Glutton for punishment, I guess. You get used to it after a while."

Buck saw Hlerv's thoughtful expression and had an unnerving vision of Dar and the Gnome joining forces to plot practical jokes.

The pull of the magic and the blue strip of light led him to the right. He took the point again with Connor. They continued on their downward slope until they reached yet another door without a lock. Again, a single word from him made it spring open.

A yawning cavern stretched out before them. The many stalactites and stalagmites made it look like the maw of some colossal creature. About a hundred feet away, a shimmering dome of light curved over a cubic glass chamber, about twenty feet on a side.

Buck's heart beat faster. The pull felt unbearable. Almost as if he were an outside observer, he watched himself move towards the crystalline box and its energy field.

"Buck?" Eric called out.

Buck kept going, heedless. He stopped about ten feet from the shimmering dome. Andyn gasped.

A nine-foot tall, hulking creature with one eye in its forehead stood next to a pedestal inside the cube. The cyclops wore chain armor and carried a pair of swords. It stood motionless, its eye closed and hands at its sides.

Is it just another statue? Buck's eyes locked on the pedestal. *I doubt it.*

A diamond lay on a velvet cushion, cut into the shape of a disk and about the size of a gold piece.

Buck barely dared to breathe. *The Eye of Truth.* He stepped forward. The shimmering field parted, then closed behind him. He heard alarmed cries from his companions.

"Buck!"

"Hey! I can't get through this thing. Buck, wait for us!"

"Andyn, Eric, Hlerv, see if you can magic this field away. Buck, for the love of God, get back here!"

He walked onwards, led by the irresistible pull, as if a giant led him by the hand. He neared the glass chamber. A doorway materialized out of the smooth surface, then closed after him the second he stepped inside.

The one-eyed giant blinked its eye. It drew its swords from their scabbards and grinned, showing wicked fangs.

Chapter Eight

Eye of Truth

She glided towards the palace on silent wings. When she neared the detection fields between the guard towers, she sent out a shunting magical force of her own. It wasn't nearly as strong as the ones in the towers, but lasted just long enough for her to skip between them. Silent, unseen, she swooped lower, then up. The guards turned as she shot past but did not see.

She veered away from another magical detector, then swooped down below a balcony.

She hovered there, holding her small wings still and using magic to levitate. No alarm went off. Still, she waited. Then, below her on another balcony, a trio of royal guards strode past.

Right on schedule.

She used magic to make herself invisible. *The detectors will find me soon if I keep it up, but can't risk a random person seeing me.*

The guards hesitated, speaking in low tones, then passed on. She sighed and flew up to the balcony above her. She eased herself up on careful hands, dropping down on the marble surface, her bare feet making no sound. She furled her wings and put a hand to her sword, peeking into the chamber beyond.

Something flared light blue under her and she winced, seeing her body fade back into view.

Damn. Should have expected that. Invisibility wards. No audible alarm though.

Through the curtains she saw three humans. Dark hair and dark eyes marked the person of Philip, King of Deran. Next to him on the royal bed sat a lovely woman with equally dark hair and cornflower blue eyes. She smiled at their visitor, a slender man in the black cassock and white tab collar of a Christian priest. The priest wore a purple skull cap with white trim on grey hair and spoke too softly for her to hear.

This is rich. She gave a wicked grin. She held down her sword and dagger to keep them from making any noise and padded forward.

The silky, translucent curtains, decorated with delicate embroidery of flowers and birds, looked flimsy enough. The elegant patterns seemed to call to her.

She smirked. *Clever. But no, I'm not touching them.*

She prepared a spell of telekinesis to shunt the curtains aside, then paused when the priest bowed and turned away towards an arched door. She used the magic to move the curtains and slipped inside.

"Come in Lady Saren," said the Papal Nuncio as he put his hand on the doorknob.

She made a face as the king and queen turned towards her. She could almost see Father Edward smirk as he turned the knob and exited.

I'll get back at him someday. He's just been lucky so far... or he has a legion of angels watching his back.

King Philip and Queen Ahlana stood. Saren bowed low.

"Your Majesties."

Ahlana shook her head and folded her into her arms when Saren straightened. "Saren, can't you come in the front door like an ordinary person?"

Saren hugged her back, a surge of affection and warmth flowing through her. "I'm supposed to test the defenses, aren't I, Majesty? This is more challenging and fun. Besides, anyone can see that I'm not ordinary."

Philip hugged her, then held her at arms-length. He fixed her with penetrating black eyes that she always had trouble meeting. "You're not ordinary. You're special, very special."

She shrugged, white bat wings ruffling behind her. "I suppose. I am glad I can use my talents to help keep you safe. Fortunately for me, my daemonic mother—may God have mercy on her black soul—left me with all kinds of little magical tricks. The only way I got this far is because I designed the security system and the guards are really getting very good. I almost had you, if it wasn't for... *His Eminence.*"

"Almost," said Ahlana with a twinkle in her eye.

"Almost," Saren muttered with a baleful look at the door. "Someday, I'll get him."

Ahlana laughed. "I think the entire Kingdom is entertained by this little game of one-upmanship between you and the Nuncio. I hear that several companies of the Royal Guard had made it into a wager, betting on when you will finally surprise Edward."

"Are you betting?" Saren asked with an arched eyebrow, smoothing her black hair away her the tiny white horns on her forehead.

Ahlana shook her head. "Not on your life. This is more fun."

"Fortunately for us," Philip added, "Your mother chose to magically enslave a paladin and that side of your heritage makes all the difference."

Saren felt a pang of longing. "I wish I had known my father. I remember so little. But I was little more than a baby after all."

"I understand Saren," Ahlana said in a gentle voice. "But God took care of you, didn't He? Melinor found you and raised you and taught you how to live a good life."

Philip smiled. "Indeed. he did. I owe him a debt for teaching you so well. If it weren't for you and Terenil, I might not be here. And look at all you've accomplished. Your father is very proud of you, I'm sure."

Saren smiled, remembering the Indidarc family. *They took me in, and Eric too, even though it might have cost them everything. They saw the right thing and just did it. I hope I'm that altruistic some day.*

The King and Queen sat, Ahlana patting the bed mattress next to her. Saren shook herself from her reverie and joined them.

"Now, speaking of that husband of yours, how is Terenil?" the Queen asked.

Saren smiled. "He is well, thank you, and sends his warmest regards."

In the mirror opposite the bed, Saren saw their reflection and marveled at the strangeness of it. Two perfectly normal humans in warm-weather sleeping clothes—and one slender, fit young woman in black leather armor and matching short skirt, white bat wings furled behind her shoulders. Tiny white horns peeked above her night-black tresses.

"So what brings you here?" asked Philip with a smile. "Besides testing my security and trying to defeat Father Edward in your little cat-and-mouse game?"

Saren ducked her head. "Actually, it is about my half-brother's group, you remember? Those free-lances who ride the pegasi. The ones found early this spring?"

"How can we forget?" Ahlana said. "What's the matter?"

Saren frowned. "Well, several things. First, your university scholars have been researching the scroll Ellen Hanford sent from Forester. Second, there's been trouble up by the northern borders. Lastly, Eric's party has disappeared."

Phillip leaned against a bedpost. "Well, pegasi are damnably hard to track, unless you use a scrying device. First things first. What did the scholars have to say?"

She shook her head. "You had better read it."

She reached inside the bodice of her leather jerkin and pulled out a tiny scroll. With a word, she enlarged it to normal size, then waved her hand to disarm two glowing symbols on the ends. She handed it to the Queen.

Ahlana read it out loud while King Philip looked over her shoulder. "Majesty: The search through the records of all your Universities, from Deorfast to Alrihan, has yielded only the following information further on the Song of the Grey Riders and the protagonists therein. The references are these:

First, of the Kingdom of Thul Mardil there is some mention at the time of the first Paragon War. The last ruler was indeed a princess named Zhinia, as theorized by Lady Hanford. She was as foul and base a ruler as any of the Corrupted Ones in that time. Her depravity knew no bounds, yet she had a hold over her people by means of clever manipulation of their fears and desires. She reportedly perished at the Battle of Three-Kingdom Lake but no body was ever found.

Second, one of the infamous names for Zhinia was the Dark Rider. She was known to ride a corrupted fell-steed of large size, armored in magical barding and as violent as her mistress. The princess was noticeable on the battlefield by her dark garb.

Thirdly, Alyssa of Tor Haldin, who reportedly slew Zhinia at the Battle of Three-Kingdom Lake, is known as Saint Alyssa by the Christian Church. She was one of the last of the decent Paragon rulers but died in an assault on her nation in the waning days of the epoch."

Saren sat back on the bed, watching the King and Queen carefully. .

"Well," said Ahlana, letting her hands drop into her lap. "That's an interesting turn of events."

Philip raised his eyebrows. "According to Lady Ellen Hanford, our lovely little Zhinia may have become a lich. Either that or someone else is using her name, which has happened in the past. Does anyone know where this nation of Thul Mardil was located?"

Ahlana bit her lip. "Yes, somewhere down near Torosc, which makes sense because that's where she defeated Margoth. The name of the lake is a little different these days: Three-Nation Lake, but it's the same one."

"Then maybe this trouble in our northern border is unrelated," mused Philip, frowning.

Saren shuddered. "The idea of a lich running around on the loose looking for revenge or something gives me chills."

Philip stood and began pacing. "We have to know more. I trust the staff at the university are still looking?"

"They have a scholar devoted to it eight hours a day," Saren replied, "but Doctor Salvatis wasn't optimistic. This took two months to find and they were working with some really obscure records."

Philip nodded. "I may have to call in a favor from Brion Aluín, in that case. The Elves may have some older records."

Saren coughed to hide her surprise. King Philip still unnerved her with the way he tossed around the names of national rulers, like the Emperor of Elven Terenai.

The King's brow furrowed. "I'll send a courier in the morning. What about the troubles in the north? I know the Duke of Darlon is in the field, looking for that bandit prince, Zyrakis."

Saren nodded. "And having some success, too. He has recaptured border posts and cleared a couple of the passes. However, there were reports of a white dragon rampaging around near the Greenwall, southwest of Eldir."

Philip stopped pacing. "White dragon?"

Saren gave a wry smile. "Which leads me to our Grey Riders. Here is a copy of a note sent to Count Telmin, who is administering Darlon in the Duke's absence. One of his staff forwarded it to us and I picked it up on my way in."

She unrolled the parchment. "Your Excellency. The northern pass is clear. A white dragon was the cause of the trouble. She is now dead. We are heading off to investigate further leads. We will return to Darlon for payment and assignment after our investigation is complete. Andyn Eleandir, Priestess of Verian."

Ahlana looked perplexed. "Further leads? What further leads? Do they think the dragon was working for someone?"

Saren shrugged. The Queen shook her head. "I'm going to have to talk to Priestess Eleandir about her reports. This doesn't tell us anything at all."

Philip's frown deepened. "I'll have to get more information from the regional commander. And this Grey Rider thing bothers me the more I think about it. In addition to all this about the Riders, Lord Hanford thinks that Margoth, or whoever is using her name, is raising an army. And the mustering-in is going on in my back yard. Frankly, all of this worries me."

Saren sat up straighter, looking at the King. *He's a paladin, just like my dad...chosen by God and endowed with special gifts. Anything that worries him is, well, frightening.*

⬧◆⬧

"Darogir of the Dark Elves, son of Ildrisana, to see Your Majesty," the Ogre rumbled.

Zhinia Margoth turned away from her table. "Very well. Send him in. We are not to be disturbed. Any interruptions will be dealt with severely."

The Ogre nodded and backed out of the throne room, massive hands held before his face.

A slender figure in dark-enameled chainmail entered and bowed. A midnight blue tunic covered the armor, the glittering insignia of a flying dragon embroidered on the cloth. A gold coronet sat atop his long silver hair, bound at the back with a twist of black cord.

Zhinia schooled her features to neutrality. *Yes, as handsome as any surface Elf: violet eyes, slim body and attractive face – even with the red sheen in his eyes. But he's a puppet, a servant to his mother. Women rule in the realms of the Dark Elves.*

"Greetings to Your Highness," Zhinia said, bowing as well.

"Greetings to Your Royal Majesty," returned Darogir, eyes glinting.

Ignoring his use of a formal address that was yet unwarranted, — *but with the conquering of Deran, soon would be* — she gathered her robes around her. She watched him for a minute. He returned her gaze without blinking. Her appearance often unnerved first-time guests: a skeletal figure with glowing pinpoints of purple light for eyes, wearing an ornate crown and rich, rotted robes, bearing a staff of twisted black wood.

Yes, he holds his composure well. I will remember that. "Well," Margoth asked, gesturing to a stone bench next to her throne, "What news of these pretenders, these Grey Riders?"

Darogir rubbed his chin. "The net grows tighter, Majesty. We are watching for them, as agreed. Our scouts report that they have been sighted in the Valley of the Spire, near the border of the nations of Astarel and Deran. When they are sighted again, we will lay our trap."

Margoth smiled. "Lord Liander Tolin has been most approving in his reports of your activities. He will, of course, take charge of the Riders when they are captured."

"Of course. Liander Tolin is a most able emissary, if I may say so."

Margoth sat back. "He has the sense to take up arms in the New Order. Your own queen has also proven to be most wise."

Darogir merely inclined his head. "Indeed. Now, Majesty, if there is nothing further, I would like to coordinate strategic sequencing with General Jerran."

Margoth stood and the dark Elf did also. "Indeed. One of my personal guard will escort you. I am honored by your visit."

"As am I, Majesty. We are glad to ally ourselves with someone of such obvious resources and brilliance."

He departed.

She smiled. *When we capture the Riders, the only real threat will be removed. Do I care about Deran? Ha. The Ja'al can have it. It's a simple bargaining chip for Thul Mardil, the real prize.* She imagined herself gloating from the ramparts of a new castle in her ancestral lands, looking towards the captive kingdom of the long-dead Alyssa of Tor Haldin.

All who oppose me will die to amuse me and my retinue, just as in the Paragon Age. We who have the power and authority will dictate to the lesser ones, who will serve, work and die as they are told. The unfit will be eliminated and everyone will have as much "freedom" I deign to give them.

A thrill of vindication and pride filled her mind.

It will be glorious.

"Where do you want it?" asked Buck Bydecy.

"Want what?" asked the cyclops, its eyebrow rising.

"My sword, of course," Buck said, trying to keep his hands from shaking. "In the neck, head or heart? That gemstone," he pointed at the diamond on the pedestal, "is the Eye of Truth and is the sole property of the family and line of Moridan Bydecy. I am Buck Bydecy. I am here to take it home and I can assume from your drawn weapons that you don't mean to let me have it."

The cyclops chuckled. "Well said, human. But you speak prematurely."

"Really?" asked Buck. He slid to his left, shield up and Khelios Giantbane ready. The sword hummed in anticipation, glowing blue along its razor edge.

The creature grinned. "You may be a Bydecy, but you have nothing of the personal integrity of Moridan."

Buck shrugged. "As if you would know."

The cyclops smiled. "I would. Can you choose, Buck Bydecy? I know who you are. You are one of the Riders Grey, as foretold by the Irial. Can you measure up to the prophecy?"

Buck froze, shocked. *How does this thing know about the Song? He's a cyclops, one of the giantkind, and they aren't exactly scholars.*

The creature pointed to the floor between them. Buck's eyes widened.

Glowing red script ran across the marble, etching letters for his eyes, letters which he recognized immediately.

For Good or Evil, all must choose or, choosing none, their lives to lose.

"How did...?"

The cyclops smirked. "Are you ready for that and what it implies?" he asked, stalking around the pedestal and the Eye of Truth. "Are you ready to stop sitting the fence and throw your token in the ring with those simpletons out there or join in with the side with real power, with real promise of all you've ever wanted?"

Buck felt cold. He licked dry lips. *To choose the side of Good or Evil... Can't I just decide not to choose?*

"I'm ready," he said with more conviction than he felt. "But how do you know all this? You're no ordinary cyclops. Most of your race can barely write their names."

The single eye in the middle of that forehead mocked him. "Why, there are others who follow your career with interest, Buck Bydecy. Other entities who have a vested interest in making sure that Moridan's lost Eye remains lost. I have been assigned here to make sure that happens. I must admit it took a while for the spells on this place to deteriorate enough for me to get in, but even Moridan's magic doesn't last forever."

Something in Buck's mind screamed at him to run for dear life. *Shit. If its masters sent it here to keep the Eye hidden and it was able to get past Moridan's magic... by the Great Mother...*

"And who are your employers, exactly?" he asked, mind whirring to figure out some kind of tactical advantage.

The creature laughed, throwing its arms up. To Buck's horror, two horns sprouted from its head and a spined tail writhed out from its backside. Black bat wings unfurled behind it.

"Any guesses?" it leered.

<hr />

"What the hell is that?" Eric asked in disbelief.

"Sweet Verian," breathed Andyn, "It's a half-Daemon. Kired-azen. In this case, a mixture of cyclops and one of the Fallen Ones."

"Hlerv, Connor, can't you figure a way inside?" Dar shouted.

Hlerv shook his head and banged a fist into the side of the chamber. "No! It's magically tuned somehow! I'd need to be a full archmage to get in there!"

"What do we do now?" asked Connor.

"We pray," said Eric, joining hands with Andyn and Dar.

Prayers in two ecclesiastical languages echoed in the chamber.

Buck felt the air suddenly lighten, as if a screen of invisible energy sprang up in front of him. The half-Daemon growled and thrust a hand towards him. A bolt of lightning lanced out. It lost cohesion about a foot away from him, then broke into a dozen smaller fingers of electricity. They spanged off the glass dome, ricocheting about the room. Two bounced off his shield, leaving his arm tingling.

Thank the Mighty Oaks for whatever that was.

With a curse, the winged horror hurled itself at him, swords slashing. Buck deflected the attacks, his shield arm aching from the impact. He struck at the Daemon's legs with Khelios, then feinted at the head and tried to stab him in the heart. He parried.

The cyclops-Daemon barked two short syllables and Buck faced two more creatures identical to the original.

Buck's heart skipped a beat. He concentrated hard, focusing his mind on Khelios.

In his altered sight, the leftmost enemy glowed red and the others faded like mist. Buck darted to the side as a blast of flame scorched the floor where he stood.

Buck charged the leftmost image. All three "creatures" swung at him but he ignored the other two, driving the real one back with stout blows. He took a cut on the leg but saw fear in the monster's eyes for the first time.

"What is that blade you carry?" he snarled.

"Khelios, Slayer of Giants," he growled. "I'll introduce your black heart to him in just a minute."

The half-Daemon took to the air, swooping up and uncorking a hail of acorn-sized flame balls. Again, that invisible screen of energy swallowed up some of the attack. Five of the tiny fireballs hit Buck on the legs, chest and helmet. He reeled backwards, bouncing off the glass walls.

Without thinking, he hurled himself to the right, hearing the twin clang of blades on the marble behind him. He tucked into a roll and leaped to his feet, breathing hard.

Those magic fire-balls hurt, but I think I'm getting my second wind.

The Kired-azen hovered in the air again, eyes blazing. "So, this will be a little harder than I thought," he hissed. "No matter. You will die all the slower for it."

It leaped forward, shouting a weird syllable. Buck's head rang. He tried to parry. A blade point pierced his leg armor and he cried out, stumbling away from the creature.

"He's losing!" cried out Connor in despair.

"Have no fear," said Andyn as the other two continued chanting. "Dar and Eric are making my protection spell more effective than it should be. By all rights, it shouldn't even penetrate that glass cage, but somehow, it's working."

"Now you die, weakling," the Daemon hissed.

It charged at him, leaping into the air.

Joko, old teacher, this had better work.

Buck pretended to stumble, then took two steps forward and tucked into a slide, slipping underneath the creature as it soared by overhead. Silver Khelios swept out in a deadly arc. With a metallic clang and a horrid ripping sound, the blade bit down through the creature's clavicle and into its chest.

The shriek of rage and agony nearly split Buck's head open. The falling Daemon ripped Khelios from his hands and the sword spun into a corner. The Daemon careened into the wall with a heavy thud.

Buck sprang on his feet in an instant, lurching for Khelios. The Daemon somehow stood up and stumbled towards him, purple ichor streaming from its wound.

Buck's hand closed on the sword. Khelios lurched in his fist and flashed so bright it dazzled him. The sword took on an insane life of its own, leaping forward and practically dragging him after it.

Khelios met the Daemon head-on, shattering one of its swords and burying itself to the hilt in its chest. Buck, Khelios, and the creature slammed into a corner in a tangled, bloody mess.

Seconds passed and Buck blinked, wondering where he was. He dragged himself to his feet. *Am I still alive?* He wondered.

"Thanks, Khelios," he gasped in a weak voice, looking at the sword with a newfound respect. He wiped the blade on the Daemon's cloak and sheathed it.

Buck gazed upward. "And thanks to whoever helped out in here."

Sound drew his attention to the outside of the glass chamber. His friends jumped up and down, their mouths open in silent shouts of joy. Andyn wiped the tears from her eyes and blew him a kiss.

"Maybe a real one later, sweetheart," he muttered.

He limped to the pedestal. It stood a little shorter than Connor, made of solid alabaster shot through with gold. On the top, a pillow of purple velvet held a single flat lens a little larger than a gold coin. He reached out a hand for it. A light tingle rushed through him as he picked it up, but nothing else happened.

Well, here it goes. It's supposed to show people's true natures.

He put it to his eye and turned toward his friends. Dar and Eric stood outlined in a warm golden glow, Dar's aura tinged with a touch of copper. Andyn radiated pure copper and a grey mist with a faint silver lining surrounded Connor. Hlerv showed up as only a flat grey with an almost imperceptible brown edge.

Buck sighed, feeling dizzy and fatigued beyond reckoning. *I sure as Hell don't know what all that means, but it confirms this is the Eye of Truth. Finally. Now we can get out of here.*

He kissed the gemstone, a sudden lightheadedness growing. The room swam in his vision. *Why is the room spinning?*

The last thing he saw as he collapsed on the floor was the glass dome shattering into a million tiny pieces.

CHAPTER NINE

Witch Storm

Brandawyn Alenar patted Amicus on the neck with a gloved hand. Close-growing willows and soran trees crowded around them, the more distant growth looming like sentinels in the thick fog beyond. Stephen and Megan rode double on Larinor next to her.

"Are you sure we can't fly?" she asked.

Stephen chuckled, leaning against the saddlebow. "Sure, if you want to smack into a tree or two, or maybe a cliff. This fog is bad and I'm not entirely sure it's natural. We'd best stay low for now."

"Too bad," Megan said from her steed behind him. "We were making good time with us on the pegasi and you and Aunt Daphne on her owl."

Stephen smiled. "Yes, but as usual, the best laid plans. Besides, she can only transform the medallion once a day for a limited amount of time. We'll be all right."

"Well," said Daphne as she strode into the woods out of the mist, "I didn't see any good campsites to the north. Let's keep going. It's another sixteen miles or so to Marolpeth and it's almost nightfall. We could do it easily in the air but with the fog we're doing no better than by horseback. We'd better find a good, safe camping spot right now so we can rest up."

Brandi gave her aunt a tired look.

Daphne grinned and swung up into the saddle behind her. "Oh, stop it. You ride. Leave the campsites to me."

They settled to a relaxed canter and struck off into the forest. Daphne dismounted often and directed them along a hunter's path so dim that Brandi often lost it.

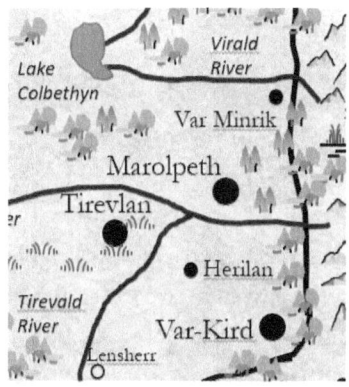

Brandi marveled. *The way she reads trail signs and guide us around potential danger spots reminds me of Dar — with about ten more years of experience.*

Finally, Daphne called a halt near a thick wall of vegetation. She eyed a tiny rivulet running out of the brush wall, then looked up at the trees beyond it and nodded. "Behind there."

Megan looked at the wall of brush. "How are we going to get through that?"

Stephen grinned and slipped a coppery ring onto a finger of his left hand. "I'm not a scout or tracker, but I have a few tricks."

He waved his hand, palm forward, and a pale green light surrounded his fingers. To Brandi's astonishment, the thorny growth parted like a curtain.

Brandi shot a glance at him. "You really have to let us know about these little goodies a tad earlier."

Stephen looked smug. "Benefits of twenty years in the field, dear niece. Let's go."

"No, Uncle Stephen," said Megan, "You *really* have to start teaching me more of those tricks."

He only smiled back at her.

The pegasi rolled their eyes and minced through the pathway. The Alenars found a small clearing sheltered by tall ironwood trees, their grey trunks soaring upward to a protecting canopy of leaves and branches. At the far end of the clearing, water trickled down a cleft in a rock wall, ending in the rivulet.

Megan looked at Daphne as she dismounted. "That's how you knew something was here. The water."

Daphne nodded and removed her helmet, tossing her hair. "The odds were good with the rivulet and the ironwoods behind the brush wall. Ironwoods tend to grow close to water and push away nearby bushes."

I don't know how she does that, but I probably should have paid more attention in botany class, Brandi thought as she slipped out of the saddle. She tried to stretch the kinks out of a sore backside, and truth be told, out of her entire body.

Amicus looked at her out of the corner of his eye and she patted him on the neck. "Yeah, I know, boy, you're tired too. And you haven't had the air under your wings today."

Even with the warm, rather humid summer nights in Terenai, Daphne set about starting a campfire, carefully banked and crafted to allow little woodsmoke. The fire comforted Brandi in her fatigued state and allowed them to heat water for washing and tea.

All four pitched in to feed, water, curry-comb and inspect and clean the wings of the pegasi. With those tasks done, Brandi and her relatives arranged themselves on their cloaks and ate dried meat and fruit and chewy trail bread.

Brandi touched a small gold cross on a chain lying against her armor. The center of it held a tiny ruby heart. She watched the fading daylight in the gemstone, remembering.

"I want you to have this," Eric had said that last day. "It shows where my love lies, with God and with you."

She took a drink from her wineskin to wash the lump from her throat. She could see him in the wan light of evening near the Deranese town of Forester as if it was yesterday. Her last words to him echoed in her brain.

"I am yours, Eric Indidarc," she had told him, tears streaming down her face, "Only God has my heart before you."

Her vision turned misty and she blinked rapidly. *Eric has my silver cross in exchange, the same cross Mother gave me as a Communion gift.* She also remembered that day, a furtive yet joyous day hiding in a neighbor's cellar while a priest in disguise gave the Sacrament to a handful of faithful.

God, please let me be with him again. Brandi sighed. She took another drink from her wineskin and watched her relatives for a moment, particularly the older two. Megan caught her eyes and nodded.

"All right," Megan said, sitting down on a large rock, "We've been patient, but you have to tell us more. No one can hear us out here and we can't stay in the dark any longer. Why are we traipsing all over creation?"

Stephen and Daphne exchanged a look. "It's not a simple tale," Daphne said.

Thankful for the distraction from her morose thoughts, Brandi sat up. She shook her head. "Wrong answer. You've dragged us along from one city to another for the past two months, looking for this sage or that text or this inscription. We have the right to know."

Stephen looked uncomfortable, his handsome face uneasy. "The less you know, the better. Suppose someone should capture you? They can't worm out of you by magic that which you don't know."

"And suppose something happens to you," countered Megan. "Who's going to complete the mission? Or isn't it important enough to finish if you and Daphne are out of action? If we're only your bodyguards on the lookout for bad guys, the mission will fail without you."

Only the sound of insects and trickling water broke the silence for a while.

Finally, Daphne stood. "Fair enough. Let me set the wards and then we'll tell you."

She went to her saddlebags and pulled out a short rod, about the thickness of her thumb and made of bluish metal for half its length, the other half a clear crystal. She eyed the area carefully, then planted the metal end into the earth near the center of the clearing.

She murmured a phrase and the crystal end flared red for a split second, then Brandi heard a low hum. A swarm of tiny red points of light skittered over the ground, passing by her and the others. They disappeared into the growth and even ran up the cliff to the source of the water. Then they vanished.

Megan shook her head. "You have the most amazing toys. I sure hope you give us the code word for this one."

Stephen's eyes twinkled. "Only if you're a good girl and eat your spinach."

Daphne sat on the ground. "Okay. You want the story, so here it is." She leaned back against the rock by the rivulet. "To put it simply, we're looking for evidence that some of the old kingdoms can be restored in Torosc."

Megan stared at her. "Are you kidding? All the old lines died out or were exterminated at the time of the founding of the Archons."

Daphne shook her head. "So we thought. However, the Church of Irial stumbled on information in a set of books and documents brought in by a free-lance party. They shared the information with the Verian hierarchy, the Lords of the Kurental Council and the Christian Curia as well, so each religion decided to send out search teams. Our task is to go into Torosc and see if we can find anyone who is descended of those old royal houses."

Brandi stared off into the wall of brush, her pulse quickening. *What if this is true? Could the Republic be overthrown? Could the land and its people be free?*

Megan looked at her aunt and uncle through narrowed eyes. "So we've been trying to find potential leaders for rebellions in Torosc."

Stephen nodded. "The Northern Alliance and Merdail could materially support such movements if they needed it."

Megan pursed her lips. "And a lot of people are interested in making sure we never find them?"

"Yes," Stephen answered. "The Archons and their allies, to start with, then the Ja'al and the other evil religions, probably in that order. Just finding history from some of the old kingdoms?" He shrugged. "That's valuable in and of itself."

"There's something more," Megan eyed the pair of them. "One of the sages we talked to wasn't a historian. He was an expert in magical relics. I checked the directory while you weren't looking."

Daphne shot an accusatory look at Stephen. "You were supposed to watch them."

Stephen made a wry face. "Children are inquisitive, my sister."

Brandi raised an eyebrow. "And?"

After another long silence, Daphne sighed. "We know that some of the relics of those royal lines survived, from what we've been able to figure out. The Sword and Cloak of the King and Queen of Loemin are on the list, as is the Crown of St. Alyssa."

"The Crown of Saint Alyssa! Where?" Megan breathed. "In Torosc? The irony of that would be too much."

Stephen shook his head. "We don't know where it is, to be honest. If we can find the old maps, we can figure out where the palace in Tor Haldin might have been. We know the city of Coastwatch was called Tor Aldin but we don't know if it's where the ancient palace might have been, or even if Alyssa ruled from there. The legends and traditions say she was Alyssa of Tor Haldin but that might just have been her hometown, not the capitol. There's also the high likelihood that the crown was taken out of the area – there are several Christian orders, including St. Terenil and St. Michael, that spirited away various relics."

"I know it's important to the history of Alenar, but I don't remember what the Crown can do." Brandawyn noted, feeling again like she should have paid more attention in her classes.

Stephen casually flicked a twig across the clearing. "Nothing much. If you die within sight of it, the wearer can raise you back to life as long as too much time doesn't pass. You can destroy evil creatures with spells such as Song of Angels, Heavenlight, or Merciful Word. You can block most malevolent magic. You're protected against things like Deathmagic and Rotting Curse. You can heal wounds, draw out poison, and inspire allies to feats of bravery. You know, minor, apprentice-level things like that."

Brandi stared at her sister in shock. *He can't be serious. That level of power is...*

Megan swallowed hard. "Those spells are *way* beyond my abilities."

"I have no doubt," Stephen continued, "High clerics and mages had a hand in the crafting of that crown and a very holy woman wore it. The point is that if we find those ancient kingdoms, we have a starting point for throwing off the yoke of the Archons and recovering those ancient relics. That's why all this is a secret."

Crickets chirped. A small animal rustled through the brush.

Daphne took a drink from her wineskin and wiped her mouth. "So far, we have two possibilities. East of Marolpeth is a remote region of Terenai where a sage named Damion Eldermain lives. He's retired, but by all accounts he did a lot of research on Torosc for Imperial Intelligence. The second possibility is a library to the south of us, near Tirevlan, in a large town named Herilan. There's an old branch of the Elven Imperial library system there. We'll head for Eldermain's home first, then to Herilan."

Megan shook her head. "Okay, suppose we find this evidence and lineage information. Then what? Lug it all the way back to Deran, to Saint Martin's?"

Stephen sat back against a tree. "No. Another one of our 'toys' is a bag with a magical token, called a Messenger Bag. All we have to do is place what we want into the bag and then activate the medallion. The information will be teleported to St. Martin's in an instant and the bag is sent back to us empty. We have a finite number of medallions so we can only do it a limited number of times. We have to be careful of what we send back."

Brandi sat quiet for a while. Her mind whirred. *Ancient kingdoms, an end to the Torosc "Republic", bags that can teleport things over vast distances, mighty holy relics... these are things of legend!*

Megan gave her aunt a sharp look. "I presume the forces of Darkness also suspect something. Otherwise, you wouldn't have come to take us away so urgently."

Daphne nodded. "We are aware that they are also trying to find the relics and the heirs."

Then there's not a moment to lose. We can do this more efficiently. Brandi stood. "We should split up. Megan and I can go one way and you two another."

Daphne raised an eyebrow at Stephen. "I'm not sure. You certainly have acquitted yourselves well, and we do have a timetable of sorts, but this is a little more than what you've done in the past."

He shrugged. "I think visiting Eldermain's home is well within their capabilities. It isn't far and we'll tell them what we need to know. You and I can go on to the library. We have the mirrors, you know."

Megan's eyes lit up. "Let me guess... Sending Mirrors?"

Brandi smiled. "I've heard of those. They had a few at the Academy."

Daphne sighed. "Well, that does change things. We can be in touch more easily with them." She reached into her pack and handed Brandi a simple metal mirror.

Brandi peered at it. The metal frame twisted like vines all around the perimeter. The symbol of an eye looked out at her from the center top of the frame. *Yes. Just like the one the professors used in their demos.*

"Just call for me," Daphne said. "And my mirror will vibrate. I'll answer. Don't make long conversations. They can only be used for a short time before they need to recharge."

Brandi hefted the mirror in her hand. *We can do this. Megan and I, together, we can make a difference on our own.*

"Thank you for your confidence in us," Megan said.

Daphne smiled. "Even though it was as one of the Grey Riders, you did find a herd of pegasi suspended in time and defeat a Ja'al high priest and his minions. That counts for something."

The enormity of their task pressed in on Brandi and she set her mouth in a firm line. "One thing is for sure," she said, looking into the fire. "The stakes in this quest just got higher."

———◈———

Andyn put away her medical kit in her backpack and sighed. "Well," she said, "That's not the worst I've seen you get hammered by an enemy, but you were pretty close." She sat back on her heels and regarded Buck.

He smiled at her and leaned back against the wall. "Thanks Andyn. Thanks, all of you."

Eric laughed. "And what did we do? We watched you and that Kired-azen beat the daylights out of each other."

Dar shook his head. "And prayed."

A lot, finished Andyn in her mind. *Verian's breath, we prayed a lot!*

Buck shivered. "Maybe that helped."

"Feel up to moving?" asked Connor.

Andyn rose with the others and helped Buck stand. The strain of the events of the day and the prayer and the healing magic caught up with her and she leaned against the wall for a moment. *He's the one who did the fighting but I feel like our roles were reversed.*

"May I see the Eye, Buck?" she asked.

He hesitated for a split second, then handed it to her. She examined the simple disk made out of solid diamond. If she peered very close, she made out the image of an eye hovering in the center of the gem.

She held it up to her eye and gasped. *I can see everyone's aura and their magic items. This really is the Eye of Truth.*

"Amazing," she said, handing it back. "What are you going to do now?"

The others watched Buck. He tossed the Eye in his hand, then gave a sheepish smile. "I know you guys have no involvement in this, but I'd appreciate it if you would come to Tyler with me so I can clear my name."

Dar laughed. "As if we'd let you go alone."

Buck had a peculiar expression on his face, halfway between embarrassment and some other emotion she thought could be tears of happiness. "Thanks," he said. He looked as if he wanted to add something but finally just nodded.

"So," Hlerv commented, "Here we are, in the Tower of Moridan, with the Eye of Truth. Now what? There's still the storm. Do we sit it out in here or do we head straight for Astarel?"

"Straight to Astarel," Eric interjected. "The white dragon knew about the Eye and it's a sure bet someone else knows. Besides, this place is creepy and no telling what else is hiding in here."

With a chorus of agreement, they filed out of the chamber, Buck taking one last look at it before exiting. Under Buck's guidance and the magical light path, they retraced their steps exactly and ended at the entrance cave.

Their pegasi whinnied at their approach. Puup fluttered up to land on Buck's shoulder. Dar grinned at Andyn.

"Nice big, warm cave. Almost as if someone put it here for flying creatures to begin with."

Andyn shook her head. "Don't put it past Moridan. He might have had a few flying creatures of his own."

They saddled their mounts and gave them a snack of high-protein grain and a little meat. Then the group slipped out of the cavern. Dar and Eric conferred, looking at the gray skies, testing the wind.

"The weather looks clear for now," Dar said. "If it keeps up, we should be in Tyler in two or three days."

Andyn nodded, feeling relieved. *It would be nice if something was easy for once.*

They negotiated the tricky downslope but all managed to launch their mounts from the mountainside without accident. The group urged their pegasi into forward flight and soared up into the summer mountain air.

———◆———

"Well, what do you know?" Keredis said, rubbing his hands together.

Farlana scowled. Daytime surface duty felt like a punishment, with the thrice-damned sunlight, even with cloudy skies. "No, I *don't* know, Keredis. Tell me and be quick about it."

The male Fallen Elf turned to her with an amused expression on his face. "Getting edgy, High Mistress?"

Her eyes narrowed. "Don't toy with me, Captain. What is it?"

He pointed between the sheltering boughs of the thicket that covered their hiding place. "It looks like our quarry is on the move."

Farlana's pulse quickened as she spied the tiny figures of five winged horses soaring away from them up to the northwest. *Queen Ildrisana will be very pleased. This, at last, would be my ticket to success, to notice from the Council.* "Get me the magic mirror, idiot. We have no time to waste."

"Farlana has done well."

The three Elf mages nodded. High Queen Ildrisana stood from her throne and floated down to their level. She gathered silver and black robes around her youthful figure, clad in a leather-and-chainmail outfit. "Is all prepared?"

One bowed. "Yes, Majesty."

She touched the platinum crown on her dark tresses and smiled. "In what direction will you drive them?"

Another mage bowed in turn. "One of our farther outposts is on the way they are heading, Majesty. Sector three. That would seem to be the best bet."

Sector three. Her smile grew more wicked. "How ironic. Andyn Eleandir will have a fit. I love it when Arachnia gifts us like this."

She whirled away from them. "Make sure the storm is strong, my obedient pets. Very strong. And alert Liander Tolin. Tell him his lady love is coming his way."

Andyn spurred Medianox faster, trying to catch up with Dar. The pegasus mare's wings and muscles strained against the storm. Andyn blinked rapidly and wiped rainwater from her eyes. A triple-forked branch of lightning sizzled past them, missing by a few hundred yards and making her hair stand on end.

This is madness! With a burst of speed, she drew level with Dar and made a frantic landing signal with her free hand.

She saw the frustration and anger in his eyes, but he nodded.

Murmuring prayers to Verian and his prophet Tolan, she followed her friends down into a clearing in the dense forest below.

Buck pulled up a prancing Shadowbane as she landed. The rain crashed down in sheets. "We've got to get out of this," he shouted as a thunderclap went off nearby, "Eric saw a rock shelf off to the west."

She nodded, spurring her mount in that direction. The group ducked under low tree branches and slid in between thick trunks, following Eric. They emerged in a clear space in a grove of pines. On the opposite side, a vast rocky ledge extended outward above their heads, leaving a somewhat dry space underneath. Rock walls soared upwards around it, disappearing in the treetops and rain above.

She lifted back the hood of her cloak. Rainwater only dripped down in spots instead of deluging the area. *It's damp, but not unbearable.*

Hlerv hopped down from Connor's mount. "Let's get a fire started. I'm freezing."

Andyn held up a hand. "No. Cold camp."

The others gaped at her in dismay but Eric and Dar nodded. "What do you mean?" asked Buck.

"This is a Witch Storm," she said, waving a hand at the sky above. "It's magically induced."

Hlerv spread his hands. "How can you tell?"

Eric flipped his hood over his helmet. "I know what normal storms look like in this area and Dar will back me up. We can't risk anyone smelling woodsmoke."

"Wonderful," groused Hlerv. "How long do these Witch Storms keep up anyway?"

"They can't go for long at this strength," Andyn replied, pulling the saddlebags off Medianox. "Only a few hours at best since they cost enormous amounts of energy. We're stuck here until then."

"Someone wants us grounded," said Eric, "Which means that if someone is looking for us, they'll be out soon, while we can't fly."

Dar nodded. "Whoever caused this storm knows we're in the area. Stay alert."

They fed the pegasi and provided them with water, then tried to make a sort of camp under the rocky overhang. Because the overhang didn't cover enough area for the pegasi to fit underneath, they resorted to ground-hitching them under a stand of trees with wide, overhanging branches. Puup flew up to sit placidly on a tree above the pegasi.

The rain tapered off soon after they finished a cold supper of jerked meat, bread and cheese.

Andyn surveyed the sky. "It'll be getting dark soon," she commented.

Dar nodded. "We'll just stay here and take off in the morning." He looked worried.

She frowned. "What's wrong?"

He scanned the area, eyes flitting from one shadow to another. "Something doesn't feel right. This place is too easy to find, right near a clearing."

"We'll just have to keep a good watch," said Eric, pushing Dar in the shoulder. "Don't worry so much."

"It's why I'm still alive," Dar retorted, eyes still moving.

Andyn drew last watch so she removed her chainmail, wrapping herself up in her cloak. She nestled under her blankets, trying to find a comfortable spot on the hard, damp earth. A spot in her throat itched and she hoped she wasn't coming down with something.

Whoever said that a free-lance mercenary's life was all glamour and adventure and riches was a stupid liar.

She dropped off to sleep.

───── ◆◯◆ ─────

A hand touched her neck and she brushed it away. "Dar, I'm going to smack you," she murmured. "No pranks today, please. I'm tired."

Another hand cupped one of her breasts and her eyes popped open. *That isn't Dar.*

An Elven man smirked at her, reddish eyes glowing. She opened her mouth to scream and a hand clamped down. She bit it, eliciting a curse.

"Attack! Everyone up!" she screamed at the top of her lungs.

A ball of light sprang into being over the middle of the camp.

Her assailant knelt down on top of her, pinning her under the blankets. She kicked her legs free, then curled up so her heels hooked under his chin. She straightened her legs and he flew off her with a grunt.

She scrambled up, hands groping for her maces. She caught a glimpse of a startled Dar and Hlerv whirling back towards the camp from their watchposts.

Dear Verian! They came from behind us! She swept up her weapons. Buck struggled with two more Dark Elves and her assailant leaped to his feet, sword flickering out. She turned and her heart sank.

The back wall of the overhang yawned open, showing a wide passageway filled with Elven warriors in shiny chainmail. Dozens of red-glowing eyes leered at them. Her heart skipped.

Connor leaped to her side as her assailant struck. She rolled away and the Halfling parried. Andyn grabbed up her armor and wriggled into it, not bothering to fasten the neck strap and just managing to get the waist belt tightened.

She turned to the entrance, murmuring a spell. She spread her fingers and extended her hand. Filmy webs shot out at the attackers, but a blue light flared from the back of the Elven ranks. Her webs disintegrated.

Another mage!

Dark Elves swarmed over the area. She parried a strike, broke one's arm with a return stroke, and got stabbed in the leg by a spear. She saw Dar cut one in half, then get hit by two swords at the same time, bleeding from his waist and arm. Buck disappeared under a pile of Elves, one of whom flew back and slammed into the ground. Eric stabbed at a trio of Elves surrounding him, keeping them at bay with his spear.

Hlerv gave the area a panicked look, then threw a dagger in the face of a nearby Elf and shouted a word. He vanished.

More Elves surged at her.

"The pegasi!" she shouted to Eric, "We can't let them get the pegasi!"

Eric risked getting skewered and stepped back, making a wide circle in the air with his hand and pointing straight up. With a rush of wings, the pegasi trotted out, snorting. Dark Elves charged at them, grabbing for bridles and saddles.

It didn't quite work out the way the Dark Elves expected.

The pegasi, unused to strange hands, bucked, reared, kicked, and buffeted the Elves with their wings. Their assailants flew out in all directions, crashing into the brush or landing in moaning heaps.

Eric's pegasus snorted, spread his pinions, and galloped out towards the glade, the other mounts following. Several Dark Elves cursed and raced after them, but Andyn knew they would get away. A familiar white pigeon flapped after the pegasi.

The Dark Elves turned their attention to the companions, cursing in Elven. Andyn fought off multiple swords and spears, dodging when she couldn't parry. She bled from a dozen minor wounds. *Too many.*

A voice shouted from the back rank of the Elves. "No killing! They are to be captured!"

A multiple twanging noise rang out. A hail of tiny crossbow bolts shot at them. She took one in the midsection and screamed. It burned like fire. Her vision grew hazy. She tried to lift her maces but it felt like they were made of stone.

The last thing she saw was a face out of her past, an object of her hatred and loathing for years.

Liander Tolin looked down at her with a mixture of admiration and triumph. She struggled to rise and kill him.

The darkness closed in.

CHAPTER TEN

Captives

At first, Eric smelled straw - old, moldy straw. Then came the scents of unwashed bodies, urine, and rotting food.

He opened his eyes and winced. The very motion brought a wave of colored lights. He closed his eyes again. He lay still for a few heartbeats on icy cold stone, listening. He heard only steady breathing nearby.

He opened his eyes again, shifting to the infrared spectrum. He stopped after a second, wincing from the interference of the light in the room. Flames danced in a fire pit beyond the bars of his cell and a few torches sputtered in wall sconces.

The chamber stood almost empty. He saw no Dark Elves so he sat up, wincing.

Eric checked his injuries: a few cuts and bruises, but his left leg seemed the worst. It felt like weak, like it couldn't support much weight. *Considering the number of whacks I took from maces, I'm was lucky it's not broken. Thank God for enchanted armor.*

He sighed. *Even so, Buck and Dar got the worst of it.* At the thought of his companions he sat up straighter and surveyed the area.

A grinning skeleton regarded him from a corner of the cell. For an insane moment, he panicked and thought that it could be one of his friends, then chided himself for such a line of thinking. *They said we were to be taken alive, and no one turns into a skeleton in less than a day. That is, without necromancy, anyway.*

Steady breathing issued from the dark lumps near him. He dragged himself between them.

Buck lay on his back, a couple of rough bandages around his leg and chest where he had been stabbed. *Got to get Andyn on that, if she's up to it.*

He moved to Connor. *He's not so bad off, but he's the only one chained to the wall.*

Eric bit his lip. *Why would they do that? Sure, he's an expert lockpick, but how can they tell if they just saw us today?* Another thought struck him and he felt a chill. *Unless someone already knows quite a bit about us.*

Dar lay on his side, also bandaged. He bore a dark bruise on the side of his face where an Elven spear haft clubbed him before the darts flew.

Eric's gaze fell on Andyn. She looked the best of all of them. He wondered why. *She has Elder blood, just like me. Dark Elves have no love for those who follow Verian, yet she is relatively untouched.*

He sat back against the wall, trying to move his injured leg as little as possible. He waited, panting from the effort, trying to figure something out, something that was nagging at him. *Now if I had a decent night's sleep, I could ready a spell to open the lock, but where could we go? We don't have any weapons and we don't even know where we are.*

Eric counted his companions. *Wait. Where's Hlerv?*

A thrill of hope surged through him. Yes, he remembered the Gnome casting a spell and winking out. In the battle and the chase for the pegasi, the Dark Elves forgot all about him. *They probably thought Hlerv a coward for running away.*

That sobered him for a moment. *What if Hlerv really did run away? After all, he doesn't owe us anything. We only hired him recently.*

He sighed. *Without any other knowledge, Hlerv is either gone for good or out there somewhere, trying to figure out a way to get to us. More than that is useless worry.*

He recalled a Scripture and felt heartened. "Fear is useless. What is needed is trust," he murmured. "Well, we need more of the latter and less of the former."

"Andyn," he whispered, nudging her. "Wake up. We've got some things to do."

She jerked away, hand flashing out for a weapon, then stared at him with wide, terrified eyes.

"It's okay. It's me. And don't bother looking for weapons. All they left us was our clothing. They even took our boots."

Andyn lifted herself up. "Where are we?"

Eric waved a hand. "Dark Elf accommodations, only for their most honored guests."

She put her head in her hands. "That bastard."

He frowned. "Are you okay? Who's the bastard?"

She shook her head, voice tense with rage. "Liander Tolin! The man who hired your father to kill my husband. He was in charge of the raiding party."

Eric gaped. "Are you sure?"

"I've memorized his face, in the event that I'd have the opportunity to smash it in," she replied savagely, lifting her face. Her look of pure hatred shocked him, completely at odds with the Andyn he knew and loved.

"Andyn," he whispered, taking her hand, "You're going to have to use your head to defeat him, not your weapons. Besides, does the Way of Verian include hate and vengeance?"

She looked down at her hands. "No," she murmured. "It doesn't. It's just..."

He gave her hand a squeeze. "Justice will win out. Just not right now and not necessarily the way we think. Keep your faith."

She looked up at him with a wry expression. "The more you talk, the more I'm convinced Brandi consecrated you as a cleric or something."

Eric chuckled. "She's too smart for that." He sat back against the stone wall. "Now as to this Liander fellow— why ally himself with Dark Elves? He knows they would hate him and probably plot to kill him. There must be some other angle."

She chewed her lip. "You're right. There must be."

"What do you know about him?"

She shrugged. "He studied as a mage. Average ability, smart, ambitious. He came from a privileged family and made some friends in the university who had unconventional ideas about magic and its use. They formed a group dedicated to researching certain forms that drew power for spells by draining intelligent creatures of life, sucking the energy from them."

Eric shuddered. "Sounds like some daemonic magic." *And I've seen that personally.*

She nodded. "The group, called the League of Knowledge, were discovered by Verian priestesses and brought before the High Council. Liander felt that he and his fellows were different, gifted and altered somehow to be able to perceive reality in a new way. He not only thought that they had the right to do whatever they liked, but that no one had the authority to tell them they were wrong. Their goal was for all in society to not only tolerate their desires, but accommodate, celebrate, and praise them. After all, they were different, and better, and special. No one had the right to judge them."

"The Council told them that they had no problem with the fact they were different," she continued, "but with their means for expressing it. They had no right to do evil in the name of their cause, no matter how beneficial they felt it was. The League were given a chance to repent and cease their activities. Some of them had committed crimes to enable their research, so they were sent to prison. Liander was not one of them, being, in the main, their spokesman. The League disbanded, Liander was fined and went off to more conventional pursuits and eventually got elected as a junior alderman of the city council. I suppose everyone thought he had reformed and given up the ideals of the League, until Larad."

He squeezed her hand. "That's all good to know. We'll make use of it somehow."

They both sat for a few moments.

"Come on," he said, "Let's wake the others up. They took quite a beating back there and will need some of your healing."

She made a face. "They took my medical kit, but I can still use spells. At least it will alleviate the pain somewhat."

She laid her hands on Buck first. Eric watched the familiar orange-gold glow radiate from her hands as she placed them on his injuries. Buck stirred and relaxed a bit.

Andyn let out a deep breath. "That's all I can do for him now."

She moved to Dar and used healing magic on him too. She checked Connor. "He doesn't look too bad... where's Hlerv?"

Eric shook his head. "I think he escaped," he whispered. "I remember him casting a spell and vanishing during the fight."

Andyn snorted. "Dabbler, he says. I can't turn myself invisible. We're going to have another talk with our Mister Hlerv."

She and Eric shook the others awake. Sore and tired, all sporting headaches, they sat up nonetheless and listened as Eric and Andyn explained their predicament.

"So, this Liander guy works for Dark Elves?" Dar asked.

Andyn nodded.

He gave her hand a gentle squeeze. "It'll be all right. We'll figure a way out of this."

They turned their heads at a deep rattling sound. The heavy, rectangular door grated inward and a group of male Dark Elves entered. Indigo-enameled chainmail glistened in the torchlight. Besides the usual swords and daggers he saw in the raiding party, these also carried wooden clubs.

All the better to bludgeon us with.

Behind them, a smiling female glided in, accompanied by a taller male Elf. The woman arranged her dark crimson robe around her, fabric swirling over a skin-tight leather outfit of long-sleeved top and short skirt. A mace hung at her silver belt and a medallion in the shape of a glowing green teardrop rested between her breasts.

Eric felt a chill again. *Priestess of Arachnia — and Arachnia's church is a member of the Ja'al Alliance.*

He looked over the male with curiosity. Liander Tolin stood a bit taller than average, as tall as Eric's five foot eight inches. Slender like most Elves, he wore simple grey robes and a plain short sword at his hip. A slim mustache graced his upper lip. He waved at the cage door and one of the guards unlocked it. The entourage entered.

"Ah, my dear Andyn," Tolin said with a gentle smile. He turned to the female dark Elf at his side. "Mardildris, I'd like to introduce Andyn Eleandir, my fiancée."

Eric shot a look at Andyn, who wore an expression somewhere between confusion and outrage.

The female Elf bowed with a mocking smile. "I am honored."

"I am *not* your fiancée," said Andyn, finding her voice. "You are a murdering, conniving - "

"See how charming she is," Liander said, grey-green eyes affectionate. He acted as if he hadn't even heard her. "The most beautiful woman in Eleth-Anor and she has traveled all this way to be with me."

Eric saw one of the guards roll his eyes and nudge one of his fellows with an elbow.

Tolin knelt down in front of Andyn and kissed her hand.

She snatched it away and stood. "What do you want?"

"Why, what we've always wanted, my dear," Liander said, rising. "To be together as man and wife."

"Never!" she spat.

Liander took her hand again. "Our life will be idyllic. I have made wondrous preparations for our future."

She jerked her hand away.

Dar rose. "Drop the romantic crap and tell us what you want."

Liander didn't even turn towards him but waved in his direction. The Elven female nodded and four Dark Elves descended on Dar with cudgels.

Dar slipped under the first blow, disabled an Elf with a kick to the knee, dodged yet another swing and hurled his assailant into a corner. The last pair swung, hitting him several times. Dar blocked, weaved and dodged.

They're getting more than they bargained for. Good.

Eric stood, but three Dark Elves wielding swords interposed themselves, grinning. He sensed Buck at his side and looked at the human.

Buck's face was frustrated, angry. "Four against one Liander? Not very sporting odds, coward."

Liander made a motion at Buck. The Elven priestess smiled at him, then raised a hand and spoke a word. A jet of azure light shot out and hit him.

Buck tried to dodge, but a blue shield covered his body. He froze in place. Eric darted to his side.

"Buck!" The warrior's eyes rolled from side to side in terror, but he didn't move.

The Dark Elves decided that Dar warranted more than four. The ranger continued to dodge and strike back, but he ended up doing more dodging and blocking than anything. Finally, a club found its way through and he went down in a heap. The cudgels continued to thump into him.

"Stop it!" Andyn screamed, throwing herself at the pileup. "Liander, what are you doing? They're killing him."

Tolin smiled. "Stop."

The beating ceased as if a door had been slammed.

"So, you see, my dear," Liander Tolin said, "I fortunately have all the resources I could want here. You also can have this, if you join me and ally with the New Order."

Andyn glared at him, then turned her back on him. He placed both hands on her shoulders.

"It is your destiny," he purred.

Andyn's jaw set and she looked at Eric out of the corner of her eye. Eric nodded very slightly.

She turned around. "Tell me of this New Order," she said. "I'm not saying I'll sign up, but you have my attention."

He beamed. "See, Mardildris, she can be reasonable."

He put his arm around Andyn. She appeared relaxed, but Eric saw one white-knuckled fist clutching her clothes.

"I have made an alliance," he said, "with a growing power in the Northern Kingdoms. She is called the Dark Rider."

Eric's heart skipped a beat.

"Her real name is Zhinia Margoth and, though a princess in her own right, she owes me quite a bit," Liander continued with a gentle smile, "You see, it was I who found her crypt, joined forces with a Dark Elf wizard to disrupt the protective spells on it, and released her from her prison. The key to all this was a medallion made by an Elven mage of Eleth-Anor in the days of old. Unfortunately, this medallion was kept in the basement of an ancient tower. Even more unfortunately, you, dear Andyn, had chosen to build your home where the tower once stood. When your idiot husband wouldn't sell and thwarted my attempts to seize it in council, I knew I had to take drastic action. Thus, the end of Larad. The house, regrettably, had to be destroyed in order to access the medallion. I'm sure you understand that it was only done because it was absolutely necessary."

I'll bet, thought Eric as Andyn nodded, a neutral expression on her face. *What is it costing her to listen to the story of her husband's death again?*

"But why would you release Margoth to begin with?" Andyn asked, eyes locked with Eric.

Liander giggled. A chill raced up Eric's spine.

Liander winked at Andyn. "It's a secret. But I can tell you, my sweet. You see, after Margoth is restored to a kingdom, I will receive a duchy of my own to rule. You shall be a duchess."

"Ah." Andyn nodded, her face still expressionless

Liander frowned, then chuckled. "Yes, I have it, right here with me. My little secret." He patted his right hip. "She won't find it. It is my final bargaining chip, shall we say, in case she decides that she isn't so grateful to me after all."

He gazed at Andyn, violet eyes bright. "Is this all not brilliant of me, my sweet?"

"Oh yes," said Andyn with enthusiasm. "Now, if you would just release me and my friends here, we'd be able to help you in your quest."

He chuckled and shook a finger at her. "No, no, no, my little Andyn. As long as you owe allegiance to Verian, you are a danger to me. This other rabble will always be a danger to me, I am afraid, because I know for a fact that the Christians do not bargain with Arachnia's loyal followers."

Andyn stood very still, fists clenched at her sides. "I will not give up Verian."

"But Andyn, my dear," he said, smiling, "the powers given by Arachnia are so much superior. I have already joined her number." His eyes glowed red and a lurid green light shone from somewhere under his tunic. Eric felt an icy cold shoot straight through to his soul.

"Sometimes," said Liander in an echoing voice, "the ceremony of transformation shreds the sanity of the subject in question. In my case, I survived unscathed."

Andyn's face paled and she took an involuntary step backward.

"You'll change your mind," Liander continued, walking back to the cell door with a careless wave of his hand. "Mardildris, we'll begin the treatments now."

Mardildris' eyes glittered and she smiled. "Certainly, Master Tolin."

———◆———

Hlerv waited in the shadows, secure in his spell but leaving nothing to chance. A troop of Dark Elves, twelve strong, marched down the ink-black passage, their forms bright in his heat-vision.

They passed through an archway. He remained where he was.

A few seconds later, two immense spiders, each the size of a small horse, strode down the passage, multiple eyes bright. The giant arachnids walked right past his little alcove with only a faint clacking noise. He suppressed a shudder.

The spiders followed their Elven masters and he counted to twenty before moving out.

Hlerv — or Handor Lervion as he had been called in a previous life — kept his eyes on the stone floor. The Elves' footprints still left a hint of warmth.

So far so good. He tiptoed on the stones, following the tracks. *The cloaking spell will keep me safe for quite a while as long as I don't try anything drastic,* he mused, *but it doesn't make me silent. I can be detected magically.*

He wore a cloak purloined from a dead Dark Elf at the campsite in the forest to make sure he smelled just like any other guard in the complex.

As for the magical? He shrugged. From what he knew of the *Gha-Ridow,* or Tall Evil Ones, as the Dwarves called them, they wouldn't waste energy on magical sentries until farther into the complex. If he kept following patrols, he might just have a chance.

And why am I doing this? he reminded himself cynically. *Oh yes. I'm a member of the famed Grey Riders. And I'm going to need them later.*

He scooted into an alcove and waited, watching the passageway. His thoughts flitted back to his ancestral home and he clenched a fist under his cloak. *Don't worry, sister. I will return for you. Bide your time and play your role.*

He continued down the passage, then stopped short as the footprints ended. Frowning, he eased forward.

A deep shaft intersected the passage, heading down into cold blackness at least ten feet across, much too far for him to leap. On the other side, he saw glowing tracks.

He muttered a curse. *One of the Dark Elves in that squad must be a mage. Only by magic they have gone to the other side.*

He reached into a side pouch and felt for an odd pair of gloves. Though also invisible by virtue of his spell, he knew that short metal claws protruded from the palm. He fitted them on with care. Dropping one now would mean a painstaking scrabble in the dirt.

He took a deep breath and began to climb, placing his boots into toeholds and digging the climbing claws into the rock wall next to the hole. He progressed slowly, working his way around the walls to the other side. He eyed every crack and crevice before using it. *It wouldn't be above the Dark Elves to hide spiders or scorpions in the sides of the passage to prevent just what I'm doing.*

His foot slipped and he desperately slammed a spiked hand into the wall, steadying himself. Sweat broke out on his brow. *Dar and the others had better appreciate this!*

He gained the opposite side of the shaft and stood there for a while, slowing his breathing and slipping the gloves off. He listened, but no sounds echoed in the passage.

The thermal footprints faded as he watched. He followed them as fast as he dared, down a sloping tunnel. This opened up into a tall, narrow cavern with phosphorescent mold clinging to slimy walls. He slipped through the cavern.

Beyond this, an intersection of six passages awaited him. More mold grew here, but it trimmed and formed so that it curled around the corner of the floor. A tiled image of a spider stared up at him from the floor, shining in the dim light.

Blast. In his infrared vision, glowed with Elven tracks leading in all directions.

He slipped inside the chamber and stepped to the left. He looked around, mulling over the situation. *Now where would I put a prison? Logically, near a barracks so I could quell any riots or foil escapes. Also, far from a storeroom or armory so they wouldn't be able to equip themselves if they did escape.*

Voices sounded from a passage to his right. He tried to melt into the wall and held still.

A female Fallen Elf in a short leather skirt with a tight, long sleeved leather jacket entered, followed by two males in chain armor.

"She will break," the female said, "or die. I don't think it will be the latter until Margoth decides it. Liander certainly doesn't know what he's getting into."

One of the males chuckled as they headed for one of the other passages. "Margoth won't let a Grey Rider live."

Hlerv felt a chill race down his spine as he sneaked along behind them.

"That shorter human with the dark hair certainly has spirit," said the other male. "He can be broken, but he doesn't look like one to give up."

The other male shrugged. "It won't matter once Margoth gets here."

They all stopped before a door in the floor. Hlerv's eyebrows rose. *Hmm. A pit room. So Dark Elves do have them in their complexes. Interesting.*

The female gestured at the door. "Catalog their gear. Report back to me tonight."

"No sooner?"

She smiled. "There's no rush. They aren't going anywhere. I'll come look at what you've found tomorrow morning."

"Yes, Lady Mardildris."

She slipped away down the dark passage.

Hlerv's mind raced as the two Elves opened the door. *I have to get in there, if for no other reason than to appropriate the more valuable magic items, like Buck's Eye of Truth.*

He shot a glance back from where they came. The Riders were probably back there somewhere. Backtracking down that passage is my next move, after seeing what's in the pit room.

He watched the Fallen Elves as they climbed down a ladder. He sat back against the stone wall, thinking. *The Fallen Elves don't know I'm in here, and if I wait and watch for a little bit, they'll make a mistake. Then I'll make sure I take full advantage of it.*

Chapter Eleven

From an Unexpected Source

Time passed. It could have been days, hours or minutes, but without the sun or moon, it became a long, interminable period of darkness. Eric had no idea how the Dark Elves could stand it, with no sun, no wind on their faces, no sounds of the outside world.

The Riders ensured darkness and silence—silence, that is, except for the sound of screams and the whip. Judging by the condescending glances and snickering of the Dark Elves, Liander controlled the Dark Elves only by the most tenuous of threads. However, when ordering them to put the Grey Riders to the torture, the warriors under his command moved readily enough.

Buck's paralysis wore off, which didn't improve the situation since the Elves kept all of them chained to the walls. They even restrained Andyn's hands, probably because Liander knew of her considerable magical abilities.

As tortures went, Eric supposed it could have gotten a lot worse. They beat or whipped them at regular intervals, then watched with cynical eyes as Andyn used her healing power to revitalize them afterwards, making no move to stop her. It made a certain warped sense: if she could heal them after the "treatments", then there was no danger of them dying. Liander could use the Riders to pressure Andyn indefinitely. Eric eventually determined how to the hours by how long it took Andyn to replenish her energies for healing. The thin gruel and tepid water they received for food didn't help anyone's energy level. He guessed they had been there for at least thirty-two hours.

Liander paid repeated visits to Andyn, each time insisting that she give up her faith in Verian and join his cause. Each time, she quietly refused or appeared to mull the proposal.

Finally, Liander's already precarious hold on reality began to crack. On a particular visit, after being rebuffed yet again, he ordered Andyn stripped naked and took the whip to her himself. Eric and the others could only strain at their bonds. Liander ignored their attempts to distract him with taunts and shouted threats.

Andyn never cried out, not once, staring ahead at the stone wall, tears streaming down her cheeks. After about ten strokes, Liander stopped. He pulled her head back and poured the contents of a tiny vial into her mouth. Her wounds glowed light blue and vanished.

"There, my pet," he said, pulling her hair back. He caressed her smooth buttocks. "You see? I hold all the power. If you do as I say, I will be gentle. If you do not, there will be more of this, and worse."

He cast the whip down. "You force me into this. As it is, I'll have you know that I have sent word to Her Majesty so that she may come and retrieve you herself. She will be far less gentle than I. Your friends, of course, you cannot save, but if you join with me, I can save you. I have an ace in the hole, don't you remember?"

He glanced at the Dark Elves and whispered something into Andyn's ear. With a last squeeze of one of her firm breasts, he left.

Eric's mind reeled. *Zhinia Margoth here?* He stared at Andyn as the prison door grated shut.

"Andyn?"

She shook her head. Finally, the iron resolve cracked. She began sobbing, her shoulders shaking as she sagged in the chains. "I'm so sorry," she sounded absolutely miserable, "This is all my fault. Liander is my—"

"Stop it!" Dar growled from the other side of the cell. "I don't want to hear this. You haven't done anything wrong! This is all Liander's doing. He's the one responsible and he'll pay for it."

"He's as nutty as Dwarven pastry," Connor added. "I think that ceremony he was talking about really sent him on the 'final quest', if you know what I mean."

"Don't give up, Andyn," Eric said.

"Yeah," added Buck, "Besides, who's going to keep us out of trouble if you join with him? We can't do a thing without you."

Her sobs subsided and she let out a deep sigh. "I'm sorry. It's hard being so strong all the time."

"Andyn," Eric asked, trying to distract her, "what did Liander whisper to you before?"

She sniffed and swallowed her tears. "He said he had something Margoth wanted. It's a medallion with a helm on one side and a lake on the other. The inscription is 'Where Light shines on Shadow, there Shadow is found.' I have no idea what it means."

Eric looked over at Dar. To his surprise, Dar looked very excited. Eric raised an eyebrow.

Dar shook his head. "Not now. I'll explain later. But I've got to get that medallion."

The door grated open and Andyn stiffened, but only a couple of guards enteree. Careful not to get within the reach of the warriors, they unshackled her and left.

Andyn picked up her clothes and put them on, a dull expression on her face. "We've got to get out of here, and soon."

"No argument there," said Connor.

They began to plan, discussing various ways that they could distract the guards and overpower them or get to Liander somehow.

The door grated again and Andyn motioned them to silence. Liander entered with five guards.

Eric stood very still. Liander's red-glowing eyes swept the room. The greenish luminescence glowed under his tunic over his heart.

"One last chance," he said to Andyn, licking his lips "You will be mine or Margoth will make you wish you weren't born."

She stood straight and tall. "I'd rather die than join myself with you. You are a weak, cowardly traitor and you wouldn't last five minutes without your Dark Elven pets to help you. I will not deal with you any longer. Kill me if you must, but there will be no deal."

"I will have you!" Liander shouted. "Now!"

He grabbed her and planted his lips on hers in a fierce kiss. She didn't resist or respond at all, just standing like a statue.

He stopped, then slapped her in the face. She didn't even flinch.

"Have it your way," he said, eyes narrowing. He grabbed the ties of her breeches.

"That's great," said Dar from his corner of the cell. "You're so repulsive you have to force yourself on a woman. You can't even convince her to join you so you take her by force. That's a real manly, strong way to do it. At least Goblins let you fight them with weapons in your hands."

Liander's face grew white and he whirled on Dar. "What did you say to me?"

Okay, Dar... nervy move. Comparing an Elf to Goblin is a very dangerous business, even if they served the same master.

"No, no, don't let us stop you," Dar said, leaning back into the bars of the cage. "You're only confirming what we already know about you. Go ahead. Prove what a great, strong servant of the 'mighty' Zhinia Margoth you are."

Liander controlled his expression and motioned to Andyn. "Chain her."

He slid over to Dar. "Brave words, human. Can you back them up?"

Dar grinned. "Let these chains down and I'll show you."

"No," Liander said, tapping his chin. "That would be exactly what you want. Instead, we will make an example of you."

He spoke to the guards in Elven. "Brand him."

"You *are* a coward," Eric replied in Elven.

Liander shrugged and answered in the same language. "As if I care what you think."

He drew a dagger and laid it along Dar's neck while the guards unchained him. The ranger winced as one guard put his arm in a painful lock.

"Come with us," Liander said. He followed the guards and the struggling Dar to the fire pit. Reaching over to a rack, he selected an iron rod with the symbol of Arachnia at the end.

"You know," he said, switching to Humana, "It is considered a sign of honor for Dark Elves to wear the mark of the Queen of Venom. I will plant one right next where your brain is located."

He thrust the symbol into the fire pit and made a motion with his hand. The flames leapt up.

"I am going to brand you," he said to Dar. "Since you insist on making an ass of yourself, that is where I will put it."

The guards pounced on Dar and forced him to bend over onto a table. The ranger struggled, but the Dark Elves put him into a vicious arm and wrist lock, holding him there.

"You know," Liander said with a wicked grin, "I could do something else with this." He brandished the red-hot brand. "But no, we need you intact. And Arachnia's sign must be visible. I hope you can explain it to whatever harlots you visit."

He whipped Dar's breeches down. Eric squeezed his eyes shut. There was a sizzling sound and Dar screamed.

Eric prayed with all his might. *Sometimes Arachnia's symbol imparts an evil curse, taking over its victim and making them do vile things. Please Lord, protect Dar. Don't let her get him.*

Liander turned to the cage. "Anyone else?" he asked, brandishing the iron. "No? Too bad. I think all of you would look great with Arachnia's sign embossed on, say, your foreheads. Try getting into your insipid churches with that."

He tossed the brand into a bucket of water. "Now," he said from the cloud of steam. "Dear Andyn, where were we?"

The guards dragged the limp form of Dar into the cage and hurled him to the floor.

Andyn rushed to his side.

The door to the prison grated open and Mardildris entered, looking grim. "Lord Tolin, there is a matter which requires your urgent attention."

He frowned. "Can't it wait?"

She jerked her head at the prisoners. "It is *very* important."

He approached and she whispered to him. He smiled smugly and turned to the Riders. "It seems that someone has absconded with some of your weapons and armor. I recall you had a cowardly companion of the Gnomish race, correct? Well, he is apparently not so cowardly after all. But have no fear. The prison is large and can hold another one of you."

The guards accompanied him and Mardildris out, the door grating shut.

Andyn bit her lip, looking at Dar's newest wound.

"Couldn't leave well enough alone, could you?" she asked.

Dar grimaced in pain. "Well, I already saw you naked twice so I had to figure out a way to return the favor."

She shook her head and held a hand over the brand. Her eyes flashed silver light. "Well, thank Verian, it's only a normal brand. Painful but not enchanted. I can't remove it myself. For now, I can take the pain away."

Dar nodded. She concentrated and a warm golden glow covered her hands, then the brand. Dar sighed and wiggled back into his breeches. "Thanks."

She regarded him for a moment, then wiped a tear from her eye and gave him a gentle kiss on the cheek. "No," she whispered, "Thank you."

Dar stared into her eyes, a mix of emotions showing on his face.

"Uh, guys," said Connor, "I believe we have a visitor. Listen."

Eric stilled, then heard a faint shuffle in front of him. With a muffled clang, a variety of weapons landed on the floor in front of the group.

"Hell," said a familiar, disembodied voice, "That shit is heavy."

"Hlerv?" Eric asked.

"The one and only," answered the wry voice. An invisible hand lifted Eric's arm. In a few seconds, one manacle clicked open. The other soon followed, then his ankle restraints.

"How did you get in here?" whispered Dar.

"Stupid Elves left the door hanging open while they did their little operation on Dar," replied Hlerv. "After all, there's no one here but them, right?"

"Thanks for coming back," Eric said.

"What else was I going to do?" asked Hlerv. "I'm a terrible cook, so it was this or starve."

Eric chuckled and shook his head, moving to the pile of weapons. He picked up his sword and a dagger from the stack. Dar already had his hand axe while Andyn carried both of her maces. Soon, the entire band was armed, Connor with his sword and magical ring and even Buck with Khelios. Unfortunately, the only armor Hlerv managed was Connor's leather jerkin and breeches.

Now we have a fighting chance, Eric mused, hefting his weapons. Elation and the desire to give back to the Dark Elves warred in his brain. *No. Revenge is useless. We have to get out of here.*

Buck tested Khelios' edge. "But no armor?"

Eric could almost see the Gnome shrug. "I know where the rest of it is so we can go get it now if you want."

"What are the passages like?" asked Dar. "Are there a lot of guards around?"

"Yes," replied Hlerv, "I've watched their patterns. It's a complicated sequence, but I think I know how they do it."

"Let's go then," said Buck, drawing Khelios.

"Hold it a minute," said Andyn, holding up her hand. "Liander and Mardildris know Hlerv is loose somewhere and they know that he has weapons. I think they're ready for us, probably on the other side of that door, then they'll drop nets on us or something."

Eric nodded. That fit with what he expected. An idea suddenly came to him. "Might you know how to do illusions, Hlerv?"

"Illusion? Me?" Despite the attempted denial, Eric detected interest in his voice.

"Yes," Eric tapped his chin. *This just might work, knowing the Dark Elves.* "Make a copy of us the way we are now. We'll have Connor open the door and we'll send our doubles out there. While Liander and his cronies are busy with the illusions, we'll jump them."

Andyn and Dar exchanged a look, eyes wide.

"Sneaky," said Dar with a grin. "I like it."

Buck gave Dar a speculative look. "I'm amazed you can smile with an Arachnia brand on your ass."

"It only hurts when I laugh."

"All right," Hlerv said. "Let's do it."

Eric heard him mutter under his breath. An exact duplicate of their group appeared in front of them. Even the dirt on their faces matched.

Connor let out a low whistle. "Nice work."

"Go, Hlerv," said Buck, walking towards the cage entrance.

Connor slipped up next to the door and gripped the handle.

Andyn nodded. He swung the door open and the illusions rushed outside, weapons up and ready.

A set of glittering nets descended on them. The outlines of their illusionary selves came alive with a thin green fire. With war cries, Dark Elves followed and a green ray of light lanced through the illusions, sizzling across the prison room.

The Grey Riders charged. Buck hit the Dark Elves with the force of a runaway horse, hurling two of them across the outside passage and skewering another. Dar slipped next to him, ducked a swing, kicked the Elf in the groin, then followed with a knee to the face. He followed that with a handaxe strike to the skull, his weapon glowing blue when it hit. Andyn's maces whirred, striking down surprised Fallen Elves with each silvery flash from her weapons.

One of the Elf warriors put up his hand and darkness enveloped the area. Andyn shouted a word and a ball of light appeared overhead.

Eric parried a thrust and shoved his attacker backwards. He saw Liander Tolin and Mardildris near the far wall, mouths open in astonishment. Mardildris recovered first, raising a hand to cast a spell.

Eric flipped his dagger at her. The blade caught her in the leg and she screamed, her spell going off into the floor with a shower of silver sparks.

For once, everything went their way. Khelios flared blue as Buck dropped two more. Connor slipped past the initial rank and stabbed another guard in the back, felling him.

Eric knocked aside a furious swing from a guard and slashed him in the leg. Liander turned towards him with hands raised for a spell, fingers glittering. Suddenly, he screamed and folded to the side. Hlerv popped into sight next to him, his sword red. Connor rushed Liander, tackling him with bruising force. The pair tumbled to the ground and Liander rolled free. The Halfling and Gnome pursued, weapons flashing.

Eric pointed at his assailant and spoke a word. Fire darts lanced out at the Elf, driving him back. He followed it with a sword thrust and the Elf dropped.

Mardildris limped to the side and tried another spell. Andyn got to her first, casting her own fire darts. Two bounced off a screen of green light surrounding the dark Elf and detonated on the floor but three got through, hitting the woman in the shoulder with sharp cracks. Mardildris stumbled backwards, a sheet of flame billowing out of her hands into the ceiling.

Liander parried Hlerv and Connor's attacks with a pair of daggers. Mardildris cursed and grabbed him, then spoke a word. A slim door of starry darkness opened next to her and she stepped through, dragging him in. The door narrowed to a line and disappeared.

All the guards lay dead. Hlerv motioned to the rest of them. "This way, hurry!"

"Damn!" Dar exclaimed. "I need that stupid medallion Liander was talking about."

"You mean this one?" asked Connor with a crooked smile.

Dar clapped a hand on the Halfling's shoulder. "You are a genius!"

"Come on!" Hlerv hissed.

Dar and Buck held onto Eric and Andyn for guidance. They followed Hlerv down smooth passages lit at intervals with glowing green crystals. Disturbing art decorated the walls: swirling patterns, dancing dragons breathing flame, or male and female Elves coupling in mid-air. They slipped through a chamber with a glittering, gem-encrusted statue of a woman riding a giant spider. The next tunnel had figures of armored Dark Elves growing out of the stone.

Eric shook his head to clear it. The patterns wavered and undulated in a mesmerizing dance.

Typical Dark Elves: confuse and distract invaders. Use power, lust and greed: three of the deadly sins. Classic bait. It's a good thing Buck can't see in the dark.

Hlerv halted them at an intersection, waiting until a group of seven Dark Elven warriors trotted past with only a whisper of sound. After a few heartbeats, he led them off down a twisting, curving passage.

"Stop," he hissed. He fiddled with a lock in the floor and lifted a trap door. "Everything is down there, in a chest against the wall."

"I'll go down," Buck offered, "and toss everything up. All I need is a light down there."

"Done," said Andyn. A ball of light sprang up inside the floor chamber and Eric shifted quickly to normal sight to avoid getting blinded.

"Give me a little warning next time, Andyn," he muttered. She whispered an apology.

Buck swarmed down the side ladder and passed armor and weapons up. Eric wiggled into his chainmail in record time, then slipped his dagger back into the thigh scabbard and replaced his sword. He grabbed up his bow, quiver and backpack. His spear went into the loop on his pack.

"Ready?" he asked, setting an arrow to his bow.

Andyn finished settling her helmet on her head and stuffing her braid inside. Her chainmail glittered under her dark green hauberk. Buck slipped his shield onto his arm and clambered up. He swept up his bow and nodded, fitting his own helm on.

"Do you have the Eye?" he asked. Buck nodded.

"We'll need light out here," Dar said.

Eric hesitated. *We have to stay hidden, but we also need to have Dar and Buck battle-ready.*

"I know what you're thinking," Andyn said to him. "We'll just have to dim the light when they had the chance and pray to Verian we can stay stealthy as long as possible. Buck dug a lantern out of Dar's pack and lit it. He shuttered it so it gave off a dim glow.

"Let's go!" Hlerv said, shutting the trap door. "They'll be here any minute."

They started out with Connor and Hlerv in the lead, followed by Dar and Buck, then Andyn and Eric.

They stopped at an intersection with two passages and a massive door at one end. The portal's lintel glowed with magical symbols and writhing figures of spiders and Elves. Eric swallowed, realizing the magnitude of their predicament.

"Hlerv, do you know how to get out of here?" asked Buck, voice unsteady.

Hlerv's eyes glittered in the half-light. "I've never been in one of these places, luckily, but I have an idea. You'd better start praying to those gods of yours, because we have about one chance in a hundred of seeing the sun again. Follow me..."

CHAPTER TWELVE

Hunted

I stink. They stink worse. Andyn gazed at her bedraggled companions. *At least we're alive.*

Dar gave her a haggard grin.

Eric took a sip from his waterskin, weighing it as if to estimate how much longer they could last. Connor leaned back against a stalagmite, eyes closed.

And, of all people, Buck and Hlerv have formed some kind of partnership. They stood in a corner, discussing something in low tones.

"We're really not doing so bad," said Eric. "Finding that supply room was a good idea, then hiding out in the casks on the cart with the giant lizards as the caravan headed out seemed to work."

Connor nodded. "Until the Fell Hounds smelled us."

"Ah, but then Hlerv got to work again. What is in those little packets he carries with him?"

"Pepper," Andyn said, opening her backpack, looking for some rejuvenating herbs. "Pepper, oregano and basil. Confuses the hell out of a creature's sense of smell, no pun intended."

Dar laughed, his voice sounding dry. "And so we've had a veritable picnic since then. Only what, three running battles with hunting parties?"

"Four," offered Connor.

"Ah. Missed one."

"But we won't have to worry about them anymore," Eric noted, standing up. "The little cave-in in the passageway near those pillars with the ancient carvings should hold them up for a while. Thanks to Connor and Hlerv."

"You're welcome," Connor replied, standing up with a groan. "You guys owe us drinks when we get back to a city."

Andyn found the herbs and sniffed them. A spicy scent redolent of woods and herbs and warm home kitchens filled her, brightening her spirits and clearing her head.

"Here," she said, handing it to Connor. "It'll work for a little while at least."

They all seemed less weary after inhaling the herb scent and looked awake when Hlerv and Buck returned.

"I think there's an underground stream nearby," Hlerv announced.

"How?" Dar asked.

"I got a look at those carvings on the stones near the place where we caved in the passage. The translation indicates there might be a waterway near here."

Buck leaned against a giant boulder. "It should be somewhere along the way we're going."

"Should be?" Andyn looked at Dar and Eric.

Eric ran a hand through his hair and replaced his helmet. "We don't have anything else. At least a water source will lead to a settlement of some kind eventually. Hlerv says water is almost as valuable as air down here and if they're not Fallen Elves, we might get out of this."

Dar hefted his backpack and slipped it on, then his own helmet. "Then let's get moving. If I'm going to die of starvation, I'd at least like to get it over with."

Andyn shook her head. *It's a wonder we're still sane: tortured by the Fallen Elves, no less than six pitched battles, hardly any sleep. We should be dead. I certainly feel dead.*

They trudged along the narrow, rough passage with Hlerv and Connor scouting ahead and the others following behind, using only Khelios' pale blue light to see. Buck's lantern had broken in one of the wild battles in the rocky tunnels.

No one spoke. It took too much energy. They also didn't react when the passage opened up into a vast darkness. Andyn could almost feel the immensity of the space above them even though she couldn't see it.

Her mind toyed with images of misshapen horrors lurking in the shadows high above them or slavering in pits along their path. *Yes. I'm well on the way to insanity now.*

Connor's hand shot up. They all crouched down low and Khelios' light dimmed to a mere glimmer. Andyn's hand moved to her maces and her heat-vision took over. Thankfully, no other outlines showed besides her companions.

Connor approached. "We hear running water."

The relief swept over Andyn so intensely she felt tears in her eyes. *Finally, a break!*

Hlerv and Connor led them carefully, slowly, along the pathway. Dar and Buck held to the backpacks of Andyn and Eric, relying on their ability to see in the dark to lead them, conserving the light until they needed it.

"Here," whispered Connor. Andyn knelt down on a sandy bank to dip her hand into cool running water. She lifted it to her mouth, reveling in the refreshing, crisp taste. She took a long, deep drink, then filled her water skin.

Buck held up his sword and concentrated. A bright blue glow surrounded them. Andyn saw a wide stream, about fifty feet across, running from left to right.

"Downstream?" Hlerv asked.

"Seems right," Dar replied. "Maybe we'll find some Dwarves or Gnomes. They have no love for the Fallen Elves."

Eric sighed. "Dwarven ale sounds really good right now. Remember, we're buying for Connor and Hlerv."

"As long as you behave yourselves," said a voice from behind them.

Andyn whirled, mace out and spell ready, but a lasso slipped around her hand and another around her neck. A strong tug jerked her to the ground and she wormed her free hand between the rope and her throat.

She heard her companions shouting and drawing weapons.

More lights flared around her and she blinked, momentarily blinded.

An array of Dwarves surrounded them. Their worn plate armor gleamed in the magical light. Several of them gripped lassos as Andyn's friends struggled against them. The others wielded battle axes, hammers or crossbows.

Tolan's Tears! There must be thirty of them.

Buck stood against a boulder, Khelios held out. He spoke in Dwarven, his eyes glimmering.

"Hold!" commanded one of the Dwarves, a grey-bearded fellow with a scar on his left cheek. The other Dwarves lowered their axes and hammers a bit. "Who speaks the tongue of The People?"

"I do," said Buck in Humana. "Wielder of Khelios Giantbane, handiwork of Lady Aalyros of Tur-Rikken."

The Dwarf's eyes widened and he gave a tight smile. "Well then, that's a little different, now, isn't it?"

⋘◆⋙

The best part of being rescued is taking a bath. Maybe we can just stay here a while. Even as she thought it, Andyn imagined living underground with the Dwarves and sighed. *Nope. As much as I like them, I need more regular sunshine and forests and open water.*

She rolled onto her side on the bed. Now, clad in only a tunic (the longest one the Dwarves could find, which meant it only reached to mid-thigh) she felt rejuvenated and refreshed. *A good long nap sure helps, and a good meal.*

She smiled, remembering their conversation with the captain of the group that found them by the river. *Kadram seems a decent enough fellow. The name of Aalyros sure changed his demeanor! And we were immediately on his good side once we told him about the battles against the Dark Elves.*

"How many did you kill?" he had asked.

Eric shrugged. "I think I stopped counting when I got to a dozen myself. I think the others did the same as I, more or less. The last couple of days have been a blur, just so you'll know."

Kadram chuckled. "Well, with six of you, that means there's seventy-odd less of those devils we'll have to deal with, and that's a cause for celebration. Come with us. Dalrikavus lies just yonder down the river, about a mile past."

He then led them to the town, not a mile from where he found them. The sight of the walled Dwarven city, with twinkling mage lights and well-armed soldiers manning the towers, almost brought Andyn to tears again. The community held shimmering fountains, bright shops, clean thoroughfares and curious citizenry numbering in the thousands. Not used to seeing visitors, they turned out by the dozens to see her and her bedraggled companions arriving with Kadram.

The captain took them to the local temple, where his wife, Tahri, worked as one of the assistants to the high priest of Kurental. The compassion and kindness shown them by the dwarven clergy warmed her heart.

She shook her head. Dwarven hospitality gave its Elven counterpart a run for its money, in her opinion. *If anyone insults Dwarves from now on in my presence, I'll give them the back of my hand.*

A knock sounded at the door and she sat up cross-legged on the bed, smoothing the tunic over her lap. "Come in."

Almina, one of the other assistants, poked her head in and smiled, black eyes shining. "You're awake."

"Yes," Andyn smiled back. "And thank you again for everything. I feel a lot better."

Almina ducked her head shyly and came inside, bearing a cloth-wrapped bundle. "We always do what we can to aid our allies in the Verian, Irial and Christian churches. You would do the same for us."

Andyn remembered some things her friends and relatives back home occasionally said about Dwarves and held her tongue. *Some people have the right combination of disrespect and just enough overweening pride to make fools of themselves. And I'll remind them of it when I get home — whenever that is.*

"Here is your gear," Almina said. "You kept it well, so repairing and cleaning weren't difficult."

Andyn stood. "I'm in your debt."

"Hush," clucked Almina. "It is nothing. Please, get ready. Tahri wanted to talk to you."

Almina left and Andyn quickly changed into her armor, boots and other gear, leaving the tunic neatly folded on the bed next to her helm. She just finished braiding her hair when she heard another knock.

Tahri smiled at her as Andyn ducked out of the room. "You look much better."

Andyn felt an instant liking for Tahri, a cheerful, ruddy-cheeked Dwarven woman with auburn hair and blue eyes. "I feel much better too. What was in that stew you fed us? It was delicious."

Tahri smiled broader. "Did you like it? Some don't appreciate it at first. We use giant lizard meat, stewed mushrooms, onions, carrots and herbs we get from surface folk."

Andyn nodded. "Very tasty and energizing."

Tahri winked. "A little Dwarven magic goes a long way too. Now, come to the temple. You mentioned something you wanted to discuss when you arrived but your state of, er, dishevelment prevented you from going into details."

Andyn took a deep breath. "Yes. Let's go then."

On impulse, she picked up her shoulder bag and followed Tahri out of the guest quarters and into the long hallways. Other Dwarven priests or acolytes nodded politely to them or bowed to Tahri, depending on their rank. Even here, deep within the guarded confines of their city, the clerics of Kurental and their associates bore weapons at their belts.

"How are your companions faring?" Tahri asked, starting up a flight of stairs.

"Very well, thank you," Andyn replied, running a hand on what she thought was a vein of gold in the marble of the staircase. "Your healers put them back together again just in time for the trainers to make them sore."

Tahri chuckled. "I'll have to have them ease up on the training then. You'll need your strength, from what I gather." She led Andyn down another hallway lit with magical lights in glass orbs. Andyn smiled.

Lights underground puzzled Dar and Buck. Not having heat vision, they naturally assumed that the underground races, like Dwarves, would have completely dark cities. Andyn explained that heat-vision was just that: the ability to detect varying levels of heat. It didn't really help with colors or textures and in addition, took some concentration and effort. Too much reliance on it gave you a headache.

Kind of like using too much magic. Besides, Dwarves are Creatures of the Light as much as Elves or Halflings or humans or Elohir. Though they can handle themselves in dark places, they disdain the True Darkness as much as anyone who opposes evil.

Tahri opened the door to an office area, nodded a greeting to the secretary and then entered a separate room, closing the door behind them.

Andyn whistled. Tahri's office looked more like a library. She said as much.

"Well," Tahri said, easing herself into a chair, "with all these brute warriors around, someone has to keep a modicum of culture." She winked.

Andyn smiled, sitting in another chair, looking out the tall window behind Tahri. The view distracted her from her hostess for a moment, showing her the vista of the great caverns beyond the city, an inky darkness dappled with shadows cast by the city lights.

"Now," said Tahri. "Tell me."

"We are agents of a human lord on the surface," Andyn explained. "In our travels on missions for him and the King of Deran, we came across a prophecy of the Church of Irial Worldmaker that seems to be about us. We have been following the words of that prophecy, trying to make sense of what it implies, but there is still much we do not know."

Tahri looked interested. "Do you have a copy?"

Andyn pulled out her copy of the Song and handed it to her. She sat in silence as the Dwarven woman read it carefully.

Tahri shuddered. "I... I don't know what to say."

Andyn blinked. "You know what this means?"

Tahri handed the scroll back to Andyn with a grim look. "The passages in your text relating to a Dark Rider. We have both histories and prophesies. In some of our most ancient texts, a Dark Rider is portrayed, a princess of vile and cruel nature. She lived in the time of the Paragon Kings and was defeated by a Meredan—holy one—of the Christians named Alyssa."

"Zhinia Margoth..." Andyn breathed.

Tahri looked at her sharply. "You know this name."

Andyn sat back in her chair. "Yes. Our scholars found information on her. They think, well, they think she has become a lich."

Tahri's mouth set in an even grimmer line. She stood and went to a book on a shelf, opening it and taking out a key. She knelt on the floor behind her desk, opened something Andyn couldn't see, and produced a flat stone with many tiny Dwarven runes running across its surface in neat lines.

"This is one of the works of *our* ancient Meredans. You would not recognize the name, but that isn't important," she said, placing a hand on it. "This also talks of a Dark Rider, who will sweep through the sun-lit lands with an army of surpassing power, aided by warriors flying on pegasi. It says if she is not stopped by those who wield the crown of light, her reign of terror will reach through forest, town and cavern."

Andyn ran her fingers over the miniscule script, feeling her insides tighten. "Yes, this sounds like Margoth, and why she was after the pegasi."

Tahri looked thoughtful. "There is a difference between your prophecy and this text which is interesting. This plaque also contains information about a magic item that the Dark Rider needs in order to make her assault on her most powerful enemies, a helmet of shadow and darkness that can teleport its bearer, and others, great distances. This is a helmet the Rider crafted in the distant past and answers to her call."

Sweet Verian help us! Dar's grandparents! The Helm of Shadows...

Tahri took the scroll back. "You know of this helmet."

Andyn nodded. "It is complex, but one of our number, Dar, is linked to it."

"But he is not of the Shadow. I have Soul-sighted him and he has no—"

Andyn shook her head. "I don't think he realizes what it is."

Tahri nodded. "Then you must tell him. He may not accept it, but you must."

Andyn stared at the stone tiles of the floor. "You're sure that this Helm of Shadows is evil?"

"I am convinced," Tahri said, trying to sound comforting. "Dar — and all of you — need to stay away from it."

Andyn shook her head. "I don't think he'll do that."

They sat in silence.

Andyn stood and bowed. "Priestess Tahri of the House of Kavatris, I need to take my leave."

"Of course," Tahri stood with her, "But before you go, I will have one of the scribes write what we know of the Helm of Shadows so that you will be forewarned. Kurental be with you."

Andyn avoided Tahri's sympathetic gaze as she left.

"It can't be true!"

Andyn sighed, feeling Dar's dismay. "I trust Lady Tahri's word. The Dwarves know much of these things and their knowledge stretches back almost as far as the Elves of Terenai."

Dar looked at Eric, Buck and Connor in turn for support. Hlerv sat like a grey-cloaked lump in the corner of the room, still as a stone.

Eric stared at her in disbelief. "The Helm... is from Margoth...?"

Andyn stayed quiet. Dar sat down on the couch in the antechamber of the men's dormitory, a stunned look on his face. "I can't believe it. I won't believe it. My grandparents would never get involved in something like that."

Andyn sat next to him. "Dar, it's highly likely they didn't even know. Did they go to Oakmoor or Alrihan to research it?"

He shook his head.

Eric leaned against the wall under a magically lit crystal lamp. "It took us quite a while to even find out who Zhinia Margoth is, let alone any items she may have crafted. I think it's almost certain that they didn't know."

"So that's it, then," said Buck. "We just drop it?"

Connor shrugged. "I say we go find it anyway. We have the medallion from Liander and that's a first step. If it's Margoth's helm, we go get it and then break it into little pieces so she can't use it. And throw the pieces in her face for good measure."

Eric grinned. "I like the way you think."

Andyn held out a scroll to Dar. "This is what the Dwarves know of it from their own records. If we went to Merdail, we might find out more, but that's a long journey and we really need to go north, not south. I've already read it and know what's in it."

Dar took it wordlessly.

"Hlerv," Andyn said, "What do you say?"

"You're probably going to give me a lot of resistance," he said his cloak, "but that Helm might be worth a lot to the right buyer — and before you get all riled up, I meant to a buyer who would destroy it. If Margoth made it, I doubt we'd be able to harm it anyway, despite what Connor might suggest."

They sat in silence for a while.

Dar shook himself. "From this, I hope that my grandparents never even found it. Either way, we can't let Margoth get it back. I agree with Connor and Hlerv, in a way. If we can't destroy it, we give it to someone who can, maybe one of the high clerics of Verian or Irial or one of the Cardinals of the Curia."

Andyn put a hand on his shoulder. "I'm sorry. This isn't what you were hoping for, but we'll help you deal with it."

He focused on her face and forced a smile. "I know you will, and thank you."

Connor, Buck and Eric nodded.

Hlerv stood. "One crisis at a time," he said. "We can't hunt for this thing if Buck has a price on his head. Let's get the Eye of Truth back to Astarel."

CHAPTER THIRTEEN
Seek and Ye Shall Find

Why wasn't I stronger? Why wasn't I braver?

He looked out from his tower room at the devastation below. He felt empty, alone, detached and cold, yearning to be gone but not able to let go.

This was my place, my home. And now, when trouble comes, I am weak. I failed them. Can they ever forgive me?

His gaze wandered over the fields and to the forest, wondering. Some had escaped while he fought the evil ones: some few, leading the surviving children into the woods.

Did any of them make it?

The silence of the place made him colder.

If not, can the dead forgive?

Brandawyn wheeled Amicus around, circling. She scanned the forest below, looking for any sign of a settlement. *That village has to be around here somewhere.*

In her mind, she went over Aunt Daphne's map of eastern Terenai. *The village of Tokkab is supposed to be around here somewhere, but the woods hide the road and it's just one long expanse of green.*

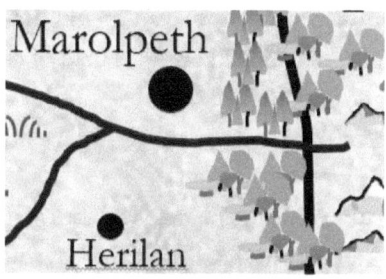

She looked across at Megan, similarly maneuvering Larinor through the afternoon sky. Her hair flew in the wind as she peered downwards. Megan caught her eye and shook her head.

Brandi flew her pegasus around in a wider circle, trying to spy a pathway through the grassy meadows and forest. Just as she turned in the other direction, she spied a thin ribbon of brown twisting through a glade. *A path or another false alarm? We've had two of the latter already.*

She swooped back towards Megan and motioned downwards. Megan pulled Larinor around to follow. Brandi winged down to the meadow. She landed in the tall grass and cantered Amicus towards the brown stripe.

"It *is* a path," she murmured, patting Amicus on the neck. "Praise be. If only it leads to a town this time instead of abandoned hunting camps."

She removed her helmet and held it in her gloved hands for a while, staring down hard-packed dirt road.

Megan pulled up beside her and voiced her thoughts for her. "I wish Dar were here."

Brandi smiled. "And I for Eric."

Megan blushed. "Well, for his tracking skills as well and, oh, you know what I mean."

Brandi's smile grew softer, remembering the feeling of being held in Eric's arms. A wistful feeling of melancholy followed the memory. "I understand, Meg," she said. "But we'll have to make do on our own."

The sisters rode their pegasi to the other side of the glade, then under the boughs of the towering trees, still following the track. Their path curved to the left, following the lap of a tall, thickly wooded hill.

They rode for almost an hour, not speaking and yet watching the surroundings. The forest hid the path from the sky, only allowing shafts of sunlight to dapple the earth in limited areas.

Then the woods thinned suddenly, so suddenly that it came as a surprise as they rounded a bend. They looked out on a field of crops, the path leading between the rows of grain.

Brandi eyed the wheat, corn and barley. "Why haven't they been harvested. They certainly look ready."

Megan gasped. "Look. Some of the fields are burned!"

Brandi's mouth tightened and she slipped the bow off her back and nocked an arrow. Megan sat up straighter in her saddle and drew a close-fitting leather mage's helmet out of her saddlebag, setting it on her head. She released the reins and flexed her fingers, guiding Larinor only with her knees. They rode with caution now, past more burned fields and then, a ruined farmhouse.

They saw the bodies soon enough— or rather, the skeletons.

"The ravens and scavengers have done their work efficiently," whispered Brandi, a slow anger growing in her.

"Elves." Megan whispered.

Brandi's eyes flicked to much larger bones. "And Trolls," she finished.

The sisters dismounted and Brandi made the sign for her pegasus to fly to safety. With a snort, Amicus led Larinor into the sky to await the return signal.

Brandi knelt by a huge skeleton and plucked a long-shafted arrow out of its ribcage. "This Troll would have been almost nine feet tall." Relying on her medical training, she assessed the condition of the remains. "It died a week or so ago."

"Do you know what kind of troll it was?" Megan asked.

"Forest Troll, I think. More slender bone structure, not as heavily built as tunnel or cavern Trolls. This one has four arms." Brandi brushed her gloved fingers over various spots on the skeleton. "Hit by five arrows from elvish longbows. And see here: some evidence of magical strikes, probably electrical and frost."

"What happened here?" Megan whispered. Brandi shook her head. They stalked forward to the wall of the burned farmhouse. Two Elven skeletons lay in the ashes of a front porch. Farther down the path, more ruined buildings stood. Sooty walls of elegant stone contrasted with blasted trees and dirty white bones. They picked their way to the village square.

"Seven Trolls so far, and fourteen Elves," Brandi whispered.

"The Trolls had a mage among them," Megan said, nodding at the damage to an arched shrine of Verian. "Those are Firestrike marks, and I see places where Darkbolts hit."

They crept through the ruins, alert for any ambush.

Megan picked up a broken spear. "Won't the army come to investigate?"

Brandi set her jaw. Sadness joined her anger. "Even if there were any survivors, it's at least a week's ride back through to Marolpeth, and it doesn't have a large garrison. If there are no survivors and this is a remote settlement near the border, visitors don't often come here."

Megan set the spear down. "It reminds me of Westhaven."

More memories rushed to Brandi's mind: a burned hamlet near the border of Deran, dead villagers — the event that started their quest for justice and ultimately led to the discovery of the pegasi of Whitehorse Peak. Then they discovered the prophecy, the Song of the Grey Riders.

I can't bring back these poor souls any more than I could the folk of Westhaven. She sighed. "Well, it's very likely that there aren't any Trolls left. They would have taken the dead with them to eat. We'll have to stay sharp. Where do you suppose Damion Eldermain's house would have been?"

Megan looked thoughtful. "Probably back in the forest. Sometimes magical experiments go a little, um, shall we say, sideways? The neighbors don't take kindly to the aftereffects."

After another hour of exploration, they found a side road that led to the west, away from the village center. By that time, they counted eleven Trolls and twenty-one Elves.

Despite the body count, Brandi felt some relief. "None of the Elf skeletons are children. Maybe some of them did get away."

"Praise God if that happened," Megan replied. "Now all we'd have to do is find them."

"With all this destruction, do we even think that Damion Eldermain is alive?" Brandi asked.

"There," Megan said. She pointed to a tall structure on a small rise just outside the town. They walked up the path towards it, warily eyeing the trees and bushes nearby.

They stopped about a dozen yards away. "Well," replied Brandi, "he's probably not here either."

The tower rose above them, about four times the height of an average house. An overgrown garden encircled it, a gravel pathway leading under an arch of white stone to an ornate, sturdy front door. Dark gashes and burns marked the wooden portal. Carvings of swirling sprites and fairies curled around the archway, evidence of either a master artist or an imaginative wizard. No less than five Troll skeletons lay among the plants and shrubs. All the plants looked limp and weak.

"What do you think?" Brandi whispered.

"The door is still intact. Maybe Eldermain survived." Megan scanned the area. "I see several places where magical spells hit, probably more of the Dark-bolts. The Troll mage was a busy fellow."

"And a dead one, hopefully," Brandi muttered, picking through the weeds towards the arch. She raised her crucifix and concentrated. *Nothing. No traps or signs of evil, but Something isn't right.*

"Well?" Megan asked, with a sidelong glance.

Brandi hesitated. She felt an icy stillness, an unnatural quiet, and a watchful-ness. "I don't like this. I can't put my finger on it, but there's something wrong." She drew her swords. "If we're going to find Mr. Eldermain, we're going to have to knock on the door."

Megan's mouth quirked in a smile. "I hope he has tea ready for us." She passed a hand in front of her face, then held it outstretched. She made it into a fist and motioned as if knocking on a door.

A wooden rapping echoed in the stillness.

"That's new," Brandi commented, eyes on the door.

"Just figured it out. I can pick up and move things too, as long as they're not large."

They waited.

"Mister Eldermain?" Brandi called out. "Hello? We are officers of the North-ern Alliance and we mean no harm. We are seeking the sage Damion Eldermain. There are no more Trolls alive. I am a medic and can heal you if you are injured."

Silence.

"You first, Mighty Armored Warrior," Megan said, her mouth quirking in a little half smile.

Brandi approached the door, her head on a swivel, then tried the handle. The door swung inward. She replaced one sword, then made a motion overhead and whispered a word. *A little extra protection, just in case.* A light blue glow settled on her and Megan, then dissipated.

She stepped inside. Megan followed her.

Brandi squinted in the gloom. The bottom floor served as a reception area or living room. A pair of finely upholstered couches, a low table, a glass display case and two bookshelves occupied the space. Brandi looked down at the red marble floor. She saw only dust.

Megan stepped next to her and nodded at a staircase that led up to the ceiling and beyond to an upper floor. "One way to go."

The bright sunlight behind them disappeared like a snuffed candle as the door swung shut.

Brandi dropped into a crouch, her swords flicking out. Her heat-vision showed her nothing.

Megan whispered arcane syllables next to her and a glittering mist stretched out into the room. "No enemies that I can see."

She brought forth three small globes of light and sent them forward. She gasped.

A chill raced down Brandi's spine. A forlorn, translucent figure stood near the staircase. It looked like a bearded, elderly human male, dressed in tattered robes.

Brandi's hand shot to her crucifix. *A wraith! I should have detected him when I scanned for evil!*

The apparition regarded them with sad eyes. He didn't move.

"Wait," she murmured. "He's not attacking."

The specter remained still in solemn quiet.

He's not evil!

"Mister Eldermain?" Megan asked.

The apparition appeared to sigh and nodded. He made a beckoning gesture and drifted towards the stairs. Without a backward glance, he floated up.

"If he's a ghost, why doesn't he just float up through the floor?" Megan whispered.

Brandi led the way to the stairs. "This ghost probably doesn't realize he's dead. He's doing the same things he did when he was alive."

The sisters followed the spirit up the stairs past an open door that looked like a bedroom, past another that led into a small kitchen, and finally to an open chamber. More bookshelves lined the walls and a display case held a bewildering assortment of crystals, scrolls and books behind a glass door.

The specter came to a desk that looked out an open window towards the forest. He pointed at a small red book.

Megan carefully picked it up and opened it. "It's a journal."

Brandi heard a very faint sigh. The ghost drifted over to another window and looked out over the ruined town, ethereal hands held behind its back.

Megan took her time reading. Totally engrossed, she sat in nearby chair.

"Um, Meg," Brandi muttered through gritted teeth. "We don't have all day. Please, just get to the last entries."

"What? Oh yes, right." Megan turned pages, then looked up at Brandi. "This is Eldermain's tower and I'm sure he's the specter. Here's what it says: '2 Augustus - The priest of Verian is very solicitous and tries to ease my pains, but I know it will eventually be for naught. I know the signs of this illness. It took my father and grandfather and it will take me. I suppose I should not be upset; these people of Tokkab and, indeed, the land of Terenai, have been very good to me. I have lived here long and have many friends among them. I only wish I had more time. But in the end, everyone runs out of that.'"

Megan turned the page. "'4 Augustus – Two hunters came in with an alarming tale. They found two giant bears in the forest, dead and butchered. Something large had fed upon them. Actually, several somethings. Everyone in the town is nervous. I can see it in their eyes. A month ago, the Kaftu war-band, fought off by the hunters and the priest. I had some small hand in it, but this is now the fourth incident this year. When will the army send someone to investigate? The woods were not so dangerous before this summer. What is going on?'"

The spectral sage turned to them with a morose expression, then floated over to Megan's side.

Megan gave him a glance and when he did nothing, she continued. "'8 Augustus... that's only eight days ago... '8 Augustus – Now we know what slew the bears. Trolls. There are over a dozen of them. They attack the town fiercely and the townspeople resist. The pain inside me is great. I am so weak. I have to help them, but now fear is like a vise on my heart. How can an old sick man turn the tide of such raging monsters? The townsfolk fight and die, retreating to my tower, asking for aid. I am paralyzed... why did I not act sooner? I see the Trolls charge them and something within me cries out. I called down fire and lightning, striking the Troll wizard. The Troll warriors become enraged and leave the Elves, rushing towards my tower. I shouted to the Elves to flee. I conjured earth-bullets and hammered the invaders, used lightning again, Brightbolts, Firedarts. Still they fought on, attacking the door, trying to climb the tower but the door is magically locked. I killed their wizard. Now all is silent. I slew them, I slew them all to avenge my friends!"

Megan read on, her voice sad. "This is the last one: '9 Augustus – I am so tired now. The Trolls are all dead, but I am so weak. I do not know if the Elves made it to Marolpeth. I saw them run to the woods, taking the surviving children with them. Did they make it? I pray to Verian with what strength I have left. Oh, why did I wait so long? Why was I so afraid? I have to go find them, to make sure they are safe. I will just rest a bit and then head after them, to make sure they are well. I —...it ends there, Bran."

Damion Eldermain fixed them with his sad eyes and Brandi felt a pain in her heart. *He looks so forlorn and sorrowful.*

"Mister Eldermain," she began, "No one can blame you for not charging out to meet the Trolls head-on. You were ill and not strong. If you had gone out of the tower, they may have killed you immediately and then massacred the townsfolk. By staying in your tower, you drew their attention to you and enabled your friends to escape. You did well."

The specter floated to the window and stared out at the forest. He sighed and shook his head, then pointed.

"You want us to find them," said Megan, standing and laying the journal on the desk.

Eldermain nodded, his face showing the first signs of hope.

Megan and Brandi exchanged a glance.

"We will find them, Mister Eldermain," Megan said. "We will find out what happened to them and bring you word. We only ask a small favor in return."

The ghost's spectral eyebrows went up.

"We are seeking ancient records of the old kingdoms of what is now Torosc," Brandi hurried on before he could react. "This is why we came to see you. We know you were knowledgeable in such things. If you can perhaps point us in the right direction..."

Eldermain smiled and nodded, bowing to them. He pointed at a small ledger on a shelf and made a motion as if handing something to them.

Brandi let out a deep breath. *Not what I had expected, but it will have to do.*

She pulled out the sending mirror, gazing into the glass, seeing her face reflected back at her. "Aunt Daphne. This is Brandawyn."

The mirror shimmered, transforming to show her aunt's face. "Yes, Brandi!"

"We have a lead..."

Chapter Fourteen

The Arm of the Law

T *hat's a few...*

Saren DeMey held her position in the top boughs of the pine tree, watching the group prowling the woods below. Elves in dark-enameled armor led two lumbering tunnel Trolls, grey-skinned and armored in nightmare helms, bearing cleavers and axes. Several of the Elves rode on the backs of horse-sized spiders. Fell wolves with red-striped fur slunk between the tree trunks, eyes glowing with fiery malevolence.

Saren extended her wings and launched herself up and back, using Eagle Magic to supplement her natural abilities. Holding forth her hand, she summoned a globe of silence around herself and winged back towards a rocky knoll about a half mile away.

A half-Elven man in a mottled green and brown cloak waited for her, accompanied by several other figures in similar raiment. She wafted down among the boulders and pines and canceled her silence spell. She slipped up next to him and squeezed his hand briefly.

She described the group. "They're looking for something... or someone, that's for sure," she finished.

Terenil DeMey squeezed her hand in return, then looked at a cloaked figure next to them. "Captain Greystone?"

A slim human woman with dark leather armor and a longbow of Elven design stepped forward. "Excellency?"

"You are certain that some pegasi were in the glade about three miles back, near the rock shelf?"

"Yes, Excellency," Sondra Greystone replied. She lifted her hood back, revealing dark brown hair and hazel eyes set in a beautiful face marred by a single pale scar that ran from hairline to jaw. "The tracks are rather distinctive, as are the small traces of feathers and horse hair."

Saren raised an eyebrow at her. "Not just some forest rangers hunting chickens on horseback?"

Sondra grinned, her scar making her appear all the more rakish and appealing, like a mischievous child. "Possible, my lady. If that is true, I suspect we will eat well tonight. However, pegasi are more likely."

Saren gave her a smirk in return. "I'm well aware of your tracking abilities, Captain. Just making sure."

"No doubt." Terenil fixed Saren with sea-grey eyes that still made her heart race. "Allowing for some oddity like chicken-hunters in an area frequented by Dark Elves—and others—the presence of horsehair and raptor feather tufts in the same area is as strong as evidence we've found. Add to that the report from the trappers a couple of days ago about winged horses in the distance during a storm and I think we have a lead."

She nodded. "It would be more than coincidence if a warband of Dark Elves were just out hunting at random, especially one as well-armed as that lot. I think we're on to something. Either the Elves know they're down and can't fly or they know they're somewhere in the vicinity."

Saren pondered their situation. *Terenil and I have a dozen elite Royal Hunters, ant their formidable Captain, plus two wizards, a healer, and two agents — all specially trained for search-and-rescue missions. More than enough to square off against a Dark Elf search party.*

"Captain," Terenil said, settling his cloak, "If you would lead us on, we will see what the Dark Elves are searching for so diligently."

"Careful now," the Dwarf said to Dar. "Your eyes will take a bit to get used to sunlight again."

"I'll take it," replied Dar, "if it means we can be far from those Dark Elves."

Rongit Kuril smiled. "This isn't the first time I've escorted surface-dwellers back to the sunlight, but you're one of the few groups who've escaped from the *Ghe-Ridow*. I've had enough run-ins with them to sympathize, Mister Cabot."

Dar stretched in the sunlight, gazing out over the forest towards the green slopes of hills curving down to a plain where a wide river sparkled in the sun. *Yes, far better than the underground, no offense to the good folk of Dalrikavus.*

Eric Indidarc stood next to him as their companions emerged from the tunnel behind him, walking between the watchtowers carved out of the mountainside. "Deorfast or Darlon?" he asked.

Dar considered this, but his concern for the pegasi weighed on his mind. "I don't think it matters. That's the Deor River, so if we go right, we end up in Deorfast. If we go left, we'll hit the Darlon Highway and the Ivory Bridge. I'd really like to go back and find the pegasi."

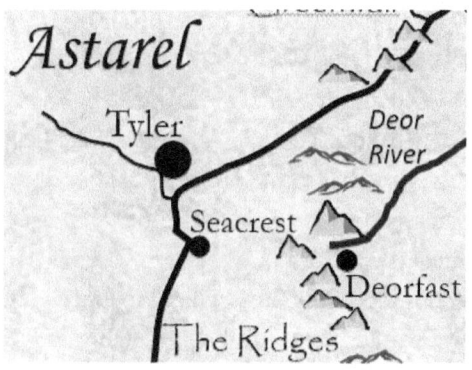

Andyn bumped him with her shoulder. "Don't worry, Dar. The pegasi know enough to stay safe and hidden until we come to find them."

"How long will they wait before they decide to go out on their own?" asked Hlerv.

Buck shrugged. "We're not sure since this situation hasn't happened before. They're specially trained and will stay somewhere near where we were captured unless the food and water run out and then they'll migrate to find it. But they'll always be always watching for us."

Dar bit his lip. "We should go back and find them."

Eric shook his head. "They're safe enough. Besides, if we return to that area, the Dark Elves will be looking for us and we don't want a repeat of our last adventure. We need some time to pass. Don't forget what our trainers told us:

pegasi have a terrific self-preservation instinct and high loyalty to their owners. They'll be fine."

Dar thought about saying something else, but decided against it. *He's right. I'm probably worrying needlessly.*

"Thank you for the escort, Master Kuril," said Andyn Eleandir, hefting her backpack. "I think we'll probably have to head towards Tyler, Astarel. Is there a town nearby where we can rest up?"

Rongit grunted. "I have a better idea. Our scouts saw a caravan on the Darlon Highway yesterday heading for Deorfast. If you head straight down towards the river, you should reach them sometime this afternoon. Offer to pay your fare or provide security and they'll take you all the way to your destination. You can get horses from there."

Dar and his companions bade farewell to the Dwarves, then shouldered their gear and headed downslope between pines and alders. The late morning sun warmed them quickly and they rolled up their cloaks to place them in their packs.

True to Rongit's word, they reached the Darlon Highway in early afternoon. The caravan approached from a couple of miles away. They waited, resting on the rocks near the river and hailed the outriders as they drew near.

The caravan master made them quite welcome. "I'm Roger Altby. We don't see folk as well-armed as you lot along the road," he said, sizing them up and stroking his beard. "And certainly none willing to join a grain caravan."

Dar nodded. "We would be glad to help. Walking to Deorfast is a bit of a stretch, and we have an appointment in Astarel."

Altby grunted but didn't inquire about their appointment. "Well, if you give me four silver a piece and agree to pull security detail for us at night, we'd be obliged. I only have two outriders and we'd sleep better with you on watch. The road is secure and there is little outward sign of danger, but it would ease my mind."

"Done," said Andyn.

Dar ended up on the back of the lead wagons with Buck and Andyn as Altby road nearby. The Darlon Highway wound along the river, a relatively smooth ride. Dar watched barges, pleasure craft and merchant vessels ply their way up the Deor River.

Andyn leaned back on her hands. "The highway is in excellent shape."

Dar flicked a leaf off his chainmail. "The Duke of Darlon takes pride in the quality of his roads. They help commercial traffic move quickly between his city and other areas in Deran, including Deorfast, up in the mountains. He has regular patrols. He also manages the river traffic."

"Interesting," said Andyn. "There sure are a lot of vessels on the water."

Altby pointed at the boats. "The Deor is very wide, almost a mile in some places. Going up river, the vessels use oars, or, if the wind is right, sails. Downriver from Deorfast is a lot easier. Still, water travel is faster than the road, but not everyone can afford to use the boats, so that's where I make my living. We'll make the hamlet of Halfdan before nightfall."

The afternoon wore on. They passed another caravan on its way to Darlon, a few individual riders (couriers, Dar decided, by their tabards and swift mounts) and a sturdy carriage with four sharp-eyed guards.

Dar turned away to regard the river again. *It is nice, in a way, to take life slower. Our lives for the last few months have been a madcap race to stay alive and thwart evil plots.*

His gaze strayed to the small pouch on a cord around Buck's neck, the pouch that held the Eye of Truth. *Things are about to get livelier in the future, I can be sure of that.*

Halfdan, it turned out, rested on the edge of the plains that stretched from Darlon to the foothills of the Greenwall Range. A small farming village, it consisted of two dozen homes, a general store and market center. The caravan reached it just as the sunlight faded.

The folk of Halfdan seemed eager to see them, coming out to talk to Altby and his assistant. Dar felt self-conscious with his armor and weapons. Shy children hid behind their mothers' skirts and young boys whispered to each other as the Grey Riders helped set up the camp.

The caravan master assigned everyone tasks and let the Riders decide on the night watch schedule. He chuckled at the way the townsfolk tried to appear like they weren't watching Dar and his friends. "Don't see a lot of your type here, I'll wager."

"At least not without horses of their own," Dar answered.

"Agreed. Be that as it may, we rise early tomorrow," Altby announced. "It will take the better part of the morning until noon to get over the river bridge and on to the foothills, then the rest of the day to get into the mountains. With luck and no accidents, we should be in Deorfast by nightfall."

"Well," said Buck, straightening up. "I thought I wouldn't see a town smaller than Wit's End and I was wrong. I wonder where the other half of Halfdan is."

Connor chuckled. "It's probably not Halfdan to begin with. It was probably Halivtan."

Dar looked at him in surprise. "Which means?"

Andyn laid out her bedroll. "'Field edge' in ancient Elven. Kind of like the word for Halfling: 'halivfae' or 'those of field magic'."

Eric smiled. "I don't see any field magic on Connor."

Connor flicked a pebble at him. "And here I thought Elves — and half-Elves — were naturally more perceptive. Halflings have a reputation for being able to raise crops out of the most barren lands."

Dar sat next to their campfire. "So, Halfling means 'people of field magic' and Dwarf means?"

"Those of Stone Magic," Andyn replied, reclining next to him. "From 'duarfae'. And before you ask, Elf comes from "ellfaen" or 'those of life magic'."

"Megan gave me a dictionary but I lost it in the Dark Elf stronghold, ," Dar said ruefully, rummaging in his backpack.

"What about human? What's the translation for that?" asked Buck.

Andyn frowned and looked at Connor and Eric, who shrugged.

"No one knows," said Eric. "Melinor thought it was because of the language, Humana, but that doesn't really explain it."

Hlerv brought out his wineskin and took a drink. "Well, I want to find the land of 'sleep magic', and I don't mean the kind you tried out on me the first time we met. I'll take dawn watch."

<hr />

"You know, we could miss the refugees by miles," Megan pointed out.

Brandi sighed. "We don't have much choice. Besides, Eldermain pointed in this direction. By the map, it's the most direct route to Marolpeth. And don't forget the campfire we found in the hollow yesterday."

Megan made a face. "That is encouraging, I have to admit. There were a lot of tracks there, so many that even we couldn't miss them. But I can't a nagging feeling we're missing something."

Brandi gave her a sidelong look. "You're beginning to sound like me."

Megan chuckled and joined her sister in walking their pegasi through the underbrush and around deadfalls. They heard only birdsong and smelled the fresh scent of trees and plants, some of them flowering now in late summer. As they continued on, heading more or less in the direction of Marolpeth, the foliage overhead grew denser. Creepers hung on the lower boughs of the trees.

It will get warmer here, that's for sure. Brandi's going to get stewed in that armor.

Brandi suddenly stopped. Megan slowed next to her, placing a hand on Larinor's head to calm him. "Bran?"

"Listen. The birds don't sing here. Eric always said to watch out for that."

Megan felt a chill.

Brandi held out her crucifix, turning in an arc and whispering under her breath. Megan followed suit, using MageSight to try to get a fix on any magical emanations. To her surprise, a flickering glow shone from under a thicket of raspberry bushes on her right.

"Anything?" Brandi asked. "I don't see hostiles."

"Over here." Megan led the way.

Her mouth dropped open. Huddled under the bush lay three small figures, each no more than a foot long. They looked like slender little people with dragonfly wings. None of them wore clothing and all appeared to be injured. There were two males and a female and one of the males still held a spear.

"*Surdara*. Hill sprites," she breathed.

Brandi used her swords to move the brambles aside and hold them there. As quickly as she dared, Megan swooped in and gathered the sprites up in her arms. None stirred and she got scratched on her arms and hands pulling them out. Her heart skipped a beat. "They're feverish and they are all cut up," she said. "Can you heal them?"

"I can try." Brandi closed her eyes and concentrated, putting one hand on each of the more severely injured sprites, a male. A golden glow lit her palms and Megan watched the wounds fade, recede and close. Brandi did the same for the female and the other male.

Megan looked around the area. Nothing out of the ordinary met her eyes. Not trusting to anything, she used AirWatcher spells to guard around them, setting them for misdirection and whisper alarms. "Who would attack hill sprites?" she muttered.

"Someone evil, that's for sure." Brandi took out a spare tunic from her saddlebag and knelt next to the sprites, who slept quietly now, fever gone. She gently laid the tunic over them. "Poor things," she said. "I wonder what happened. Those were claw and bite marks."

Megan hefted her saddlebags and sat next to the sprites. "I'm just glad we got to them in time. Why don't the birds sing here?"

Brandi shrugged. "Hill Sprites are attuned to nature. Maybe the birds were silent to avoid drawing predators to the area. We'd best stay on our guard in any case." She wet a cloth from her waterskin and gently dabbed their small foreheads. The female's eyes fluttered open.

"It's okay," Brandi said, smiling gently. "You are in no danger. We're here to help you."

The hill sprite gasped. "Esdan? Kirinar?"

Megan took the sprite's tiny hand in her own. "They live and sleep next to you. Don't worry. They will be fine."

The sprite sighed. "Praise Verian." She lay still for a few heartbeats, then fixed the sisters with golden eyes.

"We owe you our lives, travelers. I am Tinira." Megan heard the sparkle of streams and the chirp of birdsong in the sprite's voice.

"Megan and Brandawyn Alenar," said Megan with a smile.

"What happened?" asked Brandi.

Tinira sat up, putting a hand to her head. "I am charged with guarding the borders of our land. One of my scouts saw a band of Elves hurrying through the woods. Their pursuers, Trolls, were not far behind. We decided to help them and I left with ten others to assist."

She seemed to droop. "When we arrived, the Trolls, four of them, had attacked. We struck from another direction and in the confusion, the Elves escaped, slaying three of the Trolls as they did so. We were delayed by the last one and were unable to prevent the Elves from entering the Dark Moor. They...they were taken by the Hell Wisp."

Megan felt another chill. "Hell Wisp?"

Tinira nodded. "A fairy who has left the path of life to seek immortality and has thus become un-life. They have the ability to charm, confuse and enslave by use of magic. This one, a male, holds sway in a section of the Dark Moor. We tried to get to the Elves, for I have a means for dispelling the glamorie, but the wisp sent Skitterlings after us and we soon spent more time defending than rescuing. There were too many. Some of our number died, others were captured like the Elves..."

Tinira looked up at Megan, her tiny eyes sparkling with tears. "Why are you here then? Are you with the Elves?"

Megan looked at Brandi, then back at the sprite. "We are actually searching for them. It is a solemn charge to see them safe, a promise to someone who cares for them very much."

"Will you rescue my people as well?"

Brandi nodded and stood, her mouth set in a firm line. "Of course! Or die trying. How were you going to dispel the magic that holds them captive?"

Tinira stood and looked back at her companions, still sleeping under the tunic. "If you bring them with us, I will show you."

"Do you feel up to it?" asked Brandi.

Tinira fluttered her wings, then flew up into a hover. "I do now."

Megan gently lifted both of the male sprites and set them in one saddlebag, braced by a cloak so they would be comfortable. Without another word, Tinira led them away from the darker part of the forest towards a hollow, then up a rise to a sun-drenched meadow on top of a hill. She zipped ahead, making straight for a place near a boulder.

"Here," she said when the sisters approached.

A single plant grew in the sunshine, surrounded by wildflowers. It had an odd shape, with the main stem coming up out of the ground, then winding around in a circle about a hand-span in diameter. The stem then extended upwards and ended in a single rose bloom, white streaked with goldenrod. Small, three-pointed leaves clustered all around the stem, interspersed with short thorns. The very air glowed around the plant and a subtle, pleasant fragrance filled the air. Megan's heart skipped a beat.

"Is that what I think it is?" she breathed.

"*Coronam Ex Spinis*," Brandi said, kneeling down. "Crown of Thorns Rose, a plant native to Celestia. How did it get here?"

The hill sprite gave a tiny shrug. "I do not know. We have been aware of its presence for decades, but this glade has been a sacred place for us for many years before that. Verian provides what is needed in every age."

Megan suddenly felt a wild, fierce joy surge through her. *A Crown-of-Thorns, here on Damora! I've only heard legends about them and now one is here in front of us.* "Maybe this is what can defeat the hell wisp and set the captives free!"

Brandi nodded. "A holy thing, from a holy place. But it seems wrong to just take it."

Tinira laughed then, a silvery sound. "And how do you know that it wasn't allowed to grow here for just this purpose? Try to pick it up. If you are meant to have it, Verian will show you."

Brandi reached down and gently pulled on the Crown-of-Thorns where it met the earth. The plant came free easily, root ball and all. She pulled out a sack from her backpack and wrapped the roots in it.

She nodded to Tinira. "Why didn't you take it and use it?"

Tinira sighed. "We were going to but our injuries were too much and it was all we could do to hide under the bushes. Now that you're here, you should use it."

"Where is the Wisp?" asked Megan.

Tinira pointed back towards the forest. From their higher elevation, they could see now that the area where they had found the hill sprites was no more than two hundred yards from a stretch of dark woods that gradually turned to decaying, leafless trees and a dark fen, hidden by mist.

"Beware when you enter," the sprite said. "The Skitterlings will be upon you as soon as they can smell you out. Fire is deadly to them, so use it if you have it. The Wisp also has a Hulker near its lair. It may try to use its newfound slaves against you. I hope you have a way to get at the wisp without harming them."

Brandi nodded, holding the plant. "We will find a way."

Megan lifted the two male sprites out of her bag and laid them down on the grass. She then made a circular motion with her hand and pointed at the sky. Larinor snorted and leapt upward, followed by Amicus.

"You will be safe here with them?"

Tinira smiled. "Evil cannot touch us here. When they awake, we will return to our base and bring reinforcements and meet you at the edge of the moor."

Brandi handed the rose to Megan. "I'll need my hands free," she said, almost apologetic.

Megan patted her on the shoulder. "Understood. I can use magic with one hand."

Tinira waved at them as they headed off towards the dark moor.

Not the most prudent thing we've ever done, traipsing off into an undead fairy's stronghold without allies.

Using their memory of the view from the meadow, they chose their path carefully, trying to get near the edge of the fen where trees would give them cover and allow them to see ahead. The closer they approached the moorland, darker and more forbidding the woods became. All animal sounds ceased and the sunlight seemed to struggle to get through the mist and foliage.

They paused when the ground became marshy and wet and leafless trees predominated. Though the sunlight seemed hazy, far-off and feeble, they felt the heat pressing down on them. Megan wiped perspiration from her brow. The air smelled rank with decay and mold. They stood behind a cluster of trees, looking out at the moor.

"Ideas?" Brandi asked, drawing her swords.

"One, though it might not work here if the wisp is a mage," Megan answered. She closed her eyes and made a motion with her free hand, scribing a circle before her forehead, then pointing forwards. In her vision now, she saw ahead of them, as through a lens. Though she had used the Farseeing spell before, its clarity and range surprised her. Something seemed to augment her vision.

The Crown-of-Thorns?

Then she saw them. On an island in the fens, about five hundred yards from them, hidden by the mist, more than a score of Elven men, women and children stood along the shore, slack-jawed and empty-eyed. Behind them, a twisted and dark tree loomed. An impossibly intense purple light blazed at the place where the biggest boughs met; it looked like a throne.

"I'm not sure what Skitterlings look like," Megan said quietly, "but anything that can take down hill sprites is sure to be effective against flying creatures. Then there's the matter of the 'Hulker', whatever that is.

She let her enhanced sight linger, then as she felt the magic fray, returned to her normal vision. She opened her eyes and was surprised to see the Crown-of-Thorns rose glimmering faintly.

"I'm not going to ask," said Brandi with a wry look at the plant.

Megan related what she had seen with her spell. Brandi nodded. "Okay then," she leaned her swords against the tree trunk. "Hold still."

Making a wide, sweeping motion with her hands, she murmured words in Ecclesia, her eyes mere slits. Megan felt the air around her tighten, clamp down, then recede. This happened three times. Brandi repeated the spell on herself.

"My turn," said Megan. She set the plant on the moist earth and made an arc over head with one arm, whispering the arcane words. A sparkling mist floated down onto both of them. "There. We're as well-protected as we can be."

She nodded to Brandi and picked up the plant. They stepped out into the mist, picking their way over dry spots. They tried to keep close to whatever vegetation presented itself while staying out of the bogs — a tall order considering that they had to keep heading towards the wisp's misshapen tree and also watch out for enemies.

Megan kept one eye on the Crown-of-Thorns and another on the tall reeds, short bushes and sere trees along the way. *Skitterlings... do we even know what they look like? Do we guess?* She felt every nerve on edge and her breath came in shallow, almost furtive gasps.

Then the Crown-of-Thorns flashed red light. Small, dark forms, no bigger than a soup bowl, raced towards them, splashing through the shallow water or scurrying over the moist earth. Each looked like a clump of earth with wavy purple grass on top and thorny twigs poking out; tiny red dots of light glowed balefully for eyes.

Ah. So that's what they look like.

Brandi saw them too. "Stay behind me," she ordered. The first knot of creatures reached her, a dozen strong.

The rose in Megan's hands flared blue. She stared at it in wonder. *What is going on?*

Brandi moved, faster than Megan had ever seen her. Her right-hand blade flared silver and her left gold as she pirouetted, slashed, and spun. Skitterlings shrieked with thin, wailing cries and flew away from her, slashed in half or impaled. Megan lost count at eight.

The rose flared red again and she spun. Another crowd of skitterlings raced at her, hissing. Megan held the Crown-of-Thorns in one hand and extended the other horizontally, fingers splayed. She spoke a short, sharp word. The rose flared blue again.

A sheet of flame blasted out at the skitterlings, crisping most of them to embers in an eyeblink. A pair made it past and she shot them with Firedarts.

So the Rose augments spells too! Thank you Jesus!

The swamp fell silent and no more skitterlings swarmed at them. Brandi waited a few heartbeats before beckoning Megan on.

The next attack took them by surprise. Megan saw a host of tiny red dots on a small hump of earth ahead of them, then heard a thin breezy sound.

"Brandi! Look out!"

A veritable rainstorm of thorns shot out at them. Megan cried out, turning to shield her eyes. Some the thorns pinged off her mage's helmet, and others embedded themselves in her clothes, hands, and legs. Four spines stabbed into exposed skin. She almost dropped the plant.

Gritting her teeth against the pain, she called forth one of her most potent spells and hurled a fist-sized ball of flame at the hump of earth. With a thud and a roar, the ball detonated, hurling mud, sticks, ferns and Skitterling fragments in all directions.

Brandi came to her side. "Here, let me take that," she murmured, placing the Crown-of-Thorns on the earth.

Pain wracked Megan on her wrist, neck and legs where the thorns stuck her. Her limbs trembled.

"Wouldn't be surprised if there were some kind of enervating poison on those thorns," muttered Brandi. She laid gentle hands on Megan's injuries, her palms glowing. Again, the Rose flared blue.

"No wonder they took down flying hill sprites," Megan said through gritted teeth. She tried to relax as Brandi's healing magic washed over her. In a few seconds, the pain faded to a dull ache and tiredness.

Megan picked up the Crown-of-Thorns rose reverently. "Thank God for this. It's helping us, augmenting our magic, warning us of danger."

"A gift from Heaven for sure."

"Well," Megan said, eyeing the moor, "It's a sure bet the wisp knows we're here now with all that racket. Let's veer to the left. It's probably looking for us coming along a vector in line with my fireball spell, so maybe we'll take it unawares."

More quickly now, wary of another Skitterling ambush, they hustled through the swamp, twice nearly falling into bogs. Megan nearly lost a boot pulling her leg out of mud. *Maybe this end-around maneuver isn't such a great idea if we drown in the muck. Are we even close to the Wisp's tree?*

Then, as if summoned by her thoughts, the giant tree loomed up out of the misty air, surrounded the motionless Elven villagers. Without a word, the sisters crept up towards it. Brandi put away her swords and took up her bow, laying a silver-tipped arrow to it.

Megan's senses tingled and her heart thudded in her chest. Where is the Hell Wisp?

The rose flared red. The Wisp suddenly materialized from behind a large, leafy bush. Megan gasped. The ghostly image of a male fairy floated in a ball of vile purple light that crackled with electricity. The Hell Wisp cursed and thrust his hands forward.

She fired off a counterspell just as sheets of jagged ice shot out at them. The shards blasted through Megan's counterspell and struck their shields. Brandi and Megan stumbled backwards, their magic protections cracking and vanishing.

"These are my thralls!" The Wisp shouted in a thin, echoing voice. "Go find your own!"

"These people are no one's thralls!" Brandi retorted, loosing an arrow at him.

The wisp spun out of the way, then conjured a whirling column of fire, but Brandi shot another arrow at it in mid-incantation. The arrow shattered on the wisp's shield but the wisp dodged, losing control of his spell. The mini-tornado whirled off into the fen, unguided, and disappeared in a cloud of steam.

In desperation, Megan held forth the Crown-of-Thorns and cast a MuddleMind spell. The rose flared bright white and the Wisp screamed in agony, backing up madly. He fired off lightning bolts in random directions, seeming to shoot at invisible enemies. With another scream of fury, he whirled off into the fen, beyond the tree.

"Megan, quick!" Brandi led the way to the villagers. She cast a Spellbane and the Crown-of-Thorns glowed light blue in response. A shimmering field of energy floated down onto the Elves, who blinked and looked around in confusion.

"What...?" One of the males looked at them in alarm.

"There's no time to explain," Megan said. "Damion Eldermain sent us to get you. A Hell Wisp took you prisoner but we managed to drive it away. Follow us, quickly!"

To their credit, the Elves gathered their wits swiftly, as well as weapons they had discarded next to the huge tree. Megan and Brandi herded them back the way they had come.

Megan took the lead. Her head hurt. She tried to summon protective magic but her concentration failed, the words and algorithms jumbling up in her mind.

She stumbled and almost fell, but one of the Elven mothers caught her. "Are you all right?" the Elf asked.

Megan nodded. "I'll be fine if I can rest. Too much high-potency spellcasting."

They kept slogging through the fen, skirting standing water and obvious bogs. They kept to the driest areas with the children in the middle of the pack, and Brandi and some of the men bringing up the rear. Always, Megan kept her eyes open for attack.

As she expected, the Skitterlings soon charged at them from all directions. Fortunately, the Elves rose to the challenge, picking them off with arrows or hacking them to pieces when they leapt out of the tall grass. Brandi almost went down under the onslaught of six of them, but two of the Elven men came to her aid, hacking and stabbing.

Then Megan heard the sound she dreaded.

"I will make you pay!" the Hell Wisp bellowed.

Megan looked back and saw a vile sphere of purple light racing towards them through the stunted trees and fog.

"We're almost there!" called one of the mothers, pointing at green grass and healthy trees ahead. The escape became a sprint. Megan bowled over a Skitterling and stabbed it with her dagger without thinking, then raced on.

They made it out of the fen to the edge of the tangled wood.

Megan felt dizzy with relief and tiredness. Dear God, please let the sprites be on their way.

Then one of the older children screamed a warning and the refugees scurried to the side. A hulking figure, nine feet tall, lumbered out from behind a copse of trees, right in their path. It held a long spear, wore a giant bear-hide chest piece, and had a five-foot-long club in its belt. Muddy green hair waved in the breeze and it regarded them with dead black eyes. It ran a tongue over protruding fangs.

"Master say you not leave now!" the Ogre rumbled in Elven.

"Hold them for me, faithful servant!" the Wisp shouted from behind them.

Megan almost fell, exhausted. *God, help us! We can't stop so close... the normal woods are just behind that thing.*

Brandi lifted her up by her arms and stood next to her. "Hold off the Ogre as long as you can!" she yelled to the Elves. "We'll help as soon as we can."

Megan saw the exhaustion in her sister's eyes. She forced herself to stand upright and faced the Wisp as it cruised to a stop about twenty feet from them.

"I win!" said the Hell Wisp with a smirk.

Something warm hummed in Megan's hands. Wait! I forgot the Crown-of-Thorns. The rose glowed golden and bright.

Without thinking, almost in a dream, Megan plucked the rose from the plant; it felt as solid as a sling stone in her hand. She hurled it at the undead sprite.

The Wisp's eyes widened in horror. He tried to scream but the rose unerringly passed through his magical barriers as if they were mere fog. With a bright flash of golden light, the rose exploded. The Hell Wisp vanished. Only a thin veil of purple smoke remained.

Everyone in the area stared, dumbfounded.

The Ogre roared. "I kill all!" It pounded forward, then flinched. Megan heard a high whistling sound and it flinched again. Three more whistles rang out and the Ogre whirled around, its spear lashing out.

Megan's heart leaped. Weaving and darting through the tree trunks and bushes, loosing arrows without a pause, hill sprite archers sped towards them, their little bows singing.

The Ogre stumbled, lurching to the side. It tried to turn back towards the refugees but sprites swarmed around it, planting dart-like arrows in its hands, neck and head. Suddenly unable to grip its spear, the Ogre dropped its weapon from numb fingers of a hand bristling with sprite arrows. It drew its club and headed towards a sprite Megan recognized as Tinira.

Unnoticed, five sprite warriors shot down out of the trees, dagger-like swords stabbing. Impaled through the neck and temple, the Ogre spun on its heels and fell with a heavy thud.

Megan's ears rang and her head pounded as she dropped to her knees.

"Well done, Megan Alenar," said a small voice in front of her.

Tinira the sprite smiled, flanked by Esdan and Kirinar. "Now it is our turn to take care of you."

CHAPTER FIFTEEN

Justice is Blind

L iander Tolin paced the small cell. *Someday soon, my dear, we will be together. I will eliminate those insipid weaklings who fawn over you and free you from your slavery to the church of Verian. Yes, then we will be united.*

His mind worked furiously. *Naturally, Mardildris was infuriated at the loss of her prize. Word returned to Zhinia Margoth about the escape; war parties sent forth to search. Certainly, Margoth will send for me and, without the medallion, my bargaining chip is.*

Liander stopped pacing. "I couldn't care less about the damned free-lances," he muttered, "nor about my so-called future in the New Order, nor about Margoth's plans. She will put me on the rack, and worse. Andyn is the only one who matters."

With her at my side, I will be invincible — at least, once I convince her to drop her devotion to Verian. Then, Andyn, you and I will create our own new order, an order in which no priest or priestess or religion can tell us what is right or wrong, an order in which all will recognize our special nature and praise it and bow down to it!

A piercing pain in his chest made him clutch at his heart and he stood, gasping. He looked down under his tunic. The greenish tattoo of Arachnia glowed under his clothes, a reminder of old debts. *Old debts necessary for gaining power, for gaining recognition.*

Part of him wondered if it had all been worth it and maybe, just maybe, he could have taken a different path. *To appreciate the world again? To see sunlight and not cringe? To smell flowers and hear birdsong and rejoice in the natural world and all its blessings? Maybe that would be better after all.*

He felt a pang of what he might have recognized as remorse, in an earlier, cleaner life devoid of Arachnia. Some part of him regretted torturing Andyn and her friends and a small part of his mind shrank from the thought of hurting her. Yet Arachnia's influence suffused him like a heady wine. *Stupid Crossed Swords idiots! Couldn't follow instructions. All I wanted was the medallion. I shouldn't have done it, Larad didn't deserve —*

The pain hit him in the chest again and he gasped. *No! No doubting the Cause! No doubting the Mistress of Venom!*

He waited for a while, letting the pain subside, panting. *There is no return from Arachnia. She is a harsh mistress but rewards well.* The effects of the symbol inscribed on his chest increased and he felt again the intoxicating promise of power. He forgot his earlier musings and regrets.

Shaking his head angrily, he stared at the cell door, inscribed with glittering runes to prevent him from using magic to open it and with others that would alert the guards if he attempted anything more subtle. *There has to be some way of getting out! Of course, once I'm was out of the cell, I still have to escape the Dark Elf city, and for that I would practically have to teleport!*

His eyes lit up. "Of course," he whispered. "I have the means to escape, right in my chambers. Perfect!" *And I won't be telling a lie to Mardildris in any way to begin with, because everything I will tell her is absolutely true. It's just that the thing I* won't *tell her is what I need to get out of here.*

He knocked on the door, careful to keep his hand away from the stunning symbols that kept him from simply knocking the hinge pins off. "Guard! Guard!"

The small window in the center of the door opened and a bored Elven face stared back at him. "What now?"

"Tell the priestess Mardildris that I have something to offer her if she will intercede with Princess Margoth on my behalf. It will enable us to re-capture the free-lances."

The guard made a face. "She said you were not to be let out of the cell."

Liander bit back a retort. "Then she can come here to me. There is no risk to her since you will be standing guard."

The Elf hesitated. Liander shrugged and turned away, pretending not to care anymore. "Very well. I suppose she will be forgiving when she finds out you didn't tell her of this and the sell-swords escape again."

He heard a muttered curse, then the little window slammed shut. A pleased smile on his face, Liander sat back on his rickety cot and waited.

He knew Mardildris and her desire to stay in Margoth's good graces. Ildrisana, the Dark Elf Queen, made it patently obvious that Margoth's satisfaction level correlated to the amount of pain Mardildris would receive if she failed.

After a time, he heard the sound of several people approaching and he crossed his arms.

The door opened and two dark Elf soldiers entered, short swords and daggers drawn and glittering with magical fire. Behind them, Mardildris strode in, her close-fitting leathers exhibiting her physical assets to maximum effect.

She cast a haughty eye on him. "This had better be good."

"It is," Liander replied, leaning back against the wall. "I have information that tells me where the free-lances will be going next."

"Interesting." Mardildris watched him for a few heartbeats. "Why did this not come up in our discussions before?" Liander shrugged. "We had them where we wanted them, in the torture chamber. Since they weren't going anywhere, it wasn't relevant. Now, of course?"

"Of course," Mardildris swept to the other side of the cell, her cloak swirling around her. "And what is this information?" Liander smiled. "I have text from that idiotic Irial prophecy. It gives certain clues. We know the sell-swords have the same prophecy. Since they believe in its validity, they will attempt to follow it. All we have to do is use to determine where in the prophecy narrative they think they are. Then we make plans to be one step ahead of them."

He watched as Mardildris considered this. *It's highly unlikely that Margoth trusted Mardildris with any part of the Song of the Grey Riders — if the Dark Elves even have a copy.*

Mardildris held her symbol of Arachnia in one hand, toying with it. "Do you have text from the Irial prophecy that can be used to predict the next destination of the freelances?"

The symbol glowed a light green and Liander felt a magic field cover him. He answered carefully and promptly. "Yes."

"Do the free-lances have a copy of it?" asked Mardildris.

"I believe that to be true."

"Is this text in the complex?"

Liander answered directly, watching her religious symbol. "Yes, in my quarters."

He held his breath. If she asked "Is the text all you are going to get from your quarters?" he would have a hard time answering so that her spell would not detect his plan.

"Very well," she said, gathering her cloak. Liander felt the magical field disperse and he relaxed. "Guards, you will bring three more of your fellows here and we will accompany Mage Tolin to his former quarters."

She bent piercing violet eyes to Liander and spoke to the guards. "If he makes any false moves, you will run him through."

The guards bowed and left, returning quickly with three more of their number, similarly armed. Without another word, Mardildris swept out of the room.

One guard walked ahead of him while the others followed. Liander passed through the corridors in silence, past carvings of dragons, spiders, scorpions, vipers and daemons. Individual Elves or small groups passed them, either ignoring him completely or sparing him scornful looks. He ignored them in turn.

They arrived at his chamber door and Mardildris had the guard open it, then entered.

"Now," she said, "Show us this marvelous text."

Liander fought back the urge to growl in rage. Clothes littered the floor, papers lying on top of them like some bizarre carpeting. His dresser and desk drawers stood open, their contents spilled. Shards of broken glass lay all over, the only remnants of some expensive erotic crystal statues. Even his inkwell had been emptied onto the desktop.

Instead, he turned slowly to Mardildris. "Could you have made it more difficult for me to find what I'm looking for? Fire is much more efficient than this."

Mardildris smirked. "I had nothing to do with it. Her Majesty was interested in your personal effects, so she had someone go through them. Fortunately for you, they found nothing."

Liander filed away a mental note to figure out how to take revenge on Ildrisana later. "Very well, then, it will take a bit longer."

He pretended to search about, all the while putting a little more distance between himself and the guards. The Arachnia priestess and her escorts, for their part, looked either bored or impatient.

Liander made his way to his wardrobe, then knelt and lifted a board from the bottom using a hidden catch.

"Aha. Not damaged," he announced.

With his left hand he removed a thin notebook bound in red leather, while extricating a small piece of paper with his right. He turned to Mardildris with a triumphant smile, palming the paper.

"You see," he said, holding up the notebook. "The louts didn't spoil it after all."

"Here," he said, tossing the book to the nearest guard, conveniently occupying the Elf's hands in the process. "That has what you will need."

Mardildris made a face. "Give it here," she ordered.

Liander held up the small piece of paper with arcane symbols on it and pronounced the words. In the blink of an eye, a sparkling veil of stars covered him. Time and space warped. Mardildris and her troops became a swirling riot of colors and Liander lurched, trying to control his stomach.

Another second later, he stood in a dingy, dusty room with a single grimy window. He steadied himself against the wall with one hand. *Damned teleportation sickness.*

When the spinning sensation subsided, he took a deep breath and looked out the window. A crowded street stretched out before him. Pedestrians, carts and an occasional horseman jostled and pushed their way down its narrow confines, hemmed in by tall, almost ramshackle buildings.

Darlon, you were never a kind city to me, but for now, you will do.

⸻◆⸻

"That's quite a tale," said Stephen Alenar, setting his empty wine goblet down on the table.

"We're just glad we're here to tell it," said Megan wistfully. "Those Skitterlings in the swamp were very determined."

Daphne stretched in her seat, enjoying the open air and sunshine of their seats on the patio of a restaurant in Tirevlan. "Hell Wisps are very rare and quite evil. I think the fact that you arrived so quickly and unexpectedly took if off guard before it had much time to prepare defenses. I've fought one before when it did have its defense systems up and operating. A much more difficult task and nearly impossible for only two."

Brandi nodded and relaxed. "A *Coronam Ex Spinis* plant sure evens things out, though," she said.

Stephen laughed. "It would even things out quite a bit for things that are a lot more powerful than a hell-wisp, I assure you.""Really?" Megan said, surprised. She exchanged a glance with Brandi. "We heard they were powerful, and we saw what it did out there on the moor."

"Let me put it this way," Daphne offered. "Ever heard of Fallen Ones? A Crown-of-Thorns will destroy one of them, if it is used properly."

Brandi shook herself. "A magical plant that can defeat a Daemon? It doesn't seem possible."

Stephen changed the subject. "And how are all the people from Tokkab?"

"Fine," Brandi replied. "They accompanied us back to the town a day later, after Megan and I rested. The hill sprites went with us. They didn't stay, though. The town is ruined and there is nothing left for them there. Once they showed Eldermain that they were okay, they gathered up their belongings and came to Marolpeth with us."

"And Eldermain?" Daphne asked in a quiet voice.

Brandi sighed and smiled. "He gave us his book of accounts and then he closed his eyes and faded away. He seemed so joyful."

Stephen nodded. "As we all hope to leave this life."

The Alenars sat without speaking for a while.

"This isn't an isolated incident," Daphne said finally, watching her nieces. "There have been others."

Brandi looked up sharply. "What incidents?"

"Increased raids, attacks on towns, warbands penetrating a dozen miles or more into Imperial territory from the wilderness. Trolls, Ogres, Goblins, Kaftu: something is stirring them up."

Brandi pondered this. An uneasy feeling settled in her. *Could this all be an outgrowth of Zhinia Margoth's rise? Or something more sinister?*

"We've consulted with a few of the officers here in Tirevlan and gave them some suggestions to go with your report," Stephen added, "The local authorities are starting to get worried. Once in a while you'll hear of an incident, but now one a week is commonplace."

A chill raced down Brandi's spine. "What does it mean?" she asked.

Stephen shook his head. "No one is sure. Maybe Eldermain's information will help us somehow."

"Here it is, by the way," Megan said, pulling a small, blue leather-bound book from her shoulder bag. "We've already read through it and know where we have to go."

Daphne raised her eyebrows, taking the book. "And where is that?"

"Meridian, in Gorostol."

"Not close but not too far. Anything descriptive?" Stephen mused.

Megan nodded. "There's a passage on how to find the secret entrance and the way to open his safebox in the hidden library, but the location is a bit unconventional. It's under a graveyard."

Daphne rolled her eyes. "Wonderful. We'll go in the daytime."

Stephen pushed himself back from the table. "With a trip to Meridian, we'll need to make arrangements. In the meantime," he reached into his belt pouch and handed Megan a tiny scroll bound with a silver ring. "You will get this to the Papal Nuncio. Go to the Imperial Postal Service office here and use the Tele-Post."

"Tele-Post?" Megan asked, eyebrows raised. "We have to scrape and save just to send letters by Tele-Post even once but you use it every time we stop in a city."

Daphne shrugged. "As long as it's not my personal funds."

"We'll take care of it," Brandi nodded. "We have a few things of our own to mail."

Daphne stood. "We'll meet you at the fountain in the city square when the watch cries five of the clock. If we don't show up within a turn of the glass after five, go to the Cathedral of Saint Khyron and tell the arch-deacon that David of Goliath sent you."

Brandi said nothing, standing with Megan to embrace their relatives. None of her aunt's strange and obscure code words, meeting places or arcane knowledge surprised her any more, not after traveling all these days with them. The sisters left the tavern and walked up the street towards the civic center.

"Too bad we can't ride," Megan noted as they strolled through sunlit streets.

"I agree, but I also agree with Uncle Stephen," Brandi replied. They waited for a coach-and-four to pass by before crossing the street. "Airborne riders, without Imperial livery or markings from a wealthy noble house, even if ridden on the ground, would draw a lot of attention. And we don't need that."

Megan frowned and Brandi grinned. "Don't worry. Aunt Daphne's Guardian Rod will keep them safe. The glade is sheltered and it's less than three miles away."

The sisters continued down the tree-lined avenue past shops, plazas with tinkling fountains and an occasional library or chapel. Brandi liked Tirevlan. Unlike most Elven cities, it sat on a plain in the middle of one of the major sections of farmland and not in the middle of a forest or at the edge of the sea. Trees certainly grew in Tirevlan in abundance, but these were brought in and planted long ago, making the city look like a very elegant and clean human community instead of an Elven one.

Carts, wagons and riders kept to the inner section of the street, near the covered sewer trenches. Pedestrians walked on the outer edges, near the shops and stores. Everything flowed in a more or less orderly pattern, with only the calls of street vendors and occasional burst of song and conversation when a tavern door opened. It held none of the grimier hustle of the Deranese or Astarellian cities up north.

They walked up the gently sloping street without speaking. They passed clothing stores, grocers, jewellers, weaponers, tradesmen's offices, pottery shops and tinker's carts. Eventually the street leveled out and they entered a circular plaza. A trio of statues, each about twenty feet tall, faced outward from the center of the plaza as the centerpieces of a massive fountain. The lone male statue held a staff in one hand and held out the other, beckoning to an unseen congregation, his face intent and wise. One of the women knelt by a smaller statue of an injured child, her face compassionate and a gentle hand on the child's shoulder. The last statue stood tall and proud in her chainmail armor, a circlet of stars on her brow, hair flowing in the wind, a longsword and spear in her hands.

Tolan, Mindra and Cara, the greatest heroes and prophets of Verian, Brandi thought, regarding the statues. The water cascaded down between and behind the statues to a circular basin at their feet. Children giggled, laughed and splashed each other at the fountain's base, their parents not far from them, sitting on carved benches.

The traffic wound around the fountain in a counterclockwise fashion, halting occasionally to let pedestrians cross between marked lines to go to or from the fountain. Brandi and Megan followed it, their eyes on the elegant buildings of marble and alabaster along the outer edge of the massive plaza.

"There," Megan said, pointing at a building with the carved image of a scroll and falcon above the double front doors. They entered, walking down between tall white columns to a wide counter of tan wood.

"Tele-Post, please," Megan said to the dark-haired male Elf behind the counter.

The man nodded. "Government, business or private?"

"Private."

"How many items?"

"Three letters. One to Saint Martin's, Deran and the others to Hillton, Deran."

The man looked down at a ledger. "Next teleportation is at seven of the clock tonight. Is that acceptable?"

Megan nodded, holding out three sealed scroll-cases.

"Three hundred fifty gold," the man said, smiling.

Brandi marveled. *How quickly we get used to things! A few months ago, that much money was a princely sum to us: the equivalent of five months wages in a Deranese city and much more than that in the rural areas. And now we spend it to send correspondence. Aunt Daphne and Uncle Stephen have rich benefactors, that's for sure.*

The clerk took the scroll-cases, attached colored strings to each, marked on paper labels and attached those to the strings, then handed identical labels to Megan.

"Thank you," Megan said.

Brandi let out a deep sigh as they walked out. "I hope they get them."

Megan smiled. "Lord Nolan promised he would send them on and I believe him."

Brandi smiled back. She didn't worry about Lord Nolan, Baron of Forester, meeting his promises. She worried that Dar and Eric might not be able to receive the letters.

I will not think about it, she told herself firmly. *I will pray instead and they will be fine. God will guide them. The Dark Rider will not win.*

CHAPTER SIXTEEN

Out of the Shadows

"Well, Nigel, what's on the docket today?" The Honorable Ryan Hinterman, judge of the Second Court of Tyler, Astarel, settled his bulky frame into his chair. He reached for the papers on his desk.

Nigel Hawthorne's head barely cleared the desktop in front of him, but the Halfling had never let that stop him from making himself heard. Hinterman's favorite clerk pursed his lip as he read a list. "First is the case of one Buckminster Horatio Bydecy, wanted for theft, assault and battery."

The judge frowned. "I remember that one, I think. Knocked out a master jeweler and stole some gems, then turned fugitive, if I recall. How was he captured?"

Nigel handed him a folder. "He wasn't. He turned himself in. And there is a new, interesting aspect to the case as well."

Hinterman's eyebrows rose as he read the file and he stroked his beard. *Hired Marina Taggart as his counsel. Interesting. And wants the right of magical examination. Claims to have a magic item that can—*

Hinterman sat bolt upright. *A what? Truth-reading magic? That's as rare as hen's teeth, yet Bydecy claims to possess it in an artifact. Further, he charges one of the witnesses, Derek Feller, with masterminding the whole affair. Hmm...*

"Do you want to take this one yourself, Your Honor, or ask Amelia Dilende to handle it?"

"I think I'll take this one myself, Nigel," the judge said, standing and shrugging into his voluminous court robes. He picked up the folder. "I have to see this one for myself. Since it's a magical case, send for Kiara Faelin. We'll need independent verification of the magical qualities of this item Bydecy says he has."

"Five minutes?" asked Nigel.

Hinterman nodded and perused the file again. He read the city guard report, Bydecy's record (a few instances of misdemeanor tomfoolery, only one accusation of petty theft, dropped prior to trial years ago), and the records of the original testimony and information from both the jeweler and Derek Feller. *This should be most fascinating. Maybe I'll turn it into a scholarly work and publish it in the Law Journal.*

The thought of getting a leg up on his colleagues pleased him and he headed for the door from his chambers, waiting for Nigel's announcement to the court.

"All rise and pay respects to the Honorable Ryan Hinterman, Chief Magistrate of the Second Court of Tyler, Astarel," came Nigel's clear, steady voice.

Ryan Hinterman composed himself to look particularly judicial and magisterial and lumbered into the courtroom. He settled into his chair behind the bench. "Please be seated. Clerk will announce the case."

He sat back and watched the assembly as Nigel recited all the preliminaries, including rules of the court and protocols. Three bailiffs armed with sword, club and buckler stood near the back doors, armored in chainmail and wearing helmets.

The sandy-haired fellow in the prisoner's box had to be a Bydecy. He bore a striking resemblance to a greying man in the gallery and a younger man next to him. Hinterman recognized the familiar face of the city's assistant prosecutor, Darren Orvos, as well as the white-haired and stooped figure of Marina Taggart, Bydecy's counsel.

His eyes roamed the rest of the gallery. He counted two half-Elves (one male and the only female in the group), a Halfling, and another human with dark hair, all sitting behind Bydecy's relatives. Hinterman wondered who they were. *Colleagues perhaps? Some say that Buck Bydecy took the free-lance months ago.*

The judge noted two young people in the back of the room with notepads and charcoal pencils, probably news-reporters for the local journal guilds.

Nigel finished and stepped aside to his place to record the proceedings.

Ryan Hinterman began, eliciting first the prosecution and defense to present their cases. The Crown considered it a fairly straightforward issue of robbery and assault, while Counselor Taggart insisted that Bydecy had been framed by one of the witnesses. The judge watched the players carefully, looking for a sign of subterfuge.

Marina Taggart finished her case. "So, Your Honor," she said in her reedy, thin voice that somehow commanded attention in the whole of the courtroom, "we maintain that Mister Bydecy was unjustly accused and perjury used against him to levy the charges."

Hinterman steepled his fingers in front of his face. "I understand that defense counsel provides a magical item to assist in proving the innocence of the accused."

Taggart shot a glance at Bydecy in the prisoner box. "Yes, Your Honor. It has been provided to the clerk."

The two journalists at the back of the room suddenly sat up. They exchanged a glance and began to pay more attention to the proceedings.

"Very well," Hinterman announced. "Clerk will procure the item and the three decoys and place them on the table before me. Bailiff, please go into the hallway and bring in Mrs. Faelin."

Nigel brought out a locked strongbox, which he opened using a key around his neck. He laid out four small objects on the table in front of Hinterman: a polished purple stone, an obelisk of silver, a mirror with a jade diamond at the top of the frame, and a disk of pure diamond about the size of a gold piece.

Kiara Faelin, an Elven woman with short dark hair, entered and approached the bench, bowing. "I am here to serve the Crown in my capacity as wizard assisting the Second Court of Tyler," she announced.

"Very well," Hinterman said, "Court Wizard will please perform a magical examination and screening of the four items on the table to determine if any are magical. If any are, the Court requests an assessment of power and abilities of any magic items. We require that the Wizard note her assessment on the paper next to the items, sign and stamp her seal on the document, and hand it to the clerk."

Faelin nodded. She picked up each of the items in turn, closing her eyes and passing her free hand over the item. When she had finished with the last one, the diamond disk, she let out a deep breath and fixed Hinterman with aqua eyes.

She's detected something, something powerful. He sat up.

Faelin scribbled on the paper for what seemed like an eternity, stamped it with a ring on her hand, then gave it to Nigel. The clerk read it and passed it to Hinterman, his face expressionless.

Now Hinterman knew something was up. *Nigel usually looks either casual or amused in cases like this — his particularly blasé attitude towards magic.*

The judge read the paper, his excitement increasing. *Scholarly paper indeed!*

"Counselors will approach the bench," he announced. The spectators in the room murmured. The journalists scribbled furiously.

Orvos read the paper first and gave it to Taggart. "If this is true, Your Honor, well, the item can be used with impunity. This level of magical power, with such precision..."

Taggart read it, her eyebrows rising. She looked at Orvos with a flinty eye. "And why would it not be true? Kiara Faelin's reputation is beyond reproach. I move that the original witnesses be brought in to testify again."

Orvos stroked his beard momentarily, then gave a resigned shrug. "I have a feeling this isn't going to turn out as I thought, but I agree."

Hinterman nodded, satisfied. "Bailiff, please go out into the hallway and bring in the witnesses."

One of the bailiffs left and soon returned with three people. One, an older human with a trimmed beard and mustache, gave the prisoner a disdainful sneer as he entered. The second, a younger man with brown hair and dark eyes, shot a glance at the people in the courtroom before sauntering over to take a seat in the witness box. The third was a tall, lanky city guard.

Hinterman took the report of the city guard first. The prosecutor only asked a few questions, referring to details in the guard report. Marina Taggart only asked two questions, both related to Derek Feller, the apprentice to George Sarago. Hinterman dismissed the guard.

Orvos brought the jeweler forward next. Sarago answered questions clearly and quickly, but it became obvious that he had not seen his attacker and had a preferential attitude towards Derek, saving only a critical opinion for Bydecy.

Marina Taggart asked no questions.

Derek Feller sat in the witness box next. Orvos asked him to describe everything he knew about the case and the attack on Sarago. Hinterman admitted to himself that his account matched exactly with the official report. He watched the prisoner. Bydecy looked down most of the time Feller spoke, occasionally shaking his head. When he did look up, it was with an expression of disgust, anger, and a little sadness.

Marina Taggart stood. "Mister Feller, you have stated that your whereabouts at the time of the robbery were at the Three Stars Tavern, is that correct?"

"Yes. There were several witnesses who saw me there," Derek replied, his tone cool.

"For the entire afternoon?"

"Yes."

"You are sure? Two witnesses said you told them you had to visit the out-house before returning to work. They saw you go out and not return for a while."

Feller shrugged. "I had a few ales. Mister Sarago doesn't have an outhouse at the shop."

"And you left from there?"

"Yes."

She turned towards the bench. "And that's when you witnessed the accused commit the crime?"

"Yes."

"A few further questions then," Marina Taggart said, moving over to the table with halting steps. She picked up the diamond disk.

"Have you ever seen this item before?" she asked Derek Feller.

He shook his head. "No. It's not from Mister Sarago's shop, if that's what you're after."

Taggart smiled. "Not at all. Mrs. Faelin?"

She handed the disk to the wizard, who placed it over her eye.

Feller's eyes narrowed. "What's she doing?"

Taggart smiled. "Monitoring the proceedings. Your Honor, is this acceptable?"

Hinterman nodded. "Mister Feller, the disk is a magical monitoring device. The prosecutor has seen the report on it and concurs that it is legitimate."

Feller nodded, looking uneasy.

"Now," said Marina Taggart, "Did Buck Bydecy attack Mister Sarago?"

"Yes."

"Did he steal the gems and jewelry?"

"Yes."

"Did you try to stop him?"

"Yes, but he pushed me down and escaped through the back door."

"I see," said Taggart. "But you didn't do anything to Mister Sarago?"

"No."

Hinterman gestured for the disk. Kiara Faelin handed it over. The judge looked at Feller through it. The man's figure showed clearly, now outlined with a mild purple glow.

"You didn't attack him and take the valuables?" Taggart continued.

Feller stood up, angry now. "Of course not! I said it was Bydecy from the start!"

Hinterman started in surprise. A lurid red corona of light surrounded Derek Feller now. *Astounding.*

He nodded to Faelin and handed it back. The murmuring from the spectators increased and Hinterman looked up at them with a frown. "I do not need to remind the assembly that I cannot hear a case over your voices. Quiet down or the bailiff will remove you."

Silence reigned. He looked back at Taggart.

The attorney shook her head. "No further questions, Your Honor."

Hinterman addressed Derek Feller. "Both counselors were present when the diamond was examined by the court wizard. They attest that it was examined in a blind trial to avoid any improprieties. The disk is a device used to detect evil, illusion, obscurement and falsehood. I will ask you again: Did you attack Mister Sarago and steal the valuables and then frame Mister Bydecy?"

Derek Feller's mouth hung open. "I.... you... we..."

"Mister Feller? I can tell you the results of the examination via the magical gemstone. Or you can decide to alter your testimony."

Buck's former friend looked around him, then at the faces of the court wizard and the judge. His eyes hardened and he shut his mouth, sitting down suddenly.

"What are the alternatives?" he asked in a tight voice.

"Those who plead guilty get a lighter sentence," answered Hinterman in his most mild tone. "Those who do not, if they are proven guilty, receive a more severe sentence. Which would you like?"

Derek Feller looked up at the judge. "But I'm not on trial. Buck Bydecy is."

Hinterman smiled. "Not yet. But soon." He looked at Taggart.

"Motion to dismiss all charges, Your Honor," the old lady said.

"Agreed," Darren Orvos replied.

"All charges are now rescinded," Ryan Hinterman announced. "The accused is not guilty and released to go." He turned his attention to Derek Feller. "Now, as to my previous questions..."

———◆———

Kili Mikman, former spy in the service of Halkith the Grey (now deceased, and good riddance to him), stared morosely into his ale. *This is the worst mess we've ever gotten ourselves into. All because of those idiot free-lances who beat Halkith to the pegasus herd.*

Laughter drew his eyes to his traveling companion, chuckling with two human dandies at the bar. James LeFond reached for a serving wench and got a slug in the arm for his efforts. The other two men with him chortled and clapped him on the shoulder. James shrugged and grinned but Kili saw the flash of anger in his eyes.

The Stag Arms Tavern isn't the best place in Darlon, but certainly the most affordable at this point. Kili returned to contemplating the foam in his ale mug. *Correction: the second-worst mess. There was that time James tried to put the moves on the daughter of the Lord of Kiarre. That was bad.*

Kili Mikman and James LeFond, once living high as sell-swords doing the bidding of the Ja'al cult, now settled for guarding warehouses and whorehouses and occasionally knocking about people who owed other people money. Kili certainly hoped his cousin could find something better. Viddi always had connections in the seamier parts of Deranese towns.

It's about to get worse unless Viddi can do some magic.

His thoughts returned to the Grey Riders: Dar Cabot and his friends. Kili looked forward to the day when he would meet them again. He caressed the hilt of his enchanted sword. *Yes, the Scorpion's sting will very much be felt, especially by that Halfling sidekick of Cabot's – Connor Lomin.*

A furtive movement in the shadows alerted him but Kili kept his eyes down on his drink. A cloaked, Halfling-sized person joined him at the table.

"You don't need to sneak around in here, Viddi," he snarled to his cousin under his breath. "The Guard only comes in when they're looking for someone."

The hood flipped back and a round face with a slim mustache stared back at him. Viddi flicked his eyes at the room. "It's their spies and agents I'm worried about."

Kili sighed. It was no use arguing. "What do you have?"

"Where's that human that trails around after you?"

Kili looked over his shoulder at James, examining a sheet of paper with another man. It looked like a broadside or pamphlet from one of those journal guilds. He caught James' eye and motioned with his head at Viddi.

LeFond took the papers back from the other man and handed him a coin. He sauntered back to Kili, carrying his own mug.

James slouched into a chair. He brushed back his long brown hair and winked at a barmaid, who tossed her head at him and glided off into the crowd. He turned his attention to Viddi. "Who's this?"

Kili snorted. "Weren't paying attention earlier, were you? This is my cousin, Viddi."

James shrugged. "Okay. So, what do you have, Cousin Viddi?"

Kili watched his cousin's eyes narrow momentarily and then resume their normal, slightly amazed appearance. *James is a brute, but more than one brute has gone down with Viddi's knife in his back.*

"A mage is looking for freelances for a special job," Viddi said. "He won't say what it is, but it's apparently a hit on someone and a kidnapping. Five hundred gold apiece to the ones who pull it off."

Kili brightened. *Five hundred? That would help quite a bit. More than half a year's wages in Darlon.* "What do you have?"

Viddi produced a slim scroll from under his cloak. Kili unrolled it and read it, then handed it to James.

James' brow furrowed. "Liander Tolin. Sounds Elven."

Viddi nodded. "He is. He has a loft over one of the warehouses on Filbert Street."

"Can you take us to him?" asked Kili.

Viddi nodded again. "I'll meet you behind the blacksmith's shop on Filbert when the watch cries eight." He lifted his hood and slipped off into the crowd.

James eyed Viddi as he slithered away. "Are all your relatives like that?"

Kili gave him a sour look. "None of your business. Now what was all that with the journal guild flyer?"

James looked entirely too pleased with himself. "Wasn't one of those stupid freelances who took out Halkith named Bydecy?" "Yes. And...?" "Word is that he was actually on the run from Astarel. Had a bounty on him. He just went to trial a couple of days ago."

Kili smirked. "And now he's rotting in jail?"

"No," James took a swig from his mug. "He was acquitted. Seems that he was set up. But that's not the best part. He was cleared by the use of a magic item that can detect lies."

Kili almost spat his ale. "What?"

James just nodded. The Halfling watched him for a second, trying to see if he was jesting. *No. He looks too smug for that. Now, a truth-reading magic item! That would* really *set us up for a long time.*

Then he remembered something and he made a face. "Great news, if we can get a hold of it. But you're forgetting that they have pegasi to ride. We'll never get close." "Ah," said James, "that's what you might think. And you might think that pegasus-riding free-lance warriors would get some notice in the journals guilds, especially if they're privately owned. Not too many people can afford that. But nothing. Not a word. The pegasi weren't even mentioned."

Kili ran a hand over his chin. "Which means, for whatever reason, they don't have them."

"So, which one do we do? This Liander Tolin mission or go after Cabot and his crew?"

Kili considered. "Let's at least see what Tolin has to offer. We can't take all of the Riders at once and maybe this Tolin fellow would be interested in buying the truth-reading item from us after we get it. You know, maybe kill two goblins with one arrow."

James drained his ale. "Great. Barmaid!" he called out over his shoulder.

Kili sipped his own drink, mind whirring.

"You're welcome to stay as long as you'd like," Alfred Bydecy said, twisting a dishcloth in his hands.

Andyn Eleandir smiled and turned from the kitchen table and her pack, giving his hand a squeeze. "Thank you so much, Alfred, but we've already imposed on you enough. Five days is a long time to have so many house guests."

Buck's father waved a hand. "It's no trouble at all and no imposition. You've been here so long you've finally stopped calling me Mister Bydecy."

She saw the twinkle in his eye and the loneliness. She impulsively stepped over to hug him. "You have been wonderful. But you and I both know we can't stay here, right?"

Alfred hugged her back and nodded, stepping back. "I can't say as I understand all this about the Song of the Grey Riders and the pegasi and the Ja'al. But who am I to say? I never took the freelance."

"Sometimes, I don't understand it either, so don't feel bad," she continued, returning to her packing, "Besides, Jack is here for a while, so you'll have someone around, at least until his merchant ship sails again."

"You're right," Alfred said. "And I understand. You have important things to do away from here, and truth be told, I'd be holding you back. Buck needs to help you out with whatever you're doing and the Eye will come in handy, I'm sure."

He sounds like he's trying to convince himself. She finished and hefted the pack over her shoulder. "More than handy. An item that can see through obstruction and illusion and detect lies? I have a feeling Buck is going to get a lot of use out of that. Has he finished modifying his helmet yet?"

Alfred snorted. "For the fifth time. If I left him and that Halfling to it, they'd be working on it ten weeks from now."

She walked next to him. "Let's see the final product then."

They passed from her room (it used to be the room of Buck's sister, Summer, long ago) into the sitting room, where Jack Bydecy and the Riders clustered around Buck. Even Hlerv joined them, his natural reticence disappearing in the face of a new and interesting device.

Buck held an unusual helmet in his hands, speaking as he demonstrated. "So when I need to use the Eye, I rotate this arm down. The Eye, in its frame, settles down in front of my own eye. When I'm done," he continued, rotating the arm up to its bracing frame on the top of the helmet, "I put it up, out of the way. The holding frame is made of steel and connected to the helmet internal structure so it's extra strong, in case I get hit by something."

"Ah, good. So at least nothing valuable will be damaged in that case," noted Eric with a mischievous glint in his eye.

Andyn laughed and Buck gave Eric an acid look.

"And yes, Buck," she said, "your valuable brain will also be protected. Didn't you have to reinforce the frame to hold the extra weight?"

Connor nodded to her. "And we made the holding frame with an angle to it, so that a sword strike will hit and glance off."

Jack Bydecy shook his head. "I can't say as I understand the half of what you're going to need this for, but it's a sturdy helm, I'll give you that."

"Sometimes I can't even fathom it myself, Jack. But understandable or not, we have to go face it," Andyn murmured. Her eyes took in the sitting room. Unlike the rest of the house, which seemed a bit messy, the sitting room was always neat and tidy. Her gaze lingered on a small portrait of a plain-looking woman with sandy hair, sitting in a chair with two boys and a little girl.

Almost like a shrine. She felt a lump in her throat, remembering Larad, then sighed.

Dar stood. "We really should be going. The caravan master said they'd be leaving for Deorfast an hour after dawn and it's getting close."

The Riders assembled their gear and went through the front door, gathering outside the house. Andyn enjoyed the view from the Bydecy home, situated on a slight rise in the neighborhood. Through a gap in the buildings across the street and a little way down the road, she saw the Great Sea. The smell of salty air wafted lightly on the breeze.

The Riders thanked Alfred and Jack. She hugged both of them. "I will come back some day, Alfred," she told Buck's father. "I like it here."

"I hope you do, lass," he said with a little smile.

He looks so much like Buck sometimes.

Buck stepped up to his father and Alfred clapped him on the shoulder. "I always knew you didn't do it, Bucko," he told his son. "You had your moments and gave me a lot of trouble when you were a teen, but it wasn't mean or nasty trouble, and doing that crime was not like you. I'm glad it worked out."

Buck looked down, then met his father's eyes. "Thanks Da. I just didn't want anyone to say you were the father of a fugitive criminal or anything."

"Pshaw!" said Alfred. "I'd have boxed their ears for that!"

The clatter of hooves from the street caught their attention. A rider in blue and yellow livery brought his horse to a halt near their group.

"Buckminster Bydecy?" he asked.

"Here," said Buck with a wary look at him.

"I'm from the Eastwind Courier Service. I'm told you might know the whereabouts of either Dar Cabot or Eric Indidarc."

"I'm Eric."

The courier turned to him. "Then this is for you. Sign here please." He handed Eric a scroll and a notepad with a marker.

Eric signed and turned his attention to the scroll-case as the courier rode away. "It's from Saren," he breathed.

Andyn's eyebrows shot up. "Really? How did they find you?"

Eric grinned. "Maybe all the journal's guild articles about someone named Bydecy and a famous trial and a magic item that can detect lies? We have been here over a week now. That's plenty of time for someone with Saren's connections to find out where we are."

He read the instructions on the scroll-case, then took out his free-lance medallion and placed it on a symbol on the case. With a faint pop, one of the ends loosened.

He scanned the parchment, then grinned broadly. "They found them."

"Found who?" Andyn asked.

"The pegasi."

"What?" Buck exclaimed. In a rush of voices, they crowded around. Eric held up the paper.

"By Saint Michael, don't run me over! Just listen. Saren and Terenil were in the area near Darlon on a separate mission when they found evidence we had been there recently. A Dark Elf search party was there too, looking for us. I don't know what happened to the Dark Elves, but I can imagine. Anyway, they went back to Darlon and got the riding-master to come back with them. Using some methods she doesn't explain, they were able to find the pegasi and entice them to come back to Darlon. They're waiting for us there."

Andyn clapped her hands. "Yes! Finally, something goes our way—no offense to you, Buck."

He waved a hand at her. "No offense at all. I miss Shadowbane."

To soar through the air again, to ride Medianox out against the Dark Forces, to find out our destiny. Andyn sighed. "I know it sounds strange, but after being unable to fly for this long, I almost welcome the chance to follow the predictions of the Song of the Grey Riders. Almost."

"We really have to get moving then," said Dar. "If we're lucky, we'll be in Darlon in two days."

"Go then, go!" said Alfred Bydecy. "Don't stand here in the street! Get off with you."

With hurried farewells, they strode off down the avenue. Andyn spared one last look and a wave back at the figures of the elder Bydecy and his second son.

"They wanted me to join them, you know," said Buck as he walked next to her.

"Who did?"

"The Intelligence Ministry of Astarel. It seems that they liked the fact that I wasn't guilty. And the Eye of Truth didn't hurt."

She hustled down the road next to him, hefting her backpack. "What did you tell them?"

Buck shrugged. "I told them I'd consider it but I was on a special mission for the Kingdom of Deran right now anyway, which is sort of true. I don't know. It would provide stability and protection for Dad and Jack."

She trudged silently next to him. Finally, she nudged him with her shoulder. "But you don't trust them."

He shook his head. "They were ready enough to chase me out when they thought I was guilty and now I'm a hot property once I have something they want. But I have to think it over. I don't know what's going to happen later and the prophecy makes me nervous."

The salty sea air seemed a bit more chill to her now. Andyn nodded. "I know what you mean."

CHAPTER SEVENTEEN

Rumors of Shadow

Liander Tolin settled back on the couch in the private room of the Winsome Lass tavern. "Send them in."

Fenris nodded and went to the door. *As hirelings go, performs well enough,* Liander thought, *but his loyalties? Fenris' eyes always seem to be looking into the shadows or past whoever he's speaking to. He bears watching.*

Liander stayed silent as the five recruits filed into the room. He waved a hand at the chairs around the table. "Please, be seated."

He nodded to a male Halfling and a human man who entered first. He remembered them as former agents of Halkith the Grey, the unlamented Ja'al cleric who tried to swipe the pegasi of Whitehorse Peak for the Dark Rider—and had received Dar Cabot's sword in his heart for his efforts. He wondered if the pair held a grudge against the Grey Riders or merely worked for the money.

Liander smiled at the assembly and sipped from a goblet of wine at his elbow. "I have selected the five of you from the available candidates and am prepared to offer you gainful employment, should you be interested. In order that we can work together, I need you to introduce yourselves, tell us your profession, and your last assignment."

He nodded to a female Dwarf seated nearest him. She raised an eyebrow and shrugged.

"I am Zolkava. I am a warrior and have spent my last ten seasons in the service of the Church of Vardu in their light infantry. I can track targets either above or below ground. I helped a Vardu cleric in Gorostol acquire sacrifices for his ceremonies a few weeks ago. I don't care how I get my coin. It makes no difference to me."

Liander nodded to the human woman next to Zolkava. She wore robes of earth tones and a couple of colorful feathers braided into her hair. Liander noted two daggers, one strapped to each leather bracer on her wrist.

"I am Sinda," she said, bright green eyes sizing up Liander. "I used to serve the Old Faith until I had my fill of their inability to seize power for the good of the planet. I have nature magic at my disposal. My last task was the destruction of a silver mine in Merdail and the scattering of the miners."

Liander smiled at her. "Thank you, Sinda. Next?"

A male Elf with dark, shoulder-length hair and sea green eyes stretched in his seat. "Vordan is my name. I hail from Terenai, where my rather misguided kin have prohibited me from pursuing certain lines of magical study, much like our Master Tolin here. I have taken it upon myself to further my studies in a clandestine fashion. My last mission was the securing of a book of arcane knowledge from an ancient ruin in Terenai."

Liander indicated the Halfling.

"Kili Mikman," the Halfling said, "lately of the service of the Ja'al Northern Command, special operations. I was senior agent to Halkith the Grey. My last mission was the destruction of a hamlet in Deran and setting the stage for an attack on the town of Forester."

Liander watched the others carefully, noting each person's reaction, though many tried to hide them. *Word of Halkith's demise has spread. Good.*

The human next to Kili shrugged. "James LeFond, also formerly of the Ja'al service, warrior in the special operations group. Kili and I work together. When it looked like Halkith was losing his grip, we left."

"Thank you, James," Liander said with a smile. "I will give you no reason to leave our company. The rewards promise to be great."

"And they are?" Zolkava asked, giving him a piercing stare.

"Oh, I don't know," Liander replied, toying with his goblet. "How much do you think a battle-trained pegasus is worth?"

The group stared at him. Zolkava and Sinda exchanged a dubious glance.

"We're going to steal pegasi?" Sinda asked. "If they're trained, they're owned by someone, usually powerful. Not good odds there."

"I understand that two among us have first-hand knowledge of the situation." Liander looked right at Kili and James. "Care to enlighten everyone?"

Kili smirked. "You all know Halkith is dead. You might not know who did it: a bunch of amateur freelances following Verian and Christianity. In addition, they have the pegasi that Halkith was after, one for each of them."

Vordan shook his head. "They can't be amateurs if they have pegasi. Only high-ranking free-lances or lords can own those."

James snorted. "That bunch? They're amateurs all right. The only reason they even know how to ride them is because they delivered the rest of the herd to the Crown of Deran. Probably got some kind of deal on training."

"And we're going after their pegasi? You must be joking," Sinda objected. "How are we going to get close? They'll just fly away."

"We will have a few advantages," Liander said, motioning to a shelf. A scroll of paper floated to his hand. "First, the pegasi are their most potent advantage. Second, we will set up a scenario where they will feel compelled to bring them into play, using a bit of bait."

"And what is this bait?" Zolkava looked unconvinced.

"A family member," Liander said, unrolling the scroll. "One of the freelances is named Buck Bydecy. I did some research. Bydecy's father, a widower, lives in Tyler and runs a small general store. He has no family at home. An easy target. We send a couple of our number up there, grab him and then let the Riders know we have him. Then we trade or, at the worst case, take the Riders out and leave with one or more of the pegasi."

"So, you think we can just lure them close enough by threatening Bydecy's father?" Vordan asked. "Not likely. I know a bit about this Buck Bydecy from reports in the guild journals. He was put on trial in Tyler, Astarel, about a week ago for theft and assault. He was acquitted, but the interesting part is the truth-reading magic item that set him free. If that magic item has the capabilities I suspect it does, it will be very difficult for any of us to get close."

"I agree," Zolkava said, crossing her arms. "There are a dozen ways they could see us coming or sniff out the trap. Despite what you've all said, Halkith was no fool and the Riders took him out. Amateurs they may be, but they're at least competent ones."

They're skeptical and using their experience and reasoning, Liander noted. Excellent. *Just what I need.* He nodded. "We won't underestimate them. The

Dark Elves did just that and now have to deal with— well, they have problems because of it. I have a couple of items that will even the odds."

He withdrew a set of small white stones from his belt purse and laid them on the table. Smooth and odd-shaped, they appeared to be ordinary river rocks except for their pure white color and the dark purple symbols etched in their sides. "These are Manacle Stones," he explained. "I will give you the key words. They can only be used once and the effect wears off in a couple of hours if not dispelled, but they will hold a creature rooted to the spot if you can hit the target. Perfect for pinning down pegasi."

The freelancers sat up straighter in their seats. Vordan's eyes gleamed.

Sinda pursed her lip. "Yes, that would help matters."

Zolkava shook her head. "We would still need to know they were coming well in advance of their arrival. They can fly any time they want to and approach from any vector they choose. We'd need to fly ourselves for situational aware-ness."

"Good point," Liander continued, "In that case, I have just the thing for tracking them." He reached into his pouch and pulled out a small brooch in the shape of a soaring falcon. "This is a Companion Pin."

Vordan nodded, eyes glittering. "I know. I used to have one myself, a honey badger."

Kili eyed him. "What happened to it?"

Vordan made a face. "Let's just say my exit from my former homeland was precipitous and I couldn't afford to go back and get certain valuables."

Liander handed the pin to Kili. "Since you are the spy in the group, I will give it to you. Do you know how it works?"

Kili examined it minutely. "Not exactly."

"I will give you a keyword. When you pronounce it, the pin will change to a full-sized red-tailed hawk - a magical construct, but still, an airborne asset. It is completely at your command. Though it can't fight very well, it looks just like a normal hawk and has keen eyesight, which you will be able access it by shifting your vision."

Kili turned the pin over in his fingers. "So, we can see them coming and they'll never know we were there."

Liander relaxed into his seat and took up his goblet again. "Exactly. But be warned. I manufactured it myself and it is keyed to me. I am lending it to you, nothing more. Attempting to make off with it without my permission would be most unwise."

The group sat without speaking for a while.

"So," Liander said, taking a sip. "Are we clear? We have to be patient, much more patient than Halkith. But with Gariil's own luck and the blessing of Arachnia, we will have them. The hostage will ensure that. An ambush well-laid and thought out—"

"There's still one question," interrupted Sinda, crossing her arms in front of her chest. "What do you get out of it?"

Liander took a sip of wine. "Yes, that. One of the Grey Riders is my fiancée, though she has forgotten it and needs to be reminded. As long as Andyn Eleandir is with the Riders, she will not see her true destiny. Kill them all and she will return to me, where she belongs. You may do whatever you wish with the belongings of the others."

Yes. She will be my destiny and I will be hers. He smiled. He remembered her lovely face and figure and visions of their shared future danced in his mind. Arachnia's tattoo on his chest pulsed with a cold energy. *It will be glorious.*

Sinda cleared her throat. "Well, then. We have a good plan."

At the sound of her voice, he brought himself back to the present. "A very good one," he replied, setting down his goblet.

"We must begin preparations, then, Master Tolin," Kili announced suddenly, standing and giving a warning look to the others.

Liander nodded and they departed. Lost in fantasies about Andyn, he barely noticed. *Soon, my love... soon...*

━━━━◆━━━━

"I can't believe you even found Puup," Eric said, patting the neck of his pegasus. The animal nosed his side, seeking a treat. The sun shone down brightly on the Riders, attending to their animals outside the Duke of Darlon's stables near the palace. *Thank God. I thought we'd end up looking for them for months.*

Saren nodded. "The silly animal was the reason we found the pegasi in the first place. We searched all around the area where you were ambushed after we dealt with the dark Elf search party. Terenil noticed that a certain pigeon kept showing up in the area, so on a hunch we decided to feed it. It took off into the forest and slowly led us to them. There was a sheer ridge about five miles away with a ledge outside a substantial cave. The pegasi stayed there. There was plenty of forage for them at the base of the cliff and a stream nearby, so they were happy."

"See?" Buck said, petting his pigeon. "Once again, Puup proves his worth. And Connor wanted to cook him."

"Still do," said Connor with a glint in his eye.

Buck gave him a black look and Dar laughed.

Eric shook his head. *There's a debate that's going to go on for a long time.*

Terenil slipped up next to Saren. "Well, I feel sorry for good old Puup. He's a valuable asset and underrated."

Buck pointed at Terenil. "See? I have allies?"

Andyn's silvery laugh rang out as rode up to them on Medianox. "You are a band of jesters, certainly. Saren, did the pegasi give you any trouble?"

Saren shook her head. "Once we found them, we left some of our number to guard while I flew back to Darlon. After I reported what was going on, the Duke assigned his riding master to me and we flew back the next morning. They were a little skittish but the master had some techniques to coax them to follow us."

Andyn dismounted and smiled shyly at Saren. "Thank you so much for getting them for us."

Saren put her arm around Andyn. "Anyone who can put up with my brother for this long deserves a favor or two."

Eric gave Saren a sidelong look of mock disdain and she winked at him.

The Riders chuckled.

The speed at which his friends accepted his half-sister warmed Eric's heart, despite their initial discomfort at her half-Daemon appearance. *Of course, she doesn't look like a normal Daemon: her horns are ivory instead of deep purple or red and the same goes for her bat wings.*

Connor straightened from inspecting Phantom's hooves. "It was nice of the Duke to go through all that trouble."

"Not at all," Terenil answered. "You did him a great service by getting rid of the ice Balar and confounding the Dark Elves. I think he felt it was the least he could do."

186

"Well, at least everything is somewhat back to normal," Dar said, "Now at least we can figure out our next move and not have to worry about transportation, or the pegasi."

"And what is your next move?" Saren asked, leaning against the corral gate. The Riders exchanged a glance.

Now, that's the key question, isn't it? "Well," said Eric. "We could try to hunt down Liander Tolin, or go back towards Forester and see if we can pick up the trail of Margoth's forces or..." His voice trailed off.

Terenil had a half-smile on his face. "Or you can try to follow the prophecy."

And get dragged off into God-knows-where. Eric looked off into the distance, avoiding Terenil's eyes.

Terenil gave him a quizzical look. "Why do you dread it so? It was a prophecy by an Irial high priest, not in the least connected to evil, and it predicts great success."

"I think it's because it's something we can't control," Eric offered. "Without our agreement, things happen to us just as shown in the Song. We have little say in the matter."

"I see," said Terenil, nodding. "But what if it is a kind of guidebook instead of a harbinger of doom? Suppose you used it proactively."

Eric's reply died on his lips. *He has a point. We've spent so much time trying to avoid it, we've never even considered using the prophecy as an advantage.*

"You know," said Dar thoughtfully, "You might have something there."

"Well," replied Terenil, "It's just one man's opinion. Maybe you can get the opinion of some experts, say, the Order of the Three Magi."

"Maybe," murmured Eric. He raised an eyebrow at Saren. "Father wouldn't, would he?"

Saren sidled next to him and put her arm around his shoulder. She gave him a gentle hug. "I know you said that you didn't want Dad to make things happen for you in your career, just like I did, and he's kept to it. But you don't think that means he'd ignore you, do you? He's been in communication with Lord Nolan and Duke Inibe of Darlon, hearing of your exploits."

"No, I didn't think he's forgotten, but for him to use his influence like that seems like, I don't know, favoritism."

Saren gave him a look. "It's not favoritism if the subject is of interest to the Order, like a scroll from the Esten Empire that has prophetic connotations. Besides, when was the last time you saw him?"

"Just after Easter, before I left for Forester," Eric mused. "He didn't really want me to go. I'd feel odd asking for his help after insisting that I do this all on my own."

She held him at arms-length. "He didn't want me to leave either, if you recall, and this all ended well, didn't it? Well then, it's about time you did some catching up. He's still on his own, you know, after Mom passed away."

Eric felt the familiar pain in his heart and a lump in his throat, thinking of his foster mother, Anne, and how she had suffered a stroke just a year before he struck out on his own. That had led to her eventual death from a heart attack. *Dad really misses her, I know. All of us do: Saren, Emily, Brendan, the grandchildren...*

"And he misses you too," Saren said, seeming to read his mind. "He's been a visitor at Tallemar in Oakmoor several times this year already and I think he's going to move to the capitol anyway to be near us. So, what do you say?"

Eric realized the other Riders had been watching him carefully the whole time.

Dar came up and clapped him on the shoulder. "How about if I make the presentation to your dad. It wouldn't be favoritism because I'm not even from your family. So there."

Why not? Eric envisioned Melinor meeting all his friends at once and couldn't help but smile. "All right then. Dad is about to be exposed to the Grey Riders. I hope he survives."

"Well, Father?" Eric asked. "I'm curious. What do you think?"

"Frankly, I'm amazed you survived," Melinor Indidarc said to Eric, his eyes twinkling.

The Grey Riders exchanged grins.

Melinor looked over the top of the scroll of the Song of the Grey Riders at Eric and smiled. With his grey hair, neatly trimmed beard and mustache, and dark robes, Eric thought he looked as much like a kindly professor as the first day he met him. *Mom called him that sometimes: the distracted professor.*

A momentary memory of his departed foster mother's smiling face made him lose focus and he forced himself to center his thoughts.

I'm glad that Dad got to meet all of them, even if they are a bit distracted by all this. Andyn and Hlerv, in particular, hadn't stopped gazing at the interior of the audience chamber of the Order's Chapter House since their arrival. Tasteful yet splendid, the colorful tile murals on the walls depicted various scenes from the life of Christ. Hovering crystal chandeliers, lit from within by arcane fire, shone a gentle golden light on everything. Melinor let the parchment drop to the polished surface of the mahogany desk and sighed.

"Well, you're certainly right in thinking that you've been led by the nose this whole time," Melinor noted. "However, I see that Terenil's idea is probably the best way for you to deal with the prophecy and hold your own destiny at the same time."

"I think we all agree by now," said Connor. "But which way do we go? There are several things listed in the Song that we don't know how to find."

Melinor nodded. "Such as the hawk, or the Halfling toy? Or the gold-red passage? Or the crown?"

Connor nodded, looking perplexed.

Melinor steepled his fingers in front of his face and thought for a while. "Irial prophecies are arcane, but at the heart of them, they are very practical. Irial, after all, is a patron of craftsmen, farmers and artisans. Therefore, I would suggest you go with the item that is the most tangible and the easiest to track."

Dar scratched his head. "The toy?"

Melinor shrugged. "It would seem so. The hawk could be anything - a real hawk, a magic item, someone with the nickname of "Hawk". And as far as the passage or crown, the possibilities are even more varied. At least we might know where to find toys made by Halflings."

Eric looked at Connor. The other Riders followed his eyes. "Evendale," he said.

Connor nodded slowly. "I thought it might come to that." He sighed.

He exhaled. Eric sat a little straighter, his attention piqued. *Come to what? What is he talking about?* Connor looked, unsure, pained ... and lost.

"I didn't want to bring any of this up," the Halfling said, staring down at his hands, "because it was a long time ago and very irrelevant to what we were doing. I have misgivings about going to Evendale because that's where I originally came from."

Andyn leaned over and put a hand on his arm. "You don't have to tell us if you don't want to."

Connor gave a little chuckle. "After everything the rest of you have revealed? My story isn't that much, really. Don't know why I haven't said anything up until now. We all have pasts, after all." He glanced at Hlerv, who merely watched him with piercing dark eyes.

"Well," Connor said, "I was born and raised in Glen, one of the larger towns in Evendale. My father is Seamus Lomin and he's an administrator for the Irial church in Glen. He used to be a sell-sword, a long time ago, a warrior like Buck or Dar, actually. My mother is a priestess of Irial, in the Heather Temple in Glen. I have a brother, Brendan. He's married to Cerys and they have two kids. They still live in town."

He stood and began pacing. "My parents and I didn't always see eye-to-eye when I was growing up. I ran with some people of questionable background at times. Father, in particular, didn't approve. I got involved with Janey Dancy, the daughter of a local merchant. Her father was a supporter of the temple. Anyway, Janey became pregnant and we married a few months later and my daughter, Rose, was born."

Eric didn't breathe. *He has a family?*

Connor sighed. "When Rose was about nine months old, the Whispering Death overtook the Dales and Terenai."

Eric shuddered. *The Whispering Death, borne out of the wilderness. Some said it was an evil magic, not a disease. And the survivors, such as they are, can only speak in a whisper after their ordeal.* Eric felt a pang of pity at the expression on Connor's face. *I've never seen him so forlorn. That must have been awful.*

"Janey and Rose didn't make it," Connor continued, blinking rapidly. "I lost two uncles, three aunts and six cousins to it. My brother had it pretty bad but made it through. He even regained his voice somewhat. Mom and Dad nearly killed themselves trying to help everyone."

Oh, dear Jesus! Almost his entire family? Tears pricked the corners of Eric's eyes.

"I'm so sorry," said Andyn, giving him a sad smile and taking his hand again. "I know how you feel, in my own way."

Connor kissed her hand. "Thanks, Andyn. That means a lot. Well, I came down with it too, but much later when it wasn't nearly as strong. Many of the local authorities were also stricken. To distract myself from Janey and Rose, I joined up in the constabulary. It seems that they had a special need for people with my talents. I helped them stabilize the region around Glen and even went to the border forts a couple of times. There were various tribes of goblins and Ogres and Kaftu that decided to test the Army and we needed every advantage. There was a lot more crime too, as outsiders came in and tried looting the homes of the dead."

He sat down and continued. "Mother and Father eventually came to respect me for what I did. We're closer now, but it took a plague and Janey and Rose's deaths to bring it about. I haven't been back home in two years; only occasional letters."

Eric cleared his throat to get rid of the lump in it. "Connor, you know we're with you for anything. If you don't want to go back to Evendale, we'll find another way."

Connor nodded, then looked up at him with his glittering black eyes. "No, Eric, it's okay now. If going back home will somehow help us solve the riddle of the Song, then I'll do it. Janey always believed in me and she hated evil; it would honor her memory."

Melinor stood. "I honor her, and you, and your family as well, Connor Lomin. Many people perished in the evil plague and its aftermath, not only in Evendale. The chaos that ensued afterwards touched many lands. Actually..." He stopped and put a hand to his goatee, eyes slitted.

"No, this is the right time." Melinor gave them a sharp look. "What I am about to tell you is confidential, but you have to know it. Do I have your pledge to keep it secret?"

They all nodded. Melinor raised an eyebrow at Hlerv, who met his gaze for a while, then squirmed.

"Yes," Hlerv said. "No one will hear it from me."

"Good," Melinor said. "The security services of the Northern Alliance and Terenai and even farther south to Gorostol and Merdail and even across the sea have raids from the wilderness areas and heightened activities on the part of slavers, bandits, Dark Elves and criminal bands. Everyone is nervous. It seems as if a storm is brewing somewhere and all evil is agitated at its coming."

Eric felt cold. "A storm?"

Melinor nodded. "Yes, but we don't know what it is. And worse yet, there is social unrest in all the lands. Long-standing traditions and laws are being challenged, people of intellect propose new lines of inquiry with dark aspects, regardless of morality. The common folk are raised to envy and the nobility to pride and arrogance. It is as if the fabric of society is fraying."

"What does this mean for us?" asked Dar.

"I have been in council meetings with the King and Queen," Melinor replied, "and have seen firsthand the growing opposition to even basic laws and ideals regarding responsibility, criminal conduct, family, life, and the rights of the common folk. It is subtle but determined and I do not know the origin of it. I suspect that someone behind the scenes, maybe the Ja'al, are trying to distract and weaken all the lands in order to prepare for something big. This Dark Rider in the Song may be part of it. And this," he held up the medallion the Riders had taken from Liander Tolin, "this may be the key to all of it. I will write a letter of recommendation for Sidara and Simrit, two of the Order in Oakmoor. You can stop by on your way to Evendale. They are more expert in ancient history than I am and might be able to give you a clue to go on."

He walked around the desk. The Riders rose and he handed the medallion to Dar.

"Where are you staying?" he asked.

"The Golden Hart, on Hector Street," said Eric.

"Good. I know the proprietor. It is a safe place and well-regarded," Melinor replied. "I will know to reach you there if I find out more."

"However," he continued in a warning tone, "Be on your guard. If a tempest really is brewing and you are involved, you will find more enemies and fewer allies as the days continue."

Oh great. Well, it's not like we don't have enemies aplenty anyway.

Melinor suddenly smiled. "But also, fear not. People of good will of all faiths have been engaged to pray for peace and justice and their prayers will be a bounty for you. They stand ready to assist and we will apprise them of your efforts when the time is right. I, of course, will be one of your allies, as will the Order."

"Thank you, Father," Eric said simply.

Melinor gave his shoulder a squeeze. "God will guide you and help you."

Chapter Eighteen

A Dish Served Cold

"We're closing in ten minutes," said Alfred Bydecy with a smile as he wiped down the counter.

"Oh, should we come back tomorrow?" asked the young, brown-haired woman. She linked her arm with a rangy young man with long hair.

"No need," said Alfred, "If you know what you're looking for, I can help speed things a bit."

"Oh, good," said the woman with a cheerful smile of her own. "I need some fabrics for baby clothes." She gave an adoring look at the young man.

"Yes," said the man, showing white teeth as he smiled back at her. "And cloth for diapers. There will be plenty of that."

"Ah, well, I offer you congratulations! I have a fine selection of dry goods suitable for the very young." Alfred led them to a side table where the woman busied herself looking over various colors of cloth.

"Any of your own?" the man asked him.

"Oh, pshaw, yes," said Alfred with a wave of his hand. "All grown though. The early years were quite an adventure."

He turned back towards the shelves of leather purses and gloves, re-stacking a few that had gone askew. He never noticed the young man slip to the door and lock it, nor the slim hand of the woman inscribing a glowing sigil in the air behind him. He only saw colored lights followed by darkness.

"Buck, I'm so sorry," said Andyn, hanging her head. She looked miserable.

Dar put an arm around her. "Don't blame yourself. We all knew this was a possibility."

Buck sat on the edge of his bed in his room at the Golden Hart, a letter in his hand. He stared blankly at the wall.

Dar gritted his teeth. *That bastard Liander Tolin got Buck's dad. The bastards. Not content to face up to people who can fight them, are they?*

"But he's after me, and now he's pulled Alfred into this," Andyn continued. She threw her hands up in a helpless gesture. Dar gave her a quick hug.

I would react the same way if it was my past coming out to haunt us, and someday, it might, Dar thought with a sense of foreboding. "It's not your fault, Andyn. He's the one doing evil, not you."

Buck looked up at Andyn as if seeing her for the first time. He gave one of his homespun smiles and reached out to give her hand a squeeze. "Dar is right. Joko warned me about this and I've been worried about Da' all on his own. I guess it's a warning call to all of us. Besides, you threw in with me for the Eye of Truth and going to Tyler. Don't worry Andyn. I don't blame you."

Connor gave Dar a sharp look. "This begs the question of all our relatives."

Dar shook his head. "My parents work for the Count of Hillton and are well-guarded. My brothers are in large cities and in recognizable careers with guards at their workplaces. They are not easy targets."

Everyone looked at Eric, who shrugged. "Melinor? Terenil and Saren? Emily and Brendan? Even the Ja'al and Liander Tolin aren't that crazed."

"My parents and sister are safe back in Terenai. My half-siblings are likewise well-guarded. Dad's still in the Army, so he has security for everyone nearby," said Andyn, looking at Connor. "What about you?"

Connor shook his head. "My mother's position with the Church guarantees that they'd be looking out for attacks and ambushes, both for her, my dad, my brother and his family."

They all looked at Hlerv. He shrugged. "No problem here, if that's what you're asking. My family is extremely well guarded... and no, I'm not going to tell you who they are. Trust me. Liander would have to be a lot more powerful with more resources if he were going to try it."

Eric sat on the bed next to Buck and took the note from him. He pursed his lip. "This says they will have him at the ruins at Avar's Run outside Darlon in five days time. The letter is dated two days ago. I think I heard Dad saying something about the Avars when I was still training with him. Maybe he'll have something for us to go on."

"Do you think he'd help us?" Buck asked.

Eric grinned and slugged him in the shoulder. "Are you kidding? Of course. I don't think he'll swoop in and get him; the kidnappers would probably just kill your Dad outright if they saw certain death coming in the person of Melinor Indidarc. But we can ask. I'll send a message to the Duke's manor and see what he says."

"Great," said Dar. "It's getting dark outside. Let's get something to eat and wait for the return message."

They headed down to the Hartshead tavern and got dinner while Eric wrote a note and asked the manager for a courier. They ate silently, lost in their own thoughts, trying to figure out a way to deal with Liander and rescue Buck's father.

Dar considered several possible scenarios but none seemed viable. *Even with magical assistance, we need to know the lay of the land at the ruins, and I have no information on that. Hopefully, Melinor will have something.*

They had barely finished dessert when their answer came in the form of a visitor.

"Eric, didn't you save some pie for me?" asked Melinor Indidarc as he pulled up a chair.

Dar's mouth dropped open and he closed it. The Riders cleared a space for the wizard.

"I didn't think you'd come on your own, Father," Eric said.

Melinor smiled but they saw a steely glint in his eyes. "No one threatens my son's friends and gets away with it. No one. Let me see the note."

Buck blinked in shock, then gave Melinor a warm smile and handed over the note.

Dar sat quietly, sipping his wine, watching Melinor. Eric's father nodded slowly.

"Well, I can tell two things already. First, this Liander Tolin is paranoid, and from what you've already told me, deranged. This makes him unpredictable and more dangerous than usual. Rational actions are not to be expected. His warnings against involving the authorities are fairly standard for this sort of thing but with him, I'm sure he has a way of figuring out if you're by yourselves or if you have assistance. If I get involved, he might just kill Alfred outright."

"We wouldn't want to ask you to do that anyway, Father," said Eric. "This is our fight."

Too bad, thought Dar. *We could sure use his magical arsenal. But he's right. If Liander knows about us, he probably knows Eric's last name. Even though there are other Indidarcs in the Kingdoms, he's probably betting on the worst case scenario and is ready for Melinor to try something.*

Melinor gave Eric's shoulder a squeeze as he sat back in his chair. "I understand. Second, from what you've told me, what he really wants is Andyn. Everything else is secondary to him."

He looked at Andyn with a speculative eye. "You, my dear, are the bargaining chip, I'm sorry to say."

Andyn twirling her goblet in her fingers. "I know. But I'm willing to be bait if it will help Alfred."

Melinor chuckled. "That's the spirit. I think that's the only way to get Alfred away from him: make him think he's getting what he wants, then spring a trap. Also in our favor is the fact that Liander, though individually capable, is not high wizard material. The team of you should be able to take him down, even if he has help."

"How?" asked Eric.

The wizard took a paper and pencil from his shoulder bag. "By planning. Now, this is the layout of Avar's Run..."

———◦———

Kili grinned wickedly. "I see them now."

In his altered vision, a misty image formed over his real eyesight, showing what the magical hawk saw. Five winged horses soared below the clouds in the skies outside of Darlon. Kili could see the towers of the city far in the distance behind them.

"Two humans, a half-Elf male, a half-Elf wench, and a Halfling, all on pegasi," he reported. "That's all of them. Looks to be about two miles away."

Liander Tolin placed a hand on Kili's shoulder and the Halfling resisted the urge to swat it aside. "Excellent work, Mister Mikman. We will initiate phase two when they are within a mile or so."

Kili tried not to squirm. *He's technically my boss, but I hate it when people treat me like a child servant. It reminds me of Halkith the Grey – the son of a bitch.*

"Just say the word," growled Zolkava.

Liander smiled. "I admire your enthusiasm. Have a care, though. There are two tracker-scouts among them, so take that into account."

"I have," said Sinda from her post next to a tree. "The snares are set and waiting."

Kili suddenly frowned, watching through the hawk's eyes. "They are going to ground."

"Really..." Liander sounded hesitant. "Wait and see what they do."

Kili commanded the hawk to swoop around so he could get a better view of the Riders as they landed. He chafed at the time needed. "Damn it. They're hidden from view for a ... no wait. There they are."

He saw all of them now, still astride their mounts. They appeared to discuss something among themselves, then the shorter of the human men raised his arm and the pegasi took wing. "They're heading back up."

"Something's not right," Vordan said. He eyed the figure of Alfred Bydecy, bound and gagged at their feet among the trees and bushes. "Why would they stop?"

"Maybe they suspect something," offered Sinda. "But why move on afterwards? Did they see the hawk?"

"Even if they did, it is no matter," said Liander. "It looks just like a regular hawk."

James stretched and yawned. "Lord Tolin is right. Who cares? All five of them are still on their way and they'll be here soon. We just stick to the plan."

"Excellent, James." Liander beamed. "Just the sort of hard-charging initiative we need. Everyone, get to your places. James, bring along the bait."

———◄O►———

"Just remember what to look for," Connor said to his stirrup.

The disembodied voice of Hlerv floated back up to him. "I know, I know. You don't have to keep harping on it. And no, Buck, I won't lose the Eye. I promise."

Buck Bydecy kept his eyes on the nearby forest and snorted. "You better not. This piece of glass in the Eye-frame on my helmet just isn't a good substitute."

"He'll do fine," said Andyn, patting Medianox. "We just have to play our part."

"How long will the invisibility potion last?" asked Dar.

"About four hours according to Melinor," said Eric. "Or until he makes a sudden motion, like attacking someone or running."

"Which reminds me," Andyn said, motioning to the others. "Drink Melinor's potions first, then stay still so I can shield you."

Dar swallowed the blue liquid in his own tiny vial, almost choking on the flavor of cardamom, cabbage and orange peel. A magical field covered him in seconds. Andyn raised her hands and whispered arcane words. A glittering cloud sifted out from Andyn's hands to settle on them and dissipate.

Buck made a face, looking at his vial. "Tastes terrible and terrific at the same time."

Eric grinned. "That's a wizard for you."

Dar looked at his map. "Let's get in place. We'll land south of the main ruins and work our way slowly from there. Be alert for Hlerv's signal."

He raised his arm and the Riders took to the air.

———◄O►———

Excellent. A new challenge, and especially one that tests my skills in stealth and magic—well, I don't get too many opportunities like that, Hlerv thought with triumph. *Now they'll see what I can really do to ruin Tolin's plan.*

He flitted through the brush and trees, keeping his eyes alert for anyone watching. He gained the outskirts of Avar's Run fairly easily, stopping next to the tall, white-barked ghostwood trees towering overhead.

They say ghostwood trees grow best in haunted places. He shook off the eerie feeling and random thoughts and turned his attention to the low walls of the ruins. He glimpsed an abandoned set of stairs leading down into darkness under the remnants of a ruined archway and wondered.

Not now, certainly, but later, when I have a few more years under my belt. Then maybe. The Order of the Avar's were supposed to be quite rich in magic and treasures.

He remembered well Melinor's warning about the dangers of the tunnels and caverns below the ancient monastery. "Don't even think about going underground," he had told them with a dark look. "There are some creatures down there that could destroy all of you in a matter of seconds—and those are the quick, clean deaths. Stay to the plan. Andyn and Eric, especially, need extra advantages: as the spellcasters, Liander will likely go after you first since you can counter his magic."

Hlerv picked his way among the ruins, heading for a hillock mounded by large blocks of stone leaning at crazy angles. *Well, something extremely violent occurred here in ages past. Glad I wasn't around to see it.* No birdsong or animal noises sounded in the ruins, only dead silence. He took extra care with every step.

About a hundred yards from the base of the massive hillock, he stopped, feeling for the Eye of Truth in his pocket. *Too bad I have to give this back.*

He placed the Eye before his own and waited. About fifty feet away, a series of symbols glowed in the turf, spaced by about ten feet. He counted twenty in all, arranged in an arc. A couple of symbols he recognized as the work of a sorcerer, but most he didn't. Knowing Liander Tolin, they probably symbolized some baleful form of dark magic or maybe Liander had help. *Not surprising. If I were him, I'd even the odds.*

Hlerv memorized the locations of all the symbols and tried to memorize some of the patterns, then set to watching and waiting. Nothing moved.

He decided to head back when he caught motion in the trees near the left side of the hillock's base. He held up the Eye of Truth again. A vile purple light flared in his vision. A bear-like creature lumbered towards the ruins, nose in the air and sniffing. Flaring red eyes bulged in their sockets and too-long fangs protruded over its lips. Its paws ended in curved, wicked-looking talons, and a ridge of spines ran down its back. It sauntered towards Hlerv, sniffing the air.

Hlerv's eyes widened and he crept backwards. After putting some distance between them, he cut an escape route at angles to it, looking over his shoulder to make sure it didn't pick up his scent. Once he gained the shelter of the forest, he broke into a trot.

That's a Fell Bear, or I'm a Goblin bridesmaid. This is starting to get complicated.

———◇———

"Tell you what," said James Lefond as he manhandled Alfred Bydecy over the rougher rocks and crumbled stonework near the Avar ruins on the hilltop, "I'll let your kid have an even chance. After I split Dar Cabot like a melon, Buck and I can go man-to-man and see who wins."

Alfred growled something behind his gag and James raised his eyebrows.

"What, you don't think so? Don't worry. I'll go easy on him. I heard about your boy and he and I might have made a good team in the old days. Who knows? If he impresses me, I might capture him instead and have Vordan use a slave collar on him."

Alfred shot him a furious look and James laughed. "Yes, I'm sure you'll enjoy it."

They arrived at a large, flat rock and James shoved Alfred on the ground next to the rock. Liander stood atop the rock. A snuffling growl startled him.

James jerked reflexively, then swore. *That damned Fell Bear of Sinda's gives me the creeps. She's sure proud of the thing. I don't know how she managed to conjure it or mutate it or whatever it was. I'm just going to be glad when she and that damned menace are far away.*

He heard Sinda's cheerful laugh as she came around a ruined set of pillars, one arm draped over the monstrosity. "What, James, does Skurva frighten you? Poor brave warrior."

"Just keep that thing under control and away from me," he shot back. "It stinks."

The hellspawn bear's eyes twitched and it bared its fangs. Sinda laughed again and winked at James. He glared back and made an obscene gesture, which seemed to amuse her even more.

"Now, now," Liander said in a pleasant tone. "Let's keep this in control. Our real enemies are arriving soon, I can see. We must be ready for them. Are Zolkava and Kili in position?"

"Yes," answered Sinda. "They await your signal."

"Excellent," said Liander, waving a hand towards a quintet of flying creatures bearing down at them. "Our guests are here."

Dar wheeled his pegasus in the air, heading straight towards the figures below. *Let's see: Liander Tolin, another male Elf, a human woman with a hellish-looking bear, and a long-haired warrior – almost looks like James LeFond. Wouldn't that be rich?* At their feet lay a trussed-up man: Alfred Bydecy.

Andyn and Eric flew next to him. Eric tapped his helmet.

He's detected warding sigils or some kind of traps on the ground. Okay, Eric. You have the lead now.

He followed Eric and the other Riders down towards the flat rock where their enemies waited, then veered to the left. The Riders followed Eric in a precise line, curving past the woods and around the bend, then down as he landed Falcon on the turf. Dar cantered his pegasus forward and settled his helmet firmly on his head.

Sinda and Vordan cursed at almost the exact same time.

"Damn it. They're avoiding the Manacle Stones. How did they know the sigils were there?" Sinda hissed.

"Are those the ones designed to trap flying creatures?" asked James with a glare back at Sinda.

"Yes, they are." Liander said in a speculative tone. He seemed almost impressed. "I'm not sure how you did it, but well-played, my dear Andyn, well-played."

To the others on his team, he said in a low voice. "Nothing has changed. We have a backup plan. Execute it."

<hr />

"You doing all right, Da?" asked Buck. Dar could tell he was trying to remain calm.

Alfred Bydecy nodded vigorously.

Buck removed his helm and dismounted. He stepped behind his pegasus, pretending to fiddle with the saddle.

"Of course he's all right," Liander said with an expansive wave of his hands. "I do keep my word after all. Now, if you wouldn't mind, we can begin negotiations."

Dar also dismounted, hearing his other friends do so behind him.

He remembered Melinor's words. "I do not doubt that Liander knows you have pegasi and I also do not doubt that he wants to take that advantage away from you if not steal them outright. Take the option away from him and send them out of reach as soon as you can to remove them from the equation."

Dar looked back at Buck, who nodded.

Good. Hlerv has made the handoff and the Eye is back in Buck's helmet. Dar made a circular motion with his hand and pointed up and over, behind Liander and away from the arc of symbols behind Dar. Before anyone could react, the pegasi leaped up and beat their pinions, soaring away.

"Now why would you do that?" Liander asked, eyes narrowed and jaw tight.

Dar smiled. "Precautions."

"Liander," the Elven man began.

"Not now, Vordan," Liander said.

"But the pegasi—" put in the woman next to the Fell Bear.

"Later, Sinda!" Liander snapped, his suave composure broken. "I have a plan for everything. First things first!"

Dar noted the irritated looks Liander's companions shot at him. Then he recognized the long-haired human. *It is James! If he's here, can Kili Mikman be far behind?*

James Lefond smirked at him. "It's because the runt is scared we'll take away his pretty pet flying horse. Isn't that right?"

Dar ignored him. "We have come for Alfred Bydecy." *Where the hell is Kili?* He shot a look at Connor, who nodded minutely.

"Excellent," answered Liander. "I have come here to be united with my future bride. We can make an exchange."

Andyn stepped up next to Dar. "You know that I cannot let Alfred die out of concern for me. Does my own happiness mean so little to you?

Liander smiled. "You will learn happiness, my sweet. I will give it to you. Oh, the wonders of magic and power when there are no trifling morals or ethics to get in the way. You will become intoxicated with them as I have, dear Andyn. Then you and I will rule alongside the Dark Rider. You will see."

Her eyes flashed. "Serving the Dark Rider was never part of the bargain."

Liander looked at the hell-spawn bear and Alfred. "I don't think you have many options."

Eric chuckled from where he stood next to Andyn, leaning on his spear casually. "I don't think you quite understand, Liander. Even if Andyn goes with you, there's no guarantee that she will remain with you if you force her into Margoth's service. If you try, well, we know her and you'd better watch your back. I think you had just better accept what you can get and negotiate later."

Dar kept silent during this exchange and then saw what he had been hoping for: a look of surprise on Alfred's face, then a schooled indifference. The ropes binding his hands and feet loosened slightly but remained on him.

Next to him, Buck flipped down the arm on his helmet with the Eye of Truth.

Liander considered Eric's words. "That is something we'll have to work on in our marriage." He extended a hand to Andyn. "Come with me, my love."

Andyn gave one look at Dar, then sighed and walked forward.

Several things happened at once.

Buck shouted. "Invisible Halfling next to Connor!"

Vordan stepped back and waved his hands in an intricate pattern. Hlerv winked into view next to Alfred, cursing and drawing his sword. Connor dropped into a back-roll as the form of a familiar, unshaven Halfling shimmered into being next to him, slashing with a sword glowing with purple fire. Hlerv pushed Buck's father and Alfred Bydecy rolled forward towards the Riders, his bonds flying off his limbs.

"Where the hell did the Gnome come from?" James roared.

Andyn called out an arcane syllable and a globe of force shot out around her, thrusting Liander and his allies away. Sinda stumbled backwards in mid-spell, tripping over a boulder and rolling back to her feet, tendrils of dark green magic spraying out from her fingertips. Liander pulled a wand from his belt as James drew his sword.

A pair of arrows zipped out from behind a boulder, where a Dwarven woman crouched. One shaft hit Dar in the calf and he lurched to the side. He yanked it out, feeling healing magic from Melinor's potion expend itself and knit the wound closed.

Buck stood over his father, shield up and Khelios drawn, the Dwarven sword glowing golden.

Eric cast a spell of his own and several symbols on the ground near Liander flared and disappeared.

"Negotiations are over," Andyn said in a cold voice.

———◆———

"Death!" screamed James and launched himself at Dar. Sinda drew her daggers, Zolkava charged around the boulder wielding two hand axes, and the hell-bear surged forward, roaring and slobbering. Kili slashed again at Connor, who beat his attack aside with a sword that glittered like ice.

"Wait!" shouted Liander. *It's all wrong! It shouldn't be happening! Andyn can't slip away again.*

A voice echoed in Liander's head. *Slay the Riders, my servant! The rewards will be great.* Something snapped in him and he felt a searing pain over his heart, just where the brand of Arachnia lay.

"Kill them all!" he commanded in a voice not his own.

Dar whipped out his sword as James lunged forward to impale him. He banged the sword to the side, whirling as he did. As expected, his return slash whistled through empty air where James had been. The long-haired warrior rolled away and just as quickly leaped back to the attack again. Dar met him blade-to-blade and kicked his legs out from under him. James thudded into the ground and rolled.

Dar felt a tingling in the air and hurled himself to the side as a bolt of lightning blasted into the earth a foot away from him. He saw Buck standing next to his father, sword and shield up. He deflected powerful claw swipes and slashed at the hellish monstrosity that roared and battered at him. Alfred Bydecy held a dagger in his hands, looking scared but determined. The Fell Bear pounded Buck but he grimly stood firm. He weaved and blocked, thrusting Khelios into the creature's side and limbs.

Beyond them, Liander, Vordan and Sinda hurled flame and lightning and fiery darts at Andyn and Eric, who stood firm with the spells exploding on glimmering screens surrounding them. Even as he watched, the grass beneath Andyn and Eric warped and twisted, wrapping itself around their ankles, pinning them in place. Sinda laughed wildly.

James regained his feet and launched an intricate series of cuts and thrusts. Dar gave ground bit by bit, casting quick glances over his shoulder to be sure of the terrain. He saw Hlerv and Connor engaged in a whirling, dizzying dance of blades with Kili and the Dwarven woman. An axe strike wounded Hlerv but he rolled past the Dwarf and cast up a handful of grey powder at her. She growled a curse and lurched backwards, coughing. Connor tripped Kili and stabbed, but the evil Halfling grabbed his wrist, pulled and they hit the earth in a furious melee.

"You're dead," James said, stalking forward.

Dar couldn't resist a wry smile. "Eventually. We all die, James Lefond. It's just the destination afterwards that's different."

James laughed and leaped into the air, thrusting and kicking at the same time. Dar, caught off-guard, blocked the sword but took the kick in the chest, stumbling backwards to bounce painfully into a tree trunk. James lunged. Dar rolled forward past him, slashing him in the leg and receiving a cut to his own shoulder in return.

Their armors held but Dar felt a bruise starting under his enchanted chainmail.

A gurgling scream made them both turn. The hell bear collapsed in front of Buck and his father, bleeding steaming ichor from a dozen cuts and sporting Eric's spear in its side. Flaming drool spilled from its jaws onto the churned earth as it dropped.

"That evens it a little," said Eric.

"Stay back, Da!" Buck charged towards Liander and his cronies.

Dar dodged James' next attack and spun again, banging aside his enemy's sword and putting himself closer to Alfred Bydecy.

He never quite remembered what followed next, only that he and James fought like Dar had never fought before. It took all his training and experience to avoid being run through or slashed to death. As it was, he bled from four wounds and James from at least that many when they broke apart, panting.

Behind James, Dar saw a swirling, flaming melee as Liander, Sinda, Vordan, Eric, Andyn and Buck battled in a maelstrom of blades and magic. He vaguely made out Khelios lashing about, a glittering swing of Andyn's maces, flashes of light, smoke and eruptions of earth and rocks.

James wiped his brow. "Not bad, runt. Not bad at all. Too bad it's for nothing."

Dar crouched, his blade ready and easy. "Once we free Alfred and bury the lot of you, believe me, it will be worth it."

James chuckled, a wild light in his eyes. "You have no idea. I have seen what the Ja'al are planning. I have heard the Song of Kudath. The Dark Wave will destroy you all!"

He leaped at Dar in a flurry of attacks. Dar beat them aside. He slipped and felt James' sword cut into his side. Dar thrust and stabbed him in the arm, then tripped over a rock and turned it into a back-roll. He felt blood running down his ribs and felt dizzy. James raised his sword on high, then screamed and grabbed at a dagger that appeared in his side.

Alfred Bydecy stood next to a fallen pillar, picking up a large rock. "No one attacks the friends of my boy!" he shouted.

James leaped, blade extended. Just as he had done with Halkith the Grey those many weeks ago, Dar dodged to the side and thrust. His sword buried itself halfway into James.

With a surprised look in his eyes, James stared at Dar. "I don't get it. I was supposed to win. I always win..."

Dar let him fall, pulling his blade out as James hit the earth.

Alfred pounced to his side in a second, an arm around him. Dar smiled at him. "Thanks for the help."

Alfred nodded, mouth set grimly.

A scream of rage drew their attention again.

The Dwarf-woman and Kili backed away from Hlerv and Connor. Both bled profusely and Kili limped as he retreated. Connor and Hlerv split apart, stalking them.

"This deal was a load of Goblin shit!" shouted Kili. "No pegasi, no reward, and death in the bargain!"

In a fury, he grabbed a glass sphere from under his cloak and cast it down. A cloud of thick fog burst up in front of him. Hlerv and Connor coughed and choked, backpedaling. When the mist cleared, Dar glimpsed Kili and the Dwarf many yards away, fleeing as fast as they could.

Sinda reached up into the air and made a pulling motion. Thousands of leaves and twigs from the ghostwood trees shot downwards in a blinding wall of foliage. Buck, Eric and Andyn jerked backwards, the twigs striking them like darts. Eric, gritting his teeth from a dozen small wounds, held out his hands and cast a sheet of flame at the leaf-wall, burning it into ashes and smoke.

Only Vordan and Liander remained —or what had been Liander. The Elf-mage's features looked shadowed and contorted and his eyes glowed with green light.

Vordan took a deep breath. "Looks like the odds have changed, Liander. I suggest we retreat and regroup."

"No," said Liander in an echoing voice. Vordan stepped back in alarm.

"We destroy them all," the mage continued. "With Arachnia's blessing and your sacrifice."

Liander waved his hands, a cyclone of greenish-black fog enveloping him. Vordan hurled up a magical shield. A tendril of pure black lanced out from the cloud, transfixing Vordan. The Elf stared in amazement at the ebony spike that pierced his heart. He collapsed. A ghostly red light streamed out towards Liander.

The cyclone of green and black faded. *Is Liander actually larger? What the actual Hell?*

"The Dark Rider commands," he said, pointing at Eric and Buck. "You die."

Eric cast up a magical screen and Buck raised his shield. Vile green spears of light shot out at them, curving around their defenses to strike them in the sides. Both cried out and dropped.

"No!" Andyn screamed. She darted forward to kneel by them.

Dar's heart stopped in his chest. *NO! Not like Elaine!*

He charged forward in a rage, trying to lop off Liander's arms or legs or head— or all of them at once. With inhuman speed, the mage dodged or used his dagger to block. Connor joined Dar, sword flashing. Liander fought with a demonic energy and power, his hands and eyes sizzling with that vile green light.

One of Dar's attacks got through, slicing Liander in the leg. Connor followed that with a stab in the side. Liander backhanded him and the Halfling flew through the air to land on the churned earth.

Liander held out both hands towards Dar, palms glowing. Dar tried to cut them off, but a cloud of grey dust exploded in front of him. Hlerv appeared at his side, pulling him back. Liander's spell went off into a ghostwood sapling, shredding it. Splinters and shards of wood sprayed in all directions. Dar staggered backwards, dropping his sword.

Liander lurched back, coughing and choking from Hlerv's powder. Some kind of symbol pulsated on Liander's chest, above his heart.

Dar snatched up his bow and an arrow and stood protectively over Andyn where she knelt by Eric and Dar. "How bad is it?"

"Forget us, Andyn," Eric said weakly, his wound seeping a green essence. "Get him. Don't let him get away."

"No!" Andyn exclaimed in a tearful rage. "I won't lose anyone else to his evil!" She closed her eyes and golden light covered both men from her outstretched hands. The green ichor faded and disappeared, the injuries disappearing. She slumped forwards, exhausted.

Eric and Buck scrambled for their weapons.

"Too little, too late," Liander managed, leaning on a fallen pillar. "Arachnia, Princess of the gods of the Ja'al, has given me might! If you will not join me, Andyn, then you will fall like all the others."

Andyn's eyes flashed with rage. "Never!" she hissed.

Liander raised his hands again, a glittering cloud of sparkles gathering around him.

Dar put the arrow to his bow.

A small figure hurtled at Liander from behind, sword flashing. Dar loosed, aiming for the symbol under Liander's tunic.

Connor and the arrow arrived at the same time. Green light flashed in Liander's eyes, then dimmed and went out. He collapsed.

Eric and Buck struggled to their feet, aided by Hlerv and Alfred.

"You okay, Connor?" Dar asked as they strode forward to join him where Liander lay.

Connor nodded, then winced. "Think I broke a rib or something."

"He's still alive, I think," Buck said.

Liander lay in a pool of blood, Dar's arrow still in his chest. He held out a hand.

"Andyn?" said Eric without looking at her.

She shook her head as she leaned into him. "Even if I wanted to, I couldn't. I used up all the strength I had left to heal you two. It's all I can do to stand."

"Thank you," Liander said to the Riders. "Arachnia's symbol is destroyed. I am finally free."

Did I actually hear that? Dar's mouth dropped open. "What?"

Liander managed a feeble nod. "I never wanted to hurt Andyn, or even any of you, even in the Dark Elven fortress. I just made too many bad bargains with Arachnia. She is a harsh mistress."

Andyn's face showed a mix of emotions: shock, anger, sadness. "Why?"

Liander smiled. "I really did love you, Andyn, but I allowed my jealousy to take me over. Then to gain the Dark Rider's medallion, I destroyed your home. The stupid assassins weren't supposed to kill Larad, only eliminate any guards nearby! But then it was too late."

Andyn stared down at him, tears streaming down her face.

"I don't expect you to forgive me," Liander gasped, fighting for air. "Just to understand. You were everything I wanted. I spent my life in the wrong ways trying to grow so powerful and famous and rich that you would be forced to love me."

Andyn sighed, shaking her head, looking stricken. "I never loved those things, Liander."

His smile started to fade. "As I have seen this whole time. But now I am free of Arachnia forever and accept whatever judgement the gods allow."

"I forgive you," Andyn wept miserably, clinging to Eric like a lifeline.

Liander said no more. Neither did the Riders, standing on the ruined battlefield in an ancient monastery.

CHAPTER NINETEEN

New Destinations

A ndyn watched the cityscape of Darlon as the sun set in the distance. The glimmering ribbon of the Deor River reflected the red-gold of the western sky. Below her, magical lights sprang to life in the darkening streets as city workers removed the covers.

"You okay?"

Andyn turned at the voice and smiled at Eric Indidarc. He stepped up next to her, tossing a small silver object in his hand. She turned back to the city before replying. *Am I okay?*

"Yes. If I think of everything, yes," she replied.

Eric gave her a sidelong look. "Really?"

She sighed. In her mind's eye, she saw her husband smile at her, his eyes understanding. "I am, really. Larad can sleep in peace— or, actually, he's already been at peace for a long time. I'm the one who needed peace."

He nodded, looking back over Darlon's sunset. "And Liander?"

She felt a knot in her stomach at the name and let it go. "I never realized that he loved me or how truly miserable his life was. He made the choices and took the Dark Path on his own. He didn't have to. He could have asked for help. I know there's little I could have done to change him. That part just feels empty."

Eric watched the city in silence for a while. "Vengeance always does."

Now she looked at him sidelong. "Now who's the cleric, you or me?"

He chuckled. "Point and match. I still have unfinished business with my own kin regarding Larad. I haven't forgotten."

She put a hand on his arm. "You don't have to do it."

He shook his head and caught the silver brooch. "It's not for vengeance. From what you've told me of Larad, he wouldn't want that anyway. It's justice. They have hurt far too many people and the time has come to end it. Maybe not today, but someday."

How did I deserve such friends? She watched the scene below them quietly, then eyed the brooch in his hands: about the size of a gold piece, it depicted a silver circle with the figure of a soaring hawk. "I still don't know where that came from."

Eric shrugged. "Even when I found it in the grass at Avar's Run, it was this shiny, so someone dropped it there recently. Who knows? Maybe one of Liander's allies dropped it in the scuffle."

"It should come in handy. Did Melinor tell you how to use it?"

"Yes, after he performed a magical analysis to figure out what it did, he also reset the keyword. It's mine now."

"Tried it out yet?"

Eric winked and held the brooch up to his mouth, whispering a word. He held out his hand. The brooch glowed bright white, expanded and solidified into a brown hawk with black-tipped feathers, sitting on the parapet. The bird regarded them with a shiny eye.

Eric held out his arm, a leather guard on the forearm and wrist. The hawk hopped onto his arm. "I have called him Stealth."

She grinned at him. "You know this fits in with the Song: 'hawk of sharpened claw' and all that."

"I'm aware and ignoring it."

They stood for a while, not speaking. A quiet happiness filled her, the first she felt in many months. *Larad's story — and Liander's — is over. Mine future is still to be written. I will make you proud, my Larad. Pray for me to the Highest Lord.*

A mild breeze blew on the balcony and, on it, she fancied she heard her husband answer in the affirmative. She smiled.

"Hey, you two," said Dar Cabot's voice from behind them. They turned.

"Melinor is here with Lord Simrit from the Order. Everyone else is ready."

Eric whispered a word to Stealth and the hawk became a medallion again. They turned and followed him into the tower room.

"It was nice of the Duke to let us stay in the castle," Andyn said.

"I think my dad had something to do with that," Eric murmured. "But I'll take it."

Melinor stood talking to Buck Bydecy. Hlerv and Connor sat at a table, comparing notes and poring over a map.

"Ah, good," said Melinor, smiling at Andyn.

He held out a pair of envelopes to Dar and Eric. "These are for you. Lord Nolan had them sent here a few days ago but you were otherwise occupied."

Eric looked down at the letter in his hands.

"Let me know what Brandi says," Andyn whispered to him. "At least, the parts you can tell me without blushing."

He bumped her with his shoulder but kept his head down. She giggled and bit her lip. *I wonder if I can get Connor to steal the letters... or maybe Hlerv... No. Let them have their romances to themselves. I'll write something to the sisters myself.*

"We're ready then," said Melinor. "I have to say I'm immensely proud of all of you."

Andyn smiled back, then, acting on impulse, stepped forward to embrace him. She felt a surge of affection. *He's taken us all in as an extended set of foster children, Verian love him.* "And thank you for all you've done."

He patted her back, kissed the top of her head and released her. "All I've done? Nonsense. I merely pointed you in the right direction and gave you a few supplements."

The door opened, admitting a dark-skinned, slender man with black hair in the same grey robes as Melinor. A golden star winked at the left shoulder of his garment. "Now," Melinor continued. "I would like to introduce Lord Simrit of the Order of the Three Magi. One of his specialties is ancient geography and anthropology."

"Your Excellency," Andyn bowed to Simrit, who smiled at her with brilliant white teeth.

He waved a hand. "No bowing. This is an informal setting. I am simply Simrit. Come over to the table. I have some information for you."

They followed him to where Hlerv and Connor studied the map. Simrit ran his finger over Dar's medallion in his hands, tracing the shape of the mountains and lake on one side.

"This medallion is unique," he began. "I, and several other people, wish it had been found about three years ago instead of today. It shows two mountains and a lake, but the detail is significant."

He pointed at the taller of the two mountains. "Usually, in simple artwork, mountains are rather generic, but this one here, the taller one, is shown with a pair of spikes near the crest. This is not mere artistic license; this is a very specific mountain. It is called Twinspire."

He tapped the medallion with his finger. "We know from ancient records that a fortress of the Empire stood near Twinspire, but for many years we were unable to find it. The lake you see on the medallion is also depicted in detail. I know it. It is named Shadow Lake."

Andyn looked at Dar.

Dar's eyes widened, intent on the medallion. He licked his lips. "How do you know? Where is it?"

Simrit smiled. "I understand from Melinor the significance of this medallion and what it implies to you, Dar Cabot. Rest assured my sources are reliable. You are perhaps familiar with the name of Andareth Faldanor?"

Andyn nodded, surprised. "I certainly am! We studied his exploits in the academy: Half-Elf freelance cleric and wizard, Christian, now retired, I believe. He and his party, the Four Silvers, were quite famous."

Simrit nodded. "Indeed. The Four Silvers performed many a mission for local and national interests in the Northern Alliance. One of their last tasks was to destroy a stronghold of the Ja'al dedicated to Gudarta, run by a wizard named Galchimor, operating out of the wilderness near Deran and Evendale."

"A whole fortress with just four people?" Hlerv put in, frowning. "They must have been very powerful."

Melinor chuckled. "The name of their party was an inside joke. There were actually seven of them."

Simrit pointed to a place on the map. Andyn saw it was in the wilderness north of Evendale, very close to the intersection of the Evendale-Deran border at its northernmost corner. The nearest town looked to be Dwarfshire. "Lord Faldanor kept careful records, often sketching what he saw. One of the things he sketched during his mission was a mountain range near a large lake. One mountain was, we believe, Twinspire. He reported a crumbling fortress by the lake. He and his party bypassed the fortress after defeating Galchimor, but he made a point of noting its location. We believe this medallion and the fortress are linked."

Andyn looked at her companions. They silently stared at the map, a mix of emotions on their faces. She felt a mix of eagerness, apprehension and curiosity. *Did Dar's grandparents go there? Could it be possible they're still alive?*

"So that's where we have to go," Connor mused. He shook his head. "I don't know the area exactly, but I've heard of the regions north of Dwarfshire. Rough country, and dangerous. Faldanor must have had a pretty tough crew."

Simrit shrugged, looking amused. "I'm sure they didn't think of themselves that way. At least, I know his wife would probably laugh at that."

"You know Lady Faldanor?" asked Eric.

"Of course. I work with her, except I call her Sidara. She's in the Order."

Dar's eyes rested on each of his companions. "This is it then. Are you with me?"

Buck shrugged. "Do you even have to ask?"

Eric pushed him in the shoulder. "Just make sure you keep your mouth under control." Dar ducked his head and grinned.

"Also, be aware of this," Melinor added. "Faldanor's records indicated a dragon in the area. From his description, it could be a Darkwood Drake."

Oh, that's not good. Andyn suppressed a shudder. *Damn it. Nothing is easy, is it?*

Buck's eyes grew wide. "A what?"

"Evil forest dragon," Andyn told him. "Very good at hiding in the woods, greedy, cruel, and can breathe both poison and fire."

Hlerv muttered something unprintable.

Eric turned to Melinor. "Any ideas on how to handle one of those?"

Melinor nodded. "A few, but it will be a lot like the assistance I gave you for this Liander Tolin business."

"What about you, Connor? Up to going back home again?" Dar asked.

Connor stared down at the map for a long moment, then nodded. "We have to find out about the medallion. We have to find out about anything related to a Halfling toy. And most of all, we have to find out what Margoth is planning, and stop it."

"You didn't answer the question," Andyn prodded gently.

He sighed. "I would have to deal with it eventually I suppose. Just so long as you're all there."

She gave his hand a squeeze. "I wouldn't want to be anywhere else."

※

"Do you think they got the letters?" Megan asked, reining in Larinor along the cliff. Brandawyn pulled up next to her. From their vantage point, they looked down on the fortress of Tol Divvon and the seaport. To their left, Daphne and Stephen stood next to Daphne's enchanted owl, consulting a map.

"I'm sure they did," Brandi said. "Lord Nolan promised to find a way. Too bad we aren't anywhere close to a Tele-post office to reply to them, but at least they know we're still alive and thinking of them. And we know that Lord Nolan received our latest letters."

They looked out over the sunset. Ocean waves sparkled the far below them. Megan listened to the crash of the waves and cry of the seagulls. "Do you think they're safe?"

She could hear the smile in Brandi's voice. "Safe? Absolutely not. But watched over by guardian angels? Definitely. We can do our part and pray."

Then I will. Megan looked out at the sea and prayed. *God, please let me be with him again.*

Chapter Twenty

Tempest Gathering

Zhinia Margoth pulled on the reins of her Fell Steed and it stopped with a snort. Its twisting black horns gleamed in the evening light. She shot a glance at the alchemy tent, where Ralis supervised his mages. His whining, sneering voice occasionally rose above the noise of the camp.

Margoth turned her mount towards the command tent. "General Jerran," she announced, "Status report."

Jerran thumped out of his command tent, pulling on his gauntlets. "The Goblin tribes are settled in their bivouac. And yes, Highness, they are situated away from the Dark Elven battalions."

"What is the current count?"

"Just over three thousand, Highness. We expect many more in the coming weeks."

"Excellent." Margoth swept her eyes over the broad valley. Ensconced a wooded area in the Wilderness east of Stonekeep Mountain, her campfires and tents numbered in the hundreds. True to Jerran's word, Goblin banners fluttered next to the totems of the Kaftu Bloodranger Tribe.

She smiled. "You have done well. Make sure to maintain order. I will have no brawling or grudge feuds in my army."

He touched a hand to the greatsword strapped to his back and the handle glittered with red light. "I will see to it personally, Highness," he said.

"Good. Now, make an accounting of the progress of siege engine construction and testing. We need to be ready by the first week of Augustus."

"Yes, Highness." Jerran bowed and lumbered off, his plate mail clanking lightly with every step. Three Ja'al Skullhead Legionnaires fell in behind him and they moved off into the camp. Soldiers parted to let them through.

"Ralis?" Margoth called over her shoulder. "Are we on schedule?"

"Yes, Highness." Ralis scuttled to her side. He wrung his hands, noticed it, and stopped, slipping his hands into the sleeves of his robes. "I believe so, Highness." His dark, beady eyes flicked to her, then to the side. "We will be able to accelerate the process once Queen Ildrisana's wizards join us."

She peered at him. "Is there a problem?" she hissed.

"Oh! No," he gave her an unctuous smile and inclined his head. "No, no, no! We are producing the munitions and combat aids just as you ordered. It's just that the schedule depended largely on the Dark Elves helping out, as you recall from our planning meeting. Have no fear, Highness. All will be ready for Day One."

Have no fear? Well, Ralis, you will experience fear, and a lot more, if you don't step it up, Margoth mused. Instead, she nodded. "Just so. Return to your work. I will expect a progress report by morning."

"Of course, Highness." Ralis returned to the facility, hissing orders to the mages hard at work over beakers and workbenches.

Margoth rested her hands on her saddlebow, skeletal fingers clenching and unclenching. "Day One. The first step of the reconquest," she murmured. "It will take time, but then, I have a lot of that."

Yes. Excellent. A disparate group of rivals, welded into a fighting force that plays to the best strengths of each faction, augmented by magic. Ruled by my will. The teeming horde of her army seethed and swarmed with the hustle and activity of war preparations. A feeling of great satisfaction flowed through her. *I will unleash Hell onto Deran. Pegasi or no pegasi, they will feel my wrath. Thul Mardil will rise again.*

I will see to it.

The End

Sneak Peek – Book 3: Helm of Shadows

Megan Alenar looked up as her aunt approached their campfire. "Did you see anything, Aunt Daphne?"

"Lanterns on the road," Daphne Alenar said, nodding. "A couple of wagons."

"Any outriders?"

Daphne shook her head. "None that I could see. It's getting late and I don't think they'll make it to the next town, so I'm sure we'll meet them here."

Megan knew the trail custom: any campfire could be shared along the highway and those who set it first were obligated to welcome any newcomers — as long as those newcomers posed no threat and made no attack. She unrolled her blankets and sat back against a log. "It will be nice to meet someone on the trail."

"Riding flying horses in the sky doesn't lend itself well to meeting people, does it?" her sister said. Brandawyn sat on another log and stirred a pot of stew suspended over the flames. A tiny silver cross sparkled in the firelight from a chain around her neck.

Stephen Alenar rose from his seat and headed beyond their camp, towards the sheltering trees where two black winged horses cropped grass. He clucked to them and gently led them back into the shadows, so only their heads and necks showed in the firelight.

"Suspicious, Uncle Stephen?" Brandi asked him.

"Cautious," he replied, placing his recurve bow and quiver in easy reach.

Daphne sat on a nearby log, facing towards the road and away from the flames, avoiding looking into the campfire. Stephen reclined against a tree stump so that he, too, looked away from the flames into the deepening evening. He made a small, looping motion with his right hand and it glowed for a second.

Detection spell, thought Megan. She sat back, making an effort to listen to the wind in the trees overhead. *He's just taking precautions*, she told herself. *Don't be so jumpy.*

Daphne sniffed the aroma of Brandi's cooking. "These two have a future, brother," she said to Stephen. "We won't starve with them around."

Stephen just smiled.

Megan's stomach rumbled. "Brandi's the real cook. This is the third stew we've had and they've all been different and delicious."

Brandi laughed. "It's just some salt pork, herbs and dried vegetables."

"It's chemistry," replied Daphne with a smirk.

Megan heard the jingle of harness from the road. Her aunt and uncle slid ever so slightly towards their weapons. Her hand crept to her belt, resting on the magic silver dagger given to her by Dar Cabot, so many months ago. Brandi appeared unconcerned, dipping into the stew to taste it.

"Hello, the fire!" called out a male voice.

Daphne and Stephen stood as two wagons drew into view. Large, four-wheeled conveyances with domed roofs, they rumbled along the road into the firelight on muddied wheels. They bore no device or symbol that would mark them as merchants or artisans of a particular stripe, though Megan saw branches of rosemary strung along the sides. Megan counted two men on each wagon, one driver and one crossbowman.

"Greetings!" called Daphne. "Where are you bound?"

"Shark Bluff," responded the driver of the first wagon. A dark-haired, solid-looking fellow, he wore leather armor and a sword hung form his hip. "We have a load of herbs to deliver to the waterfront."

"It's a long way from here," Stephen said, gesturing southwards. "And it's getting dark. You are welcome to share our fire."

The crossbowman's eyes flickered over all of them, lingering on Megan and Brandi. He looked at the driver.

The driver gave a broad smile. "It's not quite dark yet, and we need to make all the distance we can. A lot of money riding on our delivery, you know. Thanks all the same. Any word of conditions to Shark Bluff?"

Daphne sat back down on the log, near her bow. "Clear as far as we could tell. A road-warden patrol passed by a while ago and told us of Hobgoblin bandits the closer you get to the ocean, but if you have numbers and weapons you're in no danger."

The driver nodded. "Much obliged." He clicked his tongue at the draft horses and shook the reins. The wagons lurched off down the road.

Megan dipped a bowl of stew for herself and watched the wagons from under her eyelashes as they drove away. Two additional men sat on the tailgates of each wagon, armed with maces and short spears.

Her heart beat a little faster. *Something's not right. Herb merchants, with two guards per wagon?* She tried to calm herself and tasted the stew, redolent with the flavors of onions, carrots, sage, wine, pepper and sea salt. *Yes. Brandi is definitely better at this than I am.*

"Well?" asked Brandi, sitting back against a boulder with a hunk of bread and a bowl. Her violet eyes glittered like gemstones in the firelight.

"How much did you pay for the herbs and spices back in Tol Divvon?" asked Daphne.

"Four silver," Stephen said around a mouthful of stew.

"Doesn't seem that much in demand based on that price," Daphne mused.

They ate in silence. Megan watched her older relatives as she finished dinner.

"Roads are dry," remarked Stephen, picking up his wineskin. He took a swig. "But their wheels were muddy. They've been off road recently, maybe to avoid the road wardens."

"Could be," replied Daphne.

"And that's a lot of weaponry for herb merchants. The tailgaters were wearing brigandine, as I recall. The drivers both had magical weapons, plus the doors at the back of the wagons are warded."

"One of them came back to watch us from the brush after they turned the corner," said Brandi. "He's gone now."

Daphne and Stephen exchanged a look.

"Good eyes, Brandi," said Stephen.

Brandi gave him a little smile. "You're not the only one with magic spells. What do you think?"

"Slavers?" asked Daphne.

Stephen nodded. "Vipers, most likely. Wagons looked heavy. Rosemary has a strong scent, to hide any giveaway smells."

Megan felt her stomach clench. "They have slaves then."

Daphne stood. She picked up her bow and tested the string. "Not for long."

To find out what happens next, click the links below to pick up your copy of
***Helm of Shadows,* Book 3 of the Grey Riders Series:**
Amazon: *Helm of Shadows*
Barnes & Noble: *Helm of Shadows*

Glossary

Aalyros, Lady (of Tur-Rikken) (Dw. *"bright"*) - Dwarven artisan and noblewoman from the Esten Imperial era. She crafted the sword Khelios Giantbane (q.v.), weapon of Buck Bydecy (q.v.).

Agent - A spy, bounty hunter or thief, depending on context and the particular agent's morals and ethics. Connor Lomin, an agent, tended more towards the "spy" variety. In military terms an agent would be part of a reconnaissance unit.

Alenar, Brandawyn (Brandi) - One of the original Grey Riders, a half-Elven female, trained as a soldier and combat medic/corpsman. The older sister of Megan (q.v.), she and her family were persecuted for their Christian faith and eventually fled their homeland of Torosc under tragic circumstances. During her time with Dar Cabot and his friends, she fell in love with Eric Indidarc. Reserved but kind and devoutly religious, Brandi is quite pretty, with red-gold hair and violet eyes, but doesn't see herself as attractive. Brandawyn is also ambidextrous. Her pegasus is named Amicus.

Alenar, Daphne - Ranger knight and agent of the forces of good in the Realms. The only sister of Megan and Brandi's human mother, she spirited her nieces northward away from Torosc to safety. Sometimes thought of as overly serious (like her niece, Brandawyn), she served as a devoted mother-figure to the sisters after the death of their parents. Her brother is Stephen, a scholar and wizard.

Alenar, Megan - Another of the original Grey Riders and sister of Brandawyn Alenar, she attended college in Terenai and graduated as a wizard and scholar. Possessing red-gold hair like her sibling, Megan is friendly and outgoing, somewhat vain and impetuous, yet fiercely loyal and brave. She is also very attractive, with strawberry blonde hair and amber eyes, and is fond of baubles and fancy clothes. With her sister, she fled persecution in Torosc to arrive in Deran. She is in love with Dar Cabot and, like her sister, is ambidextrous. Her pegasus is named Larinor (Elv. *"beloved scout"*)

Alenar, Stephen - Uncle of Brandawyn and Megan Alenar, he is the younger brother of Daphne Alenar. Despite being a scholar, Stephen is also a skilled warrior and wields potent magic in battle. He likes to tease both his sister and his nieces but regards them with deep and abiding affection.

Almina (Dw. *"caring"*) - Dwarven assistant cleric to Tahri (q.v.) of Dalrikavus (q.v.).

Avar's Run - A ruined monastery for mages and wizards run by a now-defunct order of Irial monks, dating back to the time of the Esten Empire (q.v.). It is located north of Darlon, Deran.

Alyssa (Saint) - Queen of Tor Haldin, a Paragon (q.v.) nation of antiquity, she was the avowed enemy of Zhinia Margoth. She is honored as a patron saint of queens and protector of children.

Arachnia - Evil Elven goddess of poison and assassination. One of the gods of the cult of the Ja'al, Arachnia is worshipped by Dark Elves (q.v.).

Archons - Evil rulers of Torosc (q.v), the Archons were a cabal of highly trained freelance mercenaries who overthrew the existing kingdoms in the area at the time of the fall of the Esten Empire (q.v), uniting them into an artificial nation. Their descendants rule at the time of *Eye of Truth*.

Astarel - Kingdom to the north of Deran, along the coast. The homeland of Buck Bydecy, it is a seafaring nation with a robust navy and an eclectic society comprised equally of Elves, humans, Dwarves and Halflings.

Blank Shield - Another name for a mercenary or free-lance. Sell-sword.

Brightbolt - A magical spell, it takes the form of an intense beam of heat and light. When used properly, it can have the effect of a rocket-propelled grenade.

Bydecy, Alfred - Shop owner in Tyler, Astarel, he is the father of Buck Bydecy. He is a widower who raised his three children on his own after the death of his wife.

Bydecy, Buckminster (Buck) - Another of the original Grey Riders, he traveled south from his home in Tyler, Astarel, in search of employment as a caravan guard and met Eric Indidarc, Dar Cabot and the rest of the Grey Riders. A tall, rangy, sandy-haired human male warrior and free-lance, Buck's easygoing nature is often mistaken for boredom. He rides a pegasus named Shadowbane.

Bydecy, Jack - Younger brother of Buck Bydecy. He is a sailor.

Bydecy (Bydeky), Moridan - A powerful wizard during the time of the Esten Empire (q.v.), Moridan constructed a hidden fortress and was known for creating very special magic items. He is one of the forebears of Buck Bydecy. He was a follower of Irial (q.v.) the god of craftsmen and creation.

Bydecy, Summer - Younger sister of Buck Bydecy. She lives with her husband in Issendar, Eldir.

Cabot, Darius (Dar) - An original Grey Rider and native of the town of Forester, Deran, Dar ran afoul of Ja'al Goblin troops in the wilds and headed back to town for help, setting the events of *Whitehorse Peak* in motion. A young, dark-haired human male, he is a ranger/scout and adept in the woods. Dar seeks to determine the fate of his grandparents, who disappeared while searching for an ancient relic in the Wilderness. His pegasus is Virasi (Elv. "*white star*")

Celestia - Homeworld of the Elohir (q.v.). The 5th planet in the 61 Virginis system, it is approximately 27.8 LY from Earth and orbits a G6 spectral class, main sequence star. It is smaller than Damora or Earth but has very similar geography and abundant water.

Cintos, Kalar - A Ja'al courier, officer and liaison to the Dark Rider, Zhinia Margoth (q.v.).

Coastwatch - Province in Torosc (q.v.) from where the Alenars (q.v) originally hailed.

Crossed Swords - Guild of assassins based in Deran and Terenai. Founded and ruled by the Hylar family, the Crossed Swords are often used by evil forces to eliminate opposition.

Crown of Thorns Rose - Otherwise known as a "*Coronam Ex Spinis*", it is a plant native to Celestia (q.v.) but occasionally can be found on Damora. As it is from an alien world populated by noble and good creatures, it has great power against the forces of Darkness.

Daemon - Evil to the core, the otherworldly race of daemons spend most of their time trying to overthrow the Elohir (q.v.) or conquer Damora. They are known as the Fallen because legend has it that they were originally Elohir who turned to the side of evil and worship of themselves (and the Dark One).

While many Daemons look like nightmarish beasts, some are very attractive and almost human-like or Elven in appearance. Daemons are also known as the Fallen Ones.

Dalrikavus (Dw. *"place of the sparkling jewel"*) - A large Dwarven city under the land of Deran, it is a haven and trading center in the underground. Despite its stark surroundings, it is a comfortable and welcoming place.

Damora - Imaginary world setting for the Grey Riders novels. The fourth planet orbiting the star 82 Eridani, it is roughly 1.15 times the size of Earth and possesses climate regions and flora/fauna similar to Earth. The parent star is a G5V spectral class, main-sequence yellow star approximately 20 light years from Earth. The technology level of Damora approximates the High Middle Ages of real life, with significant differences due to the use of magic and scientific advancement.

Dark Elf - General term used for Elves who have left the religion of the Elven god Verian (q.v) to throw in their lot with evil, usually in the cult of Arachnia (q.v.). Dark Elves have all the magical talents, beauty and intelligence of their brethren but no morals. Also known as Fallen Elves.

Darlon - Major city in Northern Deran, pop ~ 170,000. Home to people of many races, creeds and professions, it is a trading center and university town. Ruled by a duke, it controls trade, borders and access between Deran and the northernmost nations of Astarel, Elder and Rokon.

Darogir (Elv. *"killer"*) – A Dark Elf prince. One of the sons of Queen Ildrisana (q.v.), an ally of Zhinia Margoth (q.v.).

DeMey, Saren - The half-sister of Eric Indidarc by adoption, Saren DeMey was found by Melinor Indidarc as an infant and raised by him and his wife, Anne. A devout Christian, Saren appears to be a complete contradiction in terms as she is half-Daemon but fights for the forces of good. Dark-haired and dark-eyed, she transforms to a bat-winged, horned half-Daemon at will. As the wife of Terenil, the Earl of the Oakmoor (q.v.) suburb of Tallemar, she is a Countess of Deran.

DeMey, Terenil - The half-Elven husband of Saren, he is an earl and the ruler of Tallemar, a suburb of Oakmoor, Deran. A skilled wizard and soldier in his own right, he is adaptable, thoughtful and unfailingly kind. His devotion to Saren is unquestioned.

Deorfast - Large city in the mountains of northwestern Deran. It is a trading center and military installation and sits astride the Deor and Lonmar Rivers.

Deran - Constitutional monarchy in the northern lands of the Western continent of Damora. A nation built from the remnants of the Esten Empire (q.v.), Deran is also a meritocracy, where nobles are elected by their peers and the legislature based on merit and ability more than noble connections. Deran has an advanced network of roads, potent military, and several universities. The seat of the Christian Church, Saint Martin's Town (St. Martin's) is in Deran.

Dwarf - One of the major races of Damora. The term "Dwarf" comes from the ancient elvish word, *duarfaen* (Elv. *duar* = 'stone' + *fae/ fey/ fej* -= 'magic', literally "those of stone-magic"). A typical Dwarf male is about four feet six inches tall. Dwarves tend to be burly, sturdy or muscular for their size and can live for almost two hundred years. Males are often bearded (though not all are). Their main talent, as indicated by the name bestowed on them by the Elves, is in stonework and metallurgy.

Eleandir, Andyn - One of the Grey Riders, Andyn is a priestess of the Elven god Verian (q.v.) and a wizard. Andyn has honey-blonde hair and amber eyes, a trim figure and a marvelous singing voice. Rather impatient and quick-tempered, she nonetheless displays unwavering faith, mercy, warmth and a nimble mind. She is a widow and seeks her husband's murderer with fierce resolution. Her pegasus is named Medianox (Lat. "*midnight*").

Eldermain, Damion - Human sage and scholar who retired to the Elven nation of Terenai, near the town of Marolpeth (q.v.). He is an expert on the history of the southern regions of the continent, such as Torosc.

Eldir - Nation and member of the Northern Alliance, Eldir shares a border with Astarel and Deran and is located to the north of Deran. A landlocked nation, it nonetheless has several large and beautiful lakes and is heavily forested. Not surprisingly, many of its inhabitants are Elves. It is the seat of the hierarchy of the church of Verian (q.v.).

Eleth-Anor (Elv. "*dolphin bluff*") - A coastal city of the Elven Empire of Terenai, it is a major port and trading hub and the hometown of Andyn Eleandir.

Elf - One of the major races of Damora. The term "Elf" comes from the ancient word for their race, *Ellfaen* (Elv. *ell* = 'life' + *fae/ fey/ fej* -= 'magic', literally "those of life-magic"). Elves are more slender than humans and possess intriguing eye colors (such as aqua, amber or violet) and a slight point to top of the ear (though this is not usually noted if concealed under hair, hat or helm). Elves get along well with animals and have a remarkable talent for healing trees and plants. They dislike the underground but will tolerate it for short time periods. An Elf can reach the age of almost 300 years.

Elohir - Denizen of the planet of Celestia (the 5th planet orbiting the star 61 Virginis, which is a single G6 spectral class, main-sequence yellow star approximately 28 light years from Earth). Sometimes called "Celestials", the Elohir appear to be winged humans. Skin color covers the range of typical shades seen in humans (porcelain, tanned, brown, yellow, dark brown) and their eyes are the color of jewels. Their beauty is often described as 'unearthly'. All possess potent magical and martial skills but are usually reluctant to meddle in the affairs of Damorans. They are uniformly kind, wise, honest and just. Elohir live extremely long lives (~ 1000 years) if not killed in warfare with their evil kindred.

Essergil (Elv. "*hidden-deep*") - Dark Elven city in the underground below the nation of Deran, ruled by Queen Ildrisana (q.v.). Raiding parties from the city are a constant thorn in the side of the Deranese military and police.

Esten Empire - An empire formed of various kingdoms controlling much of the known world during the second age of Damora (known as the Imperial Age and denoted in calendars by the letters IY (for Imperial Year)). Due to infighting, a breakdown in the social fabric and the influence of evil, the Empire fell after over a thousand years.

Evendale - Halfling nation southeast of Deran (q.v.) and northeast of Terenai (q.v.). A republic, Evendale consists of seven districts or counties, each of which have a prescribed number of representatives (aldermen) and senators who draft laws that are approved by the High Minister, another elected position. A land with mild climate and productive farmland, Evendale nonetheless has a border with the Wilderness, which means the Halflings are always on vigilant watch, having been invaded by evil tribes from the wild lands multiple times.

Eye of Truth - Crafted by Moridan Bydecy (q.v.), the Eye of Truth is a magically-endowed diamond that is supposed to have a unique and legendary power.

Faelin, Kiara - Officer of the Second Court of Tyler, Astarel, charged with objective analysis of magical items.

<u>Faldanor, Andareth (Lord)</u> - Half-Elf healer and wizard, retired at the time of *Eye of Truth*. He and his free-lance group, the Four Silvers, defeated the evil wizard Galchimor in the wilderness near Evendale, mapping the route to Twinspire Mountain which is eventually needed by the Grey Riders. He is married to Lady Sidara of the Order of the Three Magi.

<u>Fallbrook, Larad</u> - The deceased husband of Andyn Eleandir (q.v.), Larad was assassinated by agents of the Crossed Swords Guild (q.v.) for a mysterious and nefarious purpose. He was a carpenter by trade and childhood friend of the Eleandir family.

<u>Feller, Derek</u> - A friend of Buck Bydecy (q.v.) from his teen years, he waylaid his boss (a jeweler), robbed him and then framed Buck for the crime.

<u>Firedart</u> - A magical attack spell used by wizards and sorcerers. It is essentially a small projectile of flame with a detonable core that looks rather like a tiny comet and a limited range (about 100 feet or so). It produces the effect equivalent to a 9 mm pistol bullet and rarely misses.

<u>Firefan</u> - A magic spell consisting of a sheet of flame about seven feet across at its terminus. When used by an expert practitioner, it has the effect of a burst from a flamethrower.

<u>Forester</u> - Large town along the northern border highway of Deran. Forester is ruled by a baron and controls trade along the borderlands. Its defining feature is the central town proper, which is surrounded by a tall, well-built palisade with giant, living trees as its guard towers.

<u>Free-lance</u> - Another name for sell-sword, blank-shield or mercenary. Upon graduation from training, free-lances are given a magical medallion that attests to their completion of studies. The medallion functions as a sort of ID card.

<u>Gariil</u> - The pagan deity of chance and luck, predating the arrival of Christianity to Damora. Church structure is loose and many clergy of the faith are made simply by declaring it to be so. Although associated in a minor way with fertility, Gariil temples are mostly known for being entertaining gambling houses due to the connection to luck. They are found in almost all lands in some form or another.

<u>Glen</u> - A large community in Evendale. It is the hometown of Connor Lomin (q.v.).

<u>Gnome</u> - Half-breeds resulting from the marriage of Halfling and Dwarf, Gnomes possess features from each parent: natural affinity for stone and the

underground from the Dwarves and a cheerful disposition and natural talent with all things organic from their Halfling parent. Somewhat taller than Halflings but shorter than Dwarves, Gnomes are industrious and found in all the known lands. They usually have dark hair, tan-to-dark complexions, and brown, amber or grey eyes. A typical Gnome lives about 150 years or so.

Goblin - Short, half-simian creatures who often serve as foot-soldiers for the forces of evil, looking somewhat like horned chimpanzees. Extremely agile and able to use any available weapon that is sized for them, they are also good at hiding in shadows. They dislike sunlight. Their social structure is usually a hierarchical monarchy, with the chieftain or king of a particular tribe wielding absolute authority. Goblins particularly hate Dwarves since the two races compete for underground areas and resources. They are capable miners and are about the size of a Gnome or tall Halfling (a few inches short of four feet tall).

Gorostol (Dw. "*friend alliance*") - Racially diverse and economically strong nation south of Terenai. Its capital city is Meridian.

Gudarti - The evil goddess of torture and suffering, the seductive and sadistic Gudarti is a member of the Ja'al pantheon.

Hanford, Nolan (Lord) - The titular ruler of the Deranese border town of Forester (q.v.), he is the person who originally hired the Grey Riders (q.v.) for their first mission. A tall, middle-aged man of trim physique and piercing dark eyes, he is also a paladin (q.v.) and a member of the Christian Church. He is married to Lady Ellen Hanford and has two children.

Half-Elf - The offspring of a union between an Elf (q.v.) and human, half-Elves are a mix of their parents' heritage: magically talented, strong, adaptable and capable of learning new skills quickly. If it were not for the fact that they are noticeably larger than Elves by a couple of inches in height, they would be indistinguishable from Elves due to their predilection to inherit their Elven parent's eye color, hair color and ear shape. Half-Elves live to between 100 and 150 years.

Halfling - The smallest of the races, Halflings (from the Elven for "those of hearth magic" - *haliv-fae*) prefer pastoral villages and countrysides to large cities, though they are at home in any setting. As adaptable as humans, Halflings have a talent for craftsmanship (with things other than stone) and farming. They are known for their skill in the kitchen and the durability of their finished goods. Halflings sometimes intermarry with Dwarves, producing Gnomes (q

.v.) among their children. Their hair color (blonde, brown or black), skin color (porcelain to dark brown) and eye color (blue, green, black or grey) remind the other races of miniature humans. They live about 100 years or so.

Halkith the Grey - A human cleric of the Ja'al cult (q.v.), Halkith commanded a set of bases in the Wilderness near Forester. Responsible for myriad crimes and atrocities on the Borderlands, he was slain by Dar Cabot along the Frontier Highway.

Hawthorne, Nigel - Ryan Hinterman's (q.v.) law clerk.

Hellspawn - Technical designation for an ordinary animal warped and twisted by dark magic to serve the forces of evil.

Herilan (Elv. "*red dale*") - A large town in the south-east of Terenai known for an excellent library. It takes its name for the red maple trees in the vicinity.

Hideges - A sinister frost dragon living in the northern part of Deran.

Hinterman, Ryan - Judge of the Second Court of Tyler, Astarel, who hears the case of Buck Bydecy.

Hlerv - A Gnome who meets the Grey Riders after taking on minor tasks for Buck Bydecy. Dark of hair and beard, his demeanor seems suspicious and wary. He is unwilling to give details of his past but after a rough patch, joins the Riders, lending his talents in espionage and magic to their quests.

Human - Humans on Damora (q.v) are much like real-life people of the planet Earth, with the exception that they can use magic in the same manner as Elves, Dwarves, Halflings and other denizens of the planet. They live in all climates and places that will welcome them. They have the same coloring (skin, eyes and hair) as people of Earth. Humans can live to the age of 100. The origin of the word "human" has no Damoran equivalent as it does not translate from any Elven or Dwarven syntax.

Humana - Language of the human race on Damora (q.v).

Ildrisana (Elv. "*lance-brilliant*") - Queen of an underground, hidden city of Dark Elves (q.v.), she is courted by Zhinia Margoth as an ally in her schemes and plans.

Indidarc, Eric - One of the original Grey Riders, Eric is the adopted son of Melinor Indidarc (q.v.) a famous wizard. He meets Buck Bydecy (q.v.) on his way to Forester, Deran to seek his fortune as a blank-shield freelance mercenary guard. Able to use magic and martial weapons with equal proficiency, Eric is cheerful, optimistic and friendly. He treats everyone he meets with the same courtesy and kindness, whether a beggar or noble. Eric has violet eyes and blond hair and is a half-Elf (q.v.).

Indidarc, Melinor - High Wizard of the northern kingdom of Deran, nobleman and confidante of royalty in the Kingdoms of the Northern Alliance (q.v.). He adopted both Eric and Saren (q.v) after his own children were grown. A formidable ally and genius with knowledge of magic, science, medicine, literature and history, Melinor is fluent in several languages and is singularly focussed on thwarting evil plots in the known lands. He comes off as a kind but somewhat absent-minded man. About two years prior to the events of *Whitehorse Peak* (book 1 of the Grey Riders series), his wife, Anne, died of natural causes at their home.

Inibe, Jordan - The Duke of Darlon, Deran, Lord Jordan Inibe is an old friend of Melinor Indidarc and helps him whenever the situation demands. He has a high regard for Melinor's family, including Eric.

Irial - The Halfling god of harvests, craftsmen and home, Irial is a kindly deity who sometimes counts Elves and humans among his adherents. The precepts of Irial are hospitality, kindness, courtesy, respect for people, animals and nature, and steadfastness in the face of hardship, whether caused by nature or evil designs.

Jerran - Military attache from the Ja'al to Zhinia Margoth (q.v.). He is about 7 feet tall and powerfully-built.

Ja'al - Also known as the Manipulator Church (for their penchant for twisting words, lying and otherwise using others callously for their own ends) the Ja'al are one of the evil religions on Damora. The cult is a polytheistic religion worshiping a number of harsh and cruel deities. The precepts of the Ja'al are world domination, rule of the strong over the weak, eugenics, personal gain at the cost of other people, and treachery.

Kadram (Dw. *"swordsman"*) - Captain of the city guard of Dalrikavus (q.v.), a Dwarven underground stronghold in Deran. He is married to Tahri, a high priestess of Kurental (q.v.) in Dalrikavus.

Kaftu - A race of hyena-folk similar to the creatures of African legend. Their society is matriarchal, with males only used for mating, brute labor and some specialized tasks. The balance of each tribe is female. They are cunning, vicious and greedy and view all other creatures as either obstacles or food.

Khelios (Giantbane) - A magical Dwarven sword found by the Grey Riders while battling Halkith the Grey (q.v.), it bestows two abilities on its wielder: knowledge of the Dwarven language and the ability to detect evil. It is particularly deadly to giants or any creature with giant blood (including cyclops).

Thul Mardil - The ancient name for the domain of Zhinia Margoth (q.v.). Its location has been lost to antiquity.

Kurental (Dw. "*Creator god*") - Benevolent Dwarven deity and god of stone, mountains, and creation. The main god honored by the Dwarves of Damora, his church is allied with Verian, Irial and Christianity in resistance to the evil religions.

Lefond, James - Freelance warrior formerly in the service of Halkith the Grey (q.v.). He has a high degree of animosity towards Dar Cabot.

Lomin, Connor - Another of the original Grey Riders, Connor is a Halfling who hails from Evendale (q.v.). Serious, but with a somewhat ribald sense of humor, Connor appears stoic and sober most of the time. He is knowledgeable about traps, curious about ancient ruins and secrets, and wields a broadsword, a rather heavy weapon for a Halfling. Dark-eyed and dark-haired, he has a muscular build but has an almost uncanny skill for moving unseen. He rides a pegasus named Phantom.

Mardildris (Elv. "*black lance*") - Dark Elven mage and priestess of Arachnia (q.v.) who is assigned to manage Liander Tolin (q.v.), who is the liaison between Zhinia Margoth and the Dark Elves. An arrogant woman with a penchant for torture, she is nonetheless ambitious and clearly sees Liander's role in the designs of the lich princess.

Marolpeth (Elv. "*blue grove*") - Elven town and military installation near the eastern border of Terenai.

Margoth, Zhinia - A former Paragon Queen (q.v.) who used fell and evil magics to transform herself into an undead sorceress (a lich) to avoid death near the end of the Paragon Age, Margoth is vicious, conniving, and cruel. Her ultimate goal is unknown, but her forces range near the borderlands of Deran, causing havoc. She has intimate knowledge of the Song of the Grey Riders (q.v.) since it seems to mention her; secretly, she fears its fulfillment since it implies the Grey Riders will be her doom. She appears as a skeleton with pinpoint eyes of purple light, clothed in rotting royal robes and wielding a skull-headed staff. Her standard is a fanged skull with a crown of flame.

Merdail (Dw. "*holy land*") - A powerful nation south of Terenai ruled by Dwarves. Ruggedly mountainous in some areas and verdant in others, Merdail is rich in natural resources but landlocked. It is an enemy of Torosc, with which it shares a border to the south.

Meridian - Capital city of the nation of Gorostol (q.v.), situated near a large lake.

Mikman, Kili - Halfling agent formerly in the service of Halkith the Grey. He has a particular hatred for Connor Lomin.

Mil-Tereth (Elv. "*palace-king*") - The capital of Imperial Terenai (q.v.), Mil-Tereth is a massive city within a lush forest in the center of the Elven nation. It sports many magical wonders and all the artistry for which the Elves are famed.

Mindra - An Elven heroine of the faith of Verian (q.v.), Mindra gave her life defending children during the fall of the Paragon Kingdoms. She is revered as a saintly person who can intercede with Verian on behalf of those in need.

MuddleMind - A magical attack spell that causes disorientation and confusion in its target.

Northern Alliance - A multinational alliance similar to NATO in the real world, the Alliance is composed of Deran, Astarel, Rokon, Eldir, Evendale and Terenai.

Oakmoor - The capital city of Deran, home to over a quarter of a million people. Oakmoor is based on three large hills at the confluence of the East River and Lonmar Rivers. It has several suburbs in addition to the main city proper.

Ogre - Large, human-like creatures with fangs and odd-colored hair, Ogres are brutish, violent, and not particularly smart. Their leaders are usually the more intelligent members of a particular tribe. Some of their number are smart enough to use magic. They are usually over seven feet tall and three hundred and fifty pounds. Used as shock troops by the forces of evil, Ogres are also greedy and fearless.

Orvos, Darren - Assistant prosecutor of the city of Tyler, Astarel.

Paladin - A holy warrior. Paladins are highly-trained fighters proficient with most weapons and heavy armor and adhere to a strict code of conduct and morals. Most of the good religions of Damora have paladins serving as free-lancers or special guards for high officials. Their reputation for faithfulness, bravery and skill along with the ability to use various forms of magic make them formidable agents of Light in the war against Darkness.

Papal Nuncio - The highest-ranking Christian priest on Damora, he is ranked as a cardinal and the liaison of the Pope. At the time of *Eye of Truth*, the position was held by Edward Simpson, a lean and spare man with a kindly attitude and keen insight.

Paragon (King or Queen) - The title for a ruler of a petty kingdom in a bygone age of Damora (q.v.). Paragon rulers were originally sell-swords who wrested their kingdoms from the wilds by sheer skill and force of personality. The era of their dominion was known as the Paragon Age and featured high levels of civilization at its zenith. The Age ended when most of the nations collapsed due to societal deterioration and internal stresses.

Pegasus - Identical to the flying horses of mythology, pegasi (plural) can be trained and used either as air cavalry or transport mounts. They are extremely fast and agile and can be taught simple tasks.

Puup - Buck Bydecy's pet pigeon who somehow manages to avoid getting killed despite being in or near several battles.

Ralis - Human wizard and servant of Zhinia Margoth. He is rotund, cautious and calculating.

Rountree, Joko - Dwarven master of a military academy in Tyler, Astarel, he took Buck Bydecy on as a student against his better judgement and was pleasantly surprised when his student actually graduated.

Saint Kira's Order - Christian order of laypeople, priests, nuns and brothers with special skills (i.e. magic or sell-sword professions). Dar Cabot is a lay initiate of the Order and aspires to be a knight. The Order's main goal is protection and guidance of travelers and residents in remote areas.

Saint Martin's - Major port city in Deran. It is the seat of the Christian church and the base of the Curia, the ruling council of Christianity on Damora. The Papal Nuncio makes his residence there.

Sarago - Human jeweler in the city of Tyler, Astarel. His employee, Derek Feller, framed Buck Bydecy for a crime.

Shrikes - A small guild of assassins and thieves, they are usually allied with the Crossed Swords and extend their villainy to human trafficking, drugs and extortion.

<u>Simrit (Cassel)</u> - Wizard of the Order of the Three Magi. Dark-skinned, slender and introspective, he is a Lord of Deran and a friend of the Indidarc family, including Saren and Terenil. Two of his academic specialties are geography and anthropology.

<u>Sinda</u> - A druid priestess, she joins up with Liander Tolin mainly because of a misguided belief that the Druids need to seize power and force others to worship the planet as they do.

<u>Skitterling</u> - Small and violent creatures known to haunt swamp lands and lonely desolate places. They look like clumps of earth with wavy purple grass on top and thorny twigs poking out. They move fast and tend to swarm at targets.

<u>Spellbane</u> - Magic spell used by clerics and wizards to 'turn off' existing magical effects.

<u>Taggart, Marina</u> - Criminal defense attorney hired by Buck Bydecy.

<u>Tahri</u> (Dw. *"wise one"*) - Dwarven high cleric of Dalrikavus (q.v.) and wife of Kadram (q.v.), captain of the city guard. She is a friendly, helpful soul and quite knowledgable.

<u>Tallemar</u> - A suburb of the Deranese capital city of Oakmoor. It is ruled by the DeMey's (Terenil and Saren).

<u>Terenai</u> (Elv. *"Realm of the Elves"*) - The hereditary homeland of the Elven people, Terenai lies due south of Deran and also shares borders with Evendale (q.v.), Gorostol and Merdail. A verdant and fruitful land, it is heavily forested in places. It is ruled by an Emperor (or Empress) and is the oldest of the nations on Deran. Its capital city is Mil-Tereth (Elv. *"King's Palace"*).

<u>Telepost</u> - International postal service that uses teleportation for fast delivery.

<u>Telmin, James (Count)</u> - A vassal of the Duke of Darlon, he is an adjutant and castellan who runs various aspects of the Ducal household and military forces at the Duke's command. Responsible for the hire of free-lance mercenaries (q.v) he is rather arrogant and takes a low view of sell-swords.

<u>Three Magi, Order of the</u> - Secret order of Christian mages and scholars in service of the Papal Nuncio (q.v.). Composed of extremely skilled practitioners, it counts Melinor Indidarc as one of its number (and he is one of the few publicly acknowledged members).

<u>Tinira</u> - Hill sprite and military officer, her tribe lives in the woods of Terenai near Tokkab (q.v.).

Tirevlan (Elv. "*silver vale*") - A large market city in south-central Terenai located on the plains and farmlands. It takes its name from the extensive grain farms nearby.

Tokkab (Elv. "*ten elms*") - Small village in southeastern Terenai where Damion Eldermain (q.v.) retired.

Tolan - Legendary first prophet of the Verian faith, an Elf whose mystical visions, holiness and wisdom provided much of the philosophy of the church in its earliest days. His writings form the basis of ethics and morality for all followers of Verian and he is often invoked as an intercessor with Verian for discernment in troubled times.

Tol Divvon (Elv. "*tower south*") - The southernmost major city in the Empire of Terenai. It has a huge fortress and an extensive seaport.

Tolin, Liander - Elven wizard, scholar and sometime ally of Zhinia Margoth. He was a former councilman of the Elven city of Eleth-Anor (q.v.), the home town of Andyn Eleandir and her deceased husband, Larad.

Torosc (Dw. "*nations*") - A republic (in name only) far to the south and homeland of the Alenars. It more properly describes a region which was once a collection of petty kingdoms, but fell to despotic rulers in a bygone age and was welded into a pseudo-nation of its own. It is a stronghold of evil during the time of the Grey Riders novels.

Tremane, Phillip IV - The ruling King of Deran, he is married to Queen Ahlana and is about thirty years old at the time of the novels. He and his Queen are close to the Indidarc family, including Melinor (q.v.) and Saren DeMey (q.v.). Dark-haired and dark-eyed, he is a thoughtful and just sovereign and has a common background with the Baron of Forester in that both are paladins (q.v.).

Troll - Large, brutish bipedal creatures similar to Ogres but taller and heavier. Trolls are hairless and can have four arms rather than two. Somewhat related to giants, they are considerably less sophisticated. They prefer mountains and forests and will kill and eat anything edible. Cruel, greedy and selfish, they can nonetheless be outwitted by smarter creatures. Some more intelligent of their species can learn to use rudimentary magic. Trolls have the unnerving talent of being able to blend in with trees and rocks by merely holding still and often use this ability to ambush the unwary.

Tyler - A major city of Astarel (q.v.) located on the coast just north of the border with Deran (q.v.). It is known for its large harbor, excellent fishing fleet and naval base. It is the hometown of Buck Bydecy (q.v.).

Urmum - Goblin word for "Elf", used both in the singular and plural sense. Translated literally as "Glowing Thing", probably due to the fact that Elves live in sunlight and are adept at magic.

Verian (Elv. "*Lord-highest*") - Elven god of forests and nature. Followers of Verian worship in open structures usually in groves or copses of trees. The organizational structure is somewhat loose, with a council of high priests and priestesses making decisions of doctrine and teachings every year. Andyn Eleandir (q.v.) is a priestess of Verian.

Viddi - Halfling assassin and spy, cousin of Kili Mikman (q.v.).

Vordan - A male Elven wizard on the run from authorities in Terenai. He is hired by Liander Tolin.

Whiteclaw - Another assassins' guild, the WhiteClaw originally come from Torosc but can be found almost anywhere and are often hired by the Ja'al (q.v.).

Za'Arak - Goblin word for their race, loosely translated as "The Rulers".

Zadar - Ja'al scout and assistant to Zhinia Margoth (q.v.). He is shifty and stealthy and Margoth is not entirely sure of his loyalties.

Zolkava - Mercenary warrior hired by Liander Tolin. A Dwarven tracker, she used to work for the Church of Vardu, the god of death.

About the Author

P. G. Badzey combines his love for epic fantasy with a background in the engineering profession to create the Grey Riders series of novels (*Whitehorse Peak, Eye of Truth, Helm of Shadows, Assassin Prince, The Skull Gates, Gate of Stars* and *Tower of Light*). Inspired by authors like JRR Tolkien, CS Lewis and Terry Brooks, Mr. Badzey provides a unique perspective, crafting stories of faith combined with a science-based magic system. His novels have been featured in the Midwest Book Review, US Review of Books and all have earned five-star ratings from Readers' Favorite. A member of the Orange County (CA) Writers Guild and Realm Makers, he was interviewed for No Wasted Ink and has appeared at multiple Indie Author events. He has been a book award judge for Realm Makers and currently runs a critique group. Alongside another author, he has taught seminars on Fantasy Writing at OC Libraries. Short fiction publications include *Dragonlaugh*, an online fantasy humor magazine, and *Brevity in Paradise Vol. II* and *Vol III*, the anthology of the OC Writers Guild.

Find out more about the World of the Grey Riders at
https://pgbadzey.wordpress.com

www.ingramcontent.com/pod-product-compliance
Lightning Source LLC
Chambersburg PA
CBHW022159170626
46807CB00005B/2279